# THE ONE YOU LEAST SUSPECT

Praise for Brian McGilloway

'**Poetic, humane and gripping** . . . reminded me of Bernard MacLaverty's early work. Yes, it's that good'

Ian Rankin

'**Moving and powerful**, this is an important book, which everyone should read'

Ann Cleeves

'[A] superb book . . . **thoughtful and insightful**, wrenching and utterly compelling. It says something truly profound and universal about love, loyalty and revenge . . . If you want to understand Northern Ireland, or any society that has experienced conflict, put it on your list. And **the writing is exquisite**'

Jane Casey

'An **extraordinary** novel from one of Ireland's crime fiction masters'

Adrian McKinty

'A gentle, reflective book about a violent situation seems like an oxymoron but that's what Brian McGilloway has achieved with *The Last Crossing*. **An eye-opening read**'

Sinead Crowley

'This IS important. This book is the peak of what crime fiction can do. Brian **McGilloway writes like an angel**'

Steve Cavanagh

'As **heart-stopping and thrilling** as it is exquisitely written and prescient. A work of fiction which looks unapologetically at the legacy of our troubled past'

Claire Allan

'**Utterly stunning** and beautifully written'

Liz Nugent

'A cool, controlled, **immensely powerful** novel. McGilloway brings a forensic and compassionate eye to bear on the post-Troubles settlement in this thoughtful, morally complex book'

*Irish Times*

'**Outstanding**. From its harrowing opening scene to its equally violent conclusion, this is an **utterly compelling** story of how Northern Ireland's violent history has affected generations'

*Irish Independent*

By Brian McGilloway

The Inspector Devlin series
*Borderlands*
*Gallows Lane*
*Bleed a River Deep*
*The Rising*
*The Nameless Dead*
*Blood Ties*

The DS Lucy Black series
*Little Girl Lost*
*Hurt*
*Preserve the Dead*
*Bad Blood*

Standalone titles
*The Last Crossing*
*The Empty Room*

# THE ONE YOU LEAST SUSPECT

BRIAN McGILLOWAY

CONSTABLE

First published in Great Britain in 2025 by Constable

1 3 5 7 9 10 8 6 4 2

Copyright © Brian McGilloway, 2025

The moral right of the author has been asserted.

*All characters and events in this publication, other than
those clearly in the public domain, are fictitious
and any resemblance to real persons,
living or dead, is purely coincidental.*

All rights reserved.
No part of this publication may be reproduced, stored in a retrieval system, or transmitted, in any form, or by any means, without the prior permission in writing of the publisher, nor be otherwise circulated in any form of binding or cover other than that in which it is published and without a similar condition including this condition being imposed on the subsequent purchaser.

A CIP catalogue record for this book
is available from the British Library.

ISBN: 978-1-40871-801-8 (hardcover)
ISBN: 978-1-40871-802-5 (trade paperback)

Typeset by Hewer Text UK Ltd, Edinburgh
Printed and bound in Great Britain by Clays Ltd, Elcograf S.p.A.

Papers used by Constable are from well-managed
forests and other responsible sources.

| Constable | The authorised representative |
| An imprint of | in the EEA is |
| Little, Brown Book Group | Hachette Ireland |
| Carmelite House | 8 Castlecourt Centre, Dublin 15, D15 |
| 50 Victoria Embankment | XTP3, Ireland |
| London EC4Y 0DZ | (email: info@hbgi.ie) |

An Hachette UK Company
www.hachette.co.uk

www.littlebrown.co.uk

*For David Torrans*

## Chapter One

It began with Gail's wedding. The one in the Oceanview Hotel in Moville. That was where they picked me up the first time.

I'd been working that day; I was doing six mornings a week in O'Reilly's Pub. I used to work behind the bar but gave it up for morning shifts cleaning there instead. It suited me, because Hope, my daughter, had only just started in nursery class at the local primary school and was finished at 1.30 p.m. every day. I could drop her to school, do my work, and be back to collect her before heading on home. The cleaning was easy enough mid-week; unless there'd been a big match the previous night, the place wouldn't be too bad. Not as bad as Saturday and Sunday shifts where you'd be clearing God knows what out of the toilets. But I tried not to do weekends. At least back then.

That day, it had been raining. I remember because Hope's teacher had let them out late – someone had lost their lunchbox or something – and we'd all got soaked standing outside, waiting. I'd no coat or umbrella with me, so by the time the kids appeared, my work T-shirt was clinging to me.

I'd stopped at my mother's house to drop Hope off and to borrow a dry shirt, then went and got my hair done. The bus to the reception was picking us up at 5 p.m.; all the staff had been invited. Gail had worked behind the bar in O'Reilly's for years and the boss, Mark, had offered to pay for her evening reception. He'd even laid on transport to take us down and bring us home – those of us who wanted to come home that evening. That was Mark all over, looking after the rest of us.

The wedding was great. Gail looked beautiful and her husband had scrubbed up well. I was at the table with a few of the other girls and two of the barmen. One of them, Brendan, though we all called him Benny, came over and sat next to me when I took a breather from the Macarena.

'All right, love,' he said, winking as he sat.

He looked around the room, smiling at some of the other guests, seeming to get his breath after the exertions of the dance. Yet, at the same time, I could feel his hand snaking its way over my knee and up my thigh.

'What the fuck, Benny?'

'Just checking you've got knickers on,' he said, then his hand brushed me.

'Yeah,' he said. 'There they are.'

His hand rested too long, and I squirmed a little, squeezing my legs together where I sat, though he seemed to enjoy that.

'Ask your wife if she's wearing knickers,' I snapped.

Benny had been married for eight years. He'd two kids already and the rumour was a third was coming. He'd never confirmed that for me, probably because he thought I'd be less likely to sleep with him if I knew his wife was pregnant. Mind you, it hadn't stopped me during the previous two pregnancies. In fact, our first time had been just after he'd announced that she was expecting their first.

I'd been helping behind the bar that night, covering for someone who'd called in a sickie, while my mum watched Hope. We were locking up and Benny asked did I want a night cap.

'Have you not got someone waiting for you at home?'

'Her? Huh,' he said, and that was that. We'd gone for shots, stayed in for a lock-in in a pub down the street, then ended up at a party and, a bit later, in bed.

'Knickers?' Benny said now. 'More like a chastity belt.'

I reached down and pulled his hand away, then crossed my legs away from him.

'You're at a wedding. Does that not make you feel guilty?'

'Do you?' he asked, seeming genuinely interested.

'I'm a free agent,' I said.

'You're cheating too,' he said. 'And Amy's done nothing to you. She's a pain in my hole every day.'

'Then divorce her,' I said.

'It's not that easy. The kids, you know.'

'I'd rather Hope had no da than one who was playing away from home every night.'

'But you've no problem with her ma doing it?' he grinned, believing that he'd reached a winning conclusion, then reached into his pocket and pulled out a white card which he laid on the table in front of me.

'I'm staying down. I got two keys. Room 121.'

'Someone's going to see,' I said, lifting the card from the table where he'd placed it. It was only as he got up and went back onto the dance floor, laughing, that I realised I'd put it in my bag rather than handing it back to him.

At 2 a.m., when the bus was leaving, I went to the bathroom and waited until I heard the chugging of the diesel engine and the shouts of the wedding party fade, then made my way up to the first floor.

Benny answered the door in his boxers, already holding a bottle of Aftershock.

'I missed the bus,' I said.

He laughed and danced, as if on puppet strings. His skin was absurdly white, his chest narrow and free from hair. For a moment, as I looked at him, I wondered what two women now had seen in him, at least one of whom knew he was a cheating weasel.

But I'd no lift home and enough of a buzz from the wedding that I could go a few more shots and, weasel or not, the night wouldn't be a complete waste.

He woke me at 8 o'clock the next morning and told me he'd a taxi arranged with a few other lads, so I'd need to find my own way home. One would be calling for him at 9 a.m. and he needed me out by then. We'd time for a quick one, he told me, smiling, kissing around my neck and ear, his hand already groping at me.

So it was that at 8.45, while Benny went in to get showered, I padded down to the first floor of the Oceanview, my heels in my hand, and made my way down to reception. I'd not enough money for a taxi home, but I figured if I was sitting in the foyer when the lads appeared with Benny, I could bum a lift off them, without anyone knowing he and I had spent the night together.

That was the plan anyway.

I got in the lift and pressed G, two buttons below 1, skipping the M. The motion of the lift made my stomach churn. The hotel was hot, the lift stuffy and smelling of someone's perfume. I felt sick and wanted to get out. Then, to add to my annoyance, the lift stopped at M anyway.

The doors slid open, and two men stood there. Absently, I thought they might have been guests at the wedding too, for their dress was neat, tidy, studiedly casual.

The pair stared at me, as if amused in some way.

'Are you getting in?' I asked, already reaching for the Close Doors button. Someone had once told me they weren't actually wired up, they were just to make impatient people feel better, but it was a risk I was willing to take. My head was spinning, the floor of the lift tilting in ways that made me doubt the cables holding it.

'Katie?' one of the men said. 'Katie Hamill?'

The other reached and laid his hand against the open door, preventing it from shutting.

'Do I know you?' I asked. The man who'd spoken, who knew my name, was decidedly average. He'd black hair, cropped short, and patchy black stubble which emphasised the roundness of his face. His eyes danced as if he'd just found something remarkably funny, and I couldn't help but feel that he was laughing at me.

'I know you. Katie, Katie, doing the walk of shame, eh?'

'Get lost,' I said, stabbing the Close Door button, but the second man, the quiet one, stepped into the doorway and stood with his back to the gap, keeping the door open.

'Can we have a wee word, Katie?' the black-haired one said.

'I don't talk to strangers.'

'We're not strangers,' he said, mock offended. 'Sure we know all about you, about Hope. About your mum, who's looking after that wee dote. About Brendan Barr. We know it all. We just want a word. Five minutes and then you're free to go. We can even throw you a few pound for a taxi if you need it.'

'I already have a taxi,' I said.

'You don't. Benny's taxi has four in it. There's no room for you. Besides, what will Amy think if he lands home with his bit-on-the-side on the side?'

'Who the fuck are you?'

'That's not the question you need to ask,' he said. 'The better question is, "What can we do for you?" Just give us five minutes and we'll show you.'

'No.'

'Five minutes, love,' the second man said, reaching out, as if to guide me out of the lift.

I pulled away from him. 'Don't touch me,' I said. 'Or I'll scream.'

'There's no need for all this,' the first man said, his voice lower now. 'Five minutes and you can go. Trust me, it's what Hope would want.'

The repeated mention of my daughter focused me. I looked up and saw a CCTV camera in the corner of the lift. There were others in the corridors of the hotel. Someone would see me walking with these men, would be able to trace my steps.

'Nothing is going to happen to you, Katie,' Black-Hair said. 'It's all good. We just want to talk.'

The quiet one stepped out of the lift and gestured that I should do likewise. My free hand reached into my bag and spidered around until I felt the cold hardness of my house keys. I bunched them in my fist, one sticking out between my fingers.

Then I got out and followed Black-Hair, the other man walking behind me, in step. We went through a set of double doors, into a conference room, then on across towards a second, marked Meeting Room.

Black-Hair opened the door and stepped back, allowing me to enter.

Inside were several black leather executive chairs positioned around a large table covered in pages. One chair was already pulled out, as if in invitation that I sit. It took me a second to register what was on the table. What I'd thought were documents were, in fact, photographs and, as I moved closer, I realised they were all of me: pictures of me and Hope coming home from school; pictures with my mother; pictures of me in a bus; pictures of me shopping; pictures of me dancing at the wedding the previous night, taken from inside the room; pictures of me and Benny. So many pictures of me and Benny, including one of us in a position which could only have been taken half an hour previous.

'What the fuck?' I repeated.

'We know a lot about you, Katie,' Black-Hair said, closing the door.

I could feel the heat in the room rising, could feel things slide from me. Something crept up the back of my throat and I knew I would either faint or be sick. As if anticipating this very thing, the quiet one stood next to me, holding a wastepaper basket.

As I leaned over to vomit into it, I could see the bottom of it had been lined with pictures of Benny on me. I only saw it an instant before it was awash with the remains of last night's eating.

'This happens more often that you'd think,' Black-Hair said, calm as you like, pulling out the chair next to me and sitting, fixing his trouser leg as he did. 'Now, let's you and us have a wee chat, eh?'

## Chapter Two

They let me sit for a few minutes while I gathered my breath and allowed the retching to subside.

In reality, I think they were deliberately giving me time to take in all the pictures that they had displayed. The ones of Benny and me were closest to my seat, though he also featured in some of the pictures near the top of the table as well, furthest from where I sat.

I got up and, moving slowly, traced back the images. They were in chronological order, mostly. A birthday party with Hope at the local amusement arcade; that must have been mid-August. Pictures of me sitting eating ice cream with my mum. I knew the beach where we'd been, but it was on the other side of the Inishowen peninsula. Moving backwards, pictures of me on the bus, in a taxi, standing outside work sharing a cigarette with Gail, who looked like she was in tears. I remembered that night too: it must have been June at some stage because I'd been drafted in to cover shifts for someone who'd gone on an early holiday before the schools closed and prices rocketed. Gail had been having doubts about her engagement and we'd chatted as we shared a smoke. I told her how lucky she was to have her other half ... I took a blank – I'd been at his wedding the day before and still couldn't remember his name.

Finally, at the top of the table, pictures of Benny and me, doing shots in a bar, walking to the taxi stand together, him leaning towards me. Us in the taxi, already kissing before we even made it back to my place.

And scattered throughout, like confetti, a memory of joy, pictures of Hope, smiling, playing, taking my hand. It was these pictures that wounded me most; the knowledge that someone had been filming my daughter, while I was there, and I hadn't noticed or done anything to protect her. Those images left me feeling much more vulnerable than the images of me and Benny in bed.

'She's a lovely looking kid,' Black-Hair said, seemingly having read my mind.

I could not put my thoughts in order enough to say all that I wanted and instead simply managed, 'Why?'

'We've been watching you for a while, Katie,' Black-Hair said. 'As you can see. You've a busy life.'

His accent was northern, broad but polished. Belfast, maybe, but educated Belfast – one of the posh schools. The quiet one hadn't said enough for me to make a judgement on him yet. He was watching me, his hands resting lightly on the back of one of the other chairs, in a pretence of relaxation. But he did not seem relaxed.

That made two of us.

'Why?' I asked again.

'You seem like a popular person,' Black-Hair said, leaning forward in his seat. 'Someone people feel comfortable around. Look at Gail there. Getting cold feet over Hugh and who does she go to? Her best friend? No. You, a work colleague. You're a shoulder to cry on, Katie. A friendly ear.'

'I don't know what this is about,' I said, then, nodding at the quiet one, asked, 'And why doesn't he talk? Who are you?'

My brain was finally beginning to process thoughts. Why hadn't I asked them to identify themselves from the start. 'Are you police?'

The quiet one inclined his head a little, as if indicating that such a thing should be self-evident.

'Guard or PSNI?' I asked. We were in Donegal, in the Republic where the Gardai had jurisdiction, but his northern accent made me think that, like me, he was from over the border and so maybe with the Police Service of Northern Ireland.

'It's not as simple as that.'

'I want to see some ID,' I said, folding my arms in a show of defiance I certainly did not feel.

The quiet one laughed at that, and Black-Hair smiled over towards him.

'Now you make a sound,' I said. 'I thought you were a fucking mute for a minute.'

The nervous adrenaline was making me jumpy and I was getting pissed.

'When I've something to say to you, you'll know all about it, love,' the quiet one said. English accent. He wasn't a Guard, that's for sure.

'Look, we're getting off on the wrong foot,' Black-Hair said.

'All you have are wrong feet,' I said, getting up. 'Who the hell do you think you are, taking pictures of my wee girl? Or my ma?'

I'd barely stood when I felt the pressure of English's hands on my shoulders, pushing me back down into the seat.

'We want to help you, Katie,' Black-Hair said. 'Just hear us out. Christmas is coming. We could give you a few pounds; get something nice for Hope. She's asking for a bike, isn't that right?'

She was, but I didn't know how they knew that, and I wasn't going to confirm it for the smug bastard.

'I know she is,' he said, again seeming to know what I was thinking. 'And she deserves it. She's a great wee lassie, isn't she?'

This question was directed not to me but to English, who glanced at her picture and nodded.

Black-Hair produced an envelope from his pocket and, placing it on the table, pushed it towards me, spilling some of the pictures onto the floor as he did. Absurdly, I bent to pick them up.

'Don't worry about those,' he said, laughing. 'We'll get those later. That's for you.' He indicated the envelope with a nod of his head.

I was curious to know what was inside, yet did not want to give them the satisfaction of looking.

'I don't want it, whatever it is.'

'It's five hundred quid,' he said. 'For you. Think what you could get Hope with that. No more scrimping on Santa.'

'I never scrimp,' I said. 'I'd go without before having her be disappointed.'

'I know you would,' Black-Hair agreed, his voice plaintive and sincere. 'I know how much you love her. You can see it in the pictures. And we'll be destroying all of these once we're done here, so don't be worrying about that.'

'Why bother taking them then?'

'To show you that we're serious people. I know you'd only want to work with serious people.'

'Are you offering me a job?'

Another laugh from English, though this time it seemed to annoy Black-Hair, who glanced at him sharply, then back to me.

'Kind of. We want you to stay working in O'Reilly's, but we just want you to keep that friendly ear of yours open.'

'For what?'

'Anything.'

'Like in the playground. Who's having an affair? Who's almost broke? That kind of shit? 'Cause that's all I'm hearing in any day.'

'Don't be disingenuous,' English said. 'You know what we mean.'

'Don't be what? That must be a word from English schools, 'cause I don't know that one.'

'Don't act stupid,' he said. 'Is that better?'

English was rattled, though I couldn't tell why.

Black-Hair took control again. He produced another picture and placed it on the table.

'You know this man?'

I did. It was my boss's older brother, Terry O'Reilly. Everyone knew Terry, for all the wrong reasons. He had been in and out of prison more times than I knew. If there was a gun found in the city, Terry was lifted. A bomb scare?

Terry's door was kicked down. Someone shot? Terry was in Antrim in the Serious Crime Suite within an hour.

Yet, despite the almost personalised attention Terry got from the cops, within a few days, he'd be back out, released on bail pending a file being prepared for the CPS. And none of the cases ever went anywhere.

'You're Special Branch?'

Another incline of the head. 'So, you do know Terry?' he said, putting the picture away.

'The whole town knows Terry,' I said.

'They do,' Black-Hair agreed. 'Though the only one he really trusts is his younger brother. Your boss, Mark.'

'And?'

'Terry drops into the bar at times, doesn't he?'

'You obviously know he does; it's half his.' There was no point lying; almost every question he had asked, he already knew the answer to anyway.

'And he and Mark talk.'

This time it was a statement, not a question. 'And?'

'We'd like you to use your friendly ear and if you hear anything interesting, to let us know.'

'That's it?'

'That's it,' Black-Hair agreed, his hands open, as if to indicate his honesty.

'If I hear anything interesting and tell you, you'll give me five hundred quid to buy my daughter a bike for Christmas?'

He smiled, seemingly overjoyed at my amazement.

'Do you think I'm fucking stupid?' I said.

His expression faltered a little but did not fall as I had expected.

'If I tell you anything about Terry O'Reilly, I'll not make it to Christmas. I'll be shot ten minutes later.'

'I know it's overwhelming—'

'It's not overwhelming. It's insane.' The history of Derry was littered with the dead bodies of those who had been accused of informing to the police or Special Branch against paramilitaries. Most often they were found stripped naked, tortured and shot in the head, a punishment carried out at times, it had subsequently been revealed, by others who were themselves informers. All part of the dirty war. Those days might be mostly over now, but it was still a death wish and not one I shared.

'I know what happens to touts,' I said. '*You* know what happens to them. So, no thanks. I don't want your measly five hundred. Five thousand wouldn't convince me to tout on Terry O'Reilly.'

'So, you know what he's like?'

'Of course I know what he's like. The whole fucking city knows what he's like. I told you that already.'

Black-Hair offered me a mild smile. 'You did. And you're happy to let him keep shooting people and selling drugs? You're happy for your daughter, for Hope, to grow up in a town where Terry O'Reilly and his ilk do whatever they feel like?'

'Hope needs a mother *now*. The future will see to itself.'

I was shocked to feel English's hand on my shoulder again. He'd been so quiet, I'd almost forgotten he was still standing behind me.

'We can be very useful friends to have, Katie,' he said.

'I don't need friends, thanks.'

'Ah, you only think that,' he replied, quietly.

I'd had enough. Shrugging off the weight of his hand, I stood, and lifting the envelope, threw it back at Black-Hair.

'I'm not for sale,' I said. 'You can fuck off.'

Calmly, he lifted the envelope from the ground where it fell and stood himself. 'That's fine, Katie. We'll talk again. You might change your mind.'

'I won't,' I said. 'And don't come near me or my daughter again, do you hear me?'

'Or what?' English asked. 'You'll tell Terry we spoke to you? And how do you know he'll believe you that you said no?'

'He will,' I said, though not with the confidence I'd hoped.

English moved towards me, close enough that I could feel the heat off him, smell the citrus of his aftershave.

'The thing worse than being an informer, Katie, is everyone *thinking* you're one,' he said.

## Chapter Three

It was only as I made it to reception that I realised I did not have the money they had promised for a taxi. To be honest, I'd not have taken any car they'd booked for me anyway; presumably it would have been wired up with cameras watching me. Benny and the lads were nowhere to be seen so I assumed they had already left. It was 9.30 a.m. now and I knew I'd missed taking Hope to school. I trusted my mother would have done so when she realised that I hadn't made it home.

I had to ask the receptionist for directions to the bus. As she answered, she glanced at my clothing, obviously from the night before, and curled her lip a little, as if my smell offended her.

The truth is, I felt dirty. Not just physically, though I did, for my top smelt of sweat and beer and food, and my underwear was a day old. I felt dirty because of Benny. At the start, it had been exciting, being with him. There was the added thrill of knowing he picked me over his wife, over Amy. It made me feel good. And I enjoyed it. But not now.

Besides, I could still feel the touch of English on my shoulder, the pressure and warmth of his palm. He'd not considered whether he could or should touch me. He simply had, like I was powerless. They had exposed my life for me to see, its narrowness. Me and Hope and Mum, and beaches and ice cream and Benny. And in the pictures, his bony arse arched, his skinny, white, hairless legs, the pantomime of concentration on his face, his breath on me, yeasty and sour, his grin, his moan, the roll over, the void, the mess. For the first time, they'd made me feel like *I* was being used. And I'd never felt that way before.

The bus back to Derry was stuffy, the air con seemingly not working. The air smelt stale and I noticed people notice me when they got on and avoid sitting in front or behind me. One woman even chose to stand when no other seats were available, until a young lad lifted down his bag and invited her to take the free one next to him on which it had been placed.

'This isn't me,' I wanted to shout at then. 'This, what you see. This isn't me. There's more.'

But in six months of photographs, there wasn't much more. That was what they had done to me.

As we rumbled across the border, I wondered was it deliberate. Had the whole thing been intended to break my confidence, to make me doubt myself? They'd not blackmailed me with the pictures, not threatened to use them. They were just to show their power. They could do this without my knowing. They could do what they liked. As with the fact they'd approached me in Donegal, a different country for them. Had the Gardai known they were there?

But everyone knows what happens when you get involved with them. Hands taped in front of you, stripped naked, a bag over your head to contain the mess. Shot from behind so your family couldn't have an open coffin for the wake. You'd stand there, in the darkness, suffocating, waiting for the shot. Powerless.

I could feel panic rising along with the bile that had settled in my stomach. I thought I might be sick, though knew I had nothing left to bring up. I never felt so weak. I looked around the bus, studying each face. Was one of them filming me right now? Was one of *them* Special Branch, too. Is that what they did, on a Tuesday morning? Get a bus from Donegal to Derry to watch a thirty-four-year-old woman who cleaned a pub? Who knew nothing? Was that someone's fucking job?

The whole Benny thing was over, that was for a start. I was getting angry now at them all and Benny was rolled up in there too. I was going to break it off, not that there had been anything anyway. It was casual, sporadic. But it was done now. This morning was the last time, of that I was certain.

And Hope needed me to take her to school. That was my job; our time together walking in the morning, talking about things, her friends, her teacher, her quirky questions that showed an imagination much richer than mine. Who'd win in a fight between a polar bear and a lion? Hope knew.

I was going to take control of things again. And be careful. They wouldn't catch me out again, wouldn't have anything they could use against me.

My mum said nothing when I got home except, 'Have you had breakfast yet?'

I shook my head.

She looked at me, at my outfit, took it all in. 'Get a shower and I'll make some toast,' she said, passing no comment.

'Did Hope get to school okay?'

'You know she did. She's bright as a spark that one. Sharp as a pin.'

'And they say apples don't fall far from trees,' I joked, hoping for some disagreement.

A pause. 'You used to be the same, at her age,' she said as she headed into the kitchen, the rest of her thought left hanging unsaid.

I felt better after I'd washed and got some clean clothes on. I was working at 2 p.m.; Mark had said the bar wouldn't be opening until mid-afternoon to give everyone a chance to recover after Gail's wedding.

Mum asked about the day, and I showed her some of the pictures I'd taken of Gail.

'What's her hubbie called?'

'Hugh,' I said, confidently, then realised it was only because Black-Hair had called him that and I'd assumed he would know.

'Where did you all end up?' she asked, sipping her tea and not quite meeting my gaze.

'Mark booked rooms for anyone who wanted to stay over,' I said. 'I was knackered and couldn't face the drive home last night.'

'Hope was up in the night looking for you,' she said, and I felt a pang of guilt, though also that conflict between feeling bad and annoyance at my mum that she had told me, precisely to make me guilty.

'Well, I'm here now,' I said, then realised that a consequence of the later start time for work meant that I couldn't collect her from school and still get to O'Reilly's for 2 p.m.

'Actually,' I said, glancing at my mother, hoping that she would know what I was about to say and so would offer, thereby not requiring me to ask. 'Mark wants me in at two to get the place ready for opening.'

'I'll collect her,' Mum said, with a sigh that I knew was mostly performance. Or at least I hoped it was.

I walked up town, for my wages hadn't hit my account yet and I didn't have enough for a taxi. Mum walked part of the way with me before cutting across towards the school. Like earlier, when on the bus, as I walked now, I looked around me, checking to see who was nearby, whether anyone was filming me without my realising it. I noticed the CCTV cameras perched on the lampposts, stopping for a moment to see if they would move to focus on me, then taking a few steps and stopping again to see if they followed me.

A couple walking behind me tutted as they passed me on the roadway, then retook the pavement with a glance of disdain. I realised how silly I must look. Whatever the two men who'd spoken to me earlier had done, I'd made it clear that I wasn't going to help them. They knew I wouldn't tell Terry about their approaching me; indeed, English had been the one to point out the danger in doing so. They would be done with me, their surveillance wasted. Besides, what could I tell them? I wore headphones when I worked, focusing on getting the job done before Hope finished school each day. Why they thought I'd be useful to them was beyond me.

By the time I got to work, I was feeling a little more content. That was until I went inside and saw Terry and Mark sitting at a table, having coffee.

'There she is,' Mark said, laughing. 'I hope I look a bit fresher than you, Katie.'

Behind the bar, Benny was stocking shelves, the room alive with the clattering of glass bottles clinking into the empties crate. He glanced at me when I came in and I thought he blushed. I tried not to react but was pretty sure when I looked again at Mark and Terry, the older man had been watching us both.

Immediately, I wondered if he knew. Not just about Benny and me, but about all of it. Maybe the two men this morning were his. That would explain how they got some of the images they had. Maybe it was a test, a way to prove I could be trusted, though trusted with what beyond cleaning shitty bogs and vomit was beyond me.

'All right, Terry,' I said, thinking he might find it strange if I didn't acknowledge him.

'Katie. You'd a good night last night?'

Terry was older than Mark and wirier. Where Mark had kept his hair, albeit dyed a different tone from his moustache, Terry had shaved his head, so that a fine grey stubble was all that showed. His features were pinched and weathered in contrast with Mark's softness, something which reflected on their characters, too. Mark was friendly, the public face of the bar, always joking with customers; Terry was the opposite, reserved, always watching but never getting involved in the running of the place, his interests lying beyond the bar. Even when he spoke, he did so with such economy of movement that his lips barely moved. As a result, I did not know if what he had said was intended as a question or a statement. Either way, I was convinced he was attempting to suppress a smile, but I couldn't be sure.

'Gail looked beautiful,' I said, settling for something which I hoped was vague enough to avoid confusion.

'She did,' Mark said. 'That Hugh fucker is punching above his weight.'

Mark's leg bounced where he sat, his hand, resting on his knee, seemingly unable to control whatever nervous energy was buzzing through him.

'So long as that's all he's punching,' Terry said.

Mark nodded. 'Hard to make a fist when you're on crutches,' he added.

Was that a threat? Was this what Black-Hair had wanted me to listen out for? Was that why they were at Gail and Hugh's wedding?

I thought back to the night the cops had photographed: the night Gail had spoken to me about her 'cold feet'. It had been more than that, though. I'd noticed the bruises on her arms while the two of us were washing glasses. Five small, concentric marks, a grip wide. I'd asked her what happened, already fearing the worst. She'd said nothing, but her eyes had filled, and she bunched up the drying cloth and told me she was going for a smoke.

We'd pretty much locked up anyway, so I'd gone out through the kitchen to the alleyway along which we stacked the empties crates and on which staff took their smoke breaks to see if she was okay.

Gail was dragging on her cigarette, her free arm wrapped tightly round her.

'I didn't mean to pry,' I said. 'Sorry for asking.'

She dismissed my apology with a waft of her hand as she dispersed the smoke she exhaled, then offered me a cigarette.

'I asked for it,' she said. 'I hit him first.'

She looked at me, as if trying to see if I believed her. I didn't but nor did I challenge her on the point; she needed a sympathetic ear, not a sceptical one. Instead, I shrugged and blew on the tip of my cigarette before taking another drag.

'Do you ever doubt yourself?'

'The engagement?'

She shrugged this time, then nodded. 'Yeah.'

'If you're not happy, you're not happy.'

'But I am happy. Mostly. It's just sometimes . . .'

'Maybe take a breather, then? See how things work out.'

Gail shook her head and blew out a steady stream of smoke, direct and low. I realised then that she was crying, that the content of our conversation had not really mattered at all. She was working through her own thoughts, her own feelings. I was just someone she could pretend she was discussing it with.

I moved across and hugged her, tightly, felt her lay her head against my shoulder, felt the shudders of her tears. We stood like that for a moment, then she seemed to catch her breath and straightened.

'Everything okay?'

Mark had appeared in the doorway. 'We're locking up, girls.' He saw Gail turn away and wipe her eyes, then looked at me quizzically. I shook my head, indicating it was nothing. He sized up the situation then nodded. 'In your own time, Gail.' Then he motioned that I should go back inside and followed me in. He tapped me on the shoulder as we walked.

'Is it the bruises on her arm?' he hissed.

I nodded.

'I'll get it dealt with. It'll not happen again.'

Now, as he talked about crutches, I wondered whether Hugh had been given a warning back then. Gail had not mentioned him or the bruises to me again, and the wedding had gone ahead without incident – for them at least.

The door opened as I turned to lift my dustpan and brush, and looking up, I saw Benny's expression change. His face brightened with a smile, momentarily, then darkened just as quickly.

I was just turning to see what had caused it when I felt someone grab a handful of my hair and tug.

'Whore!' his wife, Amy, screamed, pulling me to the ground.

## Chapter Four

Pain seared in my head as she pulled at my hair, tugging me to one side and causing me to lose my balance. I hit my shoulder off the edge of one of the low stools as I fell, the furniture clattering away from me across the floor. I could hear the raised voices: Benny's pleading whine; Mark's barking commands.

Though I could feel Amy tug at my head, then attempt to bang it off the floor, I could not fight back beyond trying to push her off me. Then she was lifted from me, bodily, a clump of my hair still clenched in her fist that gave with a tear and my instinctive yelp of pain.

'What the fuck is going on?' Mark snapped.

Amy rushed me again as I tried to sit up, kicking out ineffectually, connecting with the sole of my trainers and little more.

'Amy,' Benny said, trying to smother her renewed anger with a hug, which she pushed away.

'Don't. You're welcome to her, you cheating bastard,' Amy said, shoving at him.

I managed to sit up and could taste blood in my mouth, warm and sour. Amy was crying now, the tears streaming down her face, her anger turning to grief. Benny was standing with his hands on his hips, his head lowered a little, defeated. Mark looked between them, shaking his head.

Only Terry remained where he had been sitting before all

this, his coffee cup in his hand, his expression unreadable. He looked from one to the other, glancing at me in turn. I looked away, embarrassed, aware that his gaze was already sliding from me and settling on Benny.

'What's going on?' Mark asked. 'Amy? What's wrong?'

'Did you know?' Amy demanded. 'That these two fucked last night?'

'Amy,' Benny said. 'I swear to God, I don't know what you're talking about.'

'Don't you? Did she stay in your room last night?'

'What?' Benny's voice cracked as he spoke and, in that moment, I wondered how either Amy or I had ever found him attractive.

'Did she stay in your room last night?'

'No!' he said. 'I swear on the kids, Amy. She didn't.'

Something in Amy's expression hardened now and she wiped away the last of her tears defiantly. 'You swear on the kids?'

'Yeah. I swear to God,' Benny said. 'Why would I sleep with Katie when I've you, love? I'm not stupid.'

Amy sniffed as she nodded. 'You're not stupid, Benny, I'll give you that.'

As I struggled to stand, I saw her pull her phone from her pocket, unlock it and hold it out to Benny so he could see the screen.

'But you are careless, you lying fucking prick.'

I could see the blood drain from Benny's face and his hand reaching out to the back of the chair nearest him for support, even as he tried to dismiss whatever she showed him with a feeble laugh.

'That? That was her.'

'What is it, Amy?' Mark asked and Amy handed him the phone. He grimaced as he studied the image on the screen, then held the phone out so I could see it.

The image was a little blurred and at such an angle that it appeared to have been taken quickly. It showed the doorway of Benny's hotel room. He stood in his boxers while I, leaving the room, stood on tiptoe as I kissed him, my heeled shoes in my hand.

I remembered the moment, just this morning, as I was leaving the room, a last hurried, exciting kiss, the fact that we were in the corridor of the hotel making it all the more thrilling. But I could not, for the life of me, remember anyone in the corridor or walking past us. Perhaps it had been taken by someone in one of the rooms opposite.

'Her?' Amy asked. 'I know it was *her*. I can fucking see, Benny.'

Mark shook his head and motioned to return the phone to Amy, when Terry reached over and took it from him. He studied the picture, then seemed to continue scrolling in a manner which made me wonder if there were other images. Worse ones.

'No. It was her. She did stay the night, but not like you think. She landed up to my room after the bus had left, said she'd missed it and didn't have money for a taxi or for a room. She'd nowhere to go. I'd a spare bed in my room.'

'Aye right,' Amy said.

'I did!' Benny protested. 'They gave me a twin with two single beds. What could I do? I felt sorry for her. You know Katie's broke, like.'

I'd never felt as pathetic as I did then, while these people discussed my poverty, in my presence, without even addressing me. No one complained, no one defended me. And I could not defend myself for seeing Amy, seeing what our sleeping together had done to her, I felt only shame.

'She slept in your room? In a different bed?' Amy asked sceptically, though I had the impression that she was trying to convince herself, even as she seemed to doubt what he said.

'Yeah. I told her I wanted her to leave this morning in case anyone got the wrong idea. As she was leaving she turned and just kissed me. I didn't ask her to. She just did it.'

Amy and Mark both looked across at me, as if to see if I would deny it. I couldn't. I had kissed him, though it was not true to say he had resisted. Still, having hurt Amy enough already, I felt conflicted about whether to add to her anger and pain by telling her the whole truth. Benny and I were over anyway.

Only Terry did not look at me. Instead, seemingly finished with the phone, he set it down on the table and took off his glasses before looking again at Benny.

'Is that true?' Amy asked me.

I looked to Benny, who nodded lightly, willing me to back up his version of events.

'I kissed him,' I said, honestly.

'And did you ask to stay in his room?'

'I missed the bus,' I said, again trying to be honest. 'Benny let me stay over.'

I could see that Amy was struggling to reconcile her feelings on all this. Her immediate reaction to the image suggested she did not wholly trust her husband – with good cause – but the explanation she'd been offered was plausible enough for her to accept it. For her to want to accept it.

'Did you sleep with him? Did you sleep with my husband?'

And there it was, as bald as you like. There was no way I could be vague about answering this. I looked again to Benny who was now mouthing 'No' so lightly it was little more than a parting of his lips, his eyes pleading, his hands gripping the back of the chair.

'No,' I said, unable to hold her gaze, my mouth suddenly dry.

There was a moment's pause as Amy considered whether she believed me, whether she wanted to believe me. She took the proffered phone from Terry and then approached me and jabbed me in the chest, once, hard.

'Stay the fuck away from my husband. Slag.'

Then she spat on me as Mark protested and moved to pull her from me.

'I'm fine,' I said as I wiped my face with the sleeve of my T-shirt, twisting my neck to do so.

'Fucking hickeys at your age,' Amy said. 'You're a dirty bitch, too.'

I couldn't work out what she meant and turning, regarded myself in the 'Guinness is Good For You' mirror which dominated the main wall. Pulling down the collar of my T-shirt, I could see the livid bruising of a love bite with which Benny must have marked me the previous evening.

'Right,' Mark said, shepherding Amy to the door. 'Benny, go home and get this sorted, would you? Katie will cover your shift.'

I suspected he worried that Amy might begin to doubt my denial if she thought too long about the love bite. And I guessed that Amy already was, though it was easier for her to believe me a slag than her husband a cheat and her marriage a sham.

'Amy?' Terry's voice was low and gravelly, but it was enough to stop her and quieten the room. 'Who sent you this?'

Amy looked to Mark, as if wondering why Terry was speaking to her.

'What?'

'Who sent you the picture?'

Amy looked to Benny, then shrugged. 'It must have been someone at the wedding,' she said.

'But who?'

'I don't know,' Amy admitted.

'It's not from one of your contacts,' Terry persisted.

'I got it through WhatsApp,' Amy said. 'Probably someone who didn't want to fall out with me, using a different phone.'

Terry nodded, though he seemed unconvinced. He looked at me again, then to Benny, watching him as he left.

'You okay?' Mark asked me with more gentleness than I felt I deserved, once they'd gone, as he righted the stools which had been knocked over.

'My head is bleeding,' I said, pressing my hand to my scalp where Amy had tugged my hair and examining the staining on my fingers.

'She wigged you rightly,' Mark said. 'There's a first-aid kit in back. Are you okay to cover for Benny? Or do you need to go home?'

I wanted to go home; I'd not seen Hope since lunchtime the day before. But I also was aware that she did want that bike for Christmas, and I needed money to buy it. I couldn't afford to turn down work when I got it. Besides, Mark always paid me for emergency shifts, cash in hand, so it didn't impact my benefits. And someone would give you a lift home at the end of the day, saving me on taxi or bus money too.

'I'll work.'

'Good girl.'

As I made my way behind the bar to get the first-aid kit, Mark retook his seat next to Terry.

'Fuck me,' he muttered. 'Bloody women. I wasn't expecting a cat fight today!'

'See if you can find out who sent Amy that picture.'

'Some shit-stirrer probably,' Mark said, replying to his brother but glancing up at me. I busied myself with the kit, taking out some cotton wool and soaking it under the tap before looking at myself in the mirror behind the bar and dabbing at the bloody patch on my scalp.

I couldn't make out what Terry said next, though did catch the word 'Benny'.

In the mirror, I pulled back the collar of my T-shirt again and regarded the bite he had left there.

'He's not a bad lad,' Mark said in response to whatever Terry had said. 'Now, what about Millar? Everyone still good?'

I caught Terry's gaze reflected in the mirror where he watched me, so dabbing once more at my head, I pulled out my headphones from my pocket and putting them in, turned on music on my phone and went back to get my dustpan.

It was only much later that I began to wonder whether Black-Hair or English had sent that picture to Amy and whether this was their idea of a punishment for not helping them.

# Chapter Five

The shift passed as most do, a lull in the afternoon, a rush after work and a few couples coming in for food, perhaps not realising that those cooking the meals in the kitchen were, for the most part, students from the local schools, too young to be behind the bar but employed because Mark wanted to do favours for a few friends. That was the way with Mark: a young lad, wholly unskilled for kitchen work, would appear some day just because his dad was doing time and the family needed some cash to keep them going while the main breadwinner was inside. The bar staff were a rag tag of the dispossessed and the abandoned, all of whom Mark had taken under his care, myself included.

The rumour about me and Benny, and Amy's discovery, had spread and with it, I noticed a change in the way those who came to be served by me reacted. Many of the women, particularly those accompanying their partners, stood next to their man while he ordered, staring at me with barely disguised disgust, as if I might at any second make a move on their fella too. A few of the lads, on their own, jokingly asked how my head was, or whether I'd had a good night at the wedding.

'Knackered today, eh?' one asked, laughing.

But some of the men, both old and younger alike, became almost predatory themselves in their interactions with me.

One, a middle-aged regular called Kenneth, ordered his usual when he approached the bar, offering me an overly friendly wink as he did so. I remembered serving Kenneth of old, remembered the way he would delve deep in his pocket to pull out a bunch of spare coins, the care with which he would pick the change from his cupped hand, counting out the exact amount on the counter in a manner that suggested he had raided a jar of coppers, or hunted down the back of the sofa before coming up for his one shot and stout of the evening.

This time though, when I poured his pint and left it to settle, he had his money ready. He handed a note and a handful of pound coins to me on his outstretched palm, as if offering a sugar lump to a horse, then when I reached to take it, he laid his other hand on top of mine, holding mine in his. His skin was warm and damp. He held my gaze as he did so and smiled, his teeth worn and stained, his smile the wrong side of creepy.

'Keep the change. You could join me for one on your break, eh?'

I'd dealt with my fair share of letches when I was younger and had served in the bar more regularly. This was the first time in a while though and never Kenneth who came and went day after day, slipping in and out of the pub almost without notice. That he felt in a position to ask me to have a drink with him, felt I was so desperate that I might agree, unsettled me.

The shift passed this way. I texted Mum every so often to see how Hope was doing and felt a pang when she told me they'd gone to the cinema together without me. The day had been a disaster from the start, from the moment I went to the wedding in fact. I longed to be able to go back twenty-four hours, to stay with Hope rather than going to the hairdresser, to avoid Gail marrying a man who abused her, avoid my sleeping with a sad excuse for another, avoid the meeting with Black-Hair and English. I began to wonder if they had been there only for me, or had my being there been an opportunistic thing. Maybe they'd be watching everyone who worked in O'Reilly's. If Terry was their target, it made sense after all. I didn't make sense: I was a no one, I heard nothing, I knew nothing. I was the least obvious person to ask to spy on her friends, to inform.

Perhaps then, they had been watching us all and I was the one who became separated from the herd. They'd rolled the dice, perhaps hoping that threatening me would be enough to make me a tout. Besides, what was the worst they had on me? That I'd shagged Benny a few times? Well, that was kind of out now anyway. It couldn't do any more harm.

I wondered whether I should tell someone about them. The more I thought about it, the more I felt I had done nothing wrong. They had cornered me, had threatened me, had tried to blackmail me. I'd not invited it, had not approached them. I'd worked for Mark for years: he knew my loyalty; knew he could count on me when he was stuck. Hadn't I worked a shift today with a bleeding scalp and a bloody reputation?

I resolved to tell him that evening. There were three of us left at the end of shift and Mark offered to drop us home. Despite my house being the closest, he said he needed to drop Harry home first; Harry was seventeen and his dad was doing time for attempted murder of a cop. Mark was protective of him and, though I didn't understand his logic in dropping Harry before me, I accepted it. Then we dropped off another of the kitchen lads, Sean.

'You'll be ready for your bed,' Mark said as we set off, having seen Sean into the house. Mark had this habit of sitting, waiting for staff to open their front door and get inside safely before he drove off. There was something sweet about it, something protective, caring.

I'd told him as much, years back, when I'd first started in the bar. I was only young then, eighteen, and found such kindness attractive. After he dropped me home each evening, I'd turn at the door and sure enough he'd be watching me, checking I got in safe. I'd always wondered if he'd try his arm some night with me when we were alone in the car, but he never did, something for which I both respected him and, back then at least, perhaps felt a little disappointed. He'd been a good-looking man then. Still was, I supposed, even if he was a bit older now.

'It's been a long day,' I said.

He laughed, or grunted, agreement and we sat in silence for a few minutes as the streets slid past. I wondered if he was going to ask whether what Amy had said was true but when he did speak, it was not what I was expecting.

'How are *you* doing?' he said, suddenly, as we drove up the Strand Road. 'That can't have been easy.' He didn't look in my direction as he spoke.

'I— ah . . .' I didn't know what to say. How was I doing? Humiliated? Embarrassed at having been caught? Guilty?

'You handled it well,' he added, perhaps sensing I was struggling to answer. 'Benny will be getting an earful this evening, though. Good enough for him. Never mind Amy, he certainly doesn't deserve you.'

The softness in his tone surprised tears in my eyes. I nodded, stared at my hands, which were gathered in my lap. I felt tiny, felt like I was collapsing in on myself, like a black hole.

'He shouldn't be messing either of you around,' he said. 'That's not right, him a married man.'

'Was it you who told Amy?' I asked, suddenly wondering if that's what this was about. He seemed to be offended by Benny's behaviour. He'd arranged a bus home for us after all at his own expense. Perhaps he'd been seeking to avoid just this happening among the bar staff.

'Me? Jesus, no!' he laughed. 'Snitches get stitches! Not a chance. It was probably some of the day staff. There's a few of them good friends with Amy, who'd be raging at Benny for taking the piss out of her.'

'Do you ever feel like you're being watched?' I asked, broaching the subject which had been on my mind before Mark had mentioned Benny.

I looked across at him and he remained staring at the road, his hand tight on the wheel. Light and shadow shifted across his face, his expression darkening and brightening as the glare of the streetlights grew and fell away as we drove.

'All the time,' he said.

'So do I,' I said. 'I think I'm being watched all the time.'

'You are,' Mark said. 'Sure, Derry's a city with a village

mentality. This whole town is watching you. But that's a good thing. It means people have your back.'

'That's not . . .' I said and he looked over at me, sharply. I couldn't work out if it was annoyance at my disagreeing with him or curiosity over what I *had* meant. His eyes were alert, almost obsidian under the hood of his brows and the shadows that washed his face.

'*Is* someone watching you?' he asked, and I suddenly regretted ever having mentioned it.

'No. I mean I feel judged by everyone. All that nonsense with Hope's dad—'

'He was a waste of skin, Katie. You did right ditching him.'

It wasn't true to say I had ditched Hope's dad, Oran, but I appreciated Mark saying so. We'd been together almost ten years when I found out I was pregnant. At the time, I'd believed that a baby coming would cement our relationship; I was almost thirty and ready to get married, settle down and buy our own place. I thought the baby would be the catalyst Oran needed. I was right, though not in the way I'd expected. He'd stayed long enough for the free bar Mark gave us at the christening then announced he was heading to Canada with one of his sister's friends, Mandy. They were still together, as far as I could tell, based on the dual signatures on Hope's birthday card from them each year.

'Now this with Benny,' I said. 'I feel like I'm being judged all the time.'

He nodded. 'Yeah, I get that. We all are. The trick is not to take criticism from anyone you wouldn't ask for advice, eh?'

He smiled now, his face open and bright again, and I felt sure I'd avoided something.

We drove on in companionable silence until we reached the street where my mother lived and where Hope was spending the night. I'd decided to sleep over at hers, to share the bed with Hope so we could wake and make ourselves breakfast in bed the next morning.

Rather than drop me at the door and wait, engine idling as he usually did, this time at the entrance to the street, a few doors down from Mum's, Mark pulled into a parking space and killed the ignition. He twisted in his seat to look at me as I tried to release my seat belt and get out.

'You know if you're having any problems, you can come to me,' he said, reaching over and laying his hand on mine, surprising me by the intimacy of the gesture, his skin warm and soft and light. 'You know that. We loved your dad, me and Terry. The whole town did. We all miss him.'

My dad had been a footballer, not international or big league, a local who stayed local. But he'd been a good man. He'd coached the local kids, encouraged them to aim for the teams that had eluded him. He'd had trials with Newcastle when he was seventeen but didn't get selected. He had five good seasons in the local leagues before he shattered his leg in a car accident and ended his career. Mark and Terry knew him from the bar where, at the age of thirty and both chronically in pain and addicted to pain relief, he'd added alcohol to the mix and started the slow descent into liver failure, which eventually claimed him in his mid-forties, when I was fifteen. Having helped him on his way and, perhaps, riven with guilt, the pair took a proprietorial interest in our family and offered me work when I dropped out of school.

A few mates back then had suggested I head to Australia with them instead, start a new life once I turned eighteen, but I couldn't leave Mum behind on her own and, in truth, I didn't want to: this was my home. Besides, I met Oran a year or two after, we rented a place and settled into our own routine, even as friends drifted away, and our social circle constricted to the point where it was just us two. In fact, after Hope was born and he left, I realised that the only person I had to rely on was my mum. I told myself that that was enough and so, I had remained, working in O'Reilly's, a picture of my dad on the wall in Legends Corner in the bar to always remind me of the goodness of the man and the pointlessness of his loss.

'Thanks, Mark,' I said, the moment suddenly solemnised by the mention of my father.

'If you're short of cash, just ask,' he said. 'We'll never see you stuck, all right?'

I nodded, knowing that I would never ask anyone for money. That was not how I was raised. Better to go hungry than ashamed, my mum claimed, though there had been many times I wasn't convinced by her argument. Just then, his phone rang, via his radio, the sound filling the space between us. I glanced at the screen and saw the name Tel.

Mark answered but before he even had a chance to speak, I heard Terry's voice reverberate inside the car.

'Marky? Some result, lad. Two–nil! Two–nil, lad. Unbelievable!'

Mark shifted in his seat, lifting the handset and changing the setting to phone rather than Bluetooth even as, with a wink and a nod, he dismissed me from the car.

## Chapter Six

Sirens scored the city through the night as I lay next to Hope, unable to sleep despite my exhaustion. I could still feel the warmth of Mark's hand resting on mine, the gentleness of him. But the last thing I needed at the moment was the complication of another man's attention, now that the affair with Benny had become public knowledge. I just wanted to hide somewhere until it all passed. Besides, being involved with Mark would presumably just make me more attractive to Black-Hair and the English fella, make me more of a target for them to come back again and try to convince me to be a tout for them. I wouldn't do it. Still, as I drifted between sleep and wake, I swore I could feel his hand tighten on mine in a way that I did not find unpleasant.

In the morning, I saw on Twitter that there'd been a shooting in Eglinton. Two people were feared dead. Already the social media grapevine had named them as Detective Superintendent Matthew Millar and his wife, Laura. The post was accompanied by praying hands emojis and people commenting that they hoped this wasn't starting all over again. 'These people don't speak for us,' one person had written. 'Time to move on.'

We were far enough past the violence of previous years that people were genuinely shocked by such incidents now, as if the city's collective numbness had eased. I was eight by the time the Good Friday Agreement was signed, but still remembered the violence in the years before and after, especially the bombing in Omagh, a massacre so wasteful, so unnecessary, it seemed to shock people into looking more actively for peace. Most of us just wanted to get on with things now, with life. Still, that morning someone had graffitied *2–0* on one of the walls on the way into town, the numerals red and ragged as a reopening scar.

I had taken Hope into town for breakfast, as I usually did when I felt guilty about something. The streets were quiet for a mid-week morning but then many of the units we passed were boarded up and empty. Trade had moved out of town to the retail parks and the city centre was getting one facelift after another in an attempt to lure it back. Roads had been partially closed so picnic benches could be installed to encourage eating outdoors, as if the weather here would permit such a thing for more than a few weeks every year. The benches lay empty that morning, still damp from a fine mizzle of rain that had clung to the city through the night.

We walked past the bicycle shop at the top of Waterloo Street and Hope stopped and admired the various bikes sitting out on display. Her heart was set on only one though; a small, pink unicorn bike with iridescent foil on the metalwork and foil tassels hanging from the back of the seat like a tail.

The sight of it made me think of Black-Hair and English once more. I'd tried to put them from my mind, to tell myself that their meeting me had been opportunistic. But that still didn't explain how they'd known about Hope wanting a bike. It struck me suddenly that perhaps they had bugged our house, but I couldn't work out why they would bother. There was literally nothing discussed which might be of value to them; had they done so, I'd be the last person they'd have approached to inform to them.

I was uneasy about it, an aspect to the whole thing which I could not explain, could not rationalise to my own satisfaction.

'We need to go, sweetie,' I said, encouraging her along with a gentle tug of her hand.

We went to a café facing out towards the city walls and I ordered a coffee for myself and hot chocolate and a pancake stack for Hope, paying for it using my phone.

I'd barely sat down with the tray when I got a text to say that my bank account was overdrawn. There had to be some mistake; my social security payments were scheduled to have hit my account, so there was no way I could be in the red. I thought back again to the wedding, wondering if I'd overspent, bought more drinks than I remembered. But I was sure that I hadn't. Mark had bought rounds for the whole staff, so it had been a cheap evening, and I'd not wasted money on a taxi the following morning.

When we'd finished, I took Hope to the bank. Sure enough, the café bill had left me overdrawn by three pounds. I went in and asked the girl at the desk to check whether my payment was pending, but she said she couldn't tell. With a smile that seemed out of place for the circumstances, she suggested instead that I contact the Benefits team to find out what happened.

I dropped Hope off at school and, on my way to the bar to clean, phoned on my mobile. Almost an hour later, as I had started cleaning the toilets while leaving the phone sitting on hold, someone answered.

I explained my situation and the person who had answered cheerily told me they would look at my account and see what had happened.

'It might just be a glitch,' he said. 'If your circumstances haven't changed.'

'They haven't,' I said. 'Just the one child still.'

'You haven't given birth without your knowledge,' he joked, then, 'Oh.'

'That doesn't sound good.'

'Give me a second, Ms Hamill.'

The insipid music began once more. A few moments later, he returned.

'I'm afraid your benefit payments have been suspended pending an investigation.'

'Sorry, what?'

'Look, I'm sorry. I can't really say too much. You're being investigated over claims that you have undeclared earnings. Your payments have been suspended.'

'But that's rubbish,' I said. 'My circumstances haven't changed.'

'Do you have paid work, Ms Hamill?' he asked. 'Work you've not declared?'

'No,' I said, peeling off my rubber gloves, as if shedding the labour I'd been doing in that moment.

'Then everything should be okay,' he said. 'But your payments will be frozen until that investigation is complete. Money you are owed will be backdated if payments resume.'

'If? Not when?'

'Again, it's dependent on the outcome of the investigation.'

'But I'm broke.'

'I'm sorry, Ms Hamill,' he said. 'Maybe see if Citizens Advice can help you out. Is there anything else I can help you with today?'

'Can you lend me a couple of hundred?' I asked, only half joking.

He laughed. 'You have a good day, Ms Hamill,' he said, and I could imagine him somewhere, clicking off my call and moving on to the next, all fake enthusiasm and oozing sincerity.

When I came out of the toilet, I came face to face with Benny, standing in the passageway that led back out to the bar. I wondered whether he had been waiting out here for me the whole time I was in the toilet cleaning.

He shifted uneasily from foot to foot where he stood, one thin arm wrapped around him.

'All right, Katie?'

I nodded, raising my bucket filled with bleach to indicate I was laden down and not in the space for a conversation. The hint went unnoticed.

'Listen, thanks for all that, you know? With Amy,' he said.

I shook my head. 'It's fine.'

'I don't know who told her, I swear.' He raised his hands lightly in surrender as if to emphasise his innocence.

'It's fine,' I repeated, shifting the bucket and mop from one hand to the other.

'How's your head? She wigged you pretty hard.' His expression was a strange mix of concern for my wellbeing and amused pride in the forcefulness with which his wife had attacked me, and I began to suspect that he was enjoying the idea of two women fighting over him more than he was ashamed at having been caught cheating.

'It's grand,' I said, for variety. 'I need to get on.'

'Look, I was thinking. Maybe we should be more careful about things for a bit.'

'I agree,' I said, assuming he felt as I did. I was wrong.

'Even give it a few weeks and then see how things go, eh?'

Tired, I put the bucket down. 'Benny, it's over. You've a kid on the way. Amy needs you.'

'But I need you,' he said, with such sincerity I felt embarrassed for him.

I was about to suggest what he should do the next time he felt he needed someone who wasn't his wife, when I heard a loud banging coming from the bar and raised voices.

'What the fuck?' Benny asked, pushing past me and knocking over the bucket of bleachy water, which pooled out under the door. I followed him out.

An armed police response team was moving in through the bar. Three of them had circled a table at which Mark and Terry sat. The three men all had their weapons raised, their gloved fingers resting on the triggers. Two others stood behind the two brothers, and I could see they were cuffing them.

One of the cops, who was behind the bar, scattered glasses onto the floor in a search for something. He looked up when we came in then raised his gun at us.

'Get on the floor! Get on the floor!'

Benny stared at him, open mouthed, his hands slightly raised, then looked over towards Terry and Mark.

'Get down!' the cop shouted, rounding the bar, his gun raised and aimed at Benny's head. 'Get the fuck down.'

But Benny seemed to have frozen. 'What the fuck are you doing?'

At that, the cop twisted his gun and struck Benny on the side of the head, causing him to fall against the table next to me. Instinctively, I went to help him, already seeing the blood welling from the gash on his cheek.

'He didn't do anything,' I screamed.

The cop glared at me. He wore a balaclava beneath his helmet so I could only make out his eyes and the thin set of his lips. His eyes were wide, the whites threaded with veins.

'Do you want one? Shut the fuck up!'

'He's hurt,' I said. 'You assaulted him. I saw it. We all saw it.'

The cop's gaze shifted wildly from me to Benny to the team who had surrounded Mark and Terry.

'Boss, she's being difficult.'

'If she's resisting arrest, use force,' one of the others – the one cuffing Terry – shouted to him.

'Leave her out of this,' Terry said as he was pulled from his seat, his arms behind his back, his shirt pulled taut. 'She's a cleaner, for fuck's sake. She has a kid.'

The one who was pulling him towards the door shouted across, 'Cuff her and bring her in too.'

I was still coming to terms with what he had said when the cop standing over me lifted his boot and, kicking at me, shoved me off balance and onto the floor. He knelt down next to me as I protested, pulling my arms back. I could feel the loops of the plastic cable ties slip over then dig into my wrists as he tightened them, could taste the bleach in the water which had pooled where I lay and in which my face now was pressed. It stung my eyes, burned in my nose and throat, raw as my fear and anger.

## Chapter Seven

I was led out onto the street, my eyes stinging from the bleach and the sudden glare of daylight after the darkness of the pub. Instinctively, I tried to raise my hand to shield my vision, but managed little more than an ache in my shoulders as the cop leading me out pulled down on the cable ties round my wrists. A crowd had gathered at the bottom of the street, held back by two Land Rovers, one at each end, which blocked access to the bar. Cops milled around in their tactical gear, guns clenched in hand, as if anticipating trouble.

I could hear the jeers and whistles, then someone started chanting 'Two–nil! Two–nil' over and over and soon the whole crowd seemed to be joining in, the chant less a song, more a rhythmic swelling, ragged and increasingly frenzied. I thought immediately of Terry saying the same thing on the phone with Mark, and the graffiti on the wall I'd seen earlier.

As I approached the police cars, I could see that we were each being taken in separate vehicles. Mark and Terry had already been split up and someone was trying to force Terry into the car in the guise of helping him avoid hitting his head on the roof. Terry resisted the man's pressure and, stepping on the lower ledge of the car frame, raised himself up a foot and held his head high. The gesture of defiance was greeted with an immediate cheer from those assembling at either end of the street.

'Get in the fucking car,' the officer with him said and shoved him in, knocking his head off the edge of the doorframe as he did so.

Terry simply twisted his head and grinned at him, then winked across at us as the cop slammed the door shut on him.

Mark and Benny were led to separate cars while I was shepherded across to the one furthest from the bar, perhaps suggesting that I was the one they least expected to cause trouble or needed to get out of view of the crowd. It was a peculiar, public humiliation, that walk, my hands bound, guarded either side by armed police, as if I was a threat to anyone.

'I haven't done anything,' I kept repeating, over and over. To my shame, the bleach had caused my eyes to stream, and I wanted desperately to wipe away the tears, lest people thought I was crying because of my arrest, or some admission of guilt. But I could do nothing more than shake my bowed head, which I realised conveyed just the same impression anyway.

I was just being lowered into the car, my arms in agony at having been held in one position for so long, when the first piece of masonry clattered off the bonnet. The crowd had waited for the four of us to be inside the vehicles before pelting the cops still standing outside.

A second rock struck the windscreen with a sharp crack, though the glass held firm. Outside, a beer bottle skittered along the paved street and shattered against the wall of

O'Reilly's. More bottles followed, some aimed at the police, some at the cars, some at the roadway in front of us, perhaps assuming it would prevent our driving off for fear of punctured tyres.

I guessed someone had managed to lift crates of empties from one of the pubs further down the street. The police, perhaps fearing that it might not take long for someone to find petrol with which to half fill them, rushed into the vehicles. Below us, I could see the Land Rover which had blocked the roadway there reverse back and turn, ready to head down into the crowd. One by one, the police cars filed in behind it, almost bumper to bumper, so that, through the heavy tint of the glass, I could make out the back of Mark's head in the rear seat of the car in front of us. The Land Rover at the top of the street followed down, coming within inches of our rear bumper as, behind them, the crowd began to wash round us.

'Keep it tight,' our driver muttered as he inched behind the cars ahead of us. I realised they were trying not to leave a gap into which protestors could stand, thereby separating one car from the others.

There were people either side of us now, thumping on the sides and roof of the car. One fella, a scarf over his face, had lifted a broken brick and was hammering at the driver's window, the blows leaving white debris in their wake, the glass holding.

Beside me, someone was slapping on the window with the flat of their hand and offering me a thumbs up. The roof of the car was being beaten, a thudding out of rhythm, and behind it, 'Two–nil' began to swell once more.

'Fucking wankers,' the cop in the front seat said. Then he twisted to glare at me. 'Matty was a mate,' he said. 'And his missus was a star.'

Matty? I realised he meant the police officer and his wife who had been shot. I opened my mouth to speak but did not know what to say. Would 'sorry' suggest guilt? Could it be construed as a confession? The whole thing was ridiculous.

'I don't know anything about it,' I said. 'I'm sorry for your loss. But it's nothing to do with me.'

'We'll see, won't we?' he replied, then turned back in his seat.

The sound of fists thudding against the passenger windows increased as we reached the edge of the crowd at the bottom of the roadway. We crept through the first line of protestors who hit the car with increased vigour. I began to worry that they might actually stop us. There was such a frenzy in their anger, such viciousness, I could not be sure they wouldn't tear me limb from limb alongside the cops if they managed to open the car.

Then a gap widened between us and the car in front, and I felt a surge as we sped forward while those around us jumped back, fearful of being struck. In a blur, we were clear of the protests and, with the exception of a final bottle striking the rear windscreen, the sounds of their protests dulled to nothing.

'Where are you taking me?' I asked. 'I need to tell someone.'

But those in the car said nothing.

'Please, I need to tell someone where I am,' I said, leaning forward.

'Sit back,' the cop next to me said, putting out his arm and forcing me back against the seat.

'Please!' I said. 'I have a daughter.'

The front seat passenger turned and stared at me. I could see the red veins in the whites of his eyes, recognised the cruel line of his mouth. He was the one who had arrested me.

'So did the Millars. So shut the fuck up.'

Adrenaline carried me through the processing when I was brought into the station. We'd come in through heavy, solid gates, corrugated steel by the looks of it, which slid slowly shut behind us. Then I was held in the car while, one by one, Mark and Benny were taken inside, each of us kept separate from the others. As I got out of my car, I looked around to see where Terry was sitting, for I had not seen him being taken into the station and he'd been in the foremost car. But his was not parked with the rest of ours and I wondered whether he'd been taken to a different location.

Then I was led up the steps and in through a plain, grey door, set deep in a red brick wall that could have been as easily the entrance to a leisure centre as a police station.

Inside, the place hummed with activity. I was brought to someone who introduced himself as the custody officer. He asked me my details, my name and address and my date of birth, and read me my rights again.

'You've been arrested for resisting or wilfully obstructing a constable in the execution of his duty, do you understand that?'

'I didn't resist.'

He smiled and nodded. 'But you do understand?'

'Yes,' I said.

'Have you taken any drugs or alcohol in the past twenty-four hours, Katie?'

'I'd a gin and tonic at the end of my shift last night,' I said. 'That's it.'

'And nothing else? No drugs?'

'I'm not a junkie,' I croaked.

He offered me a mild smile, then, holding open a clear plastic bag, said, 'I'd like you to empty your pockets, please. And put your watch and any jewellery you're wearing into this, please. You'll get it back when you're done.'

I did as I was told.

'Now, I'm going to ask a female officer to search you, Katie, okay?'

A woman who had been standing next to the desk where I was being booked came forward. 'Will you follow me, please?'

She led me into a room a few doors down which was empty save for a single chair on which sat a plastic package.

'Please remove your clothing for me, Katie,' she said, tearing open the package and removing a blue, full-body suit like I'd seen cops wearing in TV dramas. The whole thing felt so surreal that, for a second, I felt dizzy and had to reach out to the chair to support myself.

'Take your time, Katie,' she said, standing next to me. 'When you're ready.'

I took a breath and straightened, hoping that she might step back from me or turn away, but she didn't.

I slipped off one shoe, pushing it down at the heel with my other, then repeated the process, before peeling off my jeans. Finally, I pulled my T-shirt over my head and stood, one arm wrapped around me, the other reaching for the suit.

'And your underwear, please,' the woman said, her expression impassive.

It did not even strike me to protest. I unclasped my bra and tossed it onto the chair with my other clothes, then stared at her, waiting to be allowed to dress.

'All your underwear, please, Katie.'

'I'm not hiding anything,' I said.

'Everything, please.'

I peeled off my pants and socks, then stood, exposed, while she moved around me, her hands seemingly skimming the surface of my skin without touching it.

Once she was behind me, she said, 'Now bend over, Katie, please. Touch your toes, if you can.'

'Seriously?' I asked, twisting to look at her, one arm covering my chest, the other cupped over my crotch.

'Touch your toes, please, Katie.'

I did so, standing there, exposed in a way I hadn't been since Hope's birth, humiliated beyond words. Yet, I felt only numbness, as if this was happening to someone else, someone next to me, someone who deserved this.

'Thank you, Katie,' the woman said. 'You can stand up now. Take your time.'

I straightened and again felt light-headed. The woman reached out to me and I thought it was to steady me, but in fact she was handing me the paper suit. Then she gathered up my clothes and placed them inside a plastic evidence bag which she'd lifted from the chair. She waited until I was dressed, then opened the door and directed me to leave ahead of her.

A group of male officers stood at the desk when I stepped into the corridor. A few looked me up and down, and one smiled grimly. The custody officer nodded that I should approach, then brought me behind the desk and directed me to stand against a pale painted wall. He lifted a camera, which lay on his desk, connected to his computer by a cable, and he took a picture of me, then led me across and offered me a seat next to a desk.

There, he presented me with a small black box, again attached to his computer, green light shining from a glass screen at its centre.

'Now, Katie. I'm going to take your fingerprints. Can you place each finger, one by one, on the light. Just roll your finger slightly from side to side so we get a full print.'

I did as he asked and watched as my first print appeared on the screen in front of me, in real time.

'That's excellent. And the rest,' the custody officer said. 'It beats getting ink all over your hands, eh?' he asked, joking, assuming that I would have had experience of this before.

'This is my first time being arrested,' I said. 'I've not done anything wrong.'

'You'll have a chance to talk to someone about that,' he said, watching as I did one finger after the other.

When I was finished, he produced a small plastic pack from his drawer, inside of which was something that resembled a Covid testing kit: a long, thin cotton bud and a small bottle of fluid.

'Now I'm going to take a DNA sample, Katie. I just need you to open wide for me.'

'What?'

'Just like the dentists,' he said.

Another man, one of those who'd been in the bar, started to laugh. 'Or with your boyfriend,' he said, causing the woman who'd searched me and had remained watching the booking process to grit her teeth as she looked at me.

And so, I opened my mouth and sat while he swabbed the inside of my cheek. The whole process, I realised, since I had entered the building, had been designed to make me compliant. Do this, now this, now this. I had not argued, not refused. I wondered how Mark or Terry reacted in this instance. Would they have touched their toes, without complaint? Would they have opened wide, or refused and been pinned to the ground while someone gripped their jaw?

'Cell three, please,' the custody officer said as he sealed up the swab sample he'd taken, and the woman moved forward. Taking me lightly by the arm, she led me down the corridor again, past the room where I had been stripped.

We stopped at a heavy-looking door, painted blue, in the middle of which a slit was cut that provided a glimpse to the room inside. The woman took a set of keys from her belt and unlocked the door, then stepped back.

'In you go, Katie,' she said.

I suddenly felt claustrophobic, trapped here, without anyone knowing where I was or what had happened.

'Please. My daughter. She'll be wondering—'

'Would you like us to call someone and let them know what's happened?'

The offer, made with no warmth, still elicited tears despite my best efforts.

'Please,' I managed. 'My mother. Margaret Hamill.'

She nodded as I recited my mother's mobile number and scribbled it on the back of her hand with a pen, which she'd pulled from her trouser pocket. Then she indicated that I should step into the cell.

Taking a breath, I did. The room was small, clean, white. One wall carried a low shelf on which lay a thin mattress, and which doubled as both a bench and a bed. A metal toilet and washbasin were attached to the far wall.

The door slammed behind me, and I heard the heavy thunk of the key turning and the lock shunting into place.

And after all the process and busy-ness, I was suddenly alone.

# Chapter Eight

I was not sure how long I sat there, waiting. They had taken my phone from me in the bar, and my watch along with my jewellery when I first arrived. There was a small window, high and narrow, which showed only darkness and I knew it was well past 6 p.m. at this stage, though the light had faded without my noticing.

The fluorescent light above me hummed and glared so I lay and closed my eyes. This whole thing was ridiculous; I'd done nothing wrong. I replayed the events in the bar in my head, trying to remember if I had said or done anything with which they could charge me, but in each version of it, something intruded on my thoughts, some doubt that made sweat break out on me and my stomach twist.

I just wanted to see Hope and my mum. I wanted the security of home, the knowledge that there was only us and everything outside the door did not matter, could not harm us. My world had shrunk to just us three and that was all I wanted now.

But I felt like all that had changed the moment the lift door had opened, and Black-Hair and English had stopped me. I played out scenarios in my head where I hadn't taken the lift, but instead the stairs. Or where I had come home with Benny rather than being left on my own. Or where I had gone to the wedding and come home that same evening, as had been planned. I felt like all of this was a punishment for my going to Benny's room.

I heard the thunk of the lock and sat up as a young, female officer walked into the room and handed me a folder, without comment, and then left. I could see the edge of something inside: a photograph.

I assumed it was more pictures of me, perhaps more of my time with Benny, so was confused when I opened it and found a picture of a smiling family standing outside Disneyland by the looks of it.

The husband was handsome, with a thick head of hair and bright blue eyes which carried his smile. The other adult in the image was a woman, around my age, I guessed. She had blonde hair, almost shoulder length. Her skin was tanned, youthful, her smile wide and infectious. Both inclined their heads towards the child who stood between them. She was a young girl, her hair in pigtails that sat either side of a pair of Mickey Mouse ears which she wore. She was smiling so widely, her eyes were little more than scrunched lines, her teeth gleaming. Whoever they were, they were happy.

The next image was a wedding picture of the pair, younger but no less attractive or seemingly happy. The pictures that followed were more images of either the couple or the child with one or both of her parents.

Then I turned over a picture of the three of them at a birthday party – presumably the girl's fifth – and found a picture of the woman, sitting in a car, her seat belt still across her chest. Her T-shirt was stained crimson. Her head lay at an angle, her eyes and mouth open, the side of her face and neck slick with blood.

My stomach turned as I realised who this was. I shut the folder and threw it from me, but the pictures spilled onto the floor and, while I did not want to look at them, it seemed disrespectful to leave them there, as if I did not care, did not grieve for their loss.

I scrambled over and gathered them, trying not to look but seeing an image of the man, whom I now guessed to be the shot policeman, Matthew Millar, lying on the ground outside his car. The door was still open, and he lay, one leg still inside the vehicle, as if he'd been shot just as he started to climb out. His shirt had been pulled open, perhaps by paramedics, and I could see handprints in the blood which covered his chest. His head lay back, his mouth gaping, his eyes fixed on the sky overhead. A trail of blood ran from the corner of his mouth. A section of his scalp was missing, and I could see splattered on the inside window of the car, splodges of grey and pink tissue. Despite myself, I could not stop looking. I lifted more of the pictures, but they'd become mixed up now so that one image of the murdered man was followed by one of the smiling girl, then her mother, the wound in her throat where the bullet had caught her, seemingly rupturing the artery judging by the sheer volume of blood that had pooled in the seat, coating the bottom of her legs.

In both fascination and revulsion, I looked at each picture. In life, the man looked kind. He held his daughter's hand in many of the family pictures, often had one arm across her, hugging her, protective of her. His wife was undoubtedly beautiful, and their child took after her looks. The poor child was left alone now. Had she seen this happen? Was she inside when the gunmen struck? Did she see their lights come up the drive and run to the window or the door, as Hope did sometimes when she saw me come up from the bus stop? Did she rush to welcome them home? Did she see? Did she witness the shattering of her own existence?

I thought again of the crowd, chanting 'Two–nil' and felt revulsion at them. Didn't they know? Couldn't they see? But they couldn't and they didn't. These people – the Millars – were just numbers on a score sheet to them; they hadn't existed. They were just abstract ideas: a cop and his missus.

The door unlocked again, and I looked up from where I still sat, on the floor. Black-Hair came into the room, followed by English.

'Katie, Katie,' Black-Hair said. 'You've got yourself into some trouble, I believe.'

I stared at him, then back at the pictures.

'Why?' I asked.

English came across and, gathering the images, took them from me, then moved and stood at the doorway. Black-Hair, offering me a hand, directed that I should sit on the bed. He sat next to me, the two of us looking towards the door, as if English might be able to explain to us both how we had ended up here.

'I didn't do anything wrong,' I said. 'I shouldn't be here.'

'You're right,' Black-Hair said. 'Though had we lifted the other three and not you, it might have looked odd. Lifting all four of you looks like old-fashioned intimidation.

Leaving one behind looks like someone's getting special treatment.'

It made some sort of sense to me, though I don't think anyone would have blinked twice at them not lifting me.

'So, have you thought any more about my offer?'

'I've thought about nothing but,' I said. 'Was it you sent the pictures of me and Benny to his wife? And my benefits being frozen, was that you too?'

'Your benefits?' Black-Hair asked, seeming genuinely surprised. The fact he had not even acknowledged the question about Amy suggested that it had indeed been him who had contacted her.

'Someone reported that I was earning undeclared income and so they froze my benefits.'

'That's terrible. We can sort that for you,' he said and nodded to English, who opened the door and stepped outside. 'We'll take care of that, don't you worry.'

I said, 'Thank you,' without intending to, habit being so strong.

'Now, maybe you can do us a favour in return. You saw Matthew and Laura. And their wee lassie, Louise. You saw what was done to them.'

I nodded. 'I'm sorry for them,' I said. 'And especially the wee girl. But I can't help you.'

Black-Hair raised a hand, as if to stop me before I went too far. 'I know you'd nothing to do with it. The cops here know it too, or they will once they start talking to you. But I'm more interested in whether you heard anything in the bar, before or after.'

I shook my head.

'You never heard Terry and Mark discussing a job coming up? No mention of Eglinton? Of Matthew's name?'

I shook my head with each question.

'Matthew? Matty?'

Shake, shake.

'Millar?'

I thought again of Mark and Terry at the table in the bar, just before I put on my headphones: 'Now, what about Millar? Everyone still good?' Mark had said.

I shook my head, but Black-Hair must have noticed something different this time, must have sensed the briefest pause. His expression hardened a little.

'Think carefully, Katie,' he said.

'No,' I said. 'Nothing.'

But I could not stop myself thinking of it now, of Terry and Mark, heads leaning towards each other conspiratorially as I worked. I could not forget the phone call, as Mark left me home, his hand on mine while Terry celebrated: 'Marky? Some result, lad. Two–nil! Two–nil, lad. Unbelievable!'

I'd assumed he was celebrating a football result. And perhaps he had been. But then there was the graffiti on the wall and the crowd today, outside the bar, had used the same chant to taunt the police.

Black-Hair was studying me, and I could see he knew I was thinking of something. I tried to clear my mind, tried not to think of Terry or Mark, but the more I tried, the more stubbornly I heard the chant.

'Do you even know what Terry O'Reilly does?'

I shook my head. I didn't, really. There were rumours, of course, about drugs and that. But all I really knew was that he was involved in community things, mediated when the local kids started recreational rioting with the police over the summer months when the heat was too intense and the holidays dragged on. And I knew he helped people out, when they were short, lent money to those who needed a hand.

'Community stuff,' I said, wanting to sound like I knew but keeping it vague enough to not commit myself to something that was obviously wrong. 'He works in the community.'

Black-Hair laughed coldly. 'He does that all right,' he said. 'Terry O'Reilly runs an organised crime gang that is responsible for the supply of every drug that makes its way into Derry city.'

'I don't believe that,' I said. 'I've heard Terry complaining about dealers. And Mark is death on people using in the bar. Anyone who's caught is thrown out.'

'Because you don't shit where you eat,' Black-Hair said with a smile. 'If Terry has a problem with dealers, it's with those who don't pay him a cut. Their bar is clean so the local cops can't do them for offences in their building.'

'Is that what all this is about? Drugs? Then why are we all being lifted over the shooting of your colleague?'

'Matthew Millar was leading a taskforce which was aiming to disrupt the supply chain Terry relies on. Our thinking is that Terry, alongside loyalist paramilitaries further up the country, worked together to arrange the hit on him.'

'Terry wouldn't deal with those people.'

Another cold laugh. 'Terry would deal with the devil himself if he could make some money out of it. Who do you think controls the drugs coming into the country? Who supplies Terry?'

I shrugged. 'I told you before: I don't know anything. And you can cut my benefits and send pictures of me to people all you like, but that won't change what I don't know. So go ahead and waste your time.'

I folded my arms, sure I had offered the winning argument. I was of no use as an informer as I knew nothing and therefore had nothing to inform.

'That's not true, Katie,' Black-Hair said. 'I know, for example, that Matthew Millar's name *was* mentioned in your hearing.'

I started to protest but he waved it away. 'You're a very poor liar, Katie. Now that also tells me that Terry and Mark trust you enough to feel comfortable talking in your presence.'

I couldn't think of what to say to that.

'You could be more helpful to us than you realise.'

'I already said no.'

'You saw the pictures, Katie. You saw that wee girl, left with no parents, no family. Would you want that to happen to Hope?'

I felt a sudden twist in my gut. 'Are you threatening my daughter?'

'Of course not. I'm asking you: what did she do to deserve what happened to her? Why is your wee girl different? Is she more deserving of a parent?'

'Her da was a cop,' I said, instinctively. It was how I'd been raised, how I thought. Sure, what did he expect, joining the cops? How often had I heard that after someone got shot. Even when people were commiserating, saying those days were past, at some level in the community there was still a flicker of that thought. I'd seen it in the bar, men drinking, chatting: 'It's terrible, but . . .' The rest remained unspoken but seemingly understood, as if years of violence had inured people to the point that they believed there were different levels of victim. As soon as I said it, I realised that I was no better, even though I wanted not to think that way.

'He was one of yours,' Black-Hair said. 'Joined after the changeover when they were trying to recruit more Catholics. Because he wanted to make the place better for Catholics. That was his crime; trying to make life better for his own people. And they had him shot.'

'Had him shot?'

'It was the loyalists who pulled the trigger, but Terry who identified Matthew.'

'If you know that, why do you need me? Just charge him, if he did do it, and let me go.'

'How do you prove someone identified another person?'

I shrugged.

'Exactly. We need Terry's fingers on the trigger. We need evidence of him planning. We need someone's name in his mouth, recorded.'

'And you want me to give you that? No way.'

'They left a kid with no parents, Katie.'

'They'd leave *my* kid the same way if they thought I was touting on them.'

'Don't make us do this the hard way.'

'Like what? More pictures of me and Benny?'

Black-Hair shook his head. 'Matthew was killed by the loyalists at O'Reilly's behest. He owes them one back. We know that someone in his crew is going to shoot an officer in the next few weeks. All you need to do is listen and if you hear a certain name, let me know. That's all we need. Who the target is.'

I shook my head. 'No.'

'You can save a life.'

'Aye,' I said. 'My own.'

The door opened and English came back in and resumed his position against the wall. I wondered if he'd been just outside the whole time, watching us. Or sitting somewhere viewing the CCTV footage from the camera housed in the spherical casing centred in the ceiling. Black-Hair looked to him, and he nodded.

'We've done you a good turn with the benefits problem, Katie,' Black-Hair said. 'All we're asking is one in return.'

'Take my fucking benefits,' I said, feeling like I'd agreed to something without my knowledge. 'I'd rather be poor than dead.'

'There are worse things than both.' Black-Hair stood. 'You'll hear from us again very soon. Three names: Dunne, Higgins or Shaw. Listen out for any of those names. You hear them, leave your daughter's curtains closed during the day and I'll be in touch.'

'This is ridiculous,' I said, laughing at the absurdity of it. 'I haven't agreed to this. I don't owe you anything.'

'You're not doing it for us,' Black-Hair said. 'You're doing it for Hope, for Louise Millar, for every other kid that wants to grow up in a city free from the likes of Terry O'Reilly. The man's a cancer, Katie.'

He spoke with such sincerity that, for a moment, I said nothing. Then English opened the door and Black-Hair followed him out. As he was leaving, I called, 'Can I go home now? Is that it?'

'You've not been interviewed by the police yet,' Black-Hair said.

'What was this then? I thought you interviewed me.'

'Me?' he asked, incredulously. 'I'm not even here, Katie.'

He winked as he pulled the heavy door closed behind him, the lock shunted into place once more and the silence flooded in to fill his absence.

## Chapter Nine

Sometime later, the door opened once more, and I was brought to an interview room by the woman who had strip-searched me earlier. There, I was met by a solicitor who told me he represented the O'Reillys and would be sitting in on my interview.

'Say nothing,' he said while the officers who were to interview me waited in the corridor outside.

'I've nothing to say.'

'Good. Keep it like that.'

'But I *have* nothing to say,' I protested. 'I don't know anything.'

'You know that, I know that and they know that. But we'll still have to go through the usual farce. This whole thing is a fishing expedition. They ask a few questions and see what comes up.'

'But why me?'

He shrugged. 'Because you were there when they arrived,' he said. 'Simple as that. Has anyone tried to speak to you yet, without your solicitor present?'

I wondered whether I should say anything about Black-Hair and English. But to do so, I would have to explain about the morning after the wedding and explain why I hadn't said anything before this. What could I tell him anyway? Two men came in, sorted out my problem with my benefits and asked me to listen out for three names? I panicked as I realised I couldn't remember the names. One was Shaw, I knew. One was Dunne, I thought. The third might have been Hughes, but I couldn't be sure. What if he was the one whom they discussed and I wouldn't know because I couldn't remember? What if someone was shot because I couldn't remember a name? Why had they made this my responsibility?

I became aware of the silence and realised that the solicitor, who had not even told me *his* name, was staring at me.

'Sorry?'

'Has anyone tried to speak to you without me being there?' he asked, impatiently.

'No,' I said. 'No one.'

He nodded. 'Let's get this done and get home then, shall we, Katie?'

He used my name with such familiarity, as if we were long-standing friends.

'What do I call you?' I asked, but the door had already opened, and the interviewers were on their way in.

'Before we start—' he began as they stepped into the room and I sensed he had a speech already prepared which presumably he'd already used with Benny, Mark and Terry, too. I'd no doubt of my position in the pecking order.

'To save us all time,' the woman officer said, 'having looked at body cam footage from Ms Hamill's arrest, we're satisfied that there will be no charges pressed.'

'Really?' my solicitor said. 'You didn't think to review that four hours ago when she was first brought here?'

'We've had our hands full. You're free to go, Ms Hamill.'

I looked at the lawyer. 'Is that it?'

'I'm afraid so, Katie,' he said. 'They've wasted your entire day.'

'What about the others?'

'I suspect Benny won't be far behind you,' he said, then, to the woman, added, 'My office will be making a complaint to the Ombudsman about this.'

'Of course,' she said. 'Katie, your clothes are in Custody Cell three. You can collect your personal belongings at the desk from where you'll be released.'

'And how does she get home?'

'We can get someone to drop you off,' she said to me, despite the question having been posed by the lawyer.

'In a marked police car? She'll need a taxi.'

I shook my head. 'I'll phone my mum,' I said. 'I just want to get out of here.'

It was only once I was in the taxi, which my mum had ordered and brought down to collect me, that I began to cry. She held me as she used to when I was a child and let me sob. Every part of it – the arrest, the strip-search, the isolation, the images of the dead police man and his wife, the release without charge – all of it had been designed simply to remind me how powerless I was, how little control I had over what they could do to me.

Hope and I lay together on Mum's sofa that evening and watched cartoons until she had drifted to sleep. I carried her upstairs into the spare room where Mum kept a double bed that I could use when we stayed over. There was a cot next to it, but Hope was at the age now where she slept next to me.

I showered, scrubbing at myself, trying to rinse off the smell of the cell, the tang of sweat in the interview room, the feeling of being watched, examined intimately. It had been worse than a smear test despite the fact the woman had not touched me.

The process, both its formality and administration, the use of my name and yet their titles, had all been designed to make me comply. Even my own solicitor had thought so little of me, I didn't actually know his name.

I stayed in the shower until I could cry no more and then, exhausted, I came down to the living room, dressed in the most comfortable things I could find in my mother's wardrobe.

Mum was already on the sofa, the TV playing a soap at low volume, a bottle of wine sitting on the table with two glasses next to it.

'Tea or wine, love?'

'Wine,' I said and, as she opened it and poured me a glass, I began to tell her almost everything that had happened from the night of the wedding on, leaving out only the parts of the story involving my and Benny's relationship. I knew she would not complain about my having someone but knew it would offend her faith if she discovered he was married to someone else. And I did not need judgement; I needed someone to listen. And she did.

'Those bastards,' she said when I'd finished.

'Which ones?'

'All of them. But the two who cornered you at the wedding especially.'

I nodded. It seemed strange to me that, despite being told Terry and Mark had possibly been involved in the murder of two people, and having seen how disloyal Benny was to both his wife and me, the two people for whom I felt most disdain were the two who claimed they were trying to save lives, for they were doing so by risking mine.

'So, what do I do?'

'Not cross Terry O'Reilly, for sure,' Mum said.

'What if he is involved in those deaths?'

'There's no "what if" about it. I'd say it's certain he was involved. The whole town knows he's involved. That's why you can't say anything.'

'What if they keep screwing things up for me?'

Mum took my hand, her eyes glistening. 'They cut your benefits again: I'll see you right. Your dad left enough that I can sell some things. We'll not be stuck.'

'I can't do that,' I said.

'That's what it's for. What am I going to do with it but leave it to the pair of you anyway? I may as well give it to you now when you need it.'

'But what if they do something worse?'

'Worse than strip-search you and arrest you on ridiculous charges? What could they do?'

I felt my own tears well again. 'That's the thing, Mum: I don't know. If I knew their limits, I could decide if I could accept whatever they want to do. What if they do something to Hope?'

'They're not going to hurt a child,' Mum said.

'What about you?'

'What about me? What could they do? Stop my pension? The house is mine, my money is my own. Let them try to do something.'

She raised her head defiantly, then drained her glass of wine and, moving across, lifted the bottle and brought it over. She topped up my glass and refilled her own.

'What if you agreed to tell them things and then just lied?' she said.

'What do you mean?'

'Tell them you'll give them information and then just don't. Or do give them stuff but make it up so that there's nothing they can do with it and there's no way Terry or Mark find out.'

'But if I hear them talk about one of those names, that means that person is being targeted. If I hear that and don't say, or say I heard the wrong name, someone will die because of me.'

Mum shook her head. 'I don't care about that, though,' she said. 'Because none of those people are my daughter. None of them are you.'

'And if Terry is running drugs into the city, there are people dying because of that, too.'

'Not my daughter.'

'And what about Hope? What if she ends up in some—'

I wasn't aware at that moment that I was spiralling. I'd been down each rabbit hole of whether I should or shouldn't do what Black-Hair had asked, had reached various end points, seen so many ways in which someone might die.

Mum took both my hands, as if tethering me to her. 'You raise her right and she won't. Like I raised you right. You're a good girl and don't let anyone make you feel any different.'

I curled up then on the sofa and rested my head on her lap, as I had done when I was a child, but rather than feeling that sense of safety that I had felt back then, I now felt a longing for a home which seemed already beyond my reach.

## Chapter Ten

Over the following weeks, I did not hear from or see Black-Hair or English again. The day after my release, the bar was operating as normal, though neither of the O'Reilly brothers were there. The worry gnawed at me that I had, somehow, provided Black-Hair with enough that he could challenge Mark or Terry, claim that one of their staff had confirmed they were talking about Millar. It could only have come from me.

In the end, the two of them got out soon after. Mark was not allowed home until that evening. Terry was held until the following morning. On the radio, it was said that two men were released pending further inquiries, but everyone knew that meant they'd not been able to pin anything on them and that none of those arrested had said anything.

The day after Terry got out, he was back in the pub, welcomed like a homecoming hero. Mark opened the bar to all regulars for a drink each, though did so at 2 p.m. when the lunch crowd had gone and only a handful could avail of his generosity: the hardened regulars, working their way through the afternoon race lists in the papers left lying on the bar. Those gathered around the bar raised their glasses in salute to him and, as I finished unloading the last of the clean glasses before heading home, I wondered at the incongruity of celebrating someone being released on suspicion of murdering two other people, even as I raised my own glass and welcomed Terry back.

I headed into the kitchen to get my coat and bag and heard someone behind me. Terry had followed me in, his own drink still untouched in his hand.

I felt the sweat pop on my forehead as he set down the glass and leaned against the counter as he watched me. Someone had said something to him, I was sure. I tried to steady my breathing, which was suddenly amplified, ragged and shallow.

'Well, Katie,' he said.

'Terry,' I managed, swallowing as I spoke. 'Welcome home.'

'And you,' he said, smiling. 'I heard what happened.'

'What about?' I could hear my pulse now, the thudding in my ears, realised my bag was still on the floor by my feet but didn't trust myself to bend to pick it up lest I lose my balance.

'The strip-search and that. They're bastards.'

In spite of myself, I laughed at the comment. 'They are,' I agreed.

'It was wrong,' Terry said, moving closer to me now. 'They only did it because you work here, with Mark. It shouldn't have happened.'

'It's fine,' I said, then corrected myself. 'Not fine, that's not what I meant. But it's done now so . . .'

Terry reached into his pocket and pulled out a folded white envelope, which he handed to me.

'Mark told me you were in the car the other night, when I phoned him, but Joe says you told them nothing.'

'Who's Joe?'

'The solicitor I called in to represent us all.'

I nodded. 'Thanks for doing that, Terry. But, I don't . . .' I tried to hand him back the envelope.

'Don't what?'

I didn't know what was inside, though guessed it was something which, once opened, once accepted, would tie me ever more closely with Terry and Mark. And that was not something I wanted to happen. But I couldn't tell him that, for the more closely I became tied to them, the more I would become partly to blame for whatever they did and the more attractive a target I would become for Black-Hair and English.

Terry, perhaps misunderstanding my reluctance as pride, came closer to me and took my hand in both of his, pressing the envelope into my palm.

'It's a wee bonus.'

Then he turned to go.

'Terry,' I blurted. 'I might need to get a different job.' I didn't want him thinking that I owed him, now that he had given me something. If I did leave, which was seeming like a wiser idea by the moment, he might take a spite against me, that I had broken a contract with him or something.

'Why?'

What could I say? 'My benefits are playing up and I need to earn a bit more.'

'We can sort you with extra hours in here, Katie. Don't worry, love. We look after our own.'

After he returned to the main bar, I lifted my things and left. Only when I reached the bus stop did I realise that our conversation had left me late and I'd missed my bus. Mum had collected Hope so I started walking up to hers. I did not open the envelope until I was inside the house, well away from windows or where anyone might be able to photograph me and so prove that I had taken money from Terry O'Reilly.

Inside was £200. That was the price of my silence. That same afternoon, my benefits hit my bank account and, within hours, both Terry O'Reilly and Black-Hair had paid me for services which I had not wished to give.

Mum and Hope still weren't home after I got changed so I started walking up to meet them. Sometimes, on the way back from school, Mum would take her into the playpark down the road. I guessed they were probably there now and, having missed collecting her, I could at least join her on the swings and slides.

I was just walking up towards the park when I saw Mum and Hope rounding the corner. Mum had her arms around Hope, who was cradling her right arm with her left. I could see, even from a distance, that she was crying.

I ran up to meet them and instinctively knelt to embrace Hope, but she turned from me, shielding her arm.

'What happened, love?'

'She fell off the spinning thing and I tried to grab her. Her arm twisted and she says it's sore. I think it's broken.'

Mum had worked as a nurse for years, only retiring when Dad became really ill, and she needed to be at home to care for him. If she said it was broken, she was probably right. Still, in desperation, I hoped it might not be that bad.

'How sore is it, love? From one meaning not sore at all to ten being you want to cut it off.'

Normally she laughed at that last bit but not today. 'Nine,' she said, without hesitating, the thick blobs of her tears building in her eyes once more.

'Can you grip my finger?' I asked, placing my index finger in the gap of her fist. Her fingers twitched around mine but did not close around it.

'It's broken, Katie. She needs to go to hospital,' Mum said.

'Call a taxi for us, will you?'

Mum nodded and, taking out her phone, called for us to be collected from her home.

'I need to get money to pay for it,' she said. 'I left without my purse or anything. We didn't intend to go to the playground, but she wanted to. And then she was going too fast on the roundabout things and—'

I could tell Mum was panicking now and feeling guilty. And she had no reason to. She'd only been there because I hadn't.

'I have money,' I said. 'Tell them to get us here.'

She looked at me quizzically but nodded.

We sat in the Accident and Emergency department for almost eight hours before Hope was finally seen. The place was heaving with people and there was only one free seat. Mum sat there, with Hope on her lap, while I stood next to them. When she was called in, I took her through myself. We sat with a female doctor who introduced herself to me as Dr Keys and to Hope as Hazel and, despite seeming stressed out, smiled at Hope as she asked her what happened.

I explained what Mum had told me: Hope had been on the roundabout, which had been spinning quicker than Mum had liked. She'd told Hope to get off, but she hadn't wanted to and had been clinging to the handrails on the rotating platform. Mum had taken her hand to help her down, the platform had kept spinning and Hope had twisted away from her as she pulled.

'My mum was a nurse. She thinks it's broken,' I added.

Hazel looked at me, nodding as I spoke, then, when I was done, crouched down at Hope's level. 'Is that what happened to you, love?' she asked. Hope nodded solemnly, still holding her arm.

'Can I see your arm, Hope?'

Warily, she allowed Hazel to touch her, though watched guardedly as she prodded and felt along the muscle.

'We're going to get an X-ray done, Hope, okay? It takes a picture of your insides so we can see what's been done. How does that sound?'

Again, Hope nodded, heavy eyed.

'And let's get you some pain relief too, eh?'

The machinery of the hospital kept her fascinated for the next hour while she was X-rayed and returned to the curtained cubicle. Hazel returned forty minutes later with Hope's notes.

'It's a spiral fracture,' she said, then addressed Hope. 'So that's where your bone gets broken. We're going to put a cast on you, and I'll see you back here for a check-up, okay, love? And when I see you again, I want to sign your cast. So, leave plenty of room on it for me when all your school friends want to sign their names.'

Hope smiled at her, following her words but not, perhaps, her meaning. Not until the nurse had put on the cast and it had started to dry.

As we left to head back to our own house, Mum apologised once more.

'Forget about it,' I said. 'In a few weeks it'll be like it never happened.'

## Chapter Eleven

The following morning, I had just reached the school gates when my mobile rang. It was Mark.

'I need you in quickly, Katie,' he said. 'Get a taxi down. Use Maxi Cabs. I'll pay.'

He hung up before I even had a chance to protest, by which stage, Hope had headed into the schoolyard, eager to show off her cast to her friends who had already flocked around her. She smiled and raised the plaster cast towards me, and I gave her a quick wave, blew her a kiss and called Maxi Cabs.

When I got into work, Mark was standing behind the bar. He wore the same clothes as the day before, but his shirt was stained now with blood.

'Are you okay? Are you hurt?' I asked, immediately assuming that something had happened to him and he needed my help.

'Fine,' he said, draining the glass of whiskey he held. 'Look, the lounge is a bit of a mess. We need you to clean it. I'll make sure you're sorted for the extra work, okay, love?'

He nodded, as if assuming my agreement, then indicated that I should go down the lower steps to the lounge at the back of the bar.

He did not follow.

As I walked through the empty bar, towards the lounge, my thoughts began to spiral. What if this was it? What if Terry had known all along that I had spoken to Black-Hair. What if he was waiting for me now? No one knew I was here, not Hope and not my mum. The cab driver had dropped me off, but Mark had been specific about which cab firm to use, and I knew O'Reilly's had a deal with Maxi Cabs.

I stopped at the top of the two steps into the lounge and looked down into the darkness. As best I could tell, there was no one there. I waited, listening. No breaths, no movements.

I took each step slowly, peering either side of me as I reached the bottom, lest someone was waiting there, along the wall. But there was no one. I reached over and flicked on the lights.

As they buzzed to life, I saw the mess.

All but one of the tables in the centre of the lounge had been pushed back, the chairs which usually surrounded them were overturned. That one table was covered in blood-stained rags and blood had pooled on the floor beneath it. A further bundle of rags lay balled up near my feet and only when I moved closer did I see, through the bloodstaining, the recognisable pattern of the tea towels we used in the kitchen to dry glasses.

Wrapping from bandage rolls lay scattered around the floor and the bar's first-aid kit yawned open and empty on the long cushioned seat along the back wall. Someone had been injured and had their wounds tended here, by the looks of it. But judging by the amount of blood, I wondered at what type of wounds.

'You okay with this?'

I turned to where Mark stood at the top of the stairs.

I nodded. 'What happened?'

'Aw, you know,' he said. 'A young lad said the wrong thing to someone and got himself hurt. I had to take care of him, get him patched up. It's not as bad as it looks. I'm nicking home to get showered and changed. I'll lock the main doors, so work away in here; no one will bother you. Double-bag all the rubbish and leave it out back. When Benny comes in, maybe buy some fresh tea towels and stuff and refill that medical kit. Before you dump them, wash all that stuff with bleach at a high temperature too, will you? And this.'

He peeled off his shirt and passed it to me, balled up, the cotton still warm from his body. Then he headed back up behind the bar, seemingly unembarrassed, and lifted one of the promotional T-shirts that drinks companies dropped in periodically. This one was for a cider company and was a size too small. He rubbed his belly and smiled.

'I'll need to ask for a few XLs next time, eh?' he joked.

He winked with a familiarity which surprised me, then lifted his keys and left, locking me inside.

I assumed that boil-washing the tea towels in bleach was to destroy whatever evidence might be on the cloths, before they were dumped. Mark said someone was injured and he'd patched him up, but what type of injury would leave this amount of blood? Working in the bar, you did see accidents – people falling, cutting themselves on broken glass, bleeding from fights. But this scene suggested something more than that. The position of the table and the pooling of the blood was more in keeping with a surgeon's table than a pub.

That, or a butcher's block.

I worked through the morning, unhappy as I was about the manner in which Mark had assumed that I would. I guessed Terry had told him they had given me money and so I owed them. And I worried that what I was doing here was cleaning up something criminal.

I wanted to leave; in fact, the first thing I did was try the doors to see if he really had locked me inside. But I was also aware that I was being watched by the bar's CCTV cameras. Now that I was involved, now that I had seen this, how would they react if I simply walked away? Would they trust me not to say anything to anyone?

And so, I spent the morning mopping up blood and gathering up the soiled tea towels, rinsing them and then bundling them into a pot of boiling water and bleach to clean them before bagging the lot. I wiped down all the furniture, for the blood had travelled further than the thick pool beneath the central table, and I boiled the cloths I used for that as well. I mopped up the blood until the water in the mop bucket was so dark it stained the mop itself, then drained the bucket and washed it again.

It was while doing this that I found a phone, lying on the floor, hidden from view by an overturned chair. It wasn't unusual to find phones in the bar and the general rule was to set any handsets under the counter at the bar, for inevitably someone came in looking for them the following morning. This seemed different though. The lounge had been closed the previous evening so the only people who'd have been in here were those involved in whatever had resulted in all the blood on the floor. When I picked up the phone, I could see bloody fingerprints dried onto the screen, which lit briefly to show two young fellas standing in football tops and shorts, their arms across each other's shoulders. The phone was in a transparent case and, inside the back cover, visible through the bloodstained plastic, was a bank card with the name L. Burke.

I tapped the screen again and studied the two young men in the picture, hoping that I might recognise one of them, but I did not. I wasn't sure what to do with the phone. I didn't want to leave it behind the bar, for clearly Mark had wanted whatever happened here to remain hidden. Nor could I give it to Mark, for to do so would show that I now knew the name, at least, of one of those involved. I didn't want to dump it either in case L. Burke came back for his phone. I considered keeping it, just in case, but that would surely have made me an accessory, I guessed. In the end, I felt along the bottom of the seating until I found a point where the frame of the seat was lifted off the floor tiles an inch or two and I slid the phone in there, its edge sitting flush with the bottom of the seat. In so doing, I could pretend I never found it and if Burke did return, his phone would be located with a careful search of the place.

Finally, I gathered up the waste, the rolled wadges of toilet paper covered in blood, the tangled strands of bandages twisted round themselves and the discarded wrappings into a black bag and then emptied the bins from the bathrooms on top so that anyone looking into it would not immediately see the bloodstaining. Then I double-bagged the rubbish, as Mark had instructed.

I'd hung the tea towels on the airer in the kitchen, allowing them to cool before I dumped those too, when Benny arrived. I didn't even hear him coming in through the main door, for which he had a key. I was standing at the sink, rinsing out the last of the cloths, when I heard the swinging door creak on its hinges, and I turned to see him standing there.

'What are you doing in?' he asked.

'I needed to get started early,' I said, unsure whether I should tell him that Mark had called me. 'Hope has a hospital appointment, and I need to get finished up and away.'

He nodded, absentmindedly. 'Where are the bags?'

Mark had clearly contacted him too.

'At the back door. I wasn't sure whether you'd want to carry them out front in full view of everyone.'

He shrugged. 'It's just a dump run, isn't it?' he said.

'Yeah,' I said, uncertain now whether he knew the source of the rubbish he was dumping or not. 'A dump run.'

'The back door's probably best, though,' he agreed, coming over to me. He stood a few feet from me, watching me rinse the tea towels. My hands felt slick, the cloths burning my skin even though they were already cold.

I felt his hand on my back as he moved closer, felt the pressure of him behind me as he pressed me lightly against the sink. One arm wrapped around me and rested at my waist. The other pulled back my hair as he leaned in and kissed my neck.

I shoved him backwards and turned to face him. 'What the fuck are you doing?'

He stared at me, his expression bemused. 'There's no cameras in here,' he said. 'I thought we could—'

'You thought wrong,' I said. 'You have a wife and kids.'

'Jesus, Katie,' he said. 'Okay.'

'It's done, Benny.'

'Look, Amy's forgotten about it.'

'No, she hasn't,' I said. 'And I haven't. It's done. Get rid of the rubbish. I have to go up town and buy new stuff for the medicine kit.'

Wounded, and slightly aggrieved, Benny slouched off to the back door where he gathered up the first of the bags of rubbish, took them out through the alley that ran along the rear of the bar and deposited them in his car. By the time he'd returned, I'd bagged up the tea towels, too.

The cash register in the bar was left open overnight in case anyone was ever stupid enough to try to rob the place. The float was only eighty pounds anyway so perhaps Mark figured better to lose eighty pounds than the hassle of replacing the register if someone either lifted it or broke into it expecting it to contain more.

I took £30 and left Benny to sort the rubbish while I went and bought new tea towels and bandages and tape. He was just back from the dump when I returned to the bar and he worked in silence, restocking shelves, while I gave the new tea towels a quick wash and dry to remove the starch.

Mark arrived back as I was getting ready to leave. He came into the kitchen and looked around.

'The place looks spotless, Katie. Thanks, love,' he said.

I nodded, annoyed at the pleasure I took from the compliment.

He clocked the tea towels drying and indicated them with a nod. 'Did you not dump those?'

'They're the new ones,' I said. 'I rinsed the starch out of them. Otherwise, the kitchen will have a nightmare drying glasses.'

'You're a star, too. I'll not forget this, Katie.' He reached out and laid his hand on my shoulder, gently rubbing my upper arm. His hand rested there, lingering a little longer as he smiled mildly at me.

With that he went back to the bar and, as the glow of his words faded, I thought once more of whose blood I'd cleaned from the floor and how he or she had managed to survive having lost so much of it.

# Chapter Twelve

I saw the young man from the image on the phone two days later; this time on the news. His family were appealing for calm following their son, Leon Burke's, death. The police report simply said that he was 'known to authorities' and while no details were given regarding his death, the rumour in town was that he was knifed during a drugs deal.

The day following, my day off work, I dropped Hope to school and then went into town to buy groceries. I'd too many bags to walk home and couldn't face the thought of trekking up to the bus station and then from the stop on up the hill to my house, and so I called a taxi and stood at the rank outside the supermarket and waited for it to arrive.

A silver car with a taxi light on the roof pulled up and instinctively, I opened the rear door and started loading in my groceries.

'Hamill?' I said, glancing at the driver and then stopping.

'That's right.' The accent, the dead stare, the thin line of his mouth. English.

I started to take my bags back out when he twisted in his seat.

'Don't, Katie. Get in the car. Don't make a scene.'

I looked around, hoping there might be someone to witness this, but none of those going in or out of the supermarket even glanced in my direction.

'Get in the car, Katie,' English repeated.

I looked up towards the entrance of the supermarket and saw a CCTV camera there. I stood a moment, clearly visible to it, before climbing into the rear seat of the car. If anything did happen to me, I wanted to be sure that my last moments were recorded, that someone would know with whom I had left.

English started the car and we pulled out of the parking bay.

'I don't want anything to do with you crowd,' I protested. 'I don't know anything.'

'So you keep saying.'

'It's true.'

He nodded but did not speak for the rest of the journey, even when I asked him repeatedly where we were going and told him I wanted to get out.

We crossed the border and took the road for Letterkenny. Finally, he slowed at the turning for An Grianán and took the road up to the left.

I'd not been to Grianán for some time. It was an old ring fort, positioned high on a rise that allowed you to see for miles in all directions and on one side gave views over Lough Swilly and Inch Island. The drive up to the top, where the fort was positioned, was via a spiralling roadway and it was this we took.

One car was parked in the visitor area and, as we arrived, Black-Hair got out of it and waited for us to pull to a stop next to him. He opened the rear door for me and indicated that I should get out.

'Are you going to hurt me?' I asked.

He shook his head. 'Katie, what would be the point of hurting you? I want us to be friends.'

'By kidnapping me off the street.'

He laughed. 'You were hardly kidnapped. We'll drop you and your shopping home shortly. Take a walk with me. We may as well get some benefit from the fresh air up here rather than sitting in a car, eh?'

Cautiously, I stepped out. He closed the door behind me, then set off, up towards the fort, walking along the plastic boards which had been set along the waterlogged path.

'Watch your step,' he said.

'Why am I here?'

'I thought I would have heard from you by now,' he said. 'Every day we've been watching Hope's windows, waiting to see those curtains closed, and every day you've gone in at eight a.m. on the dot and opened them.'

'I've had nothing to tell you,' I said.

'You've had nothing to tell, or you've not wanted to tell us anything?'

'You said I was to look out for names. I haven't heard any names.'

He nodded. 'You need to take some initiative, Katie, or this isn't going to work.'

'I don't want it to work. Even being here with you is putting me at risk. What if someone sees?'

'Sees two people out walking?'

'Sees me with you.'

'Are you afraid of the O'Reillys?'

'Finally, you get it.'

'No, I don't. That's the point. You've let these people terrorise your community for years, making money off the backs of kids with drugs habits.'

'*I've* let?'

'You'd rather they just keep doing what they do than help us stop them?'

'I'll tell you what they don't do. They don't follow me around taking pictures of me. They don't freeze my benefits. They don't kidnap me off the street and threaten me.'

'Threaten?'

'You don't think I know what you're doing.'

'I'm asking for your help, Katie. And in return, I've offered to help you out. We sorted your benefits problem for you and offered to help with the cost of Hope's bike. How is she, by the way? Is she still looking for a bike, even with the plaster cast? That was a nasty break.'

'Don't mention my daughter.'

Black-Hair raised his hands in placation. We'd reached the outside of the fort now and he ducked down and made his way through to the inner section. Looking round, I felt I had no choice but to follow him.

'You're the one terrorising people. I don't fear seeing Mark or Terry. But I hate seeing you and that one out there, English, with every bone in my body.'

'We're the ones keeping you safe at night, Katie.'

'Safe?'

'Safe. And I make no apology for it. I will do whatever I need to do to take people like Terry O'Reilly and all the shit they peddle, off the streets. They can tell people that it's political or "you against us", but it's not. Not really. It's about money. And you're helping that every day you hear things and say nothing.'

'I told you, I didn't hear the names you asked me to listen for.'

'What names?'

'Shaw. Dunnes, Hughes.'

'Dunne and Higgins,' Black-Hair said. 'And that's not the point. What do you know about Leon Burke?'

'Who?'

'You're a terrible liar, Katie. I mean, the worst. Leon Burke. Fifteen years old. Died two nights ago after he got stabbed in the stomach selling drugs for the O'Reillys.'

'Nothing,' I said. 'I don't know anything about him.'

'We understand he was taken somewhere after the stabbing and someone in O'Reilly's tried to patch him up and sent him home. His mother found him yesterday morning, lying in his bed. He'd lost so much blood and was bleeding so heavily internally, his heart failed. Someone had superglued the wound closed and sent him home to die rather than get him to a hospital. Can you imagine coming in some morning and Hope lying dead in her room? And some fucking scumbag could have helped her but didn't and glued her stomach closed.'

I thought of Mark standing, peeling off his bloody shirt. The table in the lounge like a surgeon's slab. I couldn't believe that Mark hadn't been trying his best to help the young fella who was wounded, but then, with the amount of blood, I couldn't understand why he hadn't taken him straight to the hospital either.

On the back of that thought, I saw again the phone, covered in bloody fingerprints. Had the young lad been holding it? Had he wanted to phone someone? His mother? An ambulance? Was he so afraid of Terry that he didn't? Or of Mark? Or was he just so trusting of them?

'If we could only place Leon with the O'Reillys on the night of the stabbing, we could put some pressure on people, start to get witnesses. Start to deal with the problem,' Black-Hair said.

'Why are you asking me?'

'Because Burke was last seen being taken into the centre of town. And the most likely place they'd have taken him is the bar. And you clean the bar.'

'Not following that night.'

'What night?'

'The night that wee lad was killed.'

Black-Hair was not convinced. '*This* is your day off, Katie. You were working the day after Leon got stabbed.'

I nodded, anxious now, caught in the lie. 'I didn't see anything, though.'

I quietly wondered whether they had been following me that day, too. Had they seen me buying new tea towels or replenishing our first-aid kit?

'I just need to place Leon Burke in the bar after he was injured,' Black-Hair said. 'That's all I'm asking, Katie. Point me towards something that can do that. Some bloodstained top, something.'

'I can't,' I said, thinking of Leon's phone, wedged under the seat. 'I'd like to help, but I can't.'

'Will I tell Leon Burke's mother that we know who allowed her son to die but we can't do anything about it because the person who could help would like to but won't?'

'I didn't kill him,' I snapped. 'It's nothing to do with me. I was happy until you pulled me into that room and showed me them pictures.'

'It's everything to do with you, Katie. You're part of it now.'

'Why?'

'Because.'

'But that's not fair.'

'Fair? Who ever said things are fair? *It's not fair!* Do you think the O'Reillys are fighting fair? You don't think they're using a carrot and stick, too? Wee payments here, a handful of cash there. A kneecapping here, a beating there.'

I thought of Terry, the money he handed me for not talking during my arrest.

'It's not my fight,' I said.

Black-Hair shook his head. 'See, Katie, the thing is, I've been all carrot and no stick up to now. I know you cleaned up the morning after Leon Burke was stabbed. We have you on camera going into the bar.'

I started to protest but he held up his hand again. 'It doesn't matter now. I thought I could trust you, Katie. Me, like an idiot, watching your fucking curtains, thinking you'd do the decent thing, because you knew it was the right thing to do.'

'I told you I didn't want to be dragged into this.'

'Too late, Katie,' he snapped. 'You're already in it. Don't say you weren't warned.'

I felt my stomach twist once more. He seemed genuinely angry now. 'What do you mean?'

'The carrot hasn't worked, Katie. The stick will. "English" will drop you and your shopping home.'

With that, he strode back over to the low doorway, crouched down and vanished. I followed him out but by the time I'd reached the plastic boards, he was already driving off. English sat in the taxi, the engine idling.

'What are you smiling at?' I snapped as I got in.

He did not answer, though nor did he seem to stop smirking the entire way home.

## Chapter Thirteen

I was outside the school five minutes early. Most of the parents waiting to collect their children either stood in pairs, chatting, or singly, staring at their phones, enjoying the last few minutes of headspace before the doors opened.

I watched as child after child was released by the teacher at the door, once they had seen the relevant parent waiting. Yet, even after the initial flow of kids had drained to a trickle, there was no sign of Hope. I knew the teacher had seen me for she glanced in my direction, nodded, and turned to address someone in the room. A moment later, the principal of the school, a woman named Marie Doherty, came round the side of the building and called me over.

'Is everything okay?' I asked. 'Has she hurt her arm again?'

'It's best we talk in my office, Ms Hamill,' Marie said.

'What's wrong?'

'Let's wait until we have a seat, eh?'

She led me in through the front doors, using her swipe card to unlock the double doors, then ensuring they closed again behind me. I followed her past the main office and a wall display of autumn with poems, pictures of chestnuts and various browned leaves glued to the wall. I remembered Hope had spent one of the days in the park picking leaves off the ground, until she found one which was covered in dog's dirt and I'd made her throw them all away and wash her hands when she got home.

Marie reached her own office and, opening the door, lead me in. I expected Hope to be there, was already smiling in expectation of tears or upset. Instead, another woman sat, a folder in her lap.

Marie took a seat next to the woman and indicated that I should sit in the other free chair in her room. I was beginning to panic now, my legs buzzing with adrenaline. 'Where's Hope?' I asked, still standing.

'Please sit, Ms Hamill.'

'Where's Hope?'

'She's with my colleague and her classroom assistant,' the other woman said.

'Who are you?'

Marie spoke up. 'This is Linda O'Hare. She's with Gateway.'

'Gateway?'

'We're social workers, supporting families.'

'And? What do you want with me? We don't need support.'

'Why don't you sit, Ms Hamill?'

'I don't want to sit,' I snapped, then felt foolish standing and, after a second, perched on the edge of the free seat, my leg already bouncing.

'We received a call from a concerned parent earlier today,' Marie began. 'Regarding Hope's broken arm.'

'What about it? She fell off the roundabout in the playground.' Even as I spoke, I knew it wasn't quite the right story, though in that moment, it hadn't seemed relevant to go into details.

'She didn't though,' Marie said. 'The parent in question claimed that Hope's grandmother had been with her and had been shouting at her and scolding her for not coming off the roundabout.'

'She'd been going too fast, Mum said,' I agreed.

'The parent claimed that Hope's gran grabbed Hope's arm and pulled her off the roundabout as it was spinning and, in doing so, twisted and broke Hope's arm.'

It was what had happened, but somehow, in retelling it as she had, Marie had made it sound worse than it had seemed before.

'It's not like that.'

'Like what?' Linda asked, leaning forward a little in her seat.

'She didn't deliberately hurt her. You're making it sound like Mum was rough with her. She was a nurse, for God's sake; she'd hardly deliberately hurt her own granddaughter.'

'Hope suffered a spiral fracture,' Linda said. 'It's an injury most commonly seen in cases of domestic abuse where a child has had its arm twisted against its natural movement.'

'I know what she suffered. I was with her in the hospital when the doctor examined her. She didn't have any concerns about it.'

'The doctor?'

I nodded. 'And who was this parent?' I demanded.

Linda straightened a little. 'We've spoken with the doctor who treated Hope. She said that when she asked Hope what had happened, you answered for her and wouldn't let Hope speak. Is that right?'

'What? She asked what happened and I told her.'

'She asked *Hope* what happened.'

'Hope's a child,' I said.

'We've spoken with Hope ourselves.'

The adrenaline was buzzing through me at such a level now, I could not remain in my seat. 'You'd no right to talk to her without a parent present.'

'The classroom assistant with Hope's class is sitting in with her as Hope's appropriate adult.'

'I didn't agree to this.'

'With the nature of the accusation, we don't need you to.'

'This is unbelievable,' I said. 'You're twisting this. You're—'

Then it struck me.

'This is them, isn't it? Black-Hair and English.'

'Who?' Marie asked.

'This is because I wouldn't agree to be a tout for them. This is the stick he was talking about.'

Marie glanced across at Linda, confused. 'I don't know what you mean, Ms Hamill.'

'Katie,' I snapped. 'I'm fucking Katie. Stop using all the fancy language and proper names. You're doing their dirty work for them. This was them. I know it was.'

Linda looked up at me. 'Ms Hamill, I know you're upset.'

'You don't know the first fucking thing about me,' I said. 'Nothing.'

Linda nodded, glanced to Marie, shifted forward in her seat, as if to stand, but did not. 'I understand you're angry, but we have to act in the best interests of Hope.'

'Interrogating her in school?'

'Hope confirmed that her grandmother was cross with her and did shout at her. She said she was afraid to come off the roundabout because it was spinning and because her granny was angry. She told us that her granny grabbed her arm and pulled her from the roundabout as it was still turning.'

'Mum was probably worried about her. We all shout when we're panicking or worried.'

'We also shout when we're angry,' Linda said. 'Hope was quite clear that her granny was "cross" with her.' She emphasised Hope's words with a twitch of her fingers.

'Who made the complaint?' I asked. 'I have a right to know who made a complaint about me.'

'We aren't in the habit of revealing who made complaints,' Linda said. 'Besides, the complaint is not about you. It's about your mother.'

'You're being used,' I said. 'Or else you're in it with them.'

'Who?'

'Black-Hair and English.'

Marie stood at this and came across to me, her hand outstretched. She touched my arm. 'Katie, I think you should sit down.'

'I don't want to!' I said, aware I sounded like a child myself.

'Katie,' she said, angling her head to catch my line of sight. 'Katie, listen. I don't know what else is happening here, but I can promise you the call which came in was from a parent. When an allegation is made that someone has deliberately hurt one of our children, we have to make a Child Protection referral to Gateway. That's what happened today; nothing else.'

'That's how they make it seem,' I said, aware that I sounded paranoid. 'I'm not mad. That's what they do. First Benny, then the benefits, now this.'

'Katie, I promise you, I'm only acting in Hope's interests here. Someone called and we had to refer it on. There's no big conspiracy.'

'There is though,' I said. 'She must be in on it then.' I pointed at Linda who had stood now, too.

'Ms Hamill, I'm here to help you. My role is Family Support.'

'My mother *is* my family support,' I said.

'Not anymore, I'm afraid.'

'What?' The comment had refocused me. I could see what they were doing but not what the aim had been. Now it was becoming clear.

'Hope cannot have unsupervised contact with her grandmother until we've concluded our investigation.'

'That's impossible,' I said. 'I need my mum to look after her when I'm working.'

'You'll need to find someone else. A neighbour or friend maybe.'

'You want me to leave Hope with a complete stranger over someone she trusts?'

Linda nodded. 'Just because she trusts her granny doesn't mean that she isn't in danger.'

'Danger? Catch yourself on. My mum is no danger to anyone.'

'That's hopefully what we'll conclude when we've reviewed all the evidence.'

'Hope will be staying with my mother,' I said. 'I'm not cutting her granny out of her life.'

'I understand your strength of feeling, Ms Hamill,' Linda said. 'But I do have to caution you that if we feel Hope is being placed in a situation in which she is not safe, we are authorised to escalate our action.'

'What the fuck does that mean?'

'It means if you put her in a position where she is unsupervised with her granny, we may have to look at finding alternative living arrangements for her until such time as we've concluded our investigation.'

'You're threatening to take my daughter from me?'

'Not at all,' Linda said. 'Not so long as you do as you've been asked.'

Was she talking about what Black-Hair had asked? Was she working with them? Or did she mean about my mother?

'What's that meant to mean?' I asked. 'What do you mean by doing as I'm asked?'

'Keeping Hope safe. She is our priority here, Ms Hamill. I assume she's yours as well.'

'Of course she is. She's my daughter, for fuck's sake.'

'Then we understand each other. As I say, my role is to support you and Hope through this process.'

'Yeah,' I said. I was about to say more but felt Marie's hand on my arm.

'Let's see if Hope is ready to go home, shall we, Katie?'

I took the hint; the longer I argued, the longer it would be before I would see Hope.

'This is all designed to keep the little people down, isn't it?' I said, after Marie had left the room to get Hope. 'All of this.'

'All what?' Linda asked. She was standing now, near the door, as if afraid I was going to attack her, her folder clasped in front of her chest.

'This. This machinery. I've no comeback, nothing I can do to question or challenge. The whole system is just being used to make those of us at the bottom of the shit heap do as we're told. All we've done is put people in suits and clipboards and pretend it's a process or a system or whatever the fuck you want to call it, but it's really just a fancy way of keeping us down and doing as we're told.'

'I'm only looking out for Hope here, Katie,' she said.

'Don't call me Katie,' I snapped. 'I'm not your friend. You people don't give a shit what happens. If I end up with a bullet in my head some evening because they find out what's going on, what happens to Hope then? You don't give a fuck.'

'Are you under threat, Ms Hamill?' she asked. 'Are you worried about someone hurting you?'

'The only ones threatening me are your crowd.'

'Ms Hamill, if you are being threatened by someone, we can go to the police.'

The comment was so absurd, I laughed. 'Aye, that would be brilliant.'

'Or your solicitor. Maybe you do need to speak with someone.'

At that the door opened and Hope came in, tentatively, looking up at me from under her fringe, her broken arm jutting out from her side due to the clumsiness of her cast.

I couldn't stop the tears from springing in my eyes when I saw her. 'Hey, love,' I said. 'You ready to go home?'

She nodded but did not speak and I could see both Marie and Linda studying me, watching my reaction.

'Come on then, love. Let's go.'

I held out my hand and took her free one. Then she hugged into my leg, once, fiercely.

'It's okay, love,' I said, stroking her hair. 'Everything is going to be okay.'

But I did not believe it would be and I could not look at either of the other women in the room as I passed them on my way out.

## Chapter Fourteen

I took Hope into town for some hot chocolate as a treat. Initially, she was quiet, seeming to think she had done something wrong, so I didn't ask her about what had happened. Instead, we talked about Christmas, about the bike she wanted, about her arm. She showed me where each of her classmates had signed her cast, most in pictures or shapes, one – Siobhan – in elongated letters with the 'b' backwards like a 'd'. Siobhan was the brightest in the class, Hope said.

As she sipped the last of her chocolate and then lifted a spoon to scoop out the molten marshmallow that remained at the bottom, she finally brought up the subject herself.

'Is Nana in trouble?' she asked.

'Why would you think that?'

'They were asking me questions about her,' she said. 'Miss and the other woman.'

'What kind of questions?'

'Did she get angry with me? Did she ever shout or scream at me? Did she ever hit me?'

'What did you say to all that?' I asked, careful not to make her feel I was judging her.

'I said she only gets cross if I'm doing something silly.'

'And what about hitting you?'

'Nana doesn't hit me.'

'What about at the playground when you hurt your arm? Did she pull you because she was angry? Or because she was trying to get you off the roundabout without you falling?'

'The second one,' Hope said, licking the back of the spoon clean of the last of the cream and chocolate. 'She was cross because I was going too fast, so she tried to take me off.'

I nodded and drank the last of my own hot chocolate, though my stomach turned a little at the sweetness of it.

'They asked if *you* ever hit me, too.'

The question surprised me. I'd assumed that, as the complaint had been made about the incident in the playground, that would be all that they would want to discuss. Clearly, I was wrong.

'What did you say?'

'That you get cross sometimes, but you'd never hit me.'

I nodded, surprised that she even thought I got cross sometimes. I supposed I must, when I was running late or our money had run out before wages day. I might get a little stressed, but I imagined us happy in our own world. And my mother was part of that world. The idea that she couldn't see Hope, or Hope her, was unbearable.

'Hope, on the day in the playground, did you see any other parents there? Anyone else from your class?'

She scrunched up her face in a pantomime of thought, then shrugged. 'I don't know. There were some people there 'cause when I fell, they came over to help Nana.'

'Do you remember anyone in particular? Were any of your classmates there? Try to think.'

Marie had claimed that a parent had made the complaint. Perhaps I could work out which parent, if indeed it had even been a parent.

She shook her head. 'I don't think so. I don't remember.'

'Did you see a man sitting, maybe on his own or with another man. Taller than me, black hair? He has stubble, like he hasn't shaved. His hair is cut short at the sides and sticks up a bit on top.'

She was already shaking her head.

'He wasn't there, or you don't remember? Which, Hope? Think really carefully. It's important.'

I could see from her expression that I was frightening her, that in not remembering, she felt she was letting me down.

'I don't know,' she said. 'I'm trying to remember, Mummy, but . . .'

I took her hand in mine and squeezed it lightly. 'It's okay, love. Not to worry.'

She stared sullenly into her empty cup, then without looking at me, asked once more, 'Is Nana in trouble?'

'No, pet,' I said. 'Nana's made of metal. Nothing can harm her.'

Yet, despite my claim, I knew that this would hurt her deeply and could not help but feel that she would see my enforcing it as nothing short of betrayal.

## Chapter Fifteen

I dropped Hope off to visit one of her classmates for an hour after dinner and walked on up to my mother's. I'd not had the nerve to phone her and had ignored her calls for I knew I had to speak to her and did not wish to do so on the phone, not least because I could not be sure that there wouldn't be someone listening in on my calls. I was also aware that, in that regard, I was becoming increasingly paranoid. As I walked up the street, I scanned the cars on either side, studied each that passed, wondering if Black-Hair or English were sitting somewhere, watching, waiting to see if I brought Hope with me to my mum's, so that they might report me again.

'I've been calling you,' Mum said when she heard me coming into the house. She was sitting in the kitchen, scrolling on her phone, a steaming mug of tea by her elbow. 'Kettle's boiled. Where's Hope?'

'In Niamh's,' I said. I thought I was going to be sick. My legs were quaking, my head light, my fingers tingling with pins and needles.

'Are you okay, love?' Mum said, looking up. 'You look like you're going to collapse. Sit down.'

'I can't,' I said. And I couldn't. I'd have vomited on the spot if I did.

'What's wrong?' Mum asked, standing herself, worried now.

'I got called into Hope's school today,' I said. 'About her broken arm.'

'Did she hurt it again?' Mum asked, her face wan. 'What's happened, Katie?'

'No. Apparently a parent called in to make a complaint.'

'About Hope?'

I shook my head.

'About you?'

Another shake.

'Me?'

I nodded. 'They said they were in the park, and that you were angry with Hope. They tried to claim that you pulled her from the roundabout because you were angry, and you broke her arm.'

Mum stared at me open mouthed. 'That's ridiculous.'

'I told them that.'

'Did they not ask Hope what happened?'

'They did,' I said. 'But I think they worded it in such a way that they used what she said to support their view.'

'How? There is no view. There's just what happened. She was going too fast, and I tried to stop her falling.'

'I know. But they asked were you cross at her going too fast, then made it look like you deliberately did it.'

Tears sprang in her eyes. 'Did Hope say I deliberately hurt her?'

'No,' I said. 'Of course not.'

'Then what's the problem? They're hardly going to believe some busybody who can't keep their nose out of other people's things over a child and her mother.'

'They've said Hope can't have unsupervised contact with you until they investigate.'

'The school said that? What right have they to tell you what to do? You're her mother!'

'No,' I said. 'It was social services.'

'Social services?'

I nodded. 'They had to get them involved once the complaint was made.'

Mum stared at me, trying to make sense of all that I had told her. Then she shook her head and went back to her seat. I moved across and sat next to her, my hand on her arm.

'I know you didn't deliberately hurt Hope,' I said. 'I know you *couldn't*. I told them that. But they don't care. They said I can't let Hope have any unsupervised contact with you.'

'What does that mean?'

'I think it means she can visit you with me, but you can't be on your own with her.'

'What about your work?'

I shrugged and started to cry myself, but Mum was too hurt to offer me any consolation.

'They'll not know,' she said, nodding, her mind made up. 'If you drop her here when you're working, who is going to know?'

'They're watching me, Ma,' I said. 'They're watching everything I do.'

'You're being paranoid,' she said. 'Why would they care about you? What good are you to them?'

'I told them that,' I said. 'But they won't leave me alone. They took me up to Grianán the other day and threatened me. They said that they'd tried to be nice and I wasn't playing ball, so they would use a stick rather than a carrot.'

'What does that even mean?'

'It means *this*. Now. What's happening. It means they're the ones reported you. They'll be watching everything I do, waiting for me to leave Hope here and then I'll lose her too.'

'And are you going to let them do this?' Mum asked, staring at me, as if I was to blame for it all.

'What can I do?'

'You can stand up for me,' she said. 'Why am I being dragged into this mess?'

'Do you not think I've tried?' I asked. 'That I'm not going over and over all this to work out how to get away from them all? Mark, Terry, those bastards who are following me.'

'Can you speak to your solicitor?'

'I don't have one.'

'What about the person who represented you when you were arrested?'

'Terry O'Reilly's solicitor? Tell him that Special Branch want me to inform on his client? Terry will have me shot.'

'Is there someone else who could help? What about going to the papers?'

I shook my head. I had considered it but to do so would simply mark me out for everyone. The fewer people who knew, the better.

'You need to do something,' Mum said. 'You can't let them destroy your life.'

'They already are,' I said. 'I need to leave work.'

'Why?'

I thought through it as I spoke, and it began to make

sense to me. 'I can't go to work if I've no childminder, right? And if I'm not working in O'Reilly's, I'm no value to that crew so they'll have to leave me alone.'

'I thought you tried to leave already.'

'I did. Terry thought I meant I needed more money, so he gave me cash in an envelope.'

'You took cash off Terry O'Reilly?' Mum asked. 'Jesus, Katie.'

'He's my boss.'

'He's not. Mark is. And he pays you for cleaning a pub. Terry giving you money means you owe him.'

I shook my head, not needing the added worry. 'Regardless, if I explain I can't work because I've no childminder, that won't look suspicious, and they'll have to let me go. And once I'm out, I'm no use to anyone.'

Mum did not look convinced, but for the first time since this had started, I believed I could see a way out that would leave everyone happy. Or at least leave us all unharmed.

## Chapter Sixteen

I took Hope with me to work the next morning, having phoned the school and told them she wasn't feeling well. She sat in one of the booths while I cleaned, variously playing with my phone and making makeshift houses out of beer-mats. I knew it wasn't ideal, but I had been left with no choice.

Mark arrived in just after 11. He glanced over at Hope, then did a theatrical double-take and stomped over to her.

'Can I see your ID, young lady?' he said. 'You're not over eighteen!'

Hope looked up at him, unsure how to respond.

'I'm four,' she said, simply.

'Four? There's no way someone as smart as you is only four!'

Hope nodded her head solemnly.

'Well, I think four-year-olds are allowed in, but only if they're having a drink. What would you like? Lemonade or Coke?'

'Coke, please,' Hope said, nodding her head as if having reached a difficult decision.

'Coke it shall be,' Mark said, heading over behind the bar. 'How's Katie?'

I had stopped mopping the floor to watch this exchange, pleased to see Hope happy and feeling all the more guilty that I was planning on leaving the source of that joy – Mark – short-staffed.

'Sorry about this,' I said, gesturing towards where Hope sat, swinging her legs, her heels drumming off the wooden frame of the booth.

'It's fine. Your mum not well?'

'A parent phoned in to school and made a complaint about her. That she'd deliberately broken Hope's arm,' I said, moving across to speak to him without Hope hearing.

'That's ridiculous,' he said. 'The whole town knows your ma dotes on that wee lassie.'

'The school had to contact social services.'

'For fuck's sake,' Mark muttered, opening the Coke and popping a straw into the bottle. 'What had they to say for themselves?'

'I'm not allowed to leave Hope with her unsupervised or they'll take her from me.'

'You're kidding?' He stood, staring at me, genuinely surprised.

I nodded. 'So, I'm going to have to finish up here, Mark. I can't work if I can't leave Hope with my mum. And I can't afford a childminder.'

'Aw, you can't leave, Katie,' he said. 'We'll sort something for you. Bring Hope in with you, sure. She's no bother.'

'She needs to be at school,' I said. 'You know yourself that I'm not always finished work on time to collect her and I can't bring her into a bar every day. That's no way for a kid to be growing up.'

'It didn't do me any harm,' Mark said, seemingly wounded by my comment.

'That's not what I mean,' I said. 'It's just ... it makes things easier if I pack up. I can work my notice if you need.'

'Jesus, Katie, I'm awful sorry to hear that,' he said. He looked over at Hope who was waiting patiently for her drink, then took it across to her. 'There you go, my lovely.'

'Thank you,' Hope said, making me proud with her manners.

'Now that'll be twenty-three pounds, please,' Mark said, his hand held out.

Hope giggled at him as she tried, without success, to catch the dancing straw in her mouth.

'I don't have any money,' she protested.

'Taking drinks without money? Right then, I'll have to make do with a high five. But not the broken arm; we don't want you breaking it twice now, do we?'

Hope shook her head as, with a smile, she slapped his open palm with her uninjured hand.

'Ahh!' Mark gripped his hand beneath his armpit in a pantomime of pain, earning more giggles from Hope. 'I think you broke *my* hand!'

As I watched the pair, I could not reconcile this Mark, kind and funny with a child, with the Mark who had supposedly allowed Leon Burke to bleed to death. The two did not equate and I began to doubt what Black-Hair had claimed. Perhaps Terry was bad – I *knew* he was bad, had heard the rumours for years about his being involved in drugs and protection rackets – but Mark? I couldn't accept that. He must have done his best to help the boy, must have thought that the wound wasn't as bad as it turned out to be.

Regardless, I still knew that I had to leave, to free myself from Black-Hair's control, and I felt I had done the difficult part in telling Mark I needed to leave. Nothing more was said about it until I was finishing up.

Benny had arrived in and was behind the bar, making two mugs of coffee while Mark and Terry had taken their usual table near the fire. Hope was sitting in the booth where she had been, colouring on a blank page with some broken crayons which Mark had dug out from a drawer in the kitchen.

'I hear you're leaving us,' Terry said as I came up from the back lounge, my coat and bag in hand.

I nodded, feeling myself well a little at the thought, even though I had chosen to hand in my notice, and I hoped it would, in the long run, get Black-Hair off my back.

'You're leaving?' Benny said, looking personally hurt. I had the impression he thought it was because of him and me.

I nodded. 'I've no childminder,' I explained, both annoyed at his presumption that he was the cause and touched by his disappointment in seeing me go.

'We were just thinking,' Mark said. 'Our Ann looks after kids during the day.'

I knew Ann a little. We'd been at school together, though she was a few years below me. She was the youngest of the O'Reillys.

'I can't afford a childminder,' I said.

Terry shook his head. 'We'll see Ann right until all this nonsense with your mother is sorted,' he said.

'I couldn't ask you to do that,' I said, panic rising now. Having found the perfect reason to leave, and thus make myself useless to Black-Hair, the last thing I needed was for that escape route to be taken from me.

'You haven't asked. We've offered,' Mark said. 'You can drop Hope off and come in to work and Ann can collect her on days you're running late or watch her on the days she's off school.'

I shook my head. 'I really appreciate the offer, but I couldn't,' I said.

'Why not?' Mark asked, clearly confused.

Thankfully, Terry interrupted. 'Well, sure, have a think about it. The offer's there,' he said. 'Benny, are those coffees making themselves?'

And with that, the moment had passed and I said my goodbyes. Mark totalled up my last pay and rounded it up with an extra fifty quid on top.

'To keep you going for a bit,' he said. 'Your job will be here whatever time you're able to come back.'

He handed me the cash and, as I took it, clasped my hand in his other. His hands, as in my memory of the night in the car, were warm and soft. He held mine a moment longer than needed. 'I'll miss you about the place, Katie,' he said, his voice thick and low.

'I'll miss yous too,' I said, and then, because of his kindness and because I felt I should, I hugged him, lightly, briefly. I stepped back and gave him an apologetic smile, but something in his expression had softened and, as he held my gaze, I felt there was something he wanted to say but could not articulate.

I took Hope to the cinema that evening with my mum. It was Cheap Tuesday and tickets were only £3, so a tenner took us all and we sneaked in sweets Mum had bought in the shop.

It was deliberate on my part; I wanted whoever was watching to see that I would not deprive my daughter of a relationship with her granny, while also showing that I was sticking to the requirements that they not be left together unsupervised.

The movie was a Disney remake of one of their own cartoons and, while Hope seemed to enjoy it, snuggled between Mum and me, my mind soon wandered.

I wanted to believe that I had beaten Black-Hair and English at their own game, that I had found the loophole which meant I could move on with my life, my family intact. I imagined how, in a few days perhaps, social services would confirm that the investigation was over, and that Hope and my mother's relationship could resume as normal.

At one stage, I got a text from Benny, asking how I was doing. I was a little surprised, as he didn't usually text me. As I began to answer it, Hope complained about the light from my phone, so I slipped out to the toilet.

Fine. Sorry to be leaving but cant see any other way at the moment, I texted.

Three dots and then: Hope this isn't about us. I wldn't want u 2 leave on my accnt.

Typical Benny, assuming everything was about him.

No. Stuck wthout mum 2 help so have 2 quit.

Three dots.

When it sorted r u coming back?

I considered how best to respond. The events with my mum had given me a way out. I needed an excuse to stay out, having now managed it.

Not sure. Might need 2 find something w better hours. 4 Hope. Don't no. Thnx for txt tho.

The three dots continued for some time, then vanished and he did not respond. I imagined he was in work, texting in between orders and perhaps someone had come to the bar. I was flattered that he had thought of me, especially when he was not looking for anything in return.

Finishing up, I went to the toilet. I was out for all of five minutes, then went back into the cinema, took my seat, and thought nothing of it.

However, that evening, as I put Hope to bed, I heard my phone chime once more. Assuming it to be Benny, finally getting a chance to respond, I waited until Hope was settled, then headed into the living room to read his message.

Instead, it was a WhatsApp message from a number I did not recognise. It contained a single grainy image. I knew straight away what it was: Mum and Hope, sitting side by side in the cinema from earlier, the seats either side of them empty. To anyone looking at it in isolation, Hope had been with Mum alone.

I knew who'd sent the message. Clearly the picture had been taken on a mobile phone by someone sitting a few rows down from Hope and Mum. How had I not seen him? I wracked my brain, trying to remember, retracing the walk from the entrance up to our seats, each step, trying to will myself to look across each row as we went. I thought I saw Black-Hair now, in my memory, but I knew I had not. If I had seen him at the time, I'd have turned and left again.

Who is this? I texted, though I was fairly sure I knew who.

Three dots.

You need to get back to your work.

I cant, I typed. No one to watch Hope.

Three dots.

Don't try to be clever. You have other options. Get back to work.

What options? Could he know about Mark's offer of his sister, Ann, as a childminder? How could he? Did they have the place bugged? Why then did they need me?

What options?

Back to work or this gets shared.

I was so frustrated. I had managed to get out and now this.

But I wuz only out for 2 mins at toilet.

Not what the picture shows.

U no I was.

Doesn't matter. Get back to work.

I stared at the phone, waiting for something to click, for some idea of how to get out of all this. But there was nothing. In anger, I started typing.

Fuck you! Fuck you! Fuck you!

Three dots, then nothing. And, in the silence that followed, I started to panic that, in lashing out at him, he would have shared the picture with social services already.

I knew then that I had no choice left. I would have to take up Mark's offer of Ann as a childminder. And I would need to give Black-Hair something in the hope it would get him off my back and let Mum return fully into our lives.

And I knew what that thing was. Or more precisely, where it was.

## Chapter Seventeen

The following morning, as I dropped Hope to school, I'd expected Marie to come out and speak to me, to say there had been a further complaint, but instead she waved and nodded, offering me an embarrassed smile as she ushered Hope into the classroom out of the rain.

I walked into town, heading straight for O'Reilly's. Mark was cleaning behind the bar himself when I went in through the staff door at the back. He looked surprised to see me and a little flushed from mopping.

'Katie,' he said. 'I wasn't expecting you.'

I nodded. 'I feel so stupid,' I said. 'I was thinking about things last night and I really can't afford not to work. If that offer still stands, for Ann to watch Hope for a bit, I'd be very grateful.'

He nodded. 'Of course. I'll drop her a line and ask her. Are you okay for today?'

'Yeah; she's at school,' I said, gesturing towards the main doors of the bar, as if her school was situated there.

'You're soaking,' Mark said, moving forward with a tea towel from behind the bar. 'Here.'

I expected him to hand me the towel, but instead, he placed it over my head like a veil and began to rub my hair dry, then seemed to realise what he had done and stopped.

'Sorry,' he said. 'I didn't . . . I shouldn't have done that. You look drenched.'

'It's fine,' I said, even though the intimacy of the gesture had caught me off guard. 'Thanks.'

He stood awkwardly, his hands in his pockets.

'It's good to have you back. The mopping is taking it out of me. I don't know how you manage it.'

'It takes it out of me too,' I said. 'Look, Mark, I need to give you back the fifty pounds you gave me yesterday. I can work the hours and take it as an advance if you like.'

'Don't be silly, Katie,' he said. 'It's fine.'

I finished drying my hair and handed him back the towel. He took it and held it in his hands, as if studying it. I got a sense he was building to saying something.

'I think I know why you wanted to leave,' he said.

'It was because of my mum,' I said. 'You know that.'

'But before then too. You were talking about looking for other work. Is it Benny?'

'No!' I said. 'Genuinely, it's not. That's all done anyway.'

'If he was hassling you, like, I'd deal with it.'

'Honestly, Mark. It's fine. I just was stuck with the whole thing with my mum.'

'Anyone hassles you, I'll deal with it. You know that, right?'

There was something endearing in his clumsy attempt at chivalry.

'I know. You have my back,' I said, because I assumed it was what he would want to hear.

He smiled. 'You know it,' he said, and chucked me beneath the chin. 'Good to have you home.'

'Thanks, Mark,' I said, taken aback by the genuine warmth he felt at my return. When I'd first started in the place, years back, there'd been something attractive about Mark. He was confident without the brashness of Terry. And he'd always treated all of us bar staff well. Over the years, though, he'd become my boss and, in his manner with me, almost like an older brother. I could see that he'd been treating me differently from the rest: the extra cash, the help with Hope, the gentleness in his actions. And I admit I was flattered by it. There was something seductive in knowing that he was looking out for me.

'I'll get started, shall I?'

He nodded. 'Great. I've up here mostly done.'

'I'll do the lounge and the toilets, sure,' I said, lifting the mop and bucket and taking it down with me while he stood in the middle of the floor, watching me.

The lounge wasn't too bad, and I assumed it had been quiet the previous evening. I wiped down the tables first and polished them, trying to see whether Leon Burke's phone was still wedged beneath the frame of the seating, where I had left it. It was.

When I knew Mark had headed to take out the empties, I started washing the floor near the seat and quickly dropped to my knees to get the handset. It was wedged more tightly than I had expected, and I realised I would need to put something in behind it and lever it out.

I heard the creak of the hinges as Mark came back in and so stood and resumed mopping, while in the main bar area, just up the steps, he hefted another crate of empties and headed back out.

I hunkered down again and taking a folded beer mat, tried to use it to prise the phone out, but the card bent and broke. I heard the creak again and only managed to stand before Mark appeared at the bar once more for the last crate. He stopped at the top of the steps and looked down.

'It's like it was only yesterday when you left,' he laughed.

'Time flies when you're having fun,' I said, a little pointlessly, smiling, as he headed down towards the rear door.

I took out my own phone this time and slid it into the space next to Burke's, then angling it, worked it against the other phone until it began to emerge from beneath the frame. I just managed to pull it out and slip it into my pocket when I heard the rear door slam shut and Mark's heavy footfalls tread through the kitchen.

I kept my hand on the phone in my pocket as he reappeared. I could feel the dried blood on it and was reminded once more of Mark, his shirt crimsoned, that morning when he called me in to clean up Leon Burke's blood. No, that wasn't him. That wasn't the Mark I knew: kind-hearted, clumsy Mark. The same Mark who had made Hope laugh and had dried my hair and, in his own awkward way, had tried to show me softness. This was the real Mark, the one whom I had seen. It made me even angrier that Black-Hair had forced me to turn against him.

And I felt desperately guilty that, in my hand, I held an object with which I planned to betray his trust.

## Chapter Eighteen

The following morning, I left Hope's curtains pulled when I took her to school.

Terry was in the bar when I arrived in and winked when he saw me. 'I heard you were back,' he said. 'More farewell tours than Sinatra, eh, girl?'

I smiled, kind of getting the reference.

Mark stood. 'I asked Ann about helping with Hope. It's all good.'

'Thanks, Mark,' I said. 'It hopefully won't be for too long. I'm hoping this whole crap with my mum gets sorted and things can go back to normal.'

'Hopefully,' he agreed. 'But it's all fine with Ann. I'll text you her number and you can sort it between you.'

All day, he followed me around the bar, finding excuses to be near me. I was just finished washing the floors when he carried me over a mug of tea.

'Milk and one sugar, isn't that right?'

I nodded, surprised that he knew, and more surprised at how something had shifted between us for him. Whatever he had felt for me before, had remained hidden beneath the veneer of being my boss. But since Benny, since he'd helped me out with money, since I'd hugged him, he was almost openly affectionate with me.

There was definitely something there, some spark between us, though different from how I felt with Benny, where we had both been satisfying a hunger in the other without any expectation that it might develop into something bigger. In fact, that had been half the attraction with Benny, the knowledge that it wouldn't get serious. Mark was in a different position, though, and his approach to me was different too, almost chaste, in fact. I knew Benny could not wait to get me in bed. I didn't get that vibe off Mark. And yet, there was undoubtedly something that he believed existed between us.

However, the last thing I needed was to get more involved with the O'Reillys. I'd been working to get myself out of their world. I had no intention of becoming even more deeply enmeshed. Yet, I could not be rude to Mark either, even as I felt guilty, not wishing to hurt his feelings, to throw his kindness back in his face. And having been nothing more than a diversion for Benny, I found something endearing in being the sole focus of Mark's attention.

Things changed a little though when Benny arrived in for his shift. I'd not seen him since I'd started back and when he spotted me, he smiled.

'The wanderer returns,' he said. 'Welcome back!'

'Thanks, Benny. And for the texts.'

'Have you not enough problems with that wife of yours?' Mark said. 'Texting another woman and you married.'

Benny seemed to think that Mark was joking with him. 'It keeps her keen. She knows she has to up her game.'

'Show her some respect,' Mark snapped. 'She's the mother of your kids.'

'I was just joking, Mark.'

'You should treat people right,' he said.

'Fuck's sake, he's only messing,' Terry said, glancing across at his brother where he sat in their usual spot.

Mark shook his head. 'Amy's a good woman. You treat her proper.'

'I am,' Benny said, his bearing that of a scolded child.

'It doesn't sound it,' Mark grumbled.

'He's fine,' Terry said. 'Here, folks, when we have you both. There's a private function in here tomorrow night in the lounge. Can you both work a shift behind the bar? Sally's tied up, Katie, and can't do her normal cover.'

'I've Hope—' I began, but Terry had already moved on.

'Ann'll look after her. I'm picky about who I want working the event. In for eight, the pair of you, okay?'

I felt I could not argue with him and so nodded. I glanced at Benny who shrugged, his attention more on Mark than Terry, clearly wondering what he had done to annoy him.

My phone buzzed and I checked my messages. It was a WhatsApp message from the same number as that which had sent me the picture of my mum with Hope.

**Taxi will collect you on William Street at 12.30 p.m.**

No sooner had I read it than it disappeared from the screen.

I looked up at the clock. I had twenty minutes to get finished and away.

'Everything okay?' Mark asked.

'Fine,' I said, aware that his increased attention also meant increased scrutiny at a time when I did not need it.

'I'm sorry about that with Benny,' he said, seemingly misunderstanding my change in mood. 'I just think he has no respect. For Amy or for you.'

And with that, he appeared to have absolved me of all responsibility for what had happened between Benny and me.

I was at William Street by 12.35 p.m. I could have made it sooner, but something in me rebelled against being told what to do by Black-Hair. Perhaps unsurprisingly, I was left to stand for a further ten minutes before the same 'taxi', which had collected me and taken me to Grianán, turned the corner and pulled up next to me. As before, English was driving.

'You're late,' I said.

'Traffic,' he muttered, though I wondered whether he had actually been parked up around the corner, making me wait.

'Where's Black-Hair?'

'Black-Hair?' he chuckled to himself. 'He's coming.'

We drove in silence, down the Strand Road, past the police station and on towards the roundabout at the top of the Buncrana Road.

'Another visit to Grianán?' I asked, for it seemed we were heading in that direction.

English said nothing, but rather than turning left, as I'd expected, he circled the roundabout and headed back up the Strand Road, then drove into the McDonald's car park. As we neared the front door of the restaurant, Black-Hair came out carrying a bag of food and a tray of three drinks. He tapped on the window of the rear passenger door with his elbow, indicating he wanted me to open the door for him, which I did. Then he handed me in the cardboard cup holder of three Cokes and slid into the seat next to me.

'Katie. I wasn't sure what you'd have, so I ordered you a burger and chips. That okay?'

'I'm not hungry.'

'I'm guessing you've not had lunch,' he said, passing me a wrapped burger, which I left on the seat, untouched. 'You want to look after yourself.'

I stared at him, disgusted.

'What?' he asked, his mouth filled with a bite from his own burger, which he'd already started. 'We've ...' He stopped, chewed and swallowed, then continued: 'We've got off on the wrong foot, Katie. I want us to be friends. Help one another.'

'The only help I need is my mother's.'

'She's not gone anywhere, Katie. And she did break Hope's arm.'

'It was an accident.'

'Maybe. But she was cross with her. I was there.'

'You're watching my child?'

'I have a duty of care to you now, Katie. It's my job to make sure you're okay. That extends to Hope.'

'The only ones threatening me are you two. And I don't even know who you are!'

'He's Black-Hair,' English said, who had driven us over to a quiet corner of the car park and was eating his own burger. 'I said no onion.'

'I told them that,' Black-Hair said. 'Is that what you call me? Black-Hair?'

'What else can I call you?'

He considered this. 'That's fair enough. So, you pulled your curtains. What have you got for us?'

'I need to know that all this shit about my mum will be dropped.'

Black-Hair nodded. 'We'll do what we can, if the information you're providing us is useful.'

'I need a guarantee.'

'You know yourself, Katie: processes take time. But I'm sure we can try to oil the wheels a bit and get things moving.'

'I can't work if Mum can't watch my kid.'

'I think we both know that's not true.'

'Have you the bar bugged?'

Black-Hair finished the burger and fished in the brown bag. He handed me across a small carton of fries.

'Have your chips at least,' he said. 'So, what have you got for us?'

'If this gets back to Terry, I'm dead. You know that, don't you? You know what you're making me do.'

'You're choosing to do, Katie. And we appreciate it. Your city appreciates it, even though they'll never know what you've done.'

'My city couldn't give a shit about me,' I said.

'When the O'Reillys and the drugs they sell are off the streets, your city will give a shit for sure.'

I knew what he was doing, trying to make it feel less like a betrayal, if I was doing this for the local community rather than for him and whatever organisation or police force he represented.

'Both O'Reillys?'

Black-Hair nodded. 'They're both equally involved. Terry's the one with the reputation, but who do you think keeps things running every time Terry spends a spell on remand?'

'I don't buy it,' I said, even as I tried to ignore the memory of Mark, his bloodied shirt held towards me to wash for him. 'Mark's a good man.'

'Don't let the whole "softly softly" shtick of his fool you.'

'I've known him for years and he's always been decent.'

'We've places to be,' English said, wiping his hands clean with a paper napkin, his meal finished.

'He's very impatient, isn't he?' Black-Hair joked. 'So, what have you got for us?'

I rummaged through my bag and took out Leon Burke's phone, which I'd wrapped in a plastic bag.

'What's this?' Black-Hair asked, opening the bag a little cautiously and peering in.

'Leon Burke's phone,' I said.

'What? Where did you get this?'

'In the bar. The morning after he was stabbed.'

'And you never thought to say?'

'I'm saying now.'

English had twisted in his seat. 'Where did you find it?'

'On the floor, in the lounge.'

'Just lying there?'

I nodded. 'Some of the chairs and that had been overturned and I think the phone was missed. If you look at the back of it, I think his fingerprints are all over it. In blood.'

Black-Hair looked to English, then to me.

'Burke was definitely in the bar, after he'd been stabbed?'

I nodded.

'Where has this been since?' English asked.

'I found it that morning and didn't know what to do with it, so I hid it under the seats.'

'And no one else saw it?' English was incredulous.

'It was under the wooden frame of the fixed seating in the booths,' I explained. 'I took it back out yesterday.'

'You've touched this then,' Black-Hair said. 'With your bare hands?'

I hadn't thought about that. 'Yeah,' I said.

'We have her prints from the arrest anyway,' English said. 'We can eliminate her that way.'

Black-Hair nodded. 'This is really good, Katie. But it's no use to us like this.'

'It ties Leon Burke to O'Reilly's bar,' I said. 'To Terry, like you wanted.'

'Did you see Terry there?'

I couldn't lie about it, nor could I name Mark. Instead, I shook my head and said nothing.

'It ties Leon to the bar if we find it *in* the bar,' Black-Hair said. 'This could have been found anywhere.'

'You'll have to take it back,' English said.

'I can't. It was hard enough getting it out in the first place.'

'You have to, Katie,' Black-Hair said. 'This has no value to us like this.'

'It has blood on it. Fingerprints,' I said. 'You can link it to the night he died.'

Black-Hair shook his head. 'We can't. The blood could have been from a nosebleed. Anyone's phone could have any number of fingerprints on them at any one time.'

'He could have dropped his phone at any time,' I said. 'Even if it *is* found in the bar, it doesn't prove he left it there that night.'

'It does,' Black-Hair said. 'If the last calls and texts he made were in the hours before he died and everything since has been unanswered, it allows us to prove the phone could only have been left there on the night of his death. Which places him at the scene. We can do a forensic sweep then for blood and, if we're lucky, tie him to the bar and to the O'Reillys.'

'I can't take it back,' I said. 'If Terry catches me, he'll kill me, if he's as bad as you say.'

'You just need to be careful,' Black-Hair said. 'Do it first thing when you're on your own.'

'I'm working a different shift tomorrow,' I said. 'Terry asked me in late.'

This got English's attention. 'Why?'

'He wants me to work the evening shift.'

'Terry did? Isn't Mark the manager of the place? Why's Terry arranging staff shifts?' Black-Hair asked.

'He said there's an event on tomorrow night. He wants me and another lad to work it.' I didn't mention Benny, still embarrassed by the fact they knew of our affair – indeed, had revealed our affair to Amy.

English looked to Black-Hair. 'It's Andy Flood. It must be.'

'His coming out party?' Black-Hair said.

'Who's Andy Flood?' I asked, genuinely confused.

'He's a key member of the O'Reilly gang,' Black-Hair said. 'He did a stretch for a killing. Attacked a young lad who was selling drugs on their patch. Hacked him to death with a machete. Left his head hanging on by a thread.'

'And he's coming out?'

'Not of the closet. Of prison,' English said.

'He did a whole stretch and never once named names,' Black-Hair said. 'They owe him.'

'Our friends might put in an appearance,' English said. 'Ross and Flood were tight.'

I looked from one man to the other, aware that there was a whole other conversation going on about which I knew nothing. I had never felt more like a pawn, as if I had found myself in the middle of someone else's war.

'Who's Ross?' I asked.

'Ross is a key paramilitary in Belfast. He is also responsible for the importation of all the drugs that hit the streets in Northern Ireland,' Black-Hair said. 'He's the top dog.'

'One person can't be responsible for every drug.'

'Take our word for it,' English said. 'He is. And anything being sold that's not coming through Ross, the person selling it doesn't last long.'

'Like Machete Boy and Andy Flood,' Black-Hair added with a laugh.

'Machete Boy? Someone who almost got his head taken off?'

'Trust me, he was no angel either,' Black-Hair said. 'The thing is, Ross and Flood became good mates inside. Ross got out last year and has started working with the O'Reillys, presumably on the recommendation of Flood.'

'The policeman and his wife who were shot. Millar?'

Black-Hair nodded at me, encouragingly, as a teacher might a student. 'That's right. We think Ross took him out for Terry. A kind of courtship gift.'

English handed me his phone. On the screen was a young man, perhaps in his late twenties. He had black hair which was shaved at the sides and back and stood in a light quiff at the front. He had a tattoo running up the left-hand side of his neck.

'That's Ross,' English said. 'Flick across to the other two.'

I swiped to the next picture, of a younger lad, maybe in his late teens. He wore grey sweatpants and a grey sweatshirt with bright blue trainers. He was dragging on a cigarette in the picture. His head was shaven, and a line cut through one of his eyebrows, like a scar.

'That's Ross's wee brother, Lucas. He's learning the trade at his brother's side. The final lad is one of Ross's lieutenants, Simon Crowley.'

I swiped. Crowley was a little older than both of them. He carried extra weight around his gut. His black T-shirt stretched across his belly while a silver chain was worn tight to his neck. He too was clean shaven, his head like a cue ball.

'Keep an eye out for any or all of them,' English said. 'Especially Ross, though.'

'And what if I see them?'

'Just keep an eye. If you can, keep an ear out too. Remember the three names?'

'Shaw, Higgins and Dunne?'

'You hear any of those names being mentioned, you let us know.'

'Better still,' Black-Hair said, reaching over the back seat of the car and rummaging in the boot. 'Here's a present for you.'

He handed me a box with a new phone in it. It looked unused, though the cellophane had been removed from the packaging.

'What the fuck is that?' I asked, refusing to take it.

'It's a phone,' Black-Hair said.

'But what does it do?'

'Make phone calls,' he said. 'It's just a phone, Katie. It's not going to blow up or anything.'

'I have a phone.'

'I'd rather you'd use this one,' Black-Hair said. 'We can follow what's happening in real time. If you leave it sitting somewhere in the bar, the speaker unobstructed, we'll have ears too.'

'You'll not hear much in a crowded bar,' I said. 'Besides, Mark and Terry will think it's strange that I suddenly have a new phone; I can't afford a bus half the time.'

'Tell them your old one fell down the toilet and you got this one cheap on the market.'

It seemed plausible and I *had* seen hacked models like this one on the markets for eighty quid.

'You need to get rid of your old phone though,' Black-Hair said. 'If they see you with two phones, they'll start asking questions you'll not want to answer.'

'And you can listen in on this *all* the time?'

Black-Hair gave me a long-suffering look. 'Katie, do you genuinely think I've nothing better to do with my days than listen in on your phone calls to your mother? We'll track what's happening tomorrow night only. And when we know you're in the bar. Beyond that, no one will be listening or looking at whatever you search up. Trust me.'

I didn't believe a word he said but saw no point in arguing with him.

'If Ross is there, send a text to your mother saying you'll be working late and can she put Hope to bed. If we see that, we'll know Ross is in the building.'

'My mum's not allowed to look after Hope,' I said. 'Unless you can change that too.'

'No,' Black-Hair said. ' That's how we'll know the message is meant for us. But get this sorted for us, Katie, and we'll do everything we can to get that problem taken care of for you. 'After all, that's what friends do. We look after each other. You're doing the right thing here, you know that.'

He handed me the phone once more and, finally, I took it from him.

'Get rid of your old phone now,' he said. 'Actually dropping it in the toilet might be a good idea.'

With that, he opened the door of the car and got out, gathering up his rubbish as he did. 'He complains about the car smelling of fast food otherwise,' he said, with a wink.

I found his attempts at friendliness disconcerting. When I thought of the havoc he had wreaked on my family this past few weeks, I wanted to smash him in the face with his phone. Instead, I offered a weak smile and felt all the worse for having done so.

'If I'm Black-Hair, who's he, by the way?' he asked, nodding towards English, who twisted to look at me with renewed interest. 'Was it English you called him the last day?'

'No,' I lied. 'He doesn't have a name.'

Black-Hair laughed. 'Proper order, too.'

With that, he closed the door and walked over towards the bins. I turned, hoping to see where he went next, which car he got into perhaps. But English had started the ignition and pulled away before Black-Hair was finished dumping the rubbish. I looked down and realised I was holding the new phone box and a carton of uneaten fries. The bag containing Leon Burke's phone lay next to me, next to the wrapped burger which Black-Hair had given me.

'I'll drop you near Hope's school,' English said. 'You should pretend to pay me, and I'll pass you back whatever cash you give me as change,' he added.

'Why?'

'So that people think you got into a real taxi,' he said. 'You get out without paying, people might get suspicious.'

'What do I do with Leon Burke's phone?' I asked.

'Put it back where it was,' he said. 'We'll come in for it at some stage. But maybe wait until after tomorrow night. The last thing we want is someone else finding it first. Get Flood's party out of the way and then hide it when you're cleaning up the day after.'

'What excuse will you give for raiding the bar? They'll know someone tipped you off.'

He shook his head. 'Don't you worry about that. We'll take care of those things. You just do what you've been told.'

*What you've been told*. Like I was a child.

I said nothing more until we got near the school. I put the new phone and Burke's phone in my handbag and left the fries sitting on the back seat, but stuffed the uneaten burger into the seat pocket in front of me. With any luck, it would leave the car stinking and he'd not be able to find the source. It was a petty victory, but a victory none the less.

'How much do I owe you?' I asked, foolishly play-acting the pretence of paying for the taxi.

'Oh, eight quid will do, love,' English said, adopting a cockney accent. If that was his instinctive idea of a cab driver, it suggested he hadn't been here long.

I handed him a twenty-pound note and watched while he fumbled with a wallet and handed me back two ten-pound notes and a small plastic card.

'What's this?' I asked, turning it over to see the logo for one of the local toy shops.

'A contribution towards Hope's bike,' he said, smiling. 'You keep delivering for us, there'll be plenty more.'

I got out of the car, the gift card clenched in my hand. It weighed less than thirty pieces of silver, but its edges were sharp as they dug into my palm.

## Chapter Nineteen

The card lay like a guilty thought in the drawer in our kitchen that evening. Hope and I had dinner together and I explained that I would be working the following evening and would have to leave her with a new childminder.

'Is this because of what I told the teacher about Nana?'

'No, pet,' I said, for I could see the notion upset her. 'Hopefully that will all be sorted soon anyway, and you and Nana can start spending more time together again. Do you remember my boss, Mark, who gave you the bottle of Coke the other day when I took you to work?'

Hope nodded, the memory eliciting a faint smile.

'Well, Mark's sister, Ann, is going to watch you for me tomorrow evening.'

'What's she like?'

'She's probably like Mark,' I said. 'I was at school with her so she's around the same age as me. She's nice.'

I didn't know if she was but knew Hope would want to be reassured. My memory of Ann from school was someone who was aggressive with other girls. Boys were afraid of her, partly because by that stage Terry already had a reputation and so no one was going to mess around his baby sister.

Once Hope went to bed, I set up the new phone, transferring my old SIM card across. Black-Hair had told me to dump my old phone, but, as I stood in the bathroom, preparing to dip it in water as instructed, I couldn't bring myself to do it. I was uneasy about the idea that they would be listening to every conversation I had with anyone if I only used the new phone. Keeping my old handset would allow me a degree of freedom there. More importantly, though, my old handset contained a lot of photographs of Hope and my mum and me over the past four years. I'd not had a chance to transfer them to the computer and didn't have a cloud account. I was worried that if I damaged the phone, I would lose all those pictures, all those memories.

Instead, I took it and hid it in the drawer of my bedside cabinet where I would have it to use if I needed, next to a penknife I kept there. It had belonged to my father, was small and probably too blunt to be useful, but it offered me a sense of protection at night when it was just Hope and me in the house. I decided to use Black-Hair's phone for any non-personal calls and to make one or two calls to my mum on it, just to give them the impression that I was using it as instructed. I could continue using my old handset for everything else.

The following evening, I booked a Maxi Cab to Ann's with Hope. I packed her blanket and a few of her favourite toys, as well as her pyjamas and a book to read her at bedtime in case the event in the bar overran.

Ann lived in the centre of the same estate as Mark and Terry. The exterior of the house belied the extravagance of the interior, though. And its owner.

She came to the door when I knocked and, opening it, immediately greeted me as an old friend.

'Katie! And this must be Hope? How are you?' she asked, looking at Hope, who regarded her warily.

Though she was roughly the same age as me, she dressed younger, wearing skin-tight black leggings and a white T-shirt that accentuated her figure. Her face was smooth and carried that strange immobility of having had work done. Her lips were fuller than I recalled, and she exuded a confidence I did not remember. She made me feel simultaneously self-conscious and grateful that I had aged as I had.

Hope bumped the offered fist in kind and nodded.

'I'm Ann. Come in, come in!'

A chandelier dominated the narrow hallway, hanging low enough that I had to duck to avoid knocking it despite my own relative lack of height. Wooden floors ran through the downstairs of the house – all white – while the walls were also white.

A large mirror in a bejewelled frame covered most of the back wall in the living room, offering a reflection of the similarly sized TV on the opposite wall.

'Your house is lovely, Ann,' I said.

She looked around it, as if taking it in for the first time alongside me, then nodded. 'It's getting there,' she said. 'So, how are you?'

I nodded. It had been so long since last we had spoken, if ever, and we had been so little in each other's orbit even then, it seemed pointless trying to answer. Where would I start?

'Fine, thanks. You?'

'Great! Keeping busy with the childminding and that.'

I looked around the room. 'It's obviously going well,' I said.

'It's grand. I'm picky about who I take on. But happy to help out with you,' she added, lest I had taken the comment as a criticism. 'I'd not see Mark or you stuck.'

'Well, I really appreciate it,' I said. I handed her the bag of Hope's belongings and explained her evening routine, what she would take for supper and her bedtime habits if I wasn't back in time.

'I'll get a taxi back anyway, so I can just lift her into the car with me if she does fall asleep,' I said.

Ann nodded, though I had a sense she wasn't really listening. 'I've asked Maxi Cabs to do a stop on the way to the bar, by the way,' she said. 'A pick-up on Carlisle Road. Just in case you're wondering.'

I nodded. 'Grand.'

'It's covered on the pub's account anyway, but just letting you know.'

Mark hadn't mentioned anyone being collected with me. It wasn't Benny, or at least I didn't think it was as he lived in a different part of town completely.

'Don't worry about it,' Ann said. 'And don't be worrying about this Little Miss. We'll have lots of fun. Hope, love, there are colouring pencils and pictures in the kitchen. Do you want to go on in?'

Hope looked to me for permission and, when I nodded my approval, headed out to colour.

I heard the pomp of a horn from outside.

'That's your taxi now,' Ann said. 'Good luck tonight.'

'Yeah, there's a party or something on, I think.'

She nodded. 'Andy's home.'

Black-Hair had been right then; it was a getting-out party for Andy Flood.

I passed Ann and went in to give Hope a hug and kiss before I left. I stopped at the door once more to thank Ann, when she surprised me.

'Listen,' she said. 'Mark's a big softie. Don't fuck him about.'

'What do you mean?' I asked, already riven with guilt over the sense of betrayal which I carried.

'He likes you. Don't be a bitch to him.'

She held my stare as she caught me off guard, both by her warning and by the suspicion that Mark must have said something about how he felt about me.

'I won't,' I said.

When I got into the taxi, the driver insisted I take the front passenger seat, then he drove me back towards town.

'We've a stop to make on Carlisle Road, apparently,' I said, as we made our way into the city centre.

The driver simply nodded and, a moment later, turned up onto Carlisle Road and turned off to the left, driving up one of the small side streets that ran off from it. He pulled up outside a small, terraced house, one of a row of six, hooted the horn twice, then did a three-point turn and parked outside the house a second time, except now facing out towards the roadway.

As he did so, the rear door of the taxi opened, and two girls climbed in. Neither spoke nor acknowledged us. Both wore party dresses, one green, one red. I studied them in the rear-view mirror. Their make-up made it hard to determine their ages; they could as easily have been in their late teens as their early thirties. They did not look at us or at each other, barely sharing more than a whispered word or two between them in a language I did not recognise, but which sounded, to me, to possibly be East European. For most of the journey, they stared out the passenger windows, impassive.

Only when we reached the bar and they got out of the car did the taxi driver speak again.

'Not much to say for themselves, those two,' he said.

'Have you met them before?' I asked.

'Ah now,' he said. 'Them that asks no questions gets told no lies.'

He nodded, as if this had answered me to his satisfaction, then drove off.

## Chapter Twenty

The bar was already busy when we arrived. Two security men stood at the door, and a sign hung off the handle saying O'Reilly's was closed for a private function. Despite this, a group stood outside smoking and the sound of music playing carried from the backroom. The two girls followed in behind me and, when we entered, it was to cheers from the lounge.

The place was rammed with men. Some were regulars whom I recognised. I'd never considered that they might be part of Terry's gang and, in one or two cases, was disappointed to find this out for the fellas had always been friendly and polite.

Then I realised that they might be looking at me and thinking exactly the same.

Terry was moving from table to table with a bag in his hand and, for a moment, I thought he was taking donations.

'No phones, gents,' he said. 'You know the drill.'

One by one, without complaint, though with some hesitation at times, each man placed his mobile into the bag.

Benny was behind the bar, and I moved round and joined him. 'What is he doing?'

'No phones allowed at these gigs,' Benny said. 'Did Mark not tell you?'

'Even for staff?' If Ross did arrive, how was I meant to contact Black-Hair if I'd no phone? Besides, if I had to hand over my phone, I'd have to explain straight away why I had a new model and not the old battered one I'd been using for years.

'Sometimes they remember us, sometimes they don't,' Benny said. 'You'll not have time to use it anyway.'

I nodded, deciding it best to change the subject off phones altogether. 'I thought it was kicking off later,' I said. 'Mark told me I'd be time enough coming in at seven.'

Benny nodded. 'He asked me in at six, but the place was already starting to fill. What's the occasion?'

'It's some guy Andy who's got out—' I began, then realised there was no plausible way for me to know so much, '... got home. So Ann said anyway, when I dropped off Hope.'

Benny nodded as he pulled one of several pints of Guinness, which he left to settle along the front of the bar while he topped up a few that had already done so. 'It's going to be a busy one. Will you throw these down to the table at the fire? Terry's standing a round of drinks.'

I placed the six Guinness on a tray and carried them down the steps to the lounge where Terry was standing with the two girls.

'Which one, Floodsy?' he was asking, presenting the two women to a group of men sitting in the booths, and, in particular, one in the centre of the booth under which I had first hidden Leon Burke's phone.

I assumed this man to be Andy Flood. There was nothing remarkable about him save the red razor marks on the sides of his neck suggested he'd had his hair freshly cut for the evening's party. His skin was pockmarked, his eyes sliding from one girl to the next, already glazed and hazy.

One of the men next to him began a chant of 'Red, Red, Red' which some of the others took up, while in the next booth, a similar chant of 'Green, Green, Green' began. I placed the tray on the table in front of Andy Flood and put the fresh pints in front of each man before lifting the empties while, around me, the braying increased.

I looked at the two women either side of Terry and recognised at once the forced smiles, the hidden terror. One was more skilled in concealing her feelings. She wore the red dress and was the older of the two, I suspected. The other looked like a rabbit in headlights.

I felt a hand grip my arm and turned to see Andy Flood's lopsided grin.

'Which one, love? What do you think?'

I looked to the two women. The one in the red dress stared straight ahead, not reacting, though I guessed she knew what he had asked. The woman in green, however, caught my eye, her gaze flicking quickly to me, then back to Flood.

'I couldn't say,' I managed.

'Pick one,' Flood insisted, still gripping my arm.

I offered a frozen smile of my own, desperate not to have to choose. 'They're both beautiful girls,' I said. 'Excuse me.'

'I said pick one.' His grip had tightened now on my wrist.

'Let go of me, please,' I said.

'Pick a colour for the man, Katie,' Terry shouted.

'Pick one,' Flood repeated. 'Green? Red? Green?'

'Andy, don't hassle the staff, lad.'

I recognised the voice. Mark. I looked to Flood to see if it would make any difference. His gaze shifted towards where Mark stood at the entrance to the kitchen.

'I'm just having a bit of craic, big man,' Flood said. 'I just want her to pick a colour.'

'Red,' I said, desperate to be away from him, not wanting to get caught in the middle of something if it all kicked off and, finally, because the woman in the red dress seemed more able to deal with whatever Flood was looking to do. Though even in that, I hated having picked either.

Flood released my arm theatrically. 'See. Good choice. The woman knows, eh, lads?'

This raised more laughs from those in his own booth.

'You can't beat experience, Floody,' the man beside him said. He was younger than Flood, with a black bar piercing in his nose. He was also the one who had started the chanting of 'Red'. 'It takes a dirt to know one,' he added.

As I passed the two women, the one in green had lowered her gaze, perhaps out of relief. Red caught my eye, briefly, then flashed her practised smile once more at the men.

'Waste not, want not,' Terry said. 'I'll have Green then!'

This raised a cheer from the other booth. 'Katie, bring down two clean empties for tip jars, love, would you?' Terry asked as I headed towards the bar.

I did as I was asked. By the time I made it back down, Flood was already being led by the woman in the red dress into the toilets while Terry led the one in green into our staff room, accessed by the door next to the kitchen area. I watched him leave, then realised Mark was still standing in the doorway of the kitchen, watching me. He smiled, almost apologetically.

I put an empty glass on each of the tables, which the men sitting there immediately began stuffing with notes.

'This one's for Red,' the one with the nose piercing shouted. 'Tips for Green over there.'

'Bags not getting sloppy seconds,' one lad shouted while another called back, 'Sloppy sixths, son. You'll wait your turn.'

As I moved back towards the bar, Mark stepped forward and took my arm. 'Everything okay, Katie?' he asked.

I nodded, not trusting myself not to say what I thought. To see Terry involved in this kind of thing didn't surprise me, but I realised that I'd expected better of Mark. I found myself questioning whether, for all his softness, he wasn't so different from his brother.

'They don't mean anything by it,' he said. 'They're harmless.'

I thought of what Black-Hair had told me, about Flood almost taking off someone's head with a machete. 'It's fine, Mark,' I lied.

## Chapter Twenty-One

As the evening pressed on, the crowd grew. Despite being marked a private event, many of our regulars were allowed in, though they seemed to know to stay in the upper part of the bar, separate from the party. I guessed that there had been nights like this before; I just hadn't witnessed them because I'd stopped working evenings since Hope was born. Instead, I cleaned up the remnants of such behaviour and, looking back now, there certainly had been mornings where I'd wondered at the events of the night before.

Witnessing it was different though. As the men got more drunk, levels of both melancholy and aggression seemed to build. When Flood first came back out of the toilet, he was given a rousing cheer. I noticed that the girl in the red dress did not reappear and, thereafter, one by one, the men at Flood's booth took their turn going into the toilet when the previous man had finished. I could see the pecking order; Flood, then the man with the pierced nose, right down to a young lad who couldn't have been more than sixteen who walked with the bravado of one much older, holding his arms from his sides as if he was carrying timber, as if to accentuate his budding muscles.

When he was finished, one or two of the men from the

other booth came over and went in, pausing to put a note in the glass on their table.

I realised after a while that I had not seen Terry since he disappeared with the woman in green, even though other men had since gone into our staff room, presumably to take their turn.

Benny must have seen me looking down, searching for him, but misunderstood my interest. 'They're fucking animals sometimes, aren't they?' he said. 'Terry's crowd.'

'How often does this happen?'

Benny shrugged. 'Not often. A few times a year. It's a shit night. But the pay's good and they tip well.'

A few minutes later, I spotted Terry again. He'd come in through the kitchen doors with two other men. Immediately on seeing him, Andy Flood stood up and lunged towards them, knocking over glasses and spilling at least one pint in the process. My first thought was that a fight was about to start, but of a sudden Flood grabbed the man next to Terry and embraced him.

'I'll clean up that drink,' I said, wadding up paper towels, and headed down into the lounge.

Flood and the other man embraced while beside them, Terry beamed like a new parent and, to the other side, a second man scanned the faces of the ones opposite. The lights of the bar shone off his head, its angles and dents clear, the skin almost burnished. I recognised him, though I could not remember his name. He was one of the men English and Black-Hair had shown me, Ross's lieutenant. Crowley, was that it?

As Flood disentangled himself from the hug and stepped back, he clasped his friend by the shoulders and, even in profile, I recognised this man to be Ross, the tattoo running up his neck unmistakable. Flood turned and called over the guy with the pierced nose who shook hands with Ross, stiffly. I couldn't work out if he disagreed with the man's politics or his friendship with Flood, but either way, he didn't like him.

Black-Hair had told me to text my mother that I would be late if either man appeared and, for once, having seen the way these men had treated the two young women, I did not think to hesitate. I cleaned up the spilled beer, sopping it up with the towels then squeezing it into a dirty glass, before repeating until it was mostly cleared up. Then I took the used paper towels and glass up to the bar behind which was my bag and the phone Black-Hair had given me.

'I'm going to the toilet,' I said. 'Can you cover?'

Benny nodded as he rinsed out dirty glasses and loaded them on the dishwasher shelf for a quick clean.

I went back down to the lounge, towards the ladies' toilets. Only when I'd gone in through the main door, which led to a short corridor going to the men's on the right and ladies, on the left, did I realise that the woman in the red dress was in the ladies'. The door opened just as I was about to enter and a young man came out, sheepishly smiling at me as he fixed his zip. Beyond, I saw the woman, her dress discarded on the floor, wiping herself by the hand sink with rolled toilet paper. She looked at me with indifference as she continued to clean herself, the livid red marks of what I took to be bites visible on her breasts.

'I'm sorry,' I said, hoping she understood my meaning but, if she did, she showed no awareness. Instead, she straightened, and threw the toilet paper into the bin while behind me, a man said, 'Are you going in, love?'

I turned to see one of the regulars standing. 'All right, Katie,' he said.

'I'm not . . . I'm not using it,' I said, meaning the toilet but immediately regretting my choice of words, lest he thought I meant the woman.

He nodded and went on in past me, allowing the door to close while the woman turned and leaned on the sink in expectation.

I felt sick. The room was suddenly close, the crescendo of noise from outside each time someone opened the door into the lounge on their way to or from the toilets oppressive. How had I ended up here? How could Mark allow this to happen? He must know, I thought. His apologetic smile showed that he did. Had he visited either girl? I'd not seen him, but then I wasn't keeping careful watch. I couldn't reconcile his kindness with all this. Had I misjudged him from the start?

There was no privacy here for me to send a text, and I was aware that I couldn't be seen using my phone, Terry having collected everyone else's at the start of the evening, so I went back out and headed across to the kitchen. It was empty, though the ovens hummed, and the place was warm with the smell of cooking food. Someone could come back in at any time to check it.

There was a porchway at the back which led out to the alleyway, where staff often gathered for a smoke when it was raining and too wet to stand outside. I realised that it was through this entrance that Terry had brought in Ross and Crowley, perhaps to keep them out of sight.

I stood in the porchway and took out the phone Black-Hair had given me. I pulled up Mum's contacts and began texting. Working late. Will—

'What the fuck are you doing?'

I looked up to see the guy with the pierced nose. Flood's right-hand man.

'I'm checking on my daughter.'

'No phones,' he said. 'Let me see what you're doing.'

He was drunk, clearly.

'Fuck off.'

'Give me your phone.'

'No.'

He moved towards me. 'Give me the fucking phone.'

I backed against the door, but it was shut tight. 'Get off me,' I hissed.

I should have shouted for help, but to do so would mean revealing I had a phone.

'Give me it,' he slurred, in close to me now, his breath warm and hazed with beer, his eyes glassy and ill focused.

'No,' I said, twisting, trying to put it in my pocket.

He grabbed for me then, his hand groping at me, pawing at my pocket.

'Give it to me!' he shouted, his spit flecking my face.

He leaned towards me, one hand on my chest, the other reaching into my trousers. Of a sudden, I felt him ripped from me, and I was pulled forward with his weight as he clung to my T-shirt.

There was a thud as he hit the side of the metal bain-marie and pans clattered to the floor.

'Get the fuck off her,' Mark roared.

'He grabbed me,' I said. 'He—'

But Mark needed no more. I saw something break in his eyes, saw his jaw tighten, his lips whiten. He turned and, lifting his foot, stomped once, twice, three times on the drunken man.

Then he knelt next to him and grabbing him by the hair, lifted his head.

'She has a phone,' the drunk man said. 'She's got a fucking—'

Mark punched him full in the face, the crack of his nose so loud I wanted to be sick. Then he punched him again and again.

'Don't touch her,' Mark shouted. 'Keep your fucking hands off her.'

The other man was done now. He tried to raise his hands, tried to speak, but blood bubbled around his teeth and onto his lips. '—phone,' he managed.

Mark looked around and lifted a copper pan which had fallen near him. He raised it and brought it down several times on the man's head, the first strike a dull thud, each one afterwards lessened by the wetness of the wound it enlarged.

'What the fuck, Mark?'

Flood and another of his men stood in the doorway, staring in disbelief.

Mark stopped and looked up at them. He seemed to catch his breath, then stood while, below him, the beaten man's moans seemed to weaken.

'He touched Katie,' Mark said. 'He was groping her.'

I didn't correct his misunderstanding, my attention instead fixed on Flood, waiting for him to react.

'He was my lad, Mark,' he said. 'He worked for me.'

'You all fucking work for me and Tel,' Mark said. 'Don't fucking forget that.'

Flood gave him a sarcastic smile. 'As if we could.'

'Any one of you fuckers ever lays a finger on this woman, I'll kill you.'

The man with Flood laid a hand on his arm, as if holding him back, though Flood himself was immobile as he considered what to do.

'Fair enough, Mark,' he said. 'You're the boss.'

And with that, he and the other man headed back out of the kitchen, meeting Terry with Ross at the doorway. Most of them went back to the lounge, but Terry came in to see what happened.

'The fuck?' he said when he saw the man lying on the ground.

'He was groping at Katie. I think he was going to try something with her.'

'He's a fucking mope anyway,' Terry said. 'Too good for the prick. You okay?' he asked, looking at me.

I nodded, trying not to be sick.

Terry nodded. 'Don't forget the cake,' he said to Mark. 'Wash your hands first, ya dirty fucker,' he added, then left, laughing.

The man on the ground had stopped moaning now.

'Is he dead?' I asked.

Mark looked at him and shook his head. 'Hard to kill a cockroach,' he said. 'Even nuclear bombs can't kill them apparently. Did you know that?'

I stared at him in disbelief. How had he gone from beating a man almost to death to sharing facts about insects?

He mistook my gaze though for he came across and took my hands in his.

'Are you sure you're okay?'

I nodded, trying unsuccessfully to suppress the shiver I felt at his touch.

'You're cold,' he said, rubbing my arms lightly. 'It's okay. He'll not bother you again. I've got your back. Remember?'

He held me away from him, smiling, as if reminding me of a joke we'd shared.

I nodded, attempting to return the smile, careful not to enflame the situation any further. I'd not seen this side of Mark before and wasn't quite sure how to deal with it.

'Do you have a phone?' Mark asked, almost gently.

I wanted to lie but was aware that the outline of its bulk was clearly visible in the pocket of my jeans.

'I didn't know we weren't meant to have one here,' I said.

Mark nodded. 'I should have told you. Who were you calling?'

'No one,' I said, but Mark was not convinced.

'Let me see.'

I could feel panic building in my chest. 'It was just my mum. I was texting her to say I was working late in case—'

'Sure, Ann's watching Hope,' Mark said.

'I forgot,' I said, rolling my eyes at my own foolishness, hoping that my nervousness would not betray my lie.

'Let me see,' he repeated, smiling as he insisted.

I took out the phone and handed it to him.

'Is this new?' he asked.

'I dropped my old one in the toilet,' I said. 'I had it in my back pocket and it fell in when I was taking my jeans down.'

Mark nodded and listened even as he turned the phone over in his hand, seemingly studying it.

'It looks expensive.'

I shook my head, gritting my teeth to stop them chattering. 'I got it in the market. One of those unlocked ones. It's a knock-off brand.'

'I'll get you a decent phone,' he said.

'This one's fine, Mark,' I said, then saw his expression cloud a little. 'But thank you. You're very good to me.'

He smiled.

'Open it for me,' he said, handing me the handset.

I swiped and looked into the camera for it to unlock. He took it from me and opened the calls history and then the messages.

'You lost all your message history,' he said.

'Yeah,' I said. 'When it went down the bog.'

He smiled, then opened the message to my mum. 'You forgot to send it,' he said, pressing send himself. I heard the whoosh as the message went.

'He surprised me,' I explained, reaching to take the phone back.

'Probably best I hold on to it until the end of the evening,' Mark said. 'We don't want a repeat of this, do we?'

He flashed me a smile, his face flecked with the blood of the man lying silent between us.

'Let's bring out the cake, eh?' he added, then headed over to the sink, rinsed his hands and face, wiped himself dry on one of the aprons hanging off the oven door and, moving across, unboxed a cake which had been sitting on the shelf next to the fridge.

'Will you grab the candles?' he asked.

And so we stood there, heads bowed together, over a cake decorated with a picture of Andy Flood and the message 'Welcome Home', as if this was the most normal thing in the world, the bloodstains on Mark's shirt still glistening by the flames of the newly lit candles.

## Chapter Twenty-Two

Mark carried the cake out to the cheers of those assembled in the lounge, though I noticed as I followed him that neither Flood, nor those at his table, joined in the celebration. I couldn't help but feel that they were staring at me, blaming me for the beating which their friend had taken. Mark had made it clear he could do what he wanted, and obviously had Terry's support, too. I, on the other hand, was a barmaid as far as they were concerned.

As Mark set the cake in front of Flood, Terry called everyone to attention.

'Floody. Andy,' he began. 'Just a few words, son, to welcome you home. All of us know Floody did a tight stretch. We know how the screws treated him. We know how the filth treated his missus and kids out here. We don't forget any of that. Nor do we forget that he did all that without complaint, without ratting out his mates. So, we looked after his family while he was gone, because they are part of our family. Floody, you're one of us. Always have been, always will.'

A chant of 'One of us!' started to echo around the bar. Flood looked ready to blow out the candles on his cake, but Terry wasn't finished.

'More than that, Floody here has helped us forge new friendships, new relationships across the country. So, a warm welcome to all our friends, old and new. And a special welcome home to Andy Flood!'

Another cheer and this time, Flood blew out the candles, allowing himself a brief smile as his friends slapped his back and cheered him on.

Terry had shifted his gaze though and was raising his half-empty glass to Ross, who was seated at a corner table, with Crowley.

Mark came and stood next to me. 'There's buffet trays in the kitchen wrapped in foil, Katie, and I've sausages and chicken in the oven. Will you take them out now and serve them, love? And when you're bringing out the food, make sure the two lads in the corner get their own plates first.'

Not Floody, the guest of honour. But Ross and his right-hand man.

I went back into the kitchen and did as I was asked, setting out sausage rolls, vol-au-vents, cocktail sausages on trays, as well as setting out the buffet trays of sandwiches. I loaded up two plates separately, then brought out the first few trays, setting them on two tables which Mark had pulled into the centre of the room. The last time I'd seen them set like that, Leon Burke's blood had been pooled beneath them.

After I served Ross and Crowley their plates, which they accepted with a dry 'Cheers, love,' I set out the rest of the food, then went back up to the bar where the orders were increasing as people bought pints to wash down the supper, using the main bar to avoid the queues in the lounge bar where Benny was now working.

Half an hour later, Terry came up. 'Lift some of those trays down there now and see if any of the punters up here want any grub,' he said. 'Grab a plate yourself, too.'

I nodded, smiled a thanks, despite being afraid that if I ate anything I'd be sick, then followed him down and brought up a tray of mixed finger food, which the regulars and two doormen happily cleared.

Soon after, Benny arrived up with a tray loaded with paper plates of slices of cake. 'Terry wants everyone to have some,' he said. 'Pass them round.'

I lifted the plates and carried them round the tables, setting one in front of each regular. One of them, Kenneth, sat alone in his usual spot near the fire. I'd not seen him since the day he'd asked me to join him for a drink after my affair with Benny came out.

'Katie,' he said. 'I wanted to show you something.'

'Give me a sec, Kenneth,' I said, passing by him and continuing to hand out plates, then going back behind the bar without returning to his table. I'd no interest in being pawed by anyone else that evening and assumed that's what he was looking for.

However, he came back up to the bar with a small notebook which he'd pulled from his pocket.

'Katie,' he said, then waited. He had a habit, for as long as I'd known him, of waiting for you to acknowledge he was speaking before he would continue.

'Kenneth,' I said.

'I wanted to show you something. I wanted to show it the day I asked you to join me for a drink but you didn't.'

I looked around the bar to see who else was near, just in case he did something weird like flashing me or something.

Instead, he opened the notebook, flicking to a particular page, then turned it round to let me see it, pointing to a neat spider diagram which covered two pages, lengthwise.

'That's you,' he said, pointing to a name near the bottom.

I squinted, for his writing was tiny, though each letter was neatly formed. I could see my name and, connected to it by a vertical line beneath, Hope's.

'What is this?'

'Your family tree on your father's side,' he explained. 'Look.'

Sure enough, as I followed the path his finger traced up the page, I saw my father's, grandfather's and grandmother's names. Then more and more, each name connected to those beneath and beside with neat black lines. There must have been over half a dozen rows of names in all.

'Where did you get this?'

'I made it.'

'Why?' I couldn't understand the attraction for someone in tracing a stranger's family tree.

'I found your great-grandfather's grave in the cemetery and started from there. I knew your dad.'

The town knew my dad, though I also assumed that, based on his age and the regularity with which Kenneth drank in O'Reilly's, he possibly had been a drinking buddy of my father. The explanation made his act a little less threatening.

'How did you find it?'

'I'm up there every day at Patricia's grave, God rest her. I like taking a walk and seeing what I can find.'

'Was Patricia your wife?'

He nodded. 'Twenty-eight years gone next month,' he said. 'And I still visit her every day.'

I felt suddenly embarrassed that I had seemingly misjudged the man. 'I'm sorry to hear that, Kenneth,' I said.

He nodded. 'It passes the time. I do grave rubbings.'

Maybe he *was* a little weird, I decided. 'What are grave rubbings?'

He held up a single finger to tell me to wait, then went across to his seat and pulled a page from his overcoat pocket before bringing it across to me. He unfolded it carefully and I could see it was a sheet of greaseproof paper. Except this one had a crayon rendering of the lettering on a grave.

'You put the sheet against the gravestone and then rub with a thick crayon,' he explained. 'You can use charcoal, but I prefer crayon. It's cleaner and the image holds better. I like things being neat.'

'Can I get served?' someone from the lounge shouted, thumping his hand on the bar.

'You better go,' Kenneth said, rolling up the paper.

'Thanks for doing that, of my dad's family,' I said, laying my hand on his arm. I felt bad that I'd been so judgemental about him. He seemed to be just a little lonely and a little bored.

He smiled, his teeth barely more than nubs. 'I'll make a copy for you. And I'll do your mum's too, if you like.'

'Can I get some pints, love? My stomach thinks my throat's been cut!'

'Your tongue certainly hasn't been,' I snapped, looking at Kenneth but answering the man. 'I'm coming in a second.'

Kenneth winked at me as the man said, 'Six Guinness and six shorts for Floody's table. Terry's paying.'

'I'll bring it down.'

He nodded, then leaned a little towards me. 'We know what you done to Mickey. We know.'

'I didn't do anything,' I said, guessing Mickey to be the guy with the nose piercing.

'You'll not be Mark's fuck buddy for ever,' he said. 'We'll not forget.'

With that, he walked away, smiling at those around him as if he had not just threatened the barmaid. Only Kenneth, who was still at the bar, had heard.

'Are you okay, Katie?' he asked.

'Fine,' I said. 'You get used to being hassled.'

'Are you with Mark O'Reilly?' he asked, and I got a sense that was of more concern to him than whatever vague threat the future held at the hands of Andy Flood and his men.

'No,' I said.

'Stay that way,' Kenneth hissed, leaning in low. 'Keep away from him.'

It seemed a strange thing to say, considering Kenneth used his bar every day and frequently joined him and Terry for a drink.

'But don't tell Mark I said that,' he said, before turning away from me.

# Chapter Twenty-Three

Kenneth's warning caught me by surprise; I'd always assumed he was Mark's friend and here he was warning me away from him. Like Flood, did he assume that Mark and I were together because of what had happened in the kitchen? And what had even happened? I tried to run through what I'd witnessed but my thoughts were everywhere, my body shaking as the adrenaline wore off.

I'd been shocked by the speed with which Mark had exploded, for sure, and the ferocity of his attack on Flood's man. I'd never considered him to be dangerous before, not really, but he clearly was. Yet, while the violence had sickened me, the fact that he had risked whatever it was Terry was trying to arrange with Ross and Flood, just for me, did make it harder for me to dismiss his actions out of hand. He clearly believed he was being gallant in jumping to my defence. And, in comparison with Hope's father, who'd dropped me at the first opportunity after she was born, there was something in Mark's actions which, if I'm being brutally honest, I found admirable. Attractive even. Not the act but the motive. Was it possible to separate the two? Mark had shown me he could be dangerous, I told myself, but not dangerous to me. Even after it had happened, he'd treated me with gentleness when he'd found out I *did* have a phone.

Someone had broken out a guitar and accordion in the lounge and the air was thick with sound and vape smoke and beer. Some of the lads were attempting a reel in one corner with Mark watching and clapping along, smiling and laughing with them.

I brought the tray of drinks down to Andy Flood's table, but the man himself had moved across and was sitting with Ross, Crowley and Terry. I set out five of the pairs of drinks with Flood's friends, then brought the last pint and chaser across to where Flood now sat.

'Shaw's the fucker, though,' Terry said, his back to me as I approached. Or at least, I was pretty sure I heard 'Shaw', though the music and noise made it difficult to distinguish. 'Sat on me for two days last time—'

He twisted to look at me, following the gaze of the others at the table who'd seen me coming across.

'Everything all right, Katie?'

'I've drinks for Andy here,' I said, setting the drinks in front of him.

Andy moved his empties across a little, indicating that I was to take them.

'What the fuck do you say to the lady?' Terry asked, playfully slapping his arm. 'Did you lose your manners inside, too?'

'Thanks,' Flood muttered, staring at Ross, who glanced between him and Terry, as if reading something in the situation which I had missed.

'Can I get anyone anything else?' I asked, stacking the empties up.

'No, love,' Ross said. Then added, after a pause: 'Thanks.'

I felt sure I was being watched as I walked away from them. At the other side of the room, Mark was moving with the music now, shifting from foot to foot in time with the beat, like a dancing bear, his shirt stippled with blood.

We locked the doors and pulled the shutters at 11.30 p.m., but the drinking and partying continued. At some point, Ross and Crowley had gone, presumably taken out the kitchen exit to avoid being seen by those outside.

After 2 a.m., I watched Flood stagger his way into the staff room, where the girl with the green dress remained. Sometime later, there was a commotion. She appeared briefly at the doorway, naked, covering her crotch with one hand while the other was held in front of her, her fingers bright with blood. She was crying, bent double. I moved to go down to her, but Benny stopped me.

'Don't get involved,' he said.

Instead, Terry went across and, grabbing her by the arm, brought her back into the room. A few minutes later, Flood reappeared, flushed and smiling.

Soon after, Mark appeared at the bar. 'Last orders, folks. Close up and we'll get everyone home, all right?'

Despite this, it was after 3 a.m. before the last of the party-goers made their way out the front door. Only then did Terry go in and bring out the two girls. Both were dressed again though I noticed the girl in green's dress was torn down the side. She winced when she walked and carried a wad of toilet roll in one hand. She continued to cry, though quietly. The girl in red stared at me as she came into the lounge. A series of bites and bruises ran up her neck and across her chest.

I had never been more ashamed to be part of something in my life.

'Get a cab for those two,' Terry said, and he lifted the two tip glasses from the tables and counted out the notes. He divided them equally, between the two girls, then took out his wallet and handed both notes each too. 'You earned that fair and square, girls,' he said.

The girl in green took hers and held on to it, the notes tight in her fist. The one in red counted through them, then folded them up and, hitching her dress, slipped them inside the waistline of her pants.

Mark came up to the bar, our coats in his hand. 'Benny, there's a cab ordered. Katie, I'm staying over with Ann tonight so I can take you to hers. I'd say Hope's long sleeping at this stage.'

What could I say but agree? I had to go to Ann's anyway and he would think it strange if I refused his offer of a lift.

I thought about the two women all the way back to Ann's. I felt nothing but revulsion at the way in which they had been treated and revulsion at the men who had done so, and equally those who had allowed it to happen; indeed, had helped it happen.

'Those two girls,' I asked, as we drove up the Strand. 'Were they prostitutes?'

'They're massage girls, I think,' Mark said, not taking his eyes off the road. 'I suspect they earn a bit extra on the side doing other things, but they're here as massage therapists.'

'They looked brutalised,' I said.

'They probably made well over a grand each this evening,' Mark said, glancing over at me now. 'They come here to make money. The one in red has been here for three years now. She has a kid at home her husband is watching. He's an engineer or something and she's making more in a month than he does in a year back home. No one's forcing anyone to do anything, if that's what you thought. Those girls are completely in control of what they do.'

It was bullshit and I knew it. 'What age was the girl in green?' I asked.

'Eighteen,' Mark said with such speed, I guessed that she was not. 'She's only new to it. She's still finding her feet.'

I said nothing, which prompted him to turn and smile.

'Good job she's working on her back then. If she hasn't found her feet?' He laughed, as if to encourage me to do likewise.

I offered him a weak smile. 'And what about Mickey?'

'Who?'

'The guy in the kitchen,' I said. 'Where is he now?'

'The fucking river, if he knows what's good for him,' Mark said. 'Don't you worry your pretty little head about that prick. He'll not be feeling anyone up again.'

Dread settled like cement in my guts. Had he been killed? Had my letting Mark believe the man had been groping me cost him his life?

'I didn't want anything to happen to him,' I said, feeling the need to distance myself from the act and acutely aware that my phone remained in Mark's pocket and was, perhaps, transmitting this whole conversation to Black-Hair and English.

'He should have known better than to touch you,' Mark said. 'He knows now.'

He laughed to himself, and, once more I felt a conflicted uneasiness about the fact he'd assigned himself the role of my protector.

We fell into an uncomfortable silence. Mark must have realised the conversation was not going well, for he laughed, as if we had already shared a joke, and then asked, 'How come you never learned to drive then?'

'I can drive,' I said. 'I have my test. But I can't afford a car.'

'I can loan you if you want one. It would save on taxis.'

'I also lost my licence,' I admitted. 'I'd had a drink or two after work one night and drove home. Some knob went into the back of me and insisted on calling the cops. When they arrived, they breathalysed us both and I ended up in court over it.'

'Fuck's sake,' Mark said. 'And you not even the one caused the accident.'

I nodded.

'The fucking cops, eh?'

We pulled up outside Ann's house and Mark cut the engine, though he did not undo his seat belt or open the door.

'Ann has a spare room made up,' he said, smiling.

'I'll have to take Hope home,' I said.

'She's asleep,' Mark said. 'I checked with Ann already. She had a bed made up for her in one of the spare rooms. We can stay over.'

*We?* Did he think we were together now? That, after what had happened in the bar, I owed him something? I began to panic, wondering how to excuse myself from having to spend the night there.

'I'm so sorry, Mark. She wakes in the middle of the night. Night terrors,' I said, which was partially true. 'If she doesn't recognise her surroundings, her own toys and that, she'll have a complete meltdown. Thanks anyway.'

He looked wounded, as if all that he had planned had been for nothing.

'Another time, maybe,' I said, immediately cursing myself for saying it. Why hadn't I just told him I wasn't interested?

'Well, don't I get something for looking after you tonight?'

I wondered what he meant and, in a moment of dread, thought he might be looking for me to have sex with him, here in the car.

I leaned in and kissed him on the cheek, though he turned his head and, taking mine in his hand, kissed me on the lips in a manner he must have thought to be sweet.

I reached for the door and opened it, undoing my seat belt. 'I need to get Hope and get home, Mark. She's an early start in the morning. Can I have my phone back now, please?'

I could hear how absurd it was, having to ask for my phone, even as I stood with my hand out. He took it from his pocket, gave it to me, then pulled it away, playfully to his mind, before giving it back.

'I need to phone a cab,' I said.

'I'll drop you,' he said, but I shook my head.

'I've it already booked and paid for,' I lied. 'I just needed to tell them the time to pick me up.'

Reluctantly, he followed me, while I phoned a cab to collect me from Ann's, trying to make it sound like I was confirming an existing booking rather than placing a new one.

Ann was still up when we came in. 'Well, how was it?'

'Fine,' I said. 'I need to get Hope. Which room is she in?'

'I've a room made up for you,' she said, looking past me to Mark.

I glanced at him long enough to see him shrug at his sister, as if they'd already reached some prior understanding on the nature of Mark's friendship with me from which I'd been excluded and which put her warning to me at the start of the evening into a different light. 'Hope gets upset if she wakes up in a strange bed,' I said. 'Thanks so much for watching her for me. Where is she?'

The 'bed' Mark claimed she was in was actually a sofa in the back room. She woke when I went in and climbed up onto me, wrapping her legs around my back and leaning her head in tight against my neck.

'Mummy,' she murmured.

Yet again I felt ashamed that I had brought her into this house, into the orbit of these people. I would have to make Black-Hair get the case against my mother dropped: this would not, could not, happen again.

'How were the girls?' I heard Ann ask Mark, in the hallway outside.

'Fine,' he said. 'One of them got roughed up a bit by Floody. The young one.'

'She'll harden up,' Ann said. 'They always do.'

'That's to cover their night and watching our Hope,' Mark said and, as I came out of the room, I caught him handing Ann an envelope.

*Our* Hope. As if she was his daughter.

Ann offered me a cold smile. 'I'm off to bed so. See you later, Katie. Remember what I said now.'

Mark looked between us, as if enjoying the fact we had a shared something private.

'What's this?' he asked. 'What did she say?'

I couldn't handle any more of them and whatever twisted perverse world they lived in. 'She told me not to be a bitch to you,' I said.

He laughed. 'Ann's always looking out for us.'

I heard the honk of a car horn outside. 'That's my taxi,' I said.

Mark stepped to one side, then followed me towards the front door. 'You can come in an hour late in the morning,' he said. 'I'll help with the cleaning up.'

'It'll be fine,' I said. 'Thanks anyway.'

As I went to leave, he stepped in my way.

'Do I not get a goodnight kiss?'

I gestured towards Hope, as I hefted her from one side to the other, effectively placing her between us, the cast on her arm lying heavy against my back.

'I'll see you tomorrow, yeah?' I said, then turned towards the taxi, aware that he was watching.

## Chapter Twenty-Four

I could not sleep that night. Images of the two women at the party, of Mickey, of Ross and Terry calmly chatting about someone they wanted to kill, all of these things merged with my own thoughts so that, in a fevered slumber, they mixed together in such a way that I awoke with a deep sense of dread and guilt, as if I had done something very wrong. I'd imagined I could still feel Mark's lips on mine and swore for a moment that he was in the bed next to me.

I rushed to the toilet in the gloom, Andy Flood's welcome home cake roiling in my stomach, and made myself sick, hoping that with each retch, I was cleaning a little more of the evening's activities from me.

As a result, and, despite his telling me to come in an hour late, I decided to go into work earlier than usual the following morning, having taken a cab straight to and from Hope's school. I stared out the window at her as she marched in through the main doors, her plaster-cast arm raised in a wave of goodbye. What had I done? How had I put us in this position? Was it because of my affair with Benny? Was that it? Some failing on my part? Some flaw in my character that allowed these people – both Black-Hair and Mark – to wriggle their way into my life, almost without my control or permission?

\* \* \*

Jamie, one of the chefs, was already in the kitchen, preparing lunches, when I reached the bar.

'What the fuck happened in here last night?' he asked.

'A party.'

'In the kitchen? There was blood all over the floor and the pans were everywhere when I came in.'

'Was there anyone around?' I asked, wondering if Mickey had lain there all night too.

Jamie shook his head. 'Keep my kitchen clean in future.'

'It wasn't my party,' I said.

'You're the fucking cleaner.'

'Not last night,' I said, having taken enough crap off people to last me a lifetime.

My resolve was short-lived, for in the cold light of morning the lounge and toilet area were even more untidy than I remembered, even though it had been barely six hours since I'd last seen them. I gathered up a black bag and began clearing up.

Once I got over to the back seating, which was out of the line of sight from the kitchen, whose door remained open, I knelt, as if lifting something from the floor. I took Leon Burke's phone from my pocket, hoping to wedge it back under the seats, where I had first hidden it. Just then, I heard Terry's voice getting louder as he made his way in through the kitchen.

'Ask Mark,' he called. 'That's his handiwork.'

Jamie must have said something, for Terry replied: 'You'll be waiting a while. He was on the promise last night, the dirty fucker.'

I panicked at his approach and shoved the phone down between the cushions on the seat instead, then began to stand, just as Terry reached the open doorway.

'Katie!' he said. 'Where's Mark?'

I shrugged. 'I don't know. I think he was staying with Ann last night. I went home with Hope.'

He stared at me bemused, then nodded. 'I'm glad you're in,' he said. 'The place is a tip and my head's banging. Stick on the coffee machine when you have a chance, love,' he said, then turned and went back into the kitchen.

'Never mind,' I heard him say to Jamie. 'Maybe he wasn't so busy,' he laughed.

Nausea washed through me, both at having almost been caught with the phone and with the thought that Terry assumed that I'd have slept with Mark the night before.

I went up and put on the coffee machine as asked, then cleared the lounge and bar area, loading the dishwasher and filling the bins. That done, I went down to face the toilets. The gents' were as I'd expected. The floor was sodden, several of the toilets splattered with vomit and the mirrors plastered with splodges of wet toilet paper that someone made and threw against the wall for whatever reason young lads do such things.

The ladies' was cleaner than I'd hoped. The girl in the red dress had gathered up all the rubbish and put it in the bin at the door. The floor needed washing but beyond that, it was neat. The staff room, however, was a different experience. Used condoms had been discarded around the floor. Blood had splattered on the staff table and wads of toilet paper, hard and crimson, lay scattered around. I had to pick up twenty-three condom wrappers, counting off each one as my pity for the girl in the green dress and my revulsion at the men who had used her grew in equal measure.

'Some of the lads got carried away,' Terry said.

I looked up from where I knelt on the floor to see that he had been watching me.

'The poor girl must have been hurt,' I said.

'Whores are going to get fucked,' he said. 'Just like the rest of us. At least they know who's fucking them *and* they get paid.'

My stomach twisted. Did he know that I was passing on information? Is that what he meant by not knowing who was fucking him?

'You want to see the tax bill we got landed with last month,' he continued. 'The government have us all over a barrel, eh?'

I nodded, wondering why he thought I would share his annoyance at his tax bill.

'And your poor mother. Those fuckers keeping her away from Hope. What's happening there?'

I realised that I hadn't spoken to my mother in two days. I'd texted her the night before, to signal to Black-Hair that Ross was in the bar, but she'd only responded with a thumbs up emoji, perhaps wondering why I was telling her that I was working late. I did not want to phone her on the handset Black-Hair had given me, for I doubted his claim that he would not be listening in, and I didn't want to reveal that my mother knew of his threat to me and his role in what happened with her and Hope. As a result, I decided to wait until I was home and could transfer my SIM card to my old phone.

Benny arrived in just before I finished up. He looked on edge, distracted by something, and I wondered whether he and Amy had had another argument.

'You okay?' I asked.

He sniffed and nodded. 'Grand,' he said.

He was transferring glasses from the dishwasher tray, to load the bar and shelves. He seemed jittery, the glasses clinking against each other as he tried and failed to hold them steady as he lifted them.

'Benny,' I said and he turned and looked at me, briefly, his eyes dropping back to the tray. His eyes were wide, the black of the pupil almost filling his iris.

'Are you sure you're okay?'

'Jesus, stop asking if I'm okay. I'm okay. I'm okay. Okay?'

'Fine,' I said. 'How's everything at home?'

'Fucking great,' he said, not trying to hide his sarcasm.

'Is Amy still suspicious about you and me?'

He shrugged. 'Arriving in at half four in the morning hasn't helped.'

'Half four?' We'd finished work at 3 and Benny only lived about a twenty-minute walk away.

'By the time I got cleared up,' he said. He was nodding to a beat I couldn't hear, his foot tapping to a second rhythm, as if there was music playing somewhere only for him. I wondered if he'd had to help move Mickey; it would explain his frazzled state at least. 'What about you? Did you have a good night? You and Mark?'

'Me and Mark? I went home.'

He looked at me and away again. 'If you say so?'

'Benny, I went home,' I repeated, annoyed at even having to explain myself to him. 'Why would you ask that?'

'No reason. Who you do is up to you,' he said, sing-songing the words.

'I'm not doing anything,' I said. 'Have you heard something?'

He looked at me again now, his eyes sliding back and forth, as if unable to still. 'I know he's interested in you, if that's what you're asking. Is there nothing going on between you?' he asked, then immediately apologised, lifting a glass and turning from me. 'Sorry. None of my beeswax.'

'No,' I said. 'There's not. But it's starting to look like everyone else thinks there is.'

Benny turned again and leaned against the shelves. His eyeline seemed to focus somewhere above me. 'I don't know what to say to you, Katie.'

I'd hoped I could count on him to be honest, perhaps foolishly had believed that the time we had spent together might have meant enough that he, at least, would be straight with me.

I finished up work quickly, keen to get away before Mark came in and had just made it to the staff exit when I felt a hand on my arm. It was Benny.

He nodded that we should move outside, into the alleyway where he sometimes went for a smoke. He took out a cigarette but did not light it.

'If you're really not interested,' he hissed, 'stay away from him. Get the fuck out of here.'

'Now?'

'For good. Get as far away from Mark O'Reilly as you can.'

'What the fuck, Benny? You're scaring me,' I said, though he had simply further confirmed my own worries.

'Talk to Leah Duffy,' he whispered, leaning towards me as if to seek shelter to light his smoke. 'From Dungiven.'

'Why?'

From inside, I could hear Mark's voice, echoing through the kitchen. 'Who's in?' he was calling.

'Get out of here,' Benny said, sparking his lighter as I rounded the corner and kept running until I was well clear of the bar.

## Chapter Twenty-Five

I took the bus home and went straight upstairs, taking the SIM card out of the phone Black-Hair had given me and putting it back into my own. I left his phone in my room and went downstairs, as far from it as I could, in the hope that if the device was still listening in on what I was saying, at such a distance, it would not be able to hear my conversation clearly.

I phoned my mum. I knew from the way she answered the phone that something wasn't right.

'Hello. Margaret Hamill.'

The formality was so unlike her, and I wondered whether the swapping of the SIM cards had perhaps changed my caller ID so she didn't know it was me.

'Mum, it's me.'

'Yes. I'm afraid it's not a good time.'

Then I knew something was definitely wrong.

'Is everything okay, Mum?'

'No, that's my daughter, Katie, you're looking for. Hope's *her* daughter.'

Why did she mention Hope? I wondered. She was clearly speaking for the benefit of whoever was with her, listening. The mention of Hope suggested it was the school or social workers there to interview her.

'Is social services there? Or the police?'

'Yes, that's right.'

Perhaps Black-Hair had kept his word and sped up the investigation. Or perhaps he'd been annoyed that I'd not used the phone to eavesdrop as he'd requested when Ross arrived the previous night and so had sent social services the picture of Mum and Hope together from the trip to the movies.

'Is it about the cinema?'

'I don't know, I'm afraid. I'll tell Katie you called.'

With that she ended the call. I was sick of it: sick of the thought that my mother was being investigated to put pressure on me; sick of having to second guess the thoughts and actions of someone who was using me.

A few weeks ago, I'd been able to do what I wanted, sleep with who I wanted, visit who I wanted. Now, for no reason, I felt I was having to walk a tightrope to keep everyone else happy. I resented it and was equally aware that all the resentment in the world changed nothing.

Guessing Mum would call me when she was done with whoever was with her, I decided to look up the girl Benny had mentioned, Leah Duffy, instead.

I opened Facebook when a message came through on the phone. It was Mark.

**Id like to take u and Hope for diner tomorrow nite ok**

Normally, I'd have assumed that as the invitation was for me *and* Hope, it was not a date, but coming so soon after he had kissed me the previous night, I couldn't be so sure, nor could I deal with it now. I ignored the message, leaving it unread, and went onto Facebook instead. There was no guarantee that Leah would even be on it, depending on her age. If she was younger than me, she'd more likely be on Snapchat or something, but I didn't have an account so couldn't check there.

There were a number of Leah Duffys listed and I went through each. Only one had a single mutual friend, Liam, one of the regulars from the bar who barely spoke to me but added me when I was a barmaid, briefly. I'd assumed it was because he fancied me, but in fact, he'd never contacted me, and I realised it was because he was running a business selling chipped Firesticks and was touting for business not sex.

I clicked on the account for that Leah Duffy and was taken to a profile page with a full-length picture of a young woman, taken in a mirror. She was pretty, maybe in her early twenties in the picture. She had long brown hair, shining in the image, her body angled towards the camera, the foot nearest raised a little at the heel to accentuate the tone in her legs. She held her camera to the side to take the picture. She wore shorts and a sports top, tucked in to accentuate her figure. Behind her, reflected in the mirror, was a bed with a pink teddy bear of some sort leaning against the pillow.

I could find out little else about her for she had last posted five years ago, in 2019, and even then it had been to share the opening of a beauty parlour owned, it seemed, by one of her friends, Catherine O'Neill. The posts before that consisted mostly of photographs of beaches and, going back to 2011, her school leaving dance.

Perhaps she simply did not post much, I thought. My own profile was similarly sparse. I tended to scroll through others, content rather than posting any of my own, partly because I had nothing I felt inclined to share and partly since Hope was born and I was wary of sharing pictures of her in a public place. Maybe the same had happened with Leah.

Or perhaps her account was locked, I realised, and the only things I could see were those which she had shared publicly. But then, her profile picture was of someone who looked and dressed as if in their early twenties. Based on her school leaving dates, she would be in her thirties now.

Yet I could see no reason why Benny would suggest I contact her, nor any way in which I could. I didn't want to send her a friend request lest she was connected with Mark in some way and he would wonder why I was suddenly contacting one of his friends. I googled her name, which brought up images of various women who I assumed shared her name. Below were links to Facebook, Insta and TikTok, all of Leah Duffys, though none were of the girl whose picture I'd just seen.

I scrolled through the results before adding 'Dungiven' to the search bar alongside Leah's name.

This time, I was taken to links to her school, which I recognised from her leaving do photographs. The next result down was a news item: *Police Appeal for Witnesses to Horror Attack.*

A ripple of panic ran through me. I clicked on the link to be taken to a story in the *Dungiven Weekly* from 9th October 2019.

> Police today issued a renewed appeal for information following an horrific attack on a young woman in Dungiven in the early hours of Sunday morning.

Leah Duffy, 24, was attacked while walking home from a local nightclub. Police say they have no motive for the attack and, so far, have made no arrests. They did confirm that Leah has suffered what they describe as 'life-changing injuries'.

'This was a brutal, unprovoked assault on a young woman, walking home after enjoying her night out,' Sergeant Ian Higgins commented. 'Someone knows something about the reason for the attack or the cowardly perpetrator. Not only was the victim viciously beaten, but we believe some form of abrasive fluid was involved in the attack, resulting in life-changing injuries for this young woman.

'I would appeal to anyone who might have seen Leah walking home, or those with mobile phone or dash-cam footage, to come forward and assist us with our inquiries.'

I texted a link to the story to Benny, asking him if this was the Leah Duffy whom he meant and why he wanted me to search her up. He read the message and, for a moment, I could see the flickering three dots signifying he was typing, but then they disappeared without reply. That he had mentioned her name in a conversation warning me away from Mark suggested that he and Leah were connected in some way, but how? Was the assault she suffered because of knowing Mark? Or had Mark assaulted her?

I phoned Benny, hoping to catch him on a smoke break, but he declined the call. Perhaps Mark was with him, I reasoned. That would explain his ghosting me. He had told me to talk to her, though, but there was no way to do so through Facebook as her account seemed to have Messenger disabled. Instead, I sent a message to the business account of her friend, Catherine, who ran a hair and nail parlour in Limavady. I reasoned if I could make an appointment and get talking to her, she might be able to help me make contact directly with Leah Duffy.

# Chapter Twenty-Six

I was buzzing with adrenaline, my thoughts skittering like midges. I needed to get moving, to burn up some of the nervous energy which was pulsing through me. I still had an hour or so before I collected Hope so walked up to my mum's, thinking that by the time I got there, whoever was with her might have left. I changed the SIM card back into Black-Hair's phone and headed out.

I was about to cross the road when a taxi pulled up next to me. I knew before even looking that English would be driving it. Sure enough, when I opened the back door, he was sitting in the driver's seat, staring ahead, waiting for me to get in.

'Are you taking me for a happy meal?' I asked. I was fed up with being at their beck and call, being picked up off the street when they felt like it.

English said nothing, but drove up through the town, drawing to a stop outside a café on Ferryquay Street. Black-Hair must have been watching for us, because he stepped out from the doorway as we pulled in against the kerb. English barely had need to stop before he was in the car, and we were moving again.

Black-Hair sat beside me in the back, perhaps to better give the impression that we were a couple in a genuine taxi.

He'd had his hair cut since last I saw him and smelled of aftershave. Something citrusy and fresh.

'Katie, you'd quite the night,' he said. 'What do you have for us?'

'Ross was there. And Crowley or whatever he's called.'

'We guessed one of them turned up from your text. You didn't get the handset close enough to record though.'

'I nearly got killed over it,' I said.

'Are you okay? We heard the argument.'

'Like you care. You didn't think to step in?'

Black-Hair looked at me, as one might a child. 'We could have, but what good would that have done, Katie? It would have put you at increased risk; they'd know we were watching them, and they'd know you were our asset.'

'Your tout, you mean.'

'That's not a word we use, Katie. An asset. You are of value. You're doing a public service.' When he felt he had flattered me enough, he added, 'So, what happened?'

'Mark beat the guy who tried to take my phone half to death. I don't know where he is.'

'Who was it?' English asked, looking in the rear-view mirror, his head inclined slightly to catch my eye.

'I don't know. Some guy, Mickey, with a nose piercing. One of those black bar things going through it.'

Black-Hair nodded. 'He's one of Andy's lads.'

'That's not what Mark said.'

'Did he kill him?'

I shrugged, feeling tears building and damned if I would let them see me cry. 'He wasn't there this morning.'

Black-Hair nodded. 'We'll check it out. What else went on? We could hear some stuff, but it was muffled and pretty unusable.'

'Mark took my phone. It was terrible. There were two prostitutes brought in from a house on Carlisle Road. They were ... they were gang raped,' I said, and I couldn't stop the tears from spilling. 'It was awful. One of them was hurt really badly.'

Black-Hair shook his head, as if in sympathy, but did not express surprise. 'Sorry you had to witness that. At least now you can see who the O'Reillys really are. This is why we need to stop them.'

'You knew?' I asked.

'Not about the girls last night,' he said.

'About them being here in the city? Working as prostitutes?'

'We've had information to that effect,' he said.

'And you haven't acted? Is this all you do? Listen in on conversations and do nothing? Sit on all that information and feel important?'

'I understand your concern for those two women, Katie, but let's say we swoop in and save them. So what? We've saved two people. They'll be deported and that'll be that. We want to take our time, gather enough to be able to target the head of the organisation bringing those girls in and then go after them. That way, instead of saving two people, we save countless women.'

'And those two girls?'

'They made their beds, in a manner of speaking,' Black-Hair said. 'Unfortunate as that sounds.'

'You people don't give a shit, do you? This is all a game to you. Running round with your camera and phones, spying.'

Black-Hair appeared frustrated, but English spoke up.

'We didn't bring those girls in. They chose to come here. Chose to work as prostitutes. They could have stayed at home. That's not on us. Soldiers die in every war.'

'But this isn't a war.'

'That's exactly what it is,' he said. 'And sometimes you have to fight dirty to win. And sometimes there will be collateral damage when you do. You want your kid to grow up in a city where she won't have to worry about drugs, about violent crime. We provide that for her. You might not like our methods, but you're more than happy to accept the benefits.'

'And what if I get hurt? Will I just be more collateral damage?'

'Some soldiers die in the field,' English said. 'Some get to die in their beds of old age. The careful ones.'

'Well, I am careful. And I'm not doing this again. Not like this. I don't want Hope anywhere near Ann O'Reilly again. So, sort out that fucking mess you made with my mother and do it now, or there's no more.'

'Katie, I know you're stressed. I understand your mother is being interviewed by some of our colleagues as we speak. To give her side of events,' Black-Hair said. 'Hopefully, with a word in the right ear, we can expedite the whole process and get Hope back where she belongs.'

'You talk about choice,' I said, leaning forward so English would know I was speaking to him. 'You didn't give me a choice.'

'You had a choice,' he said. 'And you made the right one.'

'Fuck you,' I said, jabbing my finger in his shoulder.

'Katie, what's wrong?' Black-Hair asked. 'You seem upset.'

'Look what you've got me into,' I said, the tears coming more freely now. 'Of course I'm upset. I'm trapped. *You* trapped me.'

'Katie, we're on your side,' he said. 'We want you to be happy. Because if you're happy, we know you'll continue to make the right choices.'

'I don't have any choice,' I repeated.

'That's not true. You're choosing to do good work,' Black-Hair said. 'So other girls don't have to go through what those two poor lasses last night suffered. And we are on *your* side. We'll help out with your mum, okay? It might take a day or two yet, but we'll get it sorted for you. Okay?'

I stared at him, saying nothing. Did he expect gratitude for solving a problem he created?

'Good,' he said, as if we'd reached an agreement. 'Now, what about Ross? Did you hear anything? No matter how small?'

I shook my head, feeling childish. 'Nothing. Terry made a speech and welcomed "new friends". He was looking at Ross and his man when he said it. And I had to bring them over their food on separate plates from everyone else.'

'That's interesting,' Black-Hair said. 'Anything else?'

'That name you asked me to listen out for. Shaw? I heard one of them mention Shaw.'

'Who said it?' English asked.

'I think it was Terry,' I said. 'Though it was noisy so I can't be sure.'

'Good work, Katie,' Black-Hair said. 'That's all really useful. When are you putting Burke's phone back?'

'It's already back,' I said, feeling an absurd pride in having done so.

English glanced in the rear-view mirror and nodded in admiration.

'That's brilliant,' Black-Hair said, then turned to English. 'I've always said, you want something done right, get a woman to do it.'

The condescending manner in which he spoke riled me.

'Who was Leah Duffy?'

Black-Hair tried not to react, but I could see something in the tension in his jawline, his lips thin with annoyance.

'Who?'

'Leah Duffy?'

'Never heard of her,' Black-Hair said.

Despite his denial, I could see he was lying. Leah Duffy had something to do with the O'Reillys if Black-Hair knew about her. I just needed to know what exactly her connection was.

'What about you?' I asked, tapping English on the shoulder.

'You need to stop touching me, Katie,' he said. 'Where do you want to be dropped?'

I had been going to my mother's house, but by this stage, it would make more sense for me to collect Hope and then head up to see her. Besides, it was clear that neither of them was going to tell me anything. Still, I felt as if the dynamic in the car had shifted a little and that, for once, it was them and not me who were on the back foot.

'Anywhere,' I said. 'If you get Burke's phone, will that be enough to charge Mark and Terry?'

'It will be enough for us to put some pressure on them,' Black-Hair said, which was not the answer I wanted.

'Mark's shirt was covered in blood the morning Burke died,' I said.

'That's useful to know. Are you prepared to say that in court?'

'Of course not.'

Black-Hair shrugged. 'Then we may hope Mark finds God and confesses, eh? Speaking of Mark, he seems to have taken quite the shine to you.'

'I thought you weren't listening,' I said.

'The fact he beat up someone for insulting you doesn't need much analysis,' Black-Hair said. 'If he wants to spend more time with you, that could be really helpful to all of us.'

'How would that help me?' I asked.

'The closer you are to him, the more likely you'll be able to get intel which we can use to close him and Terry down for good,' Black-Hair said. 'Isn't that what we all want?'

'I'm not a whore,' I said. 'I'm not sleeping with Mark O'Reilly to get you intel.'

Black-Hair nodded. 'I'm not suggesting that,' he said. 'Do whatever you can, Katie. Just keep yourself safe.'

Ahead of me, English reached into the glove compartment and took out an envelope which he handed back to me.

'For your efforts,' he said.

'I don't want your money. Just sort out my mother,' I said, trying to pass the envelope to Black-Hair, but he held up his hands, refusing to take it from me.

'It's your money, Katie. You earned it fair and square,' English said.

I could not dismiss the thought, as I climbed out of that car, that Terry had used the same phrase to the two girls the night before.

## Chapter Twenty-Seven

I collected Hope and went to Mum's. The police had indeed been with her, along with a social worker. They had asked about Hope's broken arm, asked about her relationship with Hope and me in general, and she had shown them the spare bedroom which she had made up for Hope for those nights when she'd had to stay over. They'd simply said they would let her know if any further action would be taken in due course.

I wanted to tell her about Black-Hair promising to help but couldn't. I was aware that the phone I carried in my bag was the one he had given me, and so, I could not be sure he wasn't listening in to our conversation.

I began to panic that Mum might say something in conversation which would make it clear that I had told her about Black-Hair and English and so I took out my phone and deliberately showed her my lifting it away from us and leaving it on the counter next to my house keys.

Despite this, she did not take the hint.

'Once they start with you, they don't let go,' she said. 'Things like this are never over, Katie.'

I shook my head quickly and pointed towards the device, then tapped my ear to indicate they might hear what she was saying and work out that she knew everything.

She widened her eyes, helpless.

I nodded.

'Anyway, hopefully it'll all be sorted soon,' I said. 'Why don't we go for a walk up the town, eh?'

'Can we get ice cream?' Hope called from the back room where she was watching TV and eating a bowl of cereal.

'You have cornflakes,' I called.

'Ice cream's better,' she said.

We walked up town and Mum said she would take us for ice cream in Fiorentini's, an old family-run ice cream parlour which we'd gone to with Dad when I was young. It was one of my fondest memories of him, from the time before he'd started drinking heavily.

Even though Dad had been well known in the town when I was a kid, we weren't wealthy by any stretch, so a family visit for ice cream was a monthly highlight. He'd shake hands and exchange smiles with the regulars, commenting on the weekend game while my mum glowed in his reflected recognition. We'd been happy together, us three. The month I started secondary school, when I was eleven, was our last such visit. Mum took me herself after that while Dad sat in O'Reilly's, nursing whiskey, and injuries to his legs and his pride in equal measure.

I was surprised the first time Mum had suggested bringing Hope for ice cream there, thinking it might bring back bad memories for her. But it was quite the reverse: we were three again, without, I only recently realised, the underlying tension which Dad's drinking had always caused. I only regretted now that Black-Hair's involvement in my life might have introduced a new source of tension for Mum.

I deliberately left my phone in her house so that we could speak more freely as we walked, always conscious of Hope listening in as she walked next to us.

'Do you think they can lip read?' Mum asked.

'How do you read lips?' Hope asked.

'I don't know,' I admitted. 'Though they've no reason to be f-o-l-l-o-w-i-n-g us anymore since I'm doing what they want.'

Mum accepted this with a non-committal grunt, though I could see her scanning the street as we walked. It reminded me of myself on that first day I met Black-Hair and English, and I realised that the thing I missed most was that loss of the security of ignorance. When I knew nothing, I was content.

As we passed the bottom of the hill leading up towards O'Reilly's, four young lads ran past us, two of them holding a crate of empty bottles between them.

'For God's sake, they must be rioting again,' Mum said. 'Are they not done with all that nonsense yet? Let's move before trouble starts.'

But I wanted to know what was happening. Had the police decided to raid the bar already? It had barely been two hours since I'd told them about the phone being placed there.

I walked up part of the way and saw that the area outside the bar was indeed cordoned off. Two white forensics vans were parked outside and a number of officers, all dressed in white forensics suits, were moving in and out of the building, carrying evidence bags and various items.

The uniformed police had set up a cordon around halfway down the street, with two Land Rovers parked at angles, shielding those working at the bar from view. Or more specifically, keeping them out of range of any missiles that might be thrown.

I could see the four young lads weaving their way through the crowd that had gathered to watch, but there seemed to be little appetite for fighting, and while one or two bottles smashed off the sides of the Land Rovers, there were no cheers.

I reached the outer edge of the crowd and nodded to a woman standing there, watching.

'What's going on?'

'They're searching O'Reilly's,' she said, a little unnecessarily. 'To do with that young Burke fella who died.'

Whatever the intel that Black-Hair got from me, there was no doubt that leaks were running both ways, for people in the city knew what the police were doing and why, almost as soon as they began to do it.

I thought it better to be well clear of the place should either Mark or Terry be brought out, so walked back down to meet Mum and Hope. And that afternoon, I tried to pretend that I was not the cause of what was happening just streets from where we sat, eating ice cream that tasted of childhood and imagining that life was normal.

When I got back to my mum's, I realised I had two missed calls on my phone. I recognised the number as Benny's. He'd left a voice message after the second.

'Hey, Katie. Benny here. Listen, the bar's been raided this afternoon and Terry and Mark taken in. If it's open again tomorrow, we'll need you to come in and cover a shift as

Gail's still on honeymoon and God knows when Mark and Terry will be back. Can you do the twelve till seven shift after you clean up, please? Text me at this number and let me know. I wouldn't ask, but we're stuck. Ann says she can watch Hope after school. Thanks.'

I knew I couldn't say no, not least because they would want to know why. And, also, I felt for Benny, who had obviously been left in charge of arranging shifts in the O'Reilly's absence. Besides, working the place when Mark wasn't there wouldn't be a problem for me. If nothing else, it would give me a chance to ask Benny about Leah Duffy.

# Chapter Twenty-Eight

The following morning, I took Hope to school and told her classroom teacher that Ann O'Reilly had my permission to collect Hope at the end of the day, in the absence of my mum being allowed to do it.

When I arrived at the bar, the police had finished with it so we were able to go in. It had been left in an even worse state than the morning after the party. All the chairs and tables in the main bar had been piled into one corner and the cushioned seating in the booths lifted out and slashed open, their padded interiors pulled out.

Behind the bar, glasses and bottles still lay scattered on the floor, many of them broken, while the big blue bin that empties were thrown into, to be sorted after a shift, lay on its side, the empties spilled right across the floor. A pool of thick liquid had gathered at the lip of the bin.

In the lounge, they had gone further, taking the cushioned bench tops off the frames, exposing years' worth of rubbish lying underneath.

Ann was already in the bar with her phone, videoing the scene. When she saw me come up with a box of black bags from the store, she stopped me with an upraised hand and continued to film, silently stepping over the broken glass as she crouched and filmed the empty shelves.

When she was done, she straightened up and fixed herself. 'Our lawyer said to record all the damage and to tote up a bill for costs and loss of earnings,' she explained.

'They trashed the place,' I said. 'What were they looking for?'

She shrugged. 'They're always out looking for something. There's nothing to find.'

'Hopefully,' I agreed. 'Have you heard from Mark?' I asked, mostly because I felt she would expect me to ask.

She shook her head. 'Our man's been in with him. He'll be fine. They'll have found nothing here.'

I nodded, aware that, having already checked the lounge, Leon Burke's phone was gone. They must have found it.

'Am I getting your kid from school?' she asked.

'If that's okay?'

She shrugged as if she couldn't care one way or the other. 'Mark would want me to help out,' she said.

I realised that, in all my conversations with her, she had never really mentioned Terry. I wondered whether she was closer to Mark or simply believed that he represented a common interest for the two of us.

'What about Terry?'

She laughed. 'Tel's been in and out of jail since I was no height. He'll be okay.' She was right.

Benny and I worked the afternoon shift together at the bar. When Kenneth arrived in, he ordered his usual drink and sat by the fire, his notebook open, neatly pencilling in a new spider diagram, which, I assumed, represented someone's family history. While he worked away in the corner, I left my phone down in the staff room, out of earshot, and used the opportunity of the quiet bar and the absence of the two O'Reillys to ask Benny more about Leah Duffy.

'She was Mark's ex-girlfriend,' he said in reply. 'They dated for about six months.'

'When?'

'A few years back – Katie, we shouldn't be chatting about this in here.'

He seemed jittery again and I wondered whether he was afraid the bar was bugged.

'Terry and Mark aren't here,' I said.

'They're always here,' Benny said.

At that Kenneth came towards the bar and Benny moved forward to serve him.

'It's Katie I want to see,' the older man said.

'I'll sort out the empties in the back then,' Benny said, seemingly just as grateful to have got away from our conversation as I was frustrated by his doing so.

'I'm doing your mum's family tree,' Kenneth said. 'Look.'

He showed me the diagram he'd been working on. Again, I could see Hope and myself, with my mum above. To one side of her was a horizontal line and the name Rosie.

'Who is Rosie?'

'Your aunt,' he said, smiling.

'I don't have an aunt Rosie. You've mixed up that one.'

Kenneth shook his head. 'Rosie was your mum's older sister. By two years. She died when she was three months old.'

'What happened to her?'

Kenneth shrugged. 'I only found her because of your grandparents' gravestone.'

To my shame, I had never visited my grandparents' graves. I knew Mum did every so often when I was younger, but it meant nothing to me. They'd both been dead long before I was born.

Kenneth flicked through his notebook and took out a sheet of tracing paper. Unfolding it, I saw the rubbing of my grandparents' tombstone and, at the bottom:

*Their daughter, Rosie.*
*An Angel in Heaven,*
*Too Good for This World.*

*Died 3rd May 1963.*

'You should ask your mum,' Kenneth said. 'I'll give you a copy of both trees when I'm done,' he added with a smile.

Just as I turned to head back to the bar, the main door opened, and Terry stepped in. The place erupted into cheers when they saw him, though I noticed Kenneth's claps were more measured.

'They've not built a jail can hold me!' Terry announced with a smile. But, as he made his way to the bar, I could tell he was angry.

'Welcome home,' I said, putting dirty glasses into the sink behind the bar. 'Any word on Mark?'

'They're still holding him. They think they have something on him.'

'What about?'

'Some bullshit, no doubt,' he said, though without conviction.

'Hopefully he'll be out soon,' I said, because it seemed the right thing to say.

He nodded. 'Thanks to you two for holding the fort today,' he added, glancing past me to Benny, who had reappeared from the kitchen, presumably at the sound of the cheering.

'No sweat.'

'The pair of you can head on. I'll be in touch about hours tomorrow. Okay?'

I looked to Benny who shrugged. 'Sounds good,' he said. 'But I can stay if you want to get home.'

Terry shook his head. 'No. I'm good. I want to check the place out anyway. See what the damage is, you know?'

'Ann filmed everything before we cleaned up,' I said.

Terry nodded, absently. 'I'll pick up on things you all missed. Head on, the pair of you.'

He had already forgotten us, moving past Benny and down towards the steps into the lounge where he stood and surveyed the room below.

Benny moved over to me, and I felt him slip something into my hand. I glanced down and saw a small, folded square of paper.

'Read it later,' he said, nodding to where Terry now stepped down into the lounge and traced the room, step by step, leaning over to shift aside the cushioned benches, as if looking for something. I had an idea what.

'He seems pissed,' Benny said. 'About the mess.'

I nodded agreement, but I suspected it wasn't about the mess. The cops had almost certainly found the phone.

And now Terry knew.

## Chapter Twenty-Nine

I managed not to read the slip of paper Benny had given me until I was well clear of the bar and was surprised to see that on it was written only 'Peak Gym'. I knew where it was, down near the community centre on my way home. I had to collect Hope first though and wondered whether Terry would have contacted Ann already and told her he was home, and I'd finished work. If so, she would be expecting me soon. I wouldn't have time to call at the gym before going to Ann's.

It was just as well I decided not to risk it, for she had Hope already waiting for me when I arrived and was clearly eager to get on with her day, making little small talk beyond some general comments about the pointlessness of Terry's arrest and agreeing with my hope that Mark would be released soon.

Once we got home and I got Hope sorted with some milk and biscuits, I changed the SIM on my phone and called Peak Gym. I'd thought about dropping in to the place to ask for Leah Duffy but realised that I didn't know for sure whether she was staff there or a customer and I didn't want anyone seeing me ask about her. Instead, if I phoned, I at least had some anonymity.

As it rang, I began to panic. What if Leah herself answered the phone? What would I say?

I heard a click, then a male voice spoke. 'Yes?'

'Can I speak to Leah Duffy, please?'

'There's no Leah Duffy here,' the man said, raising his voice over the noise of the music in the background.

'Will she be working later?' I asked, hoping to at least confirm whether she was a member of staff.

'There's no Leah works here,' he said, then ended the call.

That evening, I told Hope we were taking a walk. She wanted to visit her granny, but my mum was out for the evening with old friends of her and my dad. We headed down towards the community centre and, spotting Peak, I told Hope I wanted to make a quick stop. Benny had given me the name of the place for a reason. Perhaps Leah was a regular in the place, though I wondered if I would recognise the girl if I saw her. And even if I did, what would I say?

The sound of repeated bass notes pounded from the open door of the gym as we approached, and I could see the place was busy. As we stepped through the doorway, a lad at the main desk glanced up at us.

'You all right?' he asked.

I nodded. 'The wee one wanted to see what was in here,' I lied.

Ignoring Hope's look of shock at having been blamed for our presence, I looked past the main desk to where people were exercising, hoping that I might see someone I knew.

'She's too young,' he said, seeming to assume I wanted my four-year-old to work out. 'Paddy runs a Toddlers Exercise Class on Wednesday mornings in the community centre though, if you like.'

'Better not,' I said. 'Not till her arm heals.'

I was just going to leave when Hope tugged my hand. 'There's your friend, Mummy,' she said. 'From work.'

I felt my stomach flip and looked around expecting to see Mark standing. Instead, and with some relief, I realised she was pointing to one of several framed pictures on the wall.

I peered closer and saw that it was indeed a picture of Mark, standing at the centre of a group of people, proudly displaying a sword. He was a few years younger, his black T-shirt covered with white chalk that suggested he'd been competing in some kind of weightlifting event. A caption below the image said *Mark O'Reilly, Ulster's Strongest 2019 – Enniskillen*.

But it was the figure next to him who really grabbed my attention for I was certain that I had seen her before. I took out my phone, grateful not to have changed back the SIM card yet into the new handset, and checked my Facebook account search history. I compared the picture from Leah Duffy's profile with the figure standing next to Mark. It was the same person.

'All right, Katie?'

I turned at the voice, my heart rate spiked in panic. It took me a second to place the man who had spoken as Liam, one of the regulars in the pub. He'd clearly just finished a session in the gym, his face flushed and shining with sweat.

'Hey, Liam.'

'I didn't know you were a regular,' he said, shifting his bag to his other hand and offering an upraised palm to Hope for a high five.

'Thinking about joining,' I said. 'I could be doing with some exercise.'

'Did Mark send you down?' he asked, nodding towards the picture in front of which we stood.

'I didn't know he was a member?'

'Sure he used to own the place. Mind you, I've not seen him here in a while,' Liam admitted. 'But he used to be in all the time before he sold up.'

'Did he win that sword?' I asked, tapping on the glass over the image.

'Yeah. It's a strong man competition he won in Enniskillen. He was in some shape back then.'

'Who's she?'

I tried to sound as nonchalant as possible, but Liam's smile made me wonder whether he suspected the question was motivated more by jealousy than curiosity.

'Leah. Her and Mark were an item for a while, but that was years back too.'

'They were going out?'

'Engaged from what I remember. They met here actually.'

'Is she still a member?'

Liam shook his head. 'I've not seen her since they broke up, to be honest.'

'What happened to them?'

Liam shrugged. 'It was a few years back. She's well out of the picture, Katie, if that's what you're worried about.'

I smiled and nodded, as if this information offered me some comfort. The easiest thing to do was to play along with his notion that I was jealously guarding my supposed relationship with Mark so that, if the conversation was reported back to him, he might see my questions about his ex-girlfriend in a flattering light rather than a suspicious one.

'Don't say to Mark that I was asking, Liam, yeah?'

He smiled and winked in a way I took to mean my secret was safe with him. Besides, at worst, what could he tell Mark except that I'd been asking about someone I saw in a photograph?

Initially, I wondered how I hadn't known anything about Mark being engaged, but looking back, I realised it must have happened during the time I was off having Hope. I'd struggled in the months after she was born, not least because of Oran abandoning us, so it was almost ten months before I returned to work again. It all must have been over by then.

The first thing I did when I got home was to check Mark's Facebook page to see if he had posted anything about Leah at any stage. If, as Liam had suggested, they were engaged, he must surely have posted about the two of them. However, as I scrolled back, I realised that there was not one single picture of them, not a mention of her in his feed. Presumably if he had posted about them, he'd removed any posts which mentioned her. I could not find a copy of the image from the gym wall either, despite Mark having won the competition, and wondered whether he had deleted it too or just never posted it. But he had shared other images of his winning competitions from that period, including a post dated 6th October 2019, in which he shared images of himself and Terry at a competition in France along with a comment on what an amazing weekend the pair of them were having.

The date stuck with me; the news report on Leah Duffy's assault had been dated 9th October 2019, but had referred to the incident happening in the early hours of Sunday which, according to my calendar, was the 6th October. Based on Mark's social media feed, he'd not even been in the country when it had happened. So why had Benny pointed me in her direction?

## Chapter Thirty

The following morning, I checked again to see if Leah Duffy's friend, Catherine, who ran the beauty parlour, had read my message, but she hadn't. I looked up the business and discovered it had closed during Covid and never reopened. I'd hit a dead end there, too.

I made sure I transferred the SIM card into my new phone first thing, leaving my old handset in my underwear drawer again, then took Hope to school. We were on the way up the hill towards the gates when my phone rang. It was Terry.

'Katie, I'll need you in this morning at some stage to help sort out some of the mess from the raid. Is that okay?'

'But I cleaned it yesterday,' I said. 'Does it need redone?'

'A few spots here and there,' he said. 'We had repairs to do, so there's sawdust and stuff lying around. Okay?'

'I'm just dropping off Hope now,' I said. 'I can come straight on in then if you like?'

'No. I'll send a cab for you when we're ready. The solicitor is doing some stuff here first. Just wait at home until I send for you.'

There was something about his voice, a forced lightness that Terry did not usually have. But we were already at the school by now and I got distracted by the classroom assistant who, as she welcomed Hope at the door to the classroom, asked, 'Who's collecting this wee dote today?'

'I'm not sure,' I said. 'Either myself or Ann O'Reilly.' While I hoped Black-Hair would work quickly in getting Mum cleared, I couldn't be sure it would be done by lunchtime, nor did I know how long it would take to clean up whatever mess the workmen had left in O'Reilly's.

'Grand,' she said, smiling as she ushered Hope into the classroom where she ran to join her friends.

I went home and waited as Terry had instructed. At around 11 a.m., I heard a knock at the door. When I went out, Ann was standing there and, behind her, a Maxi Cabs car idled.

'Terry wants you in to the bar now,' Ann said, moving to step into the hallway.

'Where are you going?'

'I'll house-sit while you're at work,' she said.

'Don't be ridiculous. The house is fine. Can you step out, please?'

'I'm house-sitting,' she repeated. 'Terry asked that you leave your phone here, too.'

'I'm not leaving anything,' I said. 'What if Hope's school needs to contact me?'

'I'll answer it and call the bar,' Ann said.

'Get the fuck out of my house, Ann,' I said. 'Now.'

Ann turned towards the cab and I heard the engine cut. The driver got out and made his way up the pathway to my door. I recognised his face from the party in the bar but did not know his name.

'Katie, don't make this difficult,' Ann said. 'Leave your phone and the keys.'

'Why?'

'Because Terry wants to speak to you about something.'

There it was. What I knew this was all about. I thought I was going to pass out. The hallway felt suddenly narrow, the walls looming over me.

'What about?'

Ann shrugged and looked past me. 'Have you a Wi-Fi code?' she asked.

'Ann, what's going on?'

The cab driver had stepped into the house now too and I felt his arm on my back. 'Katie, give Ann your phone and let's go.'

'I need to put on my boots,' I said. 'And I better let my mum know I'm out for the day. She'll be wondering.'

I took my phone and typed: **Working all day. Might be late** and sent it to Mum. At the sound of the whoosh of the message sending, Ann took the phone from me.

'I'll call if anyone's looking for you.'

'Why can't I bring my phone?' I asked, my mouth dry. I was trying to find ways to delay now, hoping that Black-Hair would interpret the message, listen in and come to my rescue.

'Too many distractions in the bar,' Ann said. 'Terry's worried people are spending more time scrolling than working.'

'I'll get my boots,' I said, taking the stairs two at a time. I heard the tread behind me and turned to see the driver following me up.

'Get the fuck down,' I said. 'I'm putting on a pair of boots. I can manage that by myself.'

He glanced at Ann, who shrugged again, then stayed where he was, on the bottom step, his hand resting on the banister.

'Hurry up,' he said. 'Terry's waiting.'

I went up to my room in a blind panic. I could guess what Ann's house-sitting really meant. She, or others brought in by her, would be searching the place while I was away, looking for something that would connect me to the police. But how had they known it was me who placed Burke's phone? Were there cameras I wasn't aware of in the bar? I'd checked there weren't any in the lounge. So how did they know it was me?

Maybe he did just want to talk. Maybe he wanted to speak to all of us, all the staff. Perhaps it was to let us know what had happened. But Ann 'house-sitting' for me put the lie to that.

I was a suspect.

I had the envelope of cash which English had given me still sitting in the cabinet in the kitchen. I also had my own, old phone, sitting in the underwear drawer beside my bed. That was something I needed to get rid of, for if that was found and they checked the call records, they would ask why I was alternating between two different phones.

I considered hiding it under the mattress, but I had to assume that if they searched my house, they'd be thorough. I decided then that the best thing to do would be to swallow the bullet and actually drop it in the toilet, then leave it sitting on the windowsill. That was the story I'd told anyway for why I'd replaced it, although some one of them might wonder why it was still wet now, days later.

It was a risk I had to take, for I couldn't keep it on me. If they were searching through my house, I had to assume that they would likewise search my pockets when I got to the bar.

I pulled on thick, woolly socks and my boots and tucked the phone inside the hem of my leggings, its bulk hidden by the loose folds of the socks and the open tongue of my boots.

My plan was to go to the bathroom and soak the phone, but, as I stepped out of my bedroom, the cab driver was blocking the landing.

'Let's go,' he said.

'I need to go to the toilet,' I said.

'Let's go.'

'I need a piss,' I said, hoping the crudeness of the comment would surprise him enough that I could get past him and into the toilet.

Instead, he gripped my arm. 'Let's go,' he said, a third time.

'Let go of me!' I snapped, tugging to be loose of him, but he gripped tighter.

'Terry's waiting. Let's move.'

He directed me downstairs to where Ann had already turned on the TV, the volume unnecessarily loud. My phone was sitting in front of it, the mouthpiece directed towards the flickering screen.

'I'll take care of Hope,' Ann said, and I felt my legs go as I realised I might not see my girl again.

Perhaps the cab driver felt the change in me, for he took the weight to stop me falling and, more gently now, said, 'Let's go, Katie.'

'Tell Hope . . .' I started.

Ann looked at me expectantly.

Tell her what? That I loved her? It would sound too final, too much an admission of guilt.

'Tell her I'll be home soon,' I said. 'She likes milk and biscuits when she gets home.'

Ann nodded. 'I'll take good care of her,' she said, then turned her attention again to the TV.

## Chapter Thirty-One

I went to open the rear door of the taxi, but the driver stopped me.

'Up front,' he said.

'I feel safer in the back.'

I opened the door and climbed in. Let him try to forcibly move me in front of my neighbours, I thought. I hoped someone would phone the police if he did, though knew that they may well not. *Say nothing* was the code by which most people here lived. It had been the code by which I lived, until I was left with no choice. In fact, with some irony, I realised that if the neighbours did phone anyone, it would be Terry O'Reilly, who had positioned himself as the unofficial police force of the local community, trust in the actual police in my area being so low.

The driver had decided it wasn't worth the hassle and, slamming the door on me, climbed into the front. While he was circling the car, I look the chance to slide my phone from beneath my sock and under my leg. I had nowhere else to put it on me, no pockets or spaces in my clothes which would hide it. I'd worn leggings and my work T-shirt that morning and cursed the choice now.

I could see the driver's eyes flicking up towards the rear-view mirror to watch me as he drove, so I slid across in the seat until I was sitting behind him, shifting the phone beneath me as I did so.

'Sit in the middle,' he said.

'No,' I said.

He twisted a little in his seat as he stopped the car. 'Sit in the fucking middle.'

'Your seat belt's not working,' I lied. 'I want a seat belt that works.'

'Whiny bitch,' he muttered as he turned back to the road and I used the chance to push the phone towards the back of the seat, to the gap between the back and bottom seat cushions.

I pushed the phone in, hoping that it wouldn't fall onto the floor beneath with a clatter. Fortunately, it seemed to remain wedged in the gap, much as Leon Burke's phone had done in the bar.

The thought of Burke's phone brought the present moment crashing round me. I needed to remain calm, needed to convince Terry that I knew nothing about it, if indeed that was what they wanted to see me about.

At the bottom of the hill, the driver indicated left, away from town.

'Are we not heading to the bar?' I asked, though without response.

Instead, he took us further out of Derry until he finally turned up a country lane that led to an industrial estate. All the units were shuttered, though one, towards the far end of the site, had two cars parked outside it.

'What are we doing here?' I asked, hoping, for once, that Black-Hair was following me, was keeping me under watch.

But the driver had been watching the road behind us in the mirror throughout the journey and I guessed that, had someone been back there, he'd have spotted them.

We pulled up outside the unit and the driver killed the engine and got out. He opened the rear door and motioned that I should get out too.

'What are we doing here?' I asked.

'Get out,' he said, reaching in past me and unclicking the seat belt. I leaned back, as if to move from his touch but, in fact, to ensure my phone was pushed far enough in that he would not see it the moment I climbed out of the car.

He held on to my arm as we walked across to the unit. I could see now a doorway in the front metal shutter, and it was through this that he led me. I realised that he had not blindfolded me or made any effort to hide where we were going. The implication was clear. I tried to pull away from him, but he simply gripped my arm more firmly as he pushed me inside.

We stepped into a furniture warehouse of some sort. A staircase to the left led up to a level where finished wooden furniture was on display, while the lower level was obviously the workshop. Various pieces of industrial equipment were spotted around the place, the floor coated in sawdust.

Terry and Andy Flood were standing next to one of the machines, Terry testing the saw by pressing the button on the side while he and Andy joked about something.

'Tel,' the driver shouted. He pointed at me, as if Terry might not have spotted me, then said, 'I'll be out in the car.'

Terry and Flood came across to where I stood.

'Katie,' Terry said. 'Thanks for coming.'

'I wasn't given a choice,' I said. 'What the hell is this?'

Terry glanced at Flood, as if he had heard all this before, then shook his head. 'You're on the clock,' he said. 'You'll be paid for your hours. We can't open the pub today; the lads in fixing up the damage that was done by the cops are still there.'

'Then why am I here?'

Terry thought about it for a second, then smiled. 'Staff training. First things, though. I need you to strip off.'

'What?' I felt my legs go, my knees weaken.

'I need to know you're not wearing a wire,' he said. 'I want to talk to you about Mark and I need to know you're clean.'

'I'm not stripping,' I said.

'You are,' Terry said. 'You can do it, or me and Floody here will have to do it for you. It's best for everyone if you do it yourself.'

'And if I say no?'

Terry looked again to Flood, who lifted his tracksuit top to show the butt of a gun wedged in his waistline.

'You'll not say no,' Terry said. 'You can put your clothes back on again when you're done. But I need to know you're clean.'

I stared at them, hoping that reason might prevail, and he would change his mind, but the two of them returned my stare, waiting. Eventually, as defiantly as I could, I pulled my T-shirt over my head and kicked off my boots, peeled off my leggings.

'And the underwear,' Terry said, and I was again in the police cell, being strip-searched.

'Terry, I'm not wearing a wire. Why would you think I was?' I asked, my arms folded across my chest.

'And the underwear, Katie,' Terry said. 'Make it easy, girl.'

I unclasped my bra and let it fall. Floody stared openly at my chest as I wrapped one arm across it.

'And the pants,' he said.

'Fuck you,' I said.

'And the pants, Katie. Come on; you're dragging the hole out of this. Just do it.'

Still holding my arm across my chest, I used my free hand to push down my pants until they were around my ankles.

'Check her,' Terry said.

'If he puts a hand on me, Mark will kill him,' I said, feeling utterly powerless that I had to resort to using Mark to make the threat.

'Mark's not here,' Flood snapped.

'He'll not touch you anywhere he doesn't need to,' Terry said. 'If he does, I'll deal with it.'

'As if your word means anything,' I said, keeping one hand over my chest and the other covering my crotch.

'We've all seen enough tits and twats that yours makes no odds,' Terry said. 'Don't flatter yourself, love.'

Flood circled me, coming in close enough that I could smell the vape off his breath and, beneath that, stale sweat. He ruffled through my hair and tilted my head, as if examining my ears. His hand on the nape of my neck was damp with sweat, his touch causing me to shiver against my will.

'Check her pockets and inside her boots and socks, too,' Terry said, and I muttered a silent thanks that I'd got rid of my phone before being brought in. 'Put your pants and bra back on,' he added to me. 'We're not savages.'

Flood remained standing behind me while I had to bend to tug my pants back up from my ankles. He chuckled to himself as I did so, then began patting down my clothes.

'What the hell, Terry?' I said.

'Take a seat,' he said, nodding towards where three plain wooden chairs were placed. 'You're fine. We just want to ask you a few questions for now.'

I moved across, my hands still folded across my chest in an attempt to hide both my vulnerability and the fact my hands were shaking. I had to grit my teeth to stop the two men seeing me tremble.

'Where's Mark?' I asked.

'We want to ask you some questions, Katie. Sit.'

I moved across and took the seat he indicated. He and Flood took the two seats opposite, though so close together that our knees touched. Terry reached out and laid his hand on my leg, just above the knee, and patted me lightly.

'Just be honest with us, Katie. No one wants to hurt anyone here. We're friends, right?' he said, sitting back.

'Friends don't strip one another.'

'Depends on the friendship,' Flood said, looking to Terry for a response, though the older man's expression did not change.

'Nor do they betray one another,' Terry said.

I swallowed, but my mouth was dry, and the swallow felt like it had got stuck. 'I don't know what you're talking about.'

'You worked the party the other night,' Terry said. 'For Floody getting home.'

I nodded.

'You also came in early and cleaned up the next morning.'

I nodded again. My throat felt ready to burst but I did not want to cough to ease it in case it implied guilt or discomfort with the questions.

'Who else was in the following morning?'

'Jamie in the kitchen,' I said, then cleared my throat. 'Benny came in and helped in the bar and then you came in. Why? What's happened?'

'Have you heard the name Leon Burke?'

I knew it: this was about the phone. I wanted to deny knowing the name, but half the town had heard Burke's name after he died. Besides, I was worried he'd know I was lying.

'I've heard of him. He was the young lad who was stabbed last week.'

'He was one of our lads,' Terry said. 'You'd not have known him from the bar; he was too young to be in and out. Good lad though.'

Too young to drink but not to sell drugs or to die. I hated Terry even more in that moment.

'What about him?' I asked.

'Leon was knifed, as you say. Scum of the earth, targeting a kid like that. He came into the bar looking for attention. He was given it and sent to the hospital.'

I tried not to blink. Terry was staring at me, reading me. Burke wasn't sent to hospital; not according to Black-Hair. His wound was superglued shut and he was sent home to die in bed. But I couldn't know that.

'Right.'

'Thing is, Burke's family told us they never got his phone back. We wanted to see it, see if we could work out who he'd been meeting – who'd stabbed him, you know?'

I nodded. I guessed they wanted to wipe it, wondering at how many incriminating messages were on it. Messages that were now in the hands of the police.

'I don't see what this has to do with me, Terry,' I said.

'You were called in the morning Leon got hurt,' Terry said. Not died: *hurt*. 'If his phone had been lying around, you'd have found it, I'm guessing.'

'If it was there, I would have. But I didn't. I'm sorry,' I said. If he thought I believed they were only questioning me over whether I'd found Burke's phone, it might make me look innocent of having handed it to the police. 'It mustn't have been in the bar.'

'It was,' Terry said, and I tried and failed to suppress a shiver.

Flood looked from me to Terry, as if this was important.

'Mark remembered the phone being there that night when he was helping Leon. In fact, he remembers lifting it and setting it to one side. So, we *know* it was in the bar.'

'Okay,' I said. 'Maybe I lifted it off the floor, mixed up with the bandages and tea towels that were lying around and shoved them all into the rubbish bags without checking. I was just trying to get the place cleared.'

I cursed myself even as I said it. I'd washed the tea towels before dumping them. Mark knew that I had. Had he told Terry?

'Maybe,' Terry said, and I couldn't tell if he was stringing me along or was buying my excuse. 'What happened to the rubbish bags?'

'I left them at the back door to go to the dump.'

'Who took them?'

I shrugged, unwilling to implicate Benny. 'I'm not sure.'

'It wasn't me, and it wouldn't have been Jamie,' Terry said. 'Was it Mark or Benny?'

I shrugged again.

'Think, Katie,' Terry said. 'I know who it was, so you must remember.'

'Benny,' I said, weakly.

Terry nodded. 'You're a piece of work, too, Katie,' he said. 'So that's what happened? You picked the phone up, binned it by accident and Benny took the bags?'

'I don't know,' I said. 'I'm sorry if I did. If the phone's lost—'

'The phone's not lost,' Flood said suddenly. 'The cops have it.'

Terry leaned forward, placing his two hands on my bare legs, his thumbs rubbing my inner thigh. The movement unsettled me, the intimacy of it, the vulnerability I felt.

'See, here's my problem, Katie,' he said, leaning closer. 'That all sounds very plausible. Except, as Andy says, the cops have the phone.'

'Maybe they found it—'

'They did.'

'—in the dump,' I continued.

'In the bar,' Terry said. 'In our bar. In the bar you cleaned.'

'Terry, I swear I never found that phone.'

'Swear on your kid,' Terry said, sitting back again.

'I swear on Hope,' I said, for what else could I do. 'I swear.'

At this stage, Flood reached in and pulled the gun from his waistband and the space around me became suddenly charged, the air heavy and hard to breath.

I felt sweat break on my skin, felt a sudden chill. Acid burned my throat.

Flood laid the tip of the gun on my knee, pointed towards me. It was heavy and cold, and I could smell oil and something else. I felt beneath my legs warm as I realised I'd leaked in fear.

'She's pissed herself,' Flood said.

'I'm sorry,' I said to Terry. 'I'm sorry. I must have missed it. It must have fallen somewhere, and I missed it. That's the only explanation I can think of.'

'They found it down the side of the seats,' Terry said. 'Stuck down between two cushions.'

'I wouldn't have checked there,' I said. 'I just cleaned the floor and the furniture that had blood on it. I didn't check the cushions. I'm sorry, Terry. I swear I didn't.'

I was trying to stop more urine slipping from me but could feel the panic build in me. I hoped by sheer force of will that I could convince him.

'She's lying,' Flood said, standing now and moving behind me. I could feel the tip of his gun pressed against the back of my neck as he grabbed my hair and pulled my head back.

'She's a lying bitch,' Flood said.

'I'm not. I swear, I must have missed it. I must have missed it. I swear. I'm sorry, Terry.'

'Liar,' Flood spat at me, his face looming above mine. I felt acid burning its way up my throat. I moved my head to the side and vomited on myself. Some must have splattered backwards for Flood let go my hair and stepped away.

'Dirty fucker,' he shouted.

'Katie,' Terry said, snapping his fingers, making me look at him. He reached out and gripped my leg with one hand, his other gesturing in the air between us that I should give him my attention. 'Katie.'

'I'm sorry,' I said, then, worried it sounded like a confession, added, 'I must have missed it.'

'You didn't miss it,' Terry said. 'I *know* you didn't miss it.'

'I swear I must have,' I said, crying now, the tears mingling with the saliva still hanging from my mouth. 'I must have. Terry. I swear on Hope.'

I could feel the gun against my neck again, hard against my spine.

'I know you didn't miss it, Katie, because the night of Flood's party, I searched that place from top to bottom to make sure there was no one listening in. I swept the place, you see. Do you understand?'

I shook my head, not because I didn't know but because the longer he spoke, the longer I remained alive.

'I searched every part of the bar,' Terry said. 'To make sure the cops hadn't planted anything from the last time they raided the place. And you know what *wasn't* down the side of the seat? Leon Burke's phone.'

'I don't understand,' I said again, trying to buy time.

'Someone put Burke's phone back in the bar, *after* the party. Someone planted it in the bar between the end of Flood's coming home party and the cops raiding.'

'No,' I said, shaking my head. 'No. It must have fallen or something. It must have—'

'There were three sets of prints in the blood on the phone,' Terry said, shaking his head at me, his hand gripping my leg now, his fingers digging into my flesh. 'Three sets. Burke's, Mark's, and one other.'

'The cunt who hid the phone for the cops,' Flood said, moving beside me, the tip of the gun in my ear now.

'You betrayed us, Katie,' Terry said. 'You're a tout.'

## Chapter Thirty-Two

'I'm not a tout,' I said. 'I swear.'

'There's an envelope with five hundred pounds in cash in your kitchen cabinet,' Terry said. 'You told us you were broke.'

Ann *had* searched my house. Again, I thanked everything good that I had lifted my other phone. Though that thought reminded me that it was sitting about a hundred yards away, down the back seat of the Maxi Cab outside.

'It's money I saved. And money you gave me. Money for cleaning up. And Mark gave me something when he thought I had to leave work.'

I heard Flood snort, then he wedged the gun into my ear. 'She's lying,' he said.

'I'm not. Ask him. He gave me some cash to keep me going. When I came back, he told me to keep it.'

'Fucking someone for cash means you *are* a whore,' Flood said. 'Mickey was right.' He leaned down, the gun hurting me now. 'I haven't forgot,' he hissed.

'It doesn't look good, Katie,' Terry said. 'Leaving the job and then coming back. The envelope of cash. The new phone appearing out of nowhere.'

'It's not nowhere,' I said. 'I dropped my old one in the toilet. I got the new one in the market. It's a knock-off.'

'But the money,' Terry said. 'We never gave you five hundred pounds. Are you being paid off by the cops, Katie?'

'No,' I said. 'I swear I'm not.'

'How did they get you? That nonsense with your mother? Was that it?'

I felt sick again and began to retch though my stomach was empty.

'She's fucking guilty,' Flood said. 'Let me do it. I'll string her up for the whole town to see what happens to touts.'

'I trusted you, Katie,' Terry said. 'Your dad would be ashamed of you.'

My da. The man they'd fed drink to. They knew nothing about him.

'I'm not a fucking tout,' I spat. 'I told you.'

'If not you, then who, Katie?' Terry said. 'Who lifted Burke's phone and hid it in the bar? Who? Benny? Are you fucking him twice over, Katie?'

I shook my head. 'I don't know,' I said. 'I don't know.'

I couldn't blame Benny. Not knowing, as I did, what they would likely do to him. It was wrong.

'She's lying,' Flood said.

Terry looked to Flood and nodded. Then he stepped back and stared at me. 'I'm sorry, Katie,' he said. 'I don't believe you.'

I tried to speak, opening my mouth, but the words seemed to die on my lips.

'I . . . I . . .'

'Don't—' Terry began.

He was cut short by the buzzing of his phone. He pulled it from his pocket, raised a finger to Flood and answered.

'What have you got?'

I could hear someone talking, though the sound of my own heaving breaths made it impossible to hear what was being said. Terry's expression hardened as he stared at me, his jawline flexing with anger.

'Where did you find it?'

It was the driver. I was sure of it. He must have found my phone in the back of his car. I felt my bladder void and hung my head, ready for Flood to shoot me.

'Fucking idiot,' Terry said, hanging up the phone. 'The fucking idiot. The greedy, greedy bastard.'

As he spoke, he lifted the chair he had sat on and thrashed it across the floor, the wood splintered and cracking. He let out a roar of fury.

'I'm sorry,' I whispered.

'That stupid fucker kept Burke's bank card,' he said to Flood. 'Fuck!'

With that he turned and strode towards the wall between this unit and the adjoining one.

I didn't know what he meant, could not work out what was happening. Had I kept Burke's bank card?

Flood looked down at me, his gun aimed at my face. His glance darted towards Terry's retreating form and his tongue poked through his lips as he wondered what to do. His finger tensed on the trigger.

I lowered my head. This was it.

Flood was going to shoot me.

## Chapter Thirty-Three

Instead, Flood struck me with the gun. 'Don't fucking move,' he said. He lifted a roll of thick tape and wound it round my wrists, effectively tying me to the chair. Then he pulled off a second strip, which he ran over my mouth.

That done, he set off in the direction Terry had gone.

I began to panic, thinking I would suffocate. I tried to pull free of the binding he had put round my wrists, but it was tight around the spine of the chair. Finally, I settled myself, tried to settle my breaths, in and out through my nose, forcing myself to calm a little. I could feel my heart thud in my chest.

I sat there, alone, sobbing with relief, with fear, with the thought I would not see Hope again.

What did he mean by the bank card? Burke's? It had been inside Burke's phone case. I remembered seeing it, obscured a little by the bloody case but definitely there. And it had been inside the case when I replaced it back into the gap between the cushions in the bar. I hadn't touched it. That I knew.

I could hear muffled shouts coming from next door. It went quiet then, though I could still hear the low murmur of voices. Then, Terry reappeared at the far end of the unit, coming round the side of one of the big industrial saws.

He was wiping his hands on a rag which he carried. It was bloody and I could see his hands were similarly badged with blood.

He came across and sat opposite me again and looked at me. Then he shook his head and leaning forward, pulled off the tape from my mouth.

I gulped in air and began to feel dizzy.

'Katie, we're in a pickle,' he said, as if this was an everyday situation. 'We knew someone had betrayed us to the cops and we had to do what we did to find out who. Mark's still inside, maybe facing charges over Burke. I have to protect my brother. You understand.'

I nodded, though it was not a question. I didn't even agree; I just could do no more.

'Sometimes we have to do unpleasant things. Because the cops are sneaky fuckers. They'll try anything to get people you trust to turn on you. You can't leave yourself open to that. You understand?'

I managed another nod. My fringe hung in my eyes now, my hair and face slick with sweat, despite how cold I felt sitting here in my underwear.

'So, I'm going to ask one last time, Katie. And I want you to be honest with me. I want to know that we can trust you. Have you done a deal with the cops?'

I shook my head, too exhausted to protest and aware that all my protests to date had meant nothing to him.

'Have you anything you want to tell me? Now's the time. Confess. Confession's good for the soul, you know?'

I looked up at him. My eyes were sore, my cheeks throbbing red.

'So, have you anything you need to tell me? Get it off your chest. Now, when Floody's not here.'

'No,' I said.

He nodded, leaned forward again and patted my knee.

'Good girl,' he said. 'Get yourself dressed. Max will leave you back home.'

He moved behind me and I heard the tear of the tape as he tore it from the seat back. He helped me stand, but my legs were jelly so he held me upright a moment, his hand beneath my arm.

'Take a moment,' he said. 'Get some deep breaths into you.'

When I had steadied a little, he tore the tape off my wrists. 'Ann's collected Hope. Everyone's okay at home. All right?'

'What was the point of this?' I asked.

'I needed to know I could trust you,' Terry said. 'If you're going to be doing a line with my wee brother, I need to make sure you're not playing him? Yanking his chain as well as his . . . you know?'

He laughed as he nudged me, as if this was all a shared joke. Did Mark really imagine we were dating after one chaste kiss? Or had he told Terry how he felt, and Terry had assumed things had progressed further than they actually had? I assumed the latter, for I'd not given Mark any reason to believe we were a couple.

'You're one of us, love,' he said. 'Eh? One of us.'

If I'd had anything left to vomit, I would have done so then.

\* \* \*

Max, whom I now assumed to be the owner of Maxi Cabs, helped me to the back seat. I heard him and Terry speak after he closed the door. Heard him promise he'd be right back when he was done with me. Terry shook his head and said something.

'Eight?' Max said, his voice muffled through the car door.

Terry said something else and then Max was in the car and starting the ignition.

'Home, love,' he said.

He did not look at me as he drove, perhaps ashamed, perhaps feeling I no longer needed watching. As a result, I was able to get my phone back out and slip it inside my leggings hem on the pretext that I was tying up my boots.

As he pulled up at my house, the front door opened and Ann stepped out, passing me on the pathway.

'Hope's had her milk and biscuits,' she said. 'Your phone's on the kitchen table. See you later,' and on she went, as if she had not just violated my privacy and invaded my home and family.

I went into the house and shut and locked the door. I went across and hugged Hope where she sat, watching TV.

'You smell funny,' she said, as I held her tight.

'I do,' I said. 'I need a shower. Don't answer the door to anyone, okay?'

She nodded, her expression serious, then turned her attention again to the cartoon she was watching.

I showered, just as I had the day the police had lifted me. And I stood and wept shuddering sobs, away from Hope, out of earshot. I could have been dead. Flood wanted to kill me; I guessed he probably still did.

And Terry's comment, his reassurance that I was one of them, now simply made me feel even worse.

I stayed there until I was empty, until I could feel nothing more. Then I turned off the water, dried myself and went into my room to get changed.

I could hear voices downstairs and began to panic. Had Terry changed his mind? Was he back now, in the house, now that I had returned my phone to the underwear drawer next to my bed?

I pulled on tracksuit bottoms and a top, lifted my dad's old penknife from beside the phone and rushed down.

'Hope, I told you not to let anyone in,' I said, going into the living room.

'I let myself in,' Mum said. 'Hope and I have been on our own down here.'

My relief that it was Mum meant I missed the meaning in what she said, so she repeated it with a smile.

'Just the two of us. Unsupervised.'

'Is it over?'

She nodded, beaming. 'The cops called me this morning. I tried calling you, but it went straight to voicemail.'

'I forgot my phone,' I said.

She waved away the explanation. 'Anyway, they called today to say they'd reviewed the case and decided that no further action was necessary. I asked was I okay to watch Hope and they said yes.'

'That's great, Mum,' I said, feeling my eyes brim again.

'So, us three are going out for dinner. My treat. Okay?'

'I don't feel—'

'I'm not taking no for an answer,' she said. 'Put something decent on and we'll go out for a bite to eat.'

She was so happy and Hope so pleased to have her with us, I could not refuse, though I had no appetite to eat anything.

While it was lovely to see Mum and Hope so happy together, and I knew that it would make life undoubtedly easier, not having to interact with Ann O'Reilly anymore, I could not shake the dread I felt. Terry had let me go, despite the fact that he'd seemed not to believe me. The issue of Burke's phone remained, and I couldn't help but feel that he had only delayed whatever punishment I was to face.

I spent the meal watching the tables around us, studying faces, especially those that glanced in our direction. When the door opened, I twisted to see who might be coming in, half expecting someone masked, gun raised, to be rushing towards us. Was his punishment to kill Mum and Hope too? I felt sick at the thought that I had put them at risk.

Mum insisted that we get a taxi home and wanted to phone Maxi Cabs, but I refused. I did not want to see Max, nor to sit in his car. We walked across to City Taxis and waited there.

We were a few minutes from home, only three streets from our house, when the car slowed.

'Everyone got seat belts on?' the driver asked. 'The cops are stopping cars.'

He opened the window and leaned out, craning his neck to see what lay ahead.

'There's something going on,' he said. 'I'll have to take the long way.'

'We can walk from here,' I said, keen not to spend any more time than necessary inside a taxi after the morning's events.

Mum paid and we got out of the car. Ahead of us, the roadway was closed and a policeman was unspooling tape across the street, blocking access while others worked at setting up what looked like a white tent.

There was an alleyway just up to the right that we could take, that would bring us round to mine anyway, so we headed towards it. But as we did, I saw, briefly, the cause of the disturbance.

A naked body sat on the pavement, his arms outstretched along the upper rail of the fence he leaned against, like a scarecrow's. His head lay back, the wound in his temple clear, the blood from it having coated his neck and shoulder. Around his neck, a sign hung, on which was written one word.

*Tout.*

Mum pulled Hope towards her, shielding her from the sight. But I stepped closer, towards the tape, studying the face, immobile now beneath the orange streetlamp.

A face I knew.

A face I had kissed.

Benny.

Dead on the pavement.

# Chapter Thirty-Four

I did not sleep that night, try as I might. My nerves were shot, the mixture of the day's events and Benny's killing replaying in my mind.

I could not shift the thought of his last moments, replayed them over and over as he begged them not to kill him, swore on his wife, his kids that he wasn't an informer. Knew that he wasn't. I felt how deeply unfair it must have been when they did not believe him. Did he realise it was me? Did he know I was to blame for his death?

The guilt I felt was only made worse by the relief beneath it that I was not the one dead. And those feelings weighed on me through the night.

The doorbell rang at 8 the following morning. I went downstairs and could see through the frosted pane of the front door, a man's shape standing outside.

Was this it? I wondered. Yet, they'd hardly shoot me in broad daylight.

'Who is it?'

'Surprise,' the man said, and I knew the voice. I wanted to run, to barricade the door. But I could not.

Mark smiled as I opened the door and allowed him in.

'Welcome home,' I said.

He came towards me, surprising me as he leaned and kissed me on the mouth.

'I've morning breath,' I said, trying to pull away from him.

'I don't mind,' he murmured, kissing me again.

'Mummy,' Hope said, wandering down the stairs, trailing her teddy behind her.

I broke from Mark's embrace and went to her, lifting her and bringing her across, not in the least guilty at using her once more as a shield.

'Say hello to Mark,' I said.

'Hello, Hoppity,' he said, pulling a face which made her giggle, even as his pet name for her rankled with me.

'You got out,' I said.

'I did,' Mark said, smiling. 'They could only make up shit for so long.' He pantomimed shock at the word to Hope, making her laugh, then corrected himself. 'Stuff. Make up stuff.'

'Go get breakfast, kiddo,' I said, setting Hope down. 'What do you want?'

'Pancakes,' she said.

'I'll have some too,' Mark added, as if he was part of our family.

He sat at the table and joked with Hope while I toasted her pancakes and made us tea. When she finished and went to put on her tracksuit for school, Mark moved over next to me at the sink.

'Did you hear about Benny?' he asked.

'I saw him,' I said. 'Last night coming home. It was barbaric.'

'He sold us out,' Mark said. 'He was a tout.'

'He wasn't,' I said. 'And even if he was, he didn't deserve that,' I added, lest my initial comment draw attention to me again.

'He was,' Mark said. He stood behind me and laid his hands on my shoulders. 'I know what happened yesterday. I'm so sorry you had to go through that.'

'That was barbaric too,' I said, turning to face him, forcing him to step back a little. 'They made me strip in front of them.'

'I know,' he said.

'Your fucking brother made me strip,' I hissed again, poking at him as if it were his fault.

'We needed to know who sold us out,' Mark said. 'Leon Burke's phone—'

'I'm fucking sick of Leon Burke's phone,' I snapped. 'I heard all this yesterday.'

'No,' Mark said, moving closer to me, raising his hand as if to cover my mouth until the anger in my expression stayed him. 'Listen. Burke kept his bank card in the back of his phone.'

'I know,' I said.

I realised my mistake even as I said it.

'How?'

'What?'

'How do you know?'

'I mean, I know. People do that. I do that. That's what I mean.'

Mark nodded without comment.

'What of it?'

He raised his chin a little then continued, 'The night he

was hurt, I saw the card in his phone case. I was trying to help him, the poor cub.'

By gluing him together, I thought.

'And?' I said instead.

'The phone the cops showed me didn't have the card in it. Just the phone and case.'

'Maybe they took the card out.'

'I thought that, but it's not the type of thing they'd do.'

'What does that prove?'

'Terry spoke with you, Jamie and Benny yesterday.'

'Spoke?'

'You know what I mean. He was looking out for me. You of all people would understand that.'

I didn't disagree, didn't agree.

'When he was speaking with you three, he had someone check your houses for anything unusual.'

'Like my Christmas savings?'

He smiled, clearly having been told all this by Terry.

'They found Burke's bank card in Benny's house.'

'That's not possible,' I said. It wasn't. I knew the card was in the phone when I hid it and assumed that it was still there when the cops 'found' it.

'It is,' Mark said. 'He must have found it in the rubbish bags the morning you cleaned up, took the card to see if he could empty Leon's account, then arranged with the cops to hide the phone after the party.'

'Why would he? He has a family.'

'All rats have families,' Mark said. 'Family didn't stop him messing around with . . .' He let the comment trail off. 'He was a rat, Katie,' he concluded. 'And rats need to be killed.'

'What about Amy and his kids? She's expecting.'

'His handlers will look after them,' Mark shrugged.

'I still don't believe it.'

'He admitted it.'

I was shocked at the certainty with which Mark said it.

'He admitted working with the police?' I asked, incredulous.

Mark nodded. 'Now, get ready. I want to take you away for the day.'

'Why?'

He shrugged. 'The bar is closed as a "mark of respect" to the rat's family. I thought we could head to Donegal for a drive. We'll leave Hope at school and Ann can collect her.'

'No,' I said. 'I need to be back to get her. It's been too disruptive recently.' Whatever spark of attraction I had felt for Mark, the events of the previous day had changed my view on things. Still, I knew I needed to play nice and walk a tightrope, keeping both Black-Hair and Mark happy, even as I tried to work out a way to get myself out of this situation. 'She's not been sleeping well,' I added, lying. 'Nightmares.'

He considered this briefly, then nodded. 'Okay. I'll have you back in time to collect her. So, scoot. We need to get going.'

I went upstairs, got Hope washed, then washed and dressed myself while she padded back down to watch TV and wait with Mark.

I could hear the voices from the room below, the laughter. Mark's voice, low and soft, as if he had not seen people killed, had people killed.

When I came back down, he and Hope were standing near the door, both looking sheepish.

'What's going on?' I asked. Hope giggled and Mark looked at her, smiling.

'Nothing,' he said. 'Shall we go? Who wants a lift to school?'

'Me!' Hope shouted, raising her hand, as Mark ushered her out the door and I trailed after them.

After we dropped Hope off, Mark drove us over the border. For an absurd moment, I wondered if he was going to turn up towards Grianán, but he didn't. Instead, we went down onto the nearby Inch Island, a small bird sanctuary in Lough Swilly, which was connected by a roadway to the mainland.

He drove to the edge of the island and parked up at the shoreline, then suggested we take a walk on the beach. I could not dismiss what he had said about Benny, that he had admitted working with the police. Had he actually said that? Or had he been so beaten by Terry and Flood after the finding of the bank card that he admitted anything just to make them stop? Or, worse still, had he said it to protect me? The thought spiralled into panic, and I felt I couldn't catch my breath.

'Are you okay?' Mark asked.

'Just out of puff,' I said.

He put his arm around me as we walked and, when I shuddered at his touch, offered me his coat, mistaking my fear for cold. I wondered at how one body could house someone who was such a gentleman in his treatment of me and yet also someone who let a teenager die, who was prepared to sell drugs in our city and murder those who would try to prevent him or, at the very least, turn a blind eye to his brother doing so. The most shocking element of it all was how ordinary he was. I'd told Hope stories about monsters and trolls under bridges, and we'd laughed as we'd tried to make them sound as horrid as possible. But the truth was, the monsters look just like us.

'Hope's great,' Mark said.

'She is,' I agreed. It seemed a safe enough topic to discuss.

'I don't take it for granted, you letting me get to know her,' he added. 'You know how much family means to me.'

I grunted noncommittally, thinking again about how his family had treated me the previous day.

'You know, the cops were loading it on me pretty hard,' he said.

'What's going to happen?'

'We're going to take care of it,' he said. 'There's one of them's been leaning on us for years. Me and Tel are going to take care of it.'

'How?'

'We've our ways,' he said. 'They're trying to pin Burke on me, the fuckers. Someone needs to answer for Leon, apparently.'

'He *was* just a kid, I suppose,' I said.

'He was a junkie,' Mark said. 'He was using half of what he sold and got away with it for months. It was only a matter of time before it caught up with him.'

He stared out over the water, as if he had just said something very profound.

'Does it not bother you?' I asked. 'Selling drugs.'

'I don't sell drugs,' he said, looking at me.

'You know what I mean,' I said. 'Doing whatever it is you do. Like those two girls. Doesn't that bother you?'

'I grew up in the bar,' he said. 'Tel and me ran a gym for a while, but the bar is our lives. Our old man owned it before us.'

'That's not—' I began, but he cut me off.

'You asked me a personal question. Let me answer it.'

I nodded, a little afraid that I had angered him.

'Your old man drank himself to death in our place, you know that?'

I nodded, shocked at the seeming cruelty of the comment, then realised that he had not intended it as such. 'Dad kept selling him drink, even though he knew it was bad for him. I used to ask him why; your da was a legend, so why was he doing it? You know what my old man said?'

I shook my head, more upset than I had expected by him talking about my dad. He'd died when I was too young to *really* know who he was, to the city. I knew now, too late for him to see my pride in him.

'He said, "He can drink himself to death on the street, or he can do it in here in front of a fire with his friends round him. Which would be better? Because one way or the other, that man is drinking himself to the grave."'

'He needed help.'

'Of course he did. But he wouldn't have taken it even if it was given to him. I saw him rage when Dad told him he couldn't serve him. And he ended up drinking on the walls with the winos anyway. It's just the same now.'

'How?'

'People want to snort shit, shag someone, do whatever it is they want to do, they'll find a way to do it. It's not my job to tell someone what they do is right or wrong, no more than I'd tell someone in the bar they should or shouldn't drink. People want something and they will get it one way or the other. If we weren't supplying the town, someone of a different persuasion would be and the money would be going somewhere else. We invest in the city. We employ people here. We look after our community.'

He was convinced by his own argument, proud of his civic-mindedness.

'We're all just paying off our mortgages,' he said. 'You think fuckers in banks and politics aren't at the same? Taking shortcuts to make themselves comfortable.'

'Was Leon Burke not just taking a shortcut then? Using what he was selling?'

Mark chuckled. 'Take all the shortcuts you want. But not through my garden.'

'I feel sorry for him,' I said. 'And for Benny. He was a decent man.'

'A decent man?'

'He was. He cared about people.'

'Balls. All that caring about people is a load of balls. You care about your family and that's all.'

'It's not.'

'Do you see that bus?' Mark said, pointing towards the mainland where a red bus trundled its way towards town.

'What about it?'

'Do you see if that bus went off the road now and went in the water? It wouldn't affect you or me in the slightest.

We'd try to help the people on it, but if they died, it wouldn't matter to us. Not really. We'd still be alive. Still here. Nothing would have changed. We're all just . . . cattle in the field. Do you think the other cows mourn when one of them gets served on a plate?'

'How can you live like that?' I was horrified.

'What? You think other people feel things? People posting their shit on social media; thoughts and prayers. It's virtue signalling. We're animals, that's all. People are just glad it's not them and then they can move on.'

'Do you not have feelings for anyone?'

'My family. I'd die for Tel and Ann. I'd kill for them without a second thought. They mean something.'

I stared at the water for I could think of nothing else to say.

'And I have feelings for you,' he added. 'I have had for ages.'

He pulled me tighter to him.

'Mark, I . . .'

'Don't let me down, Katie,' he said. 'I've been let down by someone I cared about before. I've trusted you with everything now.'

He leaned down and kissed me, pulling me in tighter as his hand snaked up my sweater, groping me.

'Please stop,' I said.

He moved back from me, staring at me now.

'Are you taking the piss? You've been leading me on for weeks.'

'I've not, Mark,' I said. 'I just . . . with everything yesterday and that, I need time to think about this. It's all been so fast.'

'When you know what you want, you go after it,' he said. 'I want you, Katie. I thought you felt the same way.'

I was aware that my phone, the new phone, was in my pocket and guessed that Black-Hair would be listening. If he knew I had had a chance to get closer to Mark, to have him admit everything to me, and turned it down, I could only guess what punishment he would contrive next. And yet, I also felt sick at the thought of being with Mark, of sleeping with him and sharing my daughter, my life with him.

'I just need time to think,' I said. 'I like you, too, Mark. I just . . . I've been burned in the past, people taking advantage of me. Hope's dad, for one.'

'And the rat?' Mark said.

'I just . . . I need to take things slowly,' I said. 'Even for Hope. It's not fair introducing people to her and then taking them out of her life again. She needs stability.'

'I understand that,' Mark said. 'But believe me, I am not going anywhere if that's your worry.'

I smiled. 'Give me time,' I said, taking his hand in mine.

He kissed me once more, more gently this time.

'That's fair,' he said.

We walked along the beach, me feeling increasingly like a hostage of my own making. On the way back, we stopped at a bar for lunch. Outside, he took a picture of the two of us on his phone and I felt I had to do likewise on mine.

'I want to get a picture of you,' he said. 'Just on your own.'

I pushed my hair from my face. 'I'm a bit rough-looking,' I said.

'Not to me,' he said. He moved me across to stand at the whitewashed wall of the pub and took a few pictures, telling me to smile, not to smile, to pout. I felt like I was being made to perform for something and I did not know what.

Not then, at least.

## Chapter Thirty-Five

I left Hope's curtains pulled closed all day, hoping that Black-Hair would still be watching. I sat with the phone he had given me, saying into the handset, 'I need to speak to you,' over and over, not even aware of whether they were listening in or not. I messaged the number on which he had messaged me, then panicked in case someone would find it and deleted it again.

Finally, when I did meet him, it was not where I had expected. Hope and I took a walk into town, primarily because the house was too quiet and would not let me drown out my own thoughts.

I wanted to get a gift for my mum and went into the chemists to look for perfume. Hope was at the end of the next aisle, sifting through toys, when I heard a voice that I recognised next to me.

'This stuff's got so dear, hasn't it?'

I turned, shocked to see Black-Hair standing there.

'Great to see you, Katie,' he said as he leaned in and gave me a brief hug. 'What's up?' he whispered.

'Benny,' I managed, pulling away from him.

'Not the place for that, Katie,' he said. 'What have you got for me?'

I wasn't going to have him dictate what I could ask. 'Was he working with you?'

'I can't—'

'Did that happen because of me?'

'No,' he said, as if genuinely concerned that I might think so. 'He was a big boy. Made big boy choices.' He glanced around as he spoke, smiling mildly at someone who must have glanced in our direction. 'It's sad,' he said, a little louder now. 'Taken too young.'

'How did he have Burke's card?' I hissed. 'Did you give it to him?'

'So, what's the craic anyway?' he said. 'Any gossip?'

'Why? Why did you do that?'

'I suppose some people are more valuable to the firm than others,' he said. 'He wasn't providing any service that you couldn't, so he had to be let go. And now, with your promotion, I suppose you're even more valuable. PA to the boss? That must be a thrill. Congratulations.'

I knew what he was doing, speaking in such a way that anyone overhearing might consider us simply work colleagues, but the clinical way he could justify Benny's death frightened me.

'You're starting to sound like my boss. He said something similar about not really caring about other people.'

Black-Hair shrugged. 'Is that all you wanted?'

'Did you know what happened to me the other day?'

'Your job interview? I'm sure it was gruelling.'

'Are you fucking mad?'

'We helped you out as best we could in the run-up,' he said. 'You'll be getting a bonus for your promotion, too. So, it's brilliant news all round. We're all delighted for you.'

'What about Amy and her kids?'

'Anyway, good to see you,' he said, and turned to go.

I put out my hand and stopped him. 'My boss says they're moving forward on that new target.'

'Did he say that?'

'Just that they were going to take care of things. He was pissed off about what happened to him.'

He laughed. 'I'm sure he was. That's good to know. Anyway, best get going.'

He hugged me again, quickly, and hissed, 'Record a voice memo on your phone in future. Leave it an hour, then delete it.'

Black-Hair separated from me and nodded. 'I'll see you about, sure,' he said, then strolled down the aisle, stopping to admire a bottle of aftershave.

I replayed the conversation in my head, though still could not determine whether he had planted the card on Benny to put suspicion on him. 'He had to be let go,' he had said. Did that mean Benny *had* been informing on the O'Reillys? Mark said he'd admitted it. If that was the case, had Black-Hair sacrificed Benny to keep me alive? I wondered whether there was any other way I could know for sure that Benny had been working with them. Would he have told Amy? I'd told Mum about them contacting me. Would Benny have told his wife? Would she have wondered where the extra money was coming from in the house?

I was more valuable than him, Black-Hair had said. The boss's PA. They knew what was happening and were happy to allow me to be dragged into a relationship with

Mark because they believed it would give them better intelligence.

Is that all people had become? Value and nothing more?

And while I was valuable now, what would happen when they got someone who had access further up the ladder? Would they sacrifice me the same way they had Benny?

## Chapter Thirty-Six

The next week passed without incident. I came to work earlier in the mornings to avoid seeing Terry and, I suspect, he was steering clear of me, too. I'd not spoken to him since the interrogation in the furniture warehouse and had no interest in doing so.

I tried to attend Benny's wake, partly to ease my guilt, but was stopped at the door by a relative of Amy's who knew me. Amy had made it clear she did not want me there, nor would I be welcome at the funeral.

'The kindest thing you can do now is leave this family alone,' the woman said. 'Amy suffered enough with you and Benny.'

The blame that I felt over his death had to be outweighed by respecting Amy's wishes and so I stayed away.

Mark took me out for dinner twice during that week. On the first occasion, he did not press things with me as he dropped me home. The second night was different.

'Will I come in?' he asked, cutting off the engine and removing the keys from the ignition.

'Best not,' I said. 'It's a school night.'

'Every night's a school night,' he muttered.

'I know,' I said. 'But Hope doesn't deal well with disruption to her routine.'

'You could come to mine,' he said.

I shook my head.

'Why not?' he snapped and I saw, for a second, a hint of the anger which had left Mickey lying in a bloody mess on the floor of the kitchen in the bar.

'I'm on my period,' I said, a bald lie but one which I hoped he'd accept.

'I don't mind,' he said.

'I do. It hurts.'

'We could do other things,' he said, and in that moment, I was sitting in a car with a teenage boyfriend again, whining for something, anything to take the edge off him.

'Not tonight, Mark. You said you'd give me time.'

'I've given you time,' he said. 'All we seem to do is I give and you take.'

'I didn't—'

'I'm speaking!'

I was so taken aback that it took me a second to respond.

'Don't raise your voice at me,' I said, opening the door.

He grabbed my arm, pulling me back into the car.

'I don't like having someone take the piss out of me,' he said. 'It's not going to happen.'

'Let go of me.'

'You fucked Benny,' he spat.

'And that's why I'm being careful now,' I said. 'Let go of my hand.'

'When then? If not now?'

'Never, if you don't let go of my hand,' I said, thinking I had the advantage here.

Instead, he reached across suddenly and gripped my face, his thick hand covering my mouth.

'Don't fuck me off, Katie,' he said. 'I swear to God, don't fuck me off.'

'You're hurting me,' I mumbled.

'Don't,' he repeated. 'Do you hear me?'

I couldn't breathe, his hand wedged tight to my face. I could feel panic rising, my head dizzy, my chest heaving.

'Do you hear me?'

I nodded, terrified that Hope or my mum would be watching from the house.

'Say it,' he said, loosening his hand enough for me to catch my breath a little. 'Say it.'

'I hear you.'

'What are you not going to do?'

'Not fuck you off,' I repeated, mechanically, ready to say anything to get out of that car.

'Good girl,' he said. His expression softened. 'I don't want to hurt you, Katie. I really don't.'

I considered arguing back, pointing out that it had been his choice to grab me, but there was no point. The last thing I needed to do was enrage him.

'But you can't keep being a prick-tease. Fucking Benny and then going on like you're a virgin with me. That's not fair.'

I can do what I like, I thought. But I simply nodded.

'I'll tell you what we'll do,' he said, his voice suddenly gentle. 'I'm going to book us a surprise. Something to get us away from here for a while. And if your bleeding has stopped, we can make it special. Romantic. Okay?'

I nodded to keep him happy. I needed to get away from him, once and for all.

Mum stayed over with us that night, seeming to sense my uneasiness even though I did not tell her what had happened. I did not want to worry her, nor did I need her to tell me that I had to get Mark out of my life as quickly as possible. I knew that already. *How* I could do it was the issue. I knew that Black-Hair and English could make life difficult for me if I didn't take advantage of my closeness to Mark to feed them information. I also suspected Mark would not react well to being dumped. I'd seen him violent before, as in the bar, but this was different. I'd always thought he was respectful of women, in fact had told myself that his violence in the kitchen with Flood's man was evidence of just that. But his dismissal of the fate of the two girls in the bar at Flood's party, his temper in the car? Was that what happened to Leah Duffy? Yet, Mark had been in France when she was assaulted.

Thinking of her, I transferred my SIM into my old handset and logged on to Facebook, determined to try to track down someone who might have known her. I hoped that, if I did, perhaps they could explain what had happened and whether her relationship with Mark had resulted in the violence she'd suffered.

I was surprised then to see a reply to my message to Leah's friend, Catherine O'Neill. She'd been on holidays and had only checked the business account on her return. She'd closed up shop and worked from clients' homes now. She could do a house call the following morning if I wanted my hair done.

I did.

# Chapter Thirty-Seven

Catherine was due to call around 10 a.m. I'd taken my new phone and put it out in the back garden, hoping that doing so would keep it far enough from us that if Black-Hair was listening in, he would not hear me ask about Leah.

In the end, she was early, marching up the pathway to my door at 9.45. She was in her late twenties, pretty, confident, her skin glowing, not a hair out of place.

'Katie,' she said, coming in, pulling a small, wheeled cabin bag behind her. 'Good to meet you, love. Your house is lovely.'

It wasn't, but I appreciated her saying so.

'What do you want done today, then?' she asked, already setting out her accessories.

'I'd hoped to talk to you about Leah Duffy,' I said.

She stopped what she was doing and began repacking her things. 'I'm working,' she said.

'I'll pay.'

'Are you a journalist?'

I shook my head. 'Why?'

'I've had a few over the years. Bloody vampires, looking to write books about Leah. True crime freaks.'

'No. I'm not that. I'm with someone at the moment and I've heard Leah's name in connection with him.'

She straightened up and looked at me.

'Who?'

'Mark O'Reilly.'

Her expression did not change, but she moved to start packing things up even quicker.

'I've nothing to say about Leah. I don't know who that man is.'

'Catherine, please,' I said. 'Look.'

I had deliberately taken off the concealer I'd applied first thing, once Hope and Mum were gone, so that the bruises he'd left on my face were visible. 'He did this to me,' I said.

'I don't know what you're talking about.' She closed her bag. 'You shouldn't book people under false pretences.'

I was distracted by my phone ringing. It was Mark. I declined the call, eager not to have Catherine leave.

'Please, wait a second,' I said. 'I just want to ask—'

The phone rang again. Mark. Again I declined.

'I've other clients to see,' Catherine said, moving towards the door just behind me.

'Please,' I said, moving ahead of her. 'Please give me a second.'

'I need to go.'

Another ring. I turned off the handset completely and followed Catherine to where she was fumbling with the door handle.

'Please, Catherine,' I said. 'I've got involved with him against my wishes. A friend told me to find Leah Duffy but didn't say why. Now he's dead.'

Catherine stared at me, but at least she allowed me to speak. 'I'm sorry about your friend. I don't know what you want from me.'

'Nor do I. I just . . . I know she was with Mark and I know something bad happened to her. I suppose I was wondering if the two things were connected.'

She laughed mirthlessly.

'I just need to know what I've been dragged into. I don't want to be with him. I think he's dangerous.'

'He always was,' Catherine said. And with that comment, I knew she would tell me about Leah.

I told her I would pay her for her time, having booked her, but instead she insisted on cutting my hair while we talked; that was why she was here after all. Perhaps she felt more comfortable chatting in that way than sitting face to face with someone she did not know. For my part, it meant if Mark landed at the door, wondering why I wasn't answering the phone, I'd have a good excuse.

'Leah met him in the gym, I think. She said he came on to her pretty strong. At the start she was a bit creeped out, but she said he was really decent. Kind with her. And when one of the other guys tried it on with her one night, Mark beat the living shit out of him.'

I nodded. 'I've been there. He did the same with someone who was hassling me.'

'Did you like it?'

'No!' I said, not wholly truthful.

'Leah did,' Catherine said. 'Sadly. She thought it was really noble. Like he was standing up for her. Protecting her.'

'So she agreed to go out with him?'

Catherine nodded. 'She said she didn't think it could hurt. Then when they started dating, she really liked him.

He was a real gentleman, she said. Opening doors for her, taking her out to dinner, buying her treats.'

'Did she know what he did?'

Catherine shrugged. 'He ran a gym and his family owned a bar. He had money, like. She fell for him, to be honest. And she introduced him to us, her friends. She was so excited about us all meeting up. But when he arrived, he was nothing like the person she'd described. He was pig ignorant. When any of us girls tried to talk to him, he came across like he was bored, like we were asking stupid questions. We knew he was a bit older than us anyway and put it down to that, but he came across as a prick.'

'Did you tell Leah that?'

'Aye right. Who'd thank you for telling them their new boyfriend is an asshole? We hoped she'd find out. But they just seemed to become closer. She started cancelling nights out with us. I'd only get to see her if I called unexpectedly. But try to arrange something in advance and it was all, "I think I'm out with Mark that night." Eventually, when it was all over, she told me that he'd made her give up her friends, but in a sneaky way. Like if she said she was thinking about meeting some of us, he'd suddenly produce tickets for something he'd booked for them for that night, or he'd tell her he'd planned something and could she change her plans. He never told her not to see us, but he made sure she didn't. And then, we stopped bothering asking her to come out with us for the most part.'

'So, what happened?'

'Her and me had a row over him. It was my birthday and we'd arranged to go out and Leah never even called. I'd had a few drinks and called at hers afterwards to rid my guts to her. I could see she'd been crying. She'd bruises on her neck where he'd throttled her during sex. She'd told him to stop, and he hadn't. I wanted her to tell her brother, but she was afraid, said Mark told her he was sorry, that he got carried away. She even tried to tell me she'd enjoyed it, but I knew. She was scared of him. I told her I was going to tell Alex if she didn't.'

'Was Alex her brother?'

Catherine nodded. 'And at training college to be a cop. I told her she needed to break up with him or I'd tell Alex myself. So she broke it off. A week later, she took him back and they were strong as ever.'

'Did you tell her brother?'

'No,' she said, the regret clear. 'I threw a hissy fit and decided she could get what she deserved. She fell out with me because I was the one who told her to break it off. Said Mark didn't want her to see me. I'd only met him a handful of times, so I don't know how he knew I was a bad influence. I think Leah must have been reporting back to him everything I said. Blaming me for the break-up instead of herself.'

'Was that the last time you saw her?'

'No. She arrived at my door one evening, late, in pieces. He'd beaten her. Really done a number on her. She didn't want her family to know and had nowhere else to go. So she stayed with me.'

'Why didn't she want her family knowing?'

'She thought Alex would go after him. And by that stage, she must have had an idea what the O'Reillys were like. She was worried that Alex would be shot if he got involved. She stayed with me for four days.'

'Did Mark try to contact her?'

'He tried to call, but she didn't answer, and he didn't know where I lived, so I think she thought she was safe. I suggested she get out of the place for a while, go on holidays or move away for a bit to escape him, but she couldn't. He'd told her he wanted to take her somewhere nice and had got her passport off her to book the flights. He never gave it back to her. On day five, she answered the call and told him they were done. She'd no interest in seeing him and wanted nothing to do with him. She'd taken photographs of what he had done to her and warned him she'd send them to the police if he came near her.'

'Had she?'

Catherine nodded and when I looked, I realised she was crying. She took out her phone and after a moment's scrolling, handed it to me. I scrolled through a series of images of Leah, stripped to her underwear, showing the bruising all along her ribs and shoulders, the back of her neck, her face, one eye closed shut, her lip split. I felt sick.

'Why did he do it?'

'She'd bumped into a lad she knew in the restaurant they were in. The guy had hugged her when they met. Mark was raging. Accused her of cheating on him, shagging this lad behind his back, the whole thing.'

'What happened when she told him it was over?'

'He begged her, told her he'd booked for them to go to some competition he and his brother were in the following month in France. A romantic weekend away, all that bullshit. She said no. And she heard nothing more from him. That was it.'

'Until?'

'Until the weekend he'd booked for them to go, she went out with us to a club, just on principle, like. We all hooked up with someone except her. I told her to get a taxi home with me and the fella I was with, but she said no. Her house was like a three-minute walk out of town. You could see the light at the front of it from the taxi rank. So, she walked.'

Catherine did not speak for a moment as she gathered herself. Her tears slipped freely now.

'And that was that. Someone attacked her along the roadway and threw acid on her face. They never spoke, didn't threaten her or mention anyone. Just quiet. Punched her to the ground and poured acid on her.'

She took the phone from me and scrolled through again until she showed me a different image: Leah after the attack. The skin on the left-hand side of her face had been melted back and was red and raw. Her right eye was milky, her lip swollen at one side and thinned to nothing on the other.

'Jesus Christ,' I said. 'The poor girl. Was nobody charged?'

'No. The O'Reillys were in a different country when it happened. Mark was brought in for questioning when he came back, but his solicitor had him out in hours. Leah decided she didn't want to press charges and told me to delete the pictures of her injuries.'

'Why?'

'She was afraid something would happen to her family if she reported him. She made me swear not to.'

'She didn't tell her brother what had happened? About Mark, I mean?'

She shook her head. 'But he knew, I think.'

'Where's Leah now?'

'They've all gone,' Catherine said. 'She moved away. The last I knew, she was in Singapore or somewhere, teaching. Her mum and dad both passed away. Alex moved on too. The last I heard, he was up around Belfast somewhere.'

'The whole family destroyed.'

Catherine nodded. 'All because of that scumbag. That's Leah there with her folks,' she added. 'In happier times.'

She showed me another image, this time taken at a wedding, of Leah and her family. Leah was stunning looking, wearing a bridesmaid's dress, but she was not the one who caught my attention. Instead, it was the young man next to her, smiling at the camera, his black hair cut neatly.

'Who is he?' I asked. 'That man there. Who is he?'

But I already knew the answer.

'That's Alex,' Catherine said. 'Do you know him?'

I did. Not as Alex though.

It was Black-Hair.

## Chapter Thirty-Eight

Black-Hair was Alex Duffy, Leah's brother. I understood now his determination to get Mark O'Reilly, to make him pay for what had been done to his sister. In chasing his obsession, he had been as controlling with me as Mark had been. Still, for perhaps the first time since he and English had cornered me in the elevator the morning after Gail's wedding, I felt like I was a step ahead. I knew something now, something I felt I could use, even though I was unsure how quite yet.

Something else Catherine had said still irked me. Mark had taken Leah's passport. After Ann had searched my home on the day they'd interrogated me, I'd not thought to check if anything else was missing. Now I did.

I kept my and Hope's passports in the cupboard in the kitchen, where Ann had found the envelope of cash which Black-Hair – Alex Duffy – had given to me. I knew she'd been there; Terry had asked about the envelope after all. I went straight back to the kitchen after Catherine left and took everything out of the cabinet.

The passports were gone.

I asked Mum to stay in ours with Hope that evening. Mark had already said he was taking me to dinner and for once, I wanted to see him, determined to get to the truth. I reckoned that he'd be less likely to want to come back to mine after dinner if he thought my mum was there and if he tried to force me to go to his, I could claim I needed to let Mum get home and so come back to Hope.

He collected me around 7.

'Your hair's lovely,' he said. 'Very nice.'

Catherine had cut it up short, exposing the back of my neck and Mark laid his hand there now, rubbing the skin with his broad fingers.

'Very sexy,' he said.

He'd had his own hair trimmed too, though out of pettiness, I said nothing about it. I wanted to ask him about the passports there and then, but his proximity to me, in the car, reminded me of how easily he had grabbed me the previous evening and I decided to wait until we were in public to challenge him.

The restaurant he'd booked for us was a new bistro that had opened a few weeks earlier. The décor was deliberately run-down, with mismatched kitchen chairs at a table that looked to have been made from the remains of an old door. The prices were ridiculous and the menu almost unreadable.

'It's lovely, isn't it?' Mark asked when we sat, perhaps annoyed that I hadn't already volunteered the compliment on his choice. 'Romantic.'

'Will we order? I'm hungry.'

'Give it a minute,' he said, glancing round, and I suddenly sensed that he had arranged something. Was he going to do something mad like propose? I looked around, trying to gauge the quickest way out when Terry appeared in the doorway, all smiles and hellos to the staff and some customers sitting at the table there.

I felt Mark's hand on mine and realised he was holding me at the table. 'I asked Terry to join us,' Mark said. 'I want you two to get on and you've not spoken since the whole mess over Benny.'

'Let go of me,' I said.

Mark leaned forward, smiling through gritted teeth. 'Just sit in that fucking seat and be pleasant to my brother. Do you hear me?'

'Let go.'

He leaned in closer, as if we were sharing an intimate moment. 'If you walk out of here, by fuck you'll not walk again. Now be nice.'

By the time he let go of me, Terry had already reached the table. He stood behind me, his hands resting on my shoulder, kneading gently.

'Katie, you're looking well, love,' he said and, leaning down, kissed me on the cheek. I could smell the alcohol on his breath already. 'Good to see you again,' he said before straightening up and, moving across, embracing his brother lightly. He looked around the place: 'This is some set-up, eh, Marky?' he said.

I got the sense he was performing, every gesture big, noticeable. I wondered whether he was feeling nervous about seeing me and this was his way of covering it up, but that didn't strike me as typical of Terry. I suspected he didn't give a shit about me or what he had done to me.

He sat down opposite and smiled at me. 'We all good, Katie?'

I could feel Mark's glare and knew what was expected.

'Yeah. All good, Terry.'

Mark noticeably relaxed next to me and the tension, like a held breath, was slowly released.

'That's the girl,' he said. 'What's good to eat here?'

And that was it. His strip-searching and interrogating me was forgotten, as if a minor falling-out, easily resolved over expensive chicken curry.

Terry ordered a bottle of wine and, having polished it off, moved on to his second. Mark, too, had eased into the evening, though the conversation was mostly small talk. Whatever he had said about it being romantic, it was anything but. And that suited me fine. I could do small talk, had years of experience behind the bar dealing with drunk men who mistook friendliness for attraction and the fixity of a server's smile for a come-on.

Our waitress had just cleared away the main course dishes when I decided Mark was chilled enough for me to challenge him.

'My passports are missing,' I said simply, studying his face to see how he might react.

'Oh aye?' he said, glancing at Terry.

'Since the day of all that bullshit,' I added. 'When Ann was there.'

I was ready to see both men react with fury at the thought I was accusing their sister of stealing my things. Instead, Mark smiled sheepishly, and Terry shook his head.

'I have them,' Mark said, smiling at me.

'Why have you my and Hope's passports?' I asked, raising my voice a little until Mark growled me quiet again.

'You have to spoil everything, don't you?' Mark snapped.

'You have my daughter's passport,' I hissed. 'How did you think I'd react?'

'I thought you'd wait until I explained why,' Mark said, seemingly wounded by my impatience.

'Okay. So why?'

Mark glanced at Terry again and smiled. 'I've booked us a wee trip away like I said I would.'

I thought I was going to be sick. 'Where?'

'Spain!' Terry said. 'Marbella. You're going this Friday.'

'This weekend? In three days' time?'

Terry nodded.

'Are you going too?' I asked, my first thought fear of being stuck abroad with both O'Reillys.

'No. Just the three of us,' Mark said.

'What three?'

'You, me and Hope,' he explained, chuckling. 'A wee family trip.'

'We're not a family,' I said and watched hurt and anger flicker in his eyes.

'I'd like us to be,' he said.

'You've your work cut out for you there, lad,' Terry said to his brother, gesturing towards me with his half-empty glass.

'I don't want Hope going.'

'Why not? She likes me,' Mark argued.

I couldn't tell him the truth, that I wanted to keep her as far from him as possible.

'She has school.'

'We don't leave until late,' he countered. 'Has she ever been abroad?'

She had been, once. Mum took the three of us to Disneyland in Paris the previous summer. We'd even stayed in one of the hotels so Hope could meet the characters during breakfast. Mum told me one morning that she had secretly hoped that she and Dad could have brought me when I was young and the place had first opened, but it never happened. Still, I got to experience something of the childhood wonder of the place through Hope's responses to it all. It seemed a lifetime ago now, a world apart.

'We need her to go,' Terry said.

'You *need* my daughter to go to Spain?'

He nodded, the wine having eased his tongue. 'They tend not to check kids' suitcases,' he said.

So that was it: Mark was going to Marbella for drugs. And he was using me and Hope as cover.

'All the children in the world won't hide that you're Mark O'Reilly,' I said. 'You think the cops don't know who you are?'

I glanced at Terry and silently cursed myself for doing so, for he caught my look and stared at me, bemused.

'I'm not Mark O'Reilly,' Mark said.

'What?'

'I'm John Porter. And you and Hope are . . .' He reached into his jacket pocket and pulled out two passports that he opened and showed to me. 'Hannah and Hope Porter.'

I looked at the passports he'd presented to me. My picture and Hope's, but neither of our names.

'What the fuck is that?'

I recognised the pictures now. The one of me had been taken outside the pub, the day he'd insisted on taking shots against the whitewashed wall, my expression unsmiling. Hope's was taken recently too. I pointed at it. 'Was that taken in my house?'

He nodded, smiling at his own cleverness.

I remembered now when he had called. He and Hope had seemed to share a private joke when I came down from changing and I knew now what: he had taken her picture without my knowledge.

'You don't think this is all a bit creepy, Mark? Making my daughter a fake passport?'

He seemed genuinely disappointed in my response.

'I thought you'd be happy,' he said. 'I've arranged everything.'

'You're using my daughter as a drug mule and you thought I'd be happy?' I asked, rising, and noticed some of the other diners glance towards us.

His hand shot across and gripped mine. He squeezed tight, trying to hurt me.

'Let go of my hand,' I said, louder than necessary.

'Shut the fuck up,' Terry said. 'You're overreacting.'

Mark had stood now too and was comforting me, as if I was upset, even as he guided me to my seat again. Those around us, presumably recognising the O'Reillys, had turned back to their meals.

'She's not your kid,' I said. 'I'm not putting her at risk.'

'She won't be at risk,' Terry said. 'A new friend of ours has created some business potential for us in Spain. We're taking over some gifts to sweeten the deal; nothing illegal. That's all.'

'You won't be involved,' Mark said. 'I'll go and do whatever I have to do, and you and Hope can stay in the hotel, use the pool, do whatever you want. I've booked us into a four-star.'

'You'll be paid for your efforts,' Terry said disdainfully.

'I don't want paid,' I said.

Mark took back the passports and slid over an envelope to me. 'Two grand now and three when we come home,' he said.

'I don't want paid,' I repeated, shoving it back towards him.

'Is everything okay?' the waitress said, approaching the table warily.

'All good, love,' Terry said, glancing at his watch. 'Can you throw us down the bill?'

'You'll have a good time, Katie,' Mark said. 'And Hope will have a ball. I'd never put either of you in danger.'

I'd heard Black-Hair promise something similar. We were in danger no matter what we did, but I couldn't say that.

'Where did you get the fake passports?' I asked.

'An old guy I know,' he said. 'Creeps around graveyards, picking names of people who died when they was babies. He's a weirdo but he does good work.'

I suspected I knew who he meant too: Kenneth, with his tombstone rubbings and family trees.

I felt my phone buzz but when I checked it, there were no new notifications and I began to question whether I'd imagined it, the handset weighing like a guilty secret in my pocket.

'It's nine,' Terry said, out of nowhere and Mark nodded. 'I'll pay the bill.'

As Terry went to the counter to pay, Mark and I stood.

'I'm glad you and Tel are getting on,' Mark said. 'I want you all to be friends.'

'He strip-searched me,' I muttered.

'Jesus, let it go,' Mark snapped. 'Just fucking drop it now, would you? He trusts you. He's sending you to Marbella, isn't he?'

*He's sending.* I'd always considered Terry the crueller of the pair but thought Mark to be smarter. Yet, in that moment, it was clear who ran things.

'I'll see you tomorrow evening, okay?' Mark said.

'I'm seeing my mum,' I said.

'Afterwards?'

'I'll be getting packed,' I said.

'Thursday evening, then?'

Terry cleared his throat pointedly. 'You're busy that night. We've that appointment in Belfast with the big man.'

'Can't Floody do it?'

Terry shook his head. 'The man wants to see the organ grinders, not the monkey.'

Mark rolled his eyes, out of his brother's line of sight. 'So, are we good for Friday, then?' he asked.

I nodded, not wanting to speak because to do so would seem to make it a firm agreement. One that I had no intention of keeping. After the events at Flood's party, I'd decided that Mark was clearly dangerous, but just not to me. Now I could see that I was wrong. If I annoyed him, there was no reason why he wouldn't have me attacked just as he had Leah Duffy. I had to get away from him and in a way that meant Hope, Mum and I would still be safe.

\* \* \*

I assumed Terry would go his own way after we left the bistro but instead he walked alongside us towards Mark's car. Mark had taken my hand, as if we were two lovers strolling along the street.

When we reached the car, Terry climbed in the front passenger seat and waited. Mark stood with me for a moment and kissed me.

'This break will be good for us,' he said. 'Your thing will be done by then, won't it?'

'I . . . I don't know.'

'As good as,' he said. 'I've booked two connected rooms, so Hope can have a room to herself and can still come into us in the morning if she wants to.'

I was so taken aback by his planning, I did not speak for a moment, which he mistook as my agreement.

'I can't wait,' he whispered, opening the rear passenger door for me, the inside dark and filled with dread.

I was surprised, and a little relieved, to find that rather than dropping Terry off first, Mark drove straight to my house and, when he stopped outside, left the engine idling.

'Enjoy Spain if I don't see you,' Terry called as I stepped out of the car.

'I'll see you tomorrow,' Mark said as he walked me to the door. 'In work.'

Before I could speak, he kissed me once more and then headed back to the car.

Mum was still up when I got in and glanced at her watch when she saw me coming. 'You're home early,' she said.

'I know,' I said, trying to work out why. I couldn't help

but feel there was something I had missed. Something important. Terry and Mark should have reacted more to my showing them up in public but they'd both seemed chilled about it. Mark had brought his brother on a romantic dinner with me and then hadn't pressed to come home with me.

Then, just before I went to bed, the first reports came through of a shooting in Claudy just after 8 p.m. And there it was. The reason for the dinner, for Terry's presence, for the performance, for the sudden leaving after 9 p.m. I had been made an alibi for the O'Reillys and a restaurant full of people had seen them with me.

By the following morning, the victim had been named all over Facebook. He was Kevin Shaw, a schoolteacher apparently. The rumour was that the intended target of the attack, his wife, a high-ranking police officer, had escaped injury after her husband stepped between her and the gunman who fired on her.

For some reason, Black-Hair and English had ignored my warnings that Shaw was a target.

# Chapter Thirty-Nine

I recorded a voice message first thing that morning and then left it for an hour before deleting. It simply stated that I needed to speak to someone as soon as possible. Things were reaching a point where I could not go on.

I realised as I listened back to it that it sounded as much a suicide threat as a cry for help. I hoped that Black-Hair – Alex Duffy – would take it in that vein and contact me quickly. And I knew that for him to do so, I needed to be out of the house.

I went in to work and finished cleaning up quite quickly. The bar had been open the previous evening, though must have been quiet for I was done within an hour and got away before Terry or Mark arrived in. Later, I discovered that the police had called with them both that morning and both had offered the same alibi: they were at dinner with me. That no one even bothered coming to question me to confirm this suggested that the police were already aware of it.

I made a point of walking home, expecting that, at some stage, English would pull up alongside me. Sure enough, about ten minutes later, he did. Once more, he drove us to McDonald's, without a word, where Black-Hair was waiting for us. He climbed into the car beside me.

'We got your message,' he said as he passed me back a brown paper bag of fries. 'What's up?'

'Is the news right? That shooting in Claudy. Was it a policewoman called Shaw who was targeted?'

'Nothing happens in this city but the world knows about it,' Black-Hair said.

'I warned you that she was a target,' I said.

'Did you even know *she* was a she?'

'That's not the point,' I said. 'I told you that something was about to happen and Shaw's name had been mentioned.'

'You did,' Black-Hair said. 'And we were very grateful for that information. And you were paid well for it.'

'Why didn't you stop it?'

'It's not that easy, Katie.'

'It is,' I said. 'You knew she was the target. You put a watch on her home and when someone tries to shoot her, you step in, before someone gets killed.'

'Suppose we did,' English said. 'What then? Ross knows we have intel on his operations. He knows he needs to look for an informant. He puts pressure on the O'Reillys to find the leak in their side of things. That leads to you. Or he cuts them adrift and we're back to square one.'

'If she was such an important police officer, surely she would have protection.'

'She did,' Black-Hair said, earning a glance from English.

'You let her husband be murdered.'

'Like I said before, not every foot soldier gets to die in their beds of old age.'

'Did he even know he *was* a foot soldier?' I asked.

'We make operational decisions based on keeping our people safe and keeping channels of information open,' English said. 'That's all you need to know. What happened last night kept you safe. You're welcome.'

'You're not God,' I said. 'You don't get to decide who lives or dies.'

Black-Hair tried to calm things a little. 'What happened last night with Mark and Terry?' he said.

'Mark took me for dinner,' I said. 'Then told me he was taking me and Hope to Marbella at the weekend.'

English looked at me in the rear-view mirror. 'The three of you?'

I nodded. 'Except I'm not going.'

'Yes, you are,' English said. 'That's fantastic.'

'What the fuck are you talking about?' I snapped. 'That's my daughter he's putting at risk.'

'He's not putting anyone at risk,' English said. 'Katie, if you can get us information on who he meets, what's agreed . . . that stuff could take us right up the chain.'

'What chain?'

'The O'Reillys are working for Ross now. He's working for someone in Spain.'

'They're working *with* Ross,' I corrected.

'They may think they're all equals,' English said, 'but Ross doesn't have partners. The O'Reillys are selling what he's bringing in. That's it.'

'They think they're going over to set up a new partnership.'

English laughed. 'That's the problem when people over-estimate their position in the chain of command,' he said.

'I thought Mark and Terry were your targets.'

'They are,' Black-Hair said, and I sensed for the first time a difference in aims between them.

'There's always someone higher in the chain,' English said. 'The O'Reillys can lead us to them.'

'Meanwhile, they keep killing and supplying drugs.'

'If not them, someone else,' English said.

'I'm not going to Spain with Mark,' I said. 'That's it.'

'I understand your concerns, Katie. I do,' Black-Hair said. 'And I'd never ask you to do anything that was putting you at risk. But, ironically, the closer you are to Mark O'Reilly, the safer you are from him. The problems could begin when you refuse to go. How do you think he'd take rejection?'

I knew he was right, not that I would admit it. 'I'm not going. Whatever small pieces of information I might hear aren't worth the risk to Hope.'

'Of course,' Black-Hair said. 'Though if we could get Mark coming back into the country with drugs . . . we could take him off the board for quite a while. That would be you free too, Katie.'

'If he did bring stuff back, he'd be using me and Hope to carry it. I'm not letting that happen.'

'You give evidence against him,' Black-Hair said. 'We get you into witness protection and you can have a fresh start. You and Hope both.'

'I thought Burke's phone was the evidence you needed.'

Black-Hair glanced at English, who said, 'Your prints were all over the phone. His lawyers would challenge it in court. We need more.'

'I don't care. I'm not going.'

'Why not?' English said. 'Is it money?'

'I don't give a shit about money,' I snapped. 'He wants to have sex with me. I'm not going to stay in a hotel with him.'

'Is that it?' English laughed.

Black-Hair read the situation more clearly. 'Katie, I totally respect your right to do what you want with your body. No one's questioning that. You're right.'

I was surprised at his agreement, until he continued.

'Maybe you could string him along until we are able to lift him with product on him.'

'What do you think I've been doing?'

Black-Hair nodded. 'I know. But Katie, this takes us so close. If you were able to do this, to go to Spain with him, it would help countless people. Mark wouldn't be able to wriggle out of it if we have him, at the airport, carrying drugs. And your testimony afterwards would seal the deal. Please.'

'We need you to do this,' English said. 'We'll make sure you're well paid for whatever you can bring back for us.'

'No,' I snapped. 'I want away from the O'Reillys and I want me and Hope and my mum safe. I want a new life for us.'

'Take this trip, get us names and details. We'll get the pair of you out. You have my word on it,' English said. 'I'll see what I can do for your mum.'

'I'm not going to Spain. That's it.'

'Just think about it,' English said. 'You try to get out now, while the O'Reillys are still on the streets, what chance do you have? We can't get you protection when you've not really given us anything.'

'I gave you Burke's phone. I gave you info about Shaw.'

'But not enough to be able to stop what happened,' English said. 'That's the tragedy. Your intel has been piecemeal. Flawed. We can't convince our superiors to cough up money to create a new life for you and your kid for that. But the top men in Spain. That's information worth paying for.'

'I'm not going,' I repeated.

'As I said, think about it. We'll be in touch tomorrow. Okay? I think that will do us for today.'

Black-Hair nodded and, leaning over, offered to take my untouched bag of food from me.

'Are you finished with that?'

'I'm not hungry,' I said, then added quietly, 'Alex.'

The reaction was immediate. He stared at me and I knew he'd heard. I couldn't tell whether English had or not, though he glanced in the rear-view mirror.

'Everything okay?' he asked.

'All good,' Black-Hair said. 'I'll be in touch, Katie,' he added as he got out.

As we pulled away, I turned and saw him watching us leave, his arms hanging by his side.

We drove in silence until English pulled in a few streets short of Hope's school. He left the ignition running, wound down my window with the buttons next to him, then got out of the car and opened my door for me.

I reached over, putting my hand on the door frame to support me as I climbed out. As I did so, English closed the door on my hand, trapping it against the frame of the car. He leaned his weight on it as he spoke in the window to me.

'Listen to me,' he hissed. 'I've been working this chain for years and I won't have you fuck that up for me. I've played nice and given you money and sorted out that shit with your mother for you, but that ends now. If you don't go to Spain like you've been told, I can make your life a fucking misery. Do you understand?'

I couldn't speak, my hand was in such pain. I nodded, hoping he would stop.

'So, go to Spain, do whatever Mark O'Reilly wants, meet whoever he wants to meet, and bring back whatever he wants to bring back. Do you understand?'

I couldn't agree to it. To do so would have betrayed everything that was important to me. My daughter. Myself. My own sense of who I was.

'Do you understand?'

I bit my cheek, forcing myself not to cry out in pain. I could taste blood in my mouth, could feel the pressure on the bones in my fingers. First Mark, now English, forcing me to do what they wanted when they thought they weren't getting their way. They were as bad as each other.

'There's always someone higher up the chain, Katie,' he said. 'You think we need you. We don't need you. You're dispensable. You need *us*. And, if you want to get out, you need *me*.'

I nodded. 'I understand,' I managed.

I felt the weight shift and the door opened. 'Good girl,' he said, standing waiting for me to get out, holding the door like a gentleman.

I passed him, cradling my hand.

'Nothing's broken,' he said. 'You'd have known about it if I broke something.'

I nodded and stared at him. 'I've known men like you all my life,' I said. 'Telling me what to do, throwing their weight about.'

English smiled. 'You've never met anyone like me.'

'And they all think that, too,' I said, my anger building. 'That they're special. But you're wrong. I choose what I do. I choose who I fuck. And I choose what happens to me and my daughter.'

'Are you sure that's the way you want to play this, Katie?' English said.

'This isn't a game,' I said.

'It's all a game,' he said. 'And you've nothing left to play. If you're not going to help us, you're of no value. Remember that.'

I turned and walked away from him. My hand was in agony, and I didn't want him to see that I was struggling.

## Chapter Forty

I went home first and bandaged up my hand, then changed my SIM into my own handset, leaving Black-Hair's behind. I did not need him listening in to the conversation I was hoping to have. Then, after I collected Hope from school, instead of going home, I headed up towards the cemetery. I knew Kenneth normally arrived in the bar after his day's wanderings around 3.30, which meant he left the cemetery around 3 p.m. I hoped to meet him along the way and challenge him about the passports.

It was clear that Black-Hair and English would not be helping me get away from Mark unless I went on the trip with him. And Mark now had my old passport, which meant even if I wanted to run, I couldn't. I hoped if I was right about Kenneth having been the one who made him the false ones, I might be able to create a third option for myself.

The cemetery was walled in so that, once you'd gone through the gates, the noise and business of the streets outside disappeared and, despite its central position in town, the place offered a sense of calmness and quiet I'd not been prepared for. I'd only ever considered the place to be sad, a place of loss and burial, of final goodbyes. Walking through it now, the hush of the traffic below did nothing to distract from the birdsong and the muted heat of the autumn sun.

By the time we reached the first rows of graves, I could already see Kenneth, further up the hill, picking his way down, his notebook under his arm.

He smiled when he saw us, blinking against the sun's glare. 'Katie,' he said. 'I'm just coming down from one of your ancestor's graves.' He opened the notebook, as if to show me something.

'Did you make the passports? For Mark?'

He stopped what he was doing, closing the book gently, not catching my eye.

'Did you make a set of passports for Mark?' I repeated.

He nodded.

'Why?'

He blinked again and I could see that he was nervous speaking to me.

'He said you were okay with it. He had pictures of you and the little one.' Again, though he referred to Hope, he could not look at her. 'I'm surprised he told you where he got them.'

'He didn't,' I said. 'I guessed. Who else do I know who keeps lists of those who died young?'

Kenneth nodded in acceptance.

'Did he say why he needed them?'

A shake of the head. 'No. But he's had me make ones for him, Terry and Ann before, in case they need to get out of the country and are on a watchlist. I guessed your two were for the same reason. I thought you were okay with it,' he added, looking directly at me now, as if pleading with me to believe him.

'How much do they cost?'

He looked down again and mumbled, 'A grand each.'

'I don't have a grand,' I said. 'Nor anything near it. But I need passports.'

'Why?'

I didn't speak and he must have guessed from my expression.

'He's a thug,' he said. 'You're far too good for him.'

His comment took me by surprise and he must have seen this too, for he continued. 'You've always been good to me,' he said. 'And your father, God rest him, was a gentleman. We shared many an evening drinking together.'

'And I need one for my mother, too,' I said. 'If I'm going to leave here, I need her with me.'

Kenneth nodded. 'It's doable. I could make her one in her late sister's name,' he said. 'But it will take a while. And I'll need a picture of her. Yours, I can do in a day or two. I've already done all the hard work creating the identities and have your pictures saved, so it's just about making copies of the books now.'

'How much will it cost?'

Kenneth shrugged. 'Nothing,' he said. 'If it means keeping the little one from that man, I'm happy to help. Just keep my name out of it.'

After weeks of people trying to control me, bullying me into things I did not want, such unexpected kindness brought me to tears. I moved across and embraced Kenneth. 'Thank you,' I said.

He was awkward in the embrace, his body rigid, as if unaccustomed to hugging or uncomfortable with it. But he laid one hand lightly on my shoulder before stepping back.

'You're welcome,' he said. He scribbled a number on a page in his notebook, then tore off the strip and handed it to me. 'Send me the picture of your mother when you have one. Send it from her phone so I have a number to contact her on when it's ready. Then meet me here on Friday morning and I'll have them done for you and the little one.' With that, finally, he looked down at Hope.

'All the people in your family that came before you and your mum and granny rest here. Did you know that?'

Hope stared at him, a little afraid, and shook her head.

'They all rest here. No matter where you go, you know that home is here, because this is where your history is.'

'The past is past,' I said. 'Home is where the family is. As long as we're together, we're at home. Isn't that right, kiddo?'

Hope nodded solemnly, not fully understanding what either of us were saying.

## Chapter Forty-One

I called in with Mum that evening, keen for her to have some time with Hope. If we needed to leave quickly, she would not be able to come with us. I was worried that if she did, using her own passport, Black-Hair would be able to find out where we went by tracking her movements.

We discussed all this, in hushed tones, in the kitchen, while Hope watched cartoons on the sofa.

Mum had wept when I first told her that I thought Hope and I would have to leave quickly and might not be back for some time.

'False passports? Are you mad?'

I shrugged. 'I've no choice.'

'Use your own.'

'Mark has them. Besides, the others will be able to find me if I use my own. This way, I can get away completely and not be traced.'

My paranoia had reached such levels that I could not use the word 'police' in case someone was listening, or it triggered a surveillance device somewhere.

'But what if they can tell they're fake?'

'Then I'll be arrested and will give evidence against Mark and Terry and hope the others help me out. The man who made them is going to make one for you too, but it'll take a bit longer and you'll need to let me take a photo for it, if you want.'

I could tell she wasn't convinced and, more so, could see why.

'I'd understand if you stayed here,' I said. 'I'll arrange for Kenneth to get a new passport to you, but if you don't want to leave home, I'd understand that.'

'How long will you be gone?' she asked.

'I don't know,' I said. 'I don't know if I can come back at all.'

She nodded, tears dripping down her face. She wiped them up hurriedly, not wanting to scare Hope.

'Where are you going? How would I meet you? If they're watching passports, surely they'll be watching my phone?'

'I always wanted to go to Florence,' I said.

'Your father and I went on honeymoon there.'

'I know. So, I think I'll start there and then move on.'

'How will you live?'

I shrugged. 'Bar work. Cleaning. The same as here. I don't own the house I live in so what am I leaving behind? Just you. And that's the one thing I don't want to leave behind.'

She hugged me, using the movement to hide her sobs and I, likewise, mine.

'All I have here are the memories of your dad, if you go,' she said, finally. 'And I've happier memories of him in Florence. The good ones, when he was still himself.'

'You'll come?'

She nodded. 'What would I do here on my own without you two to torture me?'

For the second time that day, my heart sang. I'd meant what I said to Kenneth. Home was where Hope and Mum were.

'How will we meet?'

I thought of Black-Hair's first instruction to me, the day of Flood's party.

'The day before you leave, post on your Facebook account that you're working the next day. It'll mean nothing to anyone but me. I'll know then you're coming, and I'll wait at the Arrivals in the airport for each flight in from here the next day.'

She nodded. 'Wait a minute,' she said.

I heard her footfalls on the stairs and across the floor above me, then traced her returning the same way. When she came back into the kitchen, she had an envelope in her hand.

'What's that?'

'When your father's drinking started getting bad, I was worried he'd drink every penny he got. I used to take a few pound from his benefits and his club pension and put it aside, in case we ever were stuck. It was my Rainy Day fund. Now seems as good a time as any to use it. There's about four thousand pounds in there. It'll not keep you going for long, but it'll get you out of the country at least and maybe sort rent for your first month or two.'

'I can't take this,' I said, tears welling again. I'd almost preferred the expectation of people being cruel to me, for kindness wounded me.

'I'd planned on leaving it for Hope,' Mum said. 'She needs it now. You both do.'

We hugged once more, then she straightened up, and wiped her eyes. 'Let's get this passport picture taken,' she said.

After I'd taken the picture and texted it from Mum's phone to Kenneth, on the number he'd given me earlier, Hope and I got ready to go home.

'I'll see you tomorrow,' Mum said, as we were leaving. Suddenly, she grabbed me in an embrace. 'And if something goes wrong before then, run as far away as the pair of you can and don't wait for me. Keep yourself and Hope safe.'

Her comment punctured the adrenaline which had sustained me all day and, for the first time, I began to doubt myself.

## Chapter Forty-Two

I woke early Thursday morning, my mind racing about what lay ahead. I needed to pack up whatever we were taking with us and I needed to check flight times. If Mark landed unexpectedly at the house and saw suitcases packed, he'd assume we were going with him. I needed to keep everyone thinking that for as long as I could.

I'd thought I would hear something from Black-Hair, having shown him I knew his real name, but, though I checked the phone repeatedly, there were no messages, no sign that it had changed anything. I began to think that perhaps he had not heard me call him 'Alex' after all.

I was wrong.

When I arrived back to the house, having dropped Hope off, he was sitting in my kitchen, waiting for me, alone.

'How did you get in?'

No response. Instead, he laid a finger to his lips and mouthed: 'Your phone.'

I had my own handset in my coat pocket. The handset he had given me was in the living room. I went in and lifted it, then went into the kitchen and gave it to him, hoping that he would not notice that there was no SIM card in it.

Thankfully, he took it and moved across to the back door without looking. He opened it and flung the phone out onto the lawn, away from the house. Then he closed the door and came back to the table and sat.

'Why did you call me Alex?' he asked.

'Because that's your name,' I said. 'You're Alex Duffy, Leah's brother. I know why you're after Mark. I know what he did to your sister.'

'Who told you I was her brother?'

'No one,' I lied, not wishing to get Catherine in trouble. 'I was searching social media and found a picture with the two of you in it.'

'Don't lie to me,' he said. 'I've been scrubbed from online. There are no pictures of me. Who told you?'

'I'm sorry what happened to Leah.'

'Who told you?'

'But you forcing me into the same position she was in doesn't make it better.'

'I've not forced you into anything.'

I held up my bandaged hand. 'You might want to tell English that. He did this yesterday after we left you.'

He glanced at my hand and did not comment, which was response enough in itself. 'Who told you? About Leah, I mean. Was it him? Mark?' he asked instead. 'Did he admit that he arranged the acid attack?'

I shook my head. 'Benny.'

'Did *he* know about me? My real name?'

'No.' His *real* name. That suggested Benny had known him, but not by name.

'Benny was passing you info, too, wasn't he?'

Black-Hair nodded. 'He was, for a few years. We picked up on you after you started sleeping with him.'

'Why did you need me if you already had him?'

'Because people get caught. Or they get greedy. Or they start telling you any old shit hoping to get paid for nothing. We always need a few assets so we can verify one story against another. And in case one gets found out. Everyone gets careless eventually.'

'Benny didn't steal Leon Burke's bank card, did he? You planted it on him to protect me.'

'You were getting closer to Mark than Benny ever would,' he said. 'You sacrifice a pawn to protect your queen.'

'It's all a game,' I said. 'English said that yesterday. This is just a game.'

'Not to me,' Black-Hair said. 'Mark O'Reilly destroyed my sister's life.'

'And you want revenge.'

'I want justice. He manages to beat every charge against him. But coming back on a flight carrying drugs or money? That's something he can't escape.'

'And Benny's life is worth that? And that poor man, Shaw's? I warned you there was an attack planned.'

'But not the details.'

'All you needed to do was place extra security around the Shaws.'

'And the O'Reillys see or Ross sees. And they know we know. They know we have someone inside, feeding us information. Something someone tells you could save a life. But it could also cost the life of the person who gives you that information. And what's not to say that they mightn't give you something a week or a month or a year later that saves thirty lives instead? Or a hundred lives?'

'And when I stop being valuable?'

Nothing.

'English told me there was always someone higher up the chain.'

'That's the job. Keep finding someone higher up and higher up, until eventually you can cut off the head.'

'I thought you wanted Mark.'

'I do.'

'And are you prepared to let him go to get someone higher up?'

'I need you to go on that trip, Katie,' he said. 'Whatever you're thinking of doing, don't. I need you on that trip and I need Mark, red-handed, with drugs or drug money in his bags. I need something he can't get out of.'

'I'm not thinking of doing anything.'

'Did you have a pleasant visit to the cemetery yesterday afternoon? That was a strange place to take a child.'

'We were visiting my daddy's grave.'

'I know who you were visiting,' Black-Hair said. 'I watched you all afternoon, after you left me at McDonald's. Did you really think you could drop my name like that, and I'd just walk away?'

'I don't really care what you do,' I said with much more confidence than I felt.

'You should. You should care. Because if you go missing, take a trip no one knows about, whether it's tomorrow or next year, we're going to find some very interesting things in your mother's house.'

'What things?'

'All sorts of things can turn up unexpectedly. Especially

in the home of a retired nurse. Medications that went missing from hospital, stolen over years and years. I'm sure she filled up the first-aid kit in your house with stuff she lifted from work.'

She had, not that I would admit it to him. And she'd lifted boxes of antibiotics at times, in case I got a cough. But it had all been harmless, a perk of the job as she saw it.

'And what age is she now? Coming sixty? It would be a shame for her to spend her old age inside.'

'You're a bastard,' I said, because I had nothing left to say.

'We do what we have to for the people we care about.'

'I'm sure Leah would be ashamed to think you're treating another woman as badly as Mark treated her.'

'You don't know the first thing about my sister,' Black-Hair said, sitting forward. 'You know nothing. The only thing Leah will regret is that she doesn't get to pour battery acid all over that fucker, just like he had someone do to her.'

'And will you regret it,' I asked, 'when he gets away?'

'Take this trip and he won't.'

'Take this trip and he will. He's not planning on coming back.'

'I don't believe that. He wouldn't turn his back on everything he's done here.'

'Why do you think I was meeting that creep in the graveyard? Mark is arranging false passports for himself and us. He's not planning on coming back here. This trip to Marbella is a cover. He's not turning his back on what he's done here; he's going to keep running things from there. He knows you're closing in on him. Benny and Leon Burke's phone spooked him.'

'You're lying.'

'I'm not.'

'No one else has told us that's what he's thinking.'

So, they had someone else inside. Someone higher up the chain.

'He hasn't even told Terry,' I said. 'Why do you think he sent me to collect the passports?'

'He already has them?'

I nodded. 'He's not coming back. You let him get on that flight and what he did to Leah may as well be forgotten.'

I could tell he was studying me, trying to gauge if I was bluffing. I hoped I had him hooked. Now I had to try to use that to my advantage.

'He and Terry are driving up to Belfast tonight to see Ross. They have to collect whatever we're meant to be taking across to Spain. If you pulled them over on the way home, you'd have them. He'll have money, or drugs, or whatever in the car with him. That's enough for you to get him. And it keeps me and Hope safe from him.'

'They wouldn't risk going to Ross themselves.'

'Mark wanted to send Andy Flood, but Terry said Ross wanted to see the organ grinders, not the monkey. You said yourself, everyone gets careless eventually. Terry is so carried away with all this stuff with Ross, he's prepared to take that risk. If you followed them up, at a safe distance, you might be able to get Ross as well.'

'Why are you telling me this now? You could have told us yesterday.'

'Because English doesn't care about Leah. Or about Mark. He wants to keep going, higher and higher. This isn't personal for him. He just wants a big win. This is about his career. But not for you. It's about Leah for you. And Hope for me. This *matters* to us.'

Black-Hair said nothing.

'If English knew, he'd block all of this. He told me he expects me to go to Marbella and let Mark do whatever he wants to me, just to make sure he gets his intel. He'd have treated Leah the same way if she was here in my position. You know he would.'

'He's doing his job,' Black-Hair said, in his defence.

'But this is *more* than a job for you.'

Again, he said nothing.

'Look, follow them up and watch what happens. I'm not lying to you. They're meeting Ross this evening. And when we leave tomorrow, we're leaving on false passports, and we won't be back. If you want to get Mark O'Reilly, you have twenty-four hours to do it before he's gone.'

# Chapter Forty-Three

Black-Hair left by the back door, and I went out and retrieved the handset he had thrown into the yard. I transferred the SIM across, then hid my old phone back in my bedside drawer, my dad's old penknife rattling against the wood as I closed it. Then I pulled out the suitcases and began sorting through things, trying to work out what to take.

I went through each room in the house, reassessing the things I owned, the things I would want with me. I had one case to take and needed to use the space sparingly. In the end, I settled on a handful of photographs, mostly of myself and Mum and Dad when we were younger. I packed a pebble which Hope had found on the beach, shaped like a heart. And I packed a sports medal my dad had won years ago and which he'd given to me one day when I had to go to hospital, as an award for bravery.

Of all the things in the house, there was nothing else I felt I needed, nothing else that, when it came to it, mattered. I was in that frame of mind when I heard a knock at the front door. Going down, I found Mark standing outside.

'Are you not coming in to work?' he asked.

I realised that Black-Hair's visit had unsettled me to the point that I'd forgotten to go to the bar.

'I'm so sorry, Mark,' I said. 'I was caught up on getting things sorted.'

He glanced past me to where the first travel bag sat in the hall. He chuckled. 'Women and packing, eh?'

I offered my best approximation of a laugh. 'And there's two women here to pack for,' I said. 'Hope has more clothes than me.'

'I'm so glad you're coming,' he said, pulling me towards him and kissing me. He pressed himself against me to let me know the effect it was having on him.

I pulled away. 'Not here, Mark,' I said.

'There's no one about,' he said, pulling me closer again. 'Hope's at school.'

'I want it to be romantic,' I said. 'The first time. You've gone to all this effort to book us away. I want to remember that every time I think back on it.'

'This could be romantic right here,' he said.

'I want our first time together to be perfect,' I said. 'I want it to be making love, not just some meaningless shag.'

He pressed against me as he pulled me tighter and I dropped my hand to his crotch, as if to feel his presence.

'I promise you, it'll be a night to remember.'

I could see he was conflicted between his own urges and the flattery of believing I wanted to make love to him, as if it was a lifelong commitment I was making to him. In the end, his ego won.

'I can't wait,' he said. 'It's going to be amazing.'

I moved away from him. 'I'll get my things and come in and get the place cleaned,' I said. 'Sorry again for forgetting.'

'Don't worry about it,' he said. 'Though it would help if you'd cover the shift this afternoon. Tel and I are away tonight. Gail's back from honeymoon so you two can compare notes on romantic holidays.'

'I can do that,' I said. 'I need to get Mum to collect Hope.'

'Ann can do it,' he said.

'No. We're away this weekend, so it'll be nice for Hope and her granny to have some time together first.'

I went upstairs, aware that Mark was following behind me. My own suitcase lay on the bed, yawning open, its contents visible. He looked through what I had packed, taking out the medal and pictures.

'We're only going for a few days,' he said.

'I was showing those to Hope earlier,' I lied. 'The medal is for her on the plane. My dad won it when they topped the league back in the day. He gave it to me when I was eight and had to go to hospital after I split myself. He said it was for bravery. So, I thought, if Hope gets nervous on the plane, it'll be her medal for bravery now.'

I deliberately pulled off my top in front of him and then rooted slowly through one of my drawers to find my O'Reilly's Bar T-shirt, which I pulled on. It had had the desired effect, drawing Mark's attention away from my suitcase and, more importantly, the money that Mum had given to me, which I had hidden in it for now.

'Shall we go?' I asked.

Mark glanced once more at the case, then nodded. I closed the door behind me before leaving, almost as a way to ensure he would not go back in.

## Chapter Forty-Four

I was genuinely pleased to see Gail when I arrived in the bar. She was tanned from her break, though the tell-tale smell of St Moritz suggested she'd topped it up before coming to work.

'I didn't get out of the room as much as I'd hoped,' she confessed to me in one of the quieter periods of the afternoon. 'You know what holidays are like? Sun, sand and sex.'

The comment actually made me feel sick with dread at the prospect of being caught in that same situation with Mark if Black-Hair didn't act on what I had told him.

I could see the risks. If he went back to speak to English, he would surely talk Black-Hair out of arresting Mark on the way home from Belfast. He wanted whoever was supplying in Spain; he'd made that clear. Arresting Mark and Terry now would screw up his chances of achieving that and would alert them, and Ross, to the fact they were being watched or that the police had inside information.

That in itself could cause me a problem. They had already suspected me once of being an informer. Benny's death had drawn a line under that suspicion until now, but a second leak, after Benny's death, would convince them that it was someone close to them. And I guessed that there were very few people who knew that they were going to Belfast: myself and Andy Flood were the only ones I knew.

What I needed then was for Black-Hair to lift them and hold them long enough to allow Hope and me to get out of the country. I was aware that that exposed Mum, though, so I could only pray that Kenneth might come into the bar later so I could explain to him how quickly I needed her passport done, too.

But seeing Gail had also forced me to realise just how much my life had changed in the weeks since she'd been gone. The last time I'd seen her, I was a little drunk, at her wedding, trying to orchestrate a reason to justify spending the night with Benny. Now, weeks later, Benny was dead, and I was trying to arrange to leave the country using fake identities and set the police on my boss.

And, in truth, I wished for those days again, even if, had I had the chance, I would not have gone for that first drink with Benny, would not have brought such harm to his family and so have avoided falling under the gaze of Black-Hair and English, too.

They were as bad as each other, the cops and the O'Reillys. I wanted nothing to do with either of them. And, I wanted both of them to pay for what they had done. The people they had killed or let die. Millar, Leon Burke, Benny, Shaw. Each a pawn sacrificed in a bigger game that they hadn't even realised they were playing. At least here, now, I knew the game I was in. And, whether I succeeded or not, I finally felt like I was making my own moves instead of being shifted around by Black-Hair or Mark.

But then, perhaps every pawn imagines itself to be a queen.

\* \* \*

Kenneth came in around half three, as was his habit. He came to the bar, smiling mildly.

'Welcome back, Gail,' he said. 'The place wasn't the same without you!'

'Charmer,' Gail said, already pouring him his whiskey and stout.

He glanced in my direction only once and only long enough to offer me a quick wink. Try as I might to get his attention, he went back to his seat and even when, later on, I went down to lift his empties, he read his notebook and did not look at me or speak.

I began to wonder whether he'd lied to me when he said he would help. Perhaps Mark had got to him? Or he had gone to Mark, selling me out for a few free drinks each afternoon.

But I had to trust him, had to believe in his decency.

'Busy today?' I asked.

'Always busy,' he said. 'But I'm on top of everything I need to be.'

He nodded, satisfied with his own answer, then turned back to his notebook.

Later, when things got quiet, Gail came across and leaned on the bar next to me.

'Sad news about Benny,' she said. She was being guarded in her sympathies, and I was unsure whether the 'sad news' she mentioned meant his death or the supposed revelation that he was an informer.

I nodded. I felt I had to be careful what I said about Benny in the bar. Many people who had joked with him when he worked there now thought of him as the enemy in death. He was a tout, a snitch, a rat. But he was a husband, a father, a friend of sorts. And that counted for something.

'It is,' I said. 'Poor Amy.'

Gail looked at me askance. 'Poor Amy? Did you not shag him at my wedding?'

The way in which she asked did not seem judgemental, rather as if we were sharing a secret.

'I'd had a lot to drink,' I said.

'Wasn't the first time either, I've heard,' Gail said. 'Spill the tea. What happened?'

And with that, Benny had gone from being a murder victim to the subject of idle gossip, as if his life's whole value lay in the entertainment of a scandalous story and no more.

Through that evening, I waited, wondering how I would know if my plan had worked, and Black-Hair had intercepted Terry and Mark on the road from Belfast. I checked my phone, left the TV in the corner turned on, the volume loud enough that a Breaking News story would be heard, although I knew it would hardly appear on the TV even if the pair were arrested.

Each time the door opened, I looked up, alternately expecting either Mark and Terry or the police to come in. Fear and excitement merged in my stomach and I couldn't settle.

Then, around 10 p.m., Andy Flood came into the bar, followed by two other men. He came round the bar, ignoring both Gail and me, reached up and rang the bell we used to indicate last orders.

'Drink up, folks. Bar's closing!' he called, then turned to us. 'We're closing early. Get the place cleared up.'

'Where's Tel and Mark?' Gail asked, presumably not having met Flood before.

'There's been an incident. So shut your mouth and get this place closed up. Now.'

The presence of Flood and his men seemed to speed everyone up and some of the customers stood, leaving their drinks sitting. One or two loitered while they drained their pints and one fella, who'd been drinking all afternoon, announced he was going to the toilet first.

'The fuck you are,' Flood said, nodding towards one of the pair who'd come in with him. He, in turn, went across and, gripping the drunk man, pulled him out through the doorway and tossed him on the street.

Once the customers had gone, Flood and the other two went down through the bar and into the staff area, as if looking for something. They appeared a few moments later, while Gail and I washed up the last few glasses.

'You can go home,' Flood said to Gail. 'Call the bar before you come to work tomorrow, just in case.'

'What's happened?' Gail asked.

Flood ignored her and turned to me. 'You need to go straight home.'

'I have to call to my mum's to collect Hope.'

'Did you not hear what I said? You need to go home. We'll take you.'

I began to panic then. Had something happened that had revealed who I was, who I'd been speaking to? Why was he taking me home? Were we even going there? I imagined, instead, being driven out to the furniture warehouse again.

'Is Mark okay?' I asked.

His expression didn't change. 'Get your things. We're leaving.'

## Chapter Forty-Five

I was put into the back of the car with Flood next to me. He was on his phone, most of the time. His two men sat up front. Only once during the journey did anyone talk, and it was when the front-seat passenger turned and spoke to Flood.

'Any word on Mickey since?'

'He's hoping to move on to spoon-feeding next week,' Flood said, not looking up. 'They're taking out the tube on Monday, all being well.'

'Fuck's sake,' the other man said.

'I know. Over nothing.'

'He'd want to see this.'

Flood chuckled to himself. 'Aye. Wait long enough and everyone gets what they deserve.'

I could feel the sweat breaking and I reached for the door handle to steady myself.

'Where are we going?' I asked.

'Your house.'

'Why?'

'Just shut the fuck up, love,' Flood said. 'I'm trying to think.'

My thoughts raced as I sat there, the streetlights slipping past us, each one seeming to count down to whatever waited for me in my own home. I was just glad Hope was with Mum and prayed for the first time in I don't know how long that she hadn't decided to bring Hope back to sleep in her own room.

'What's happening?' I asked. I tried to keep my voice steady, but I could hear the shake and knew it made me sound worried.

The fact that none of the three men responded made me feel even worse.

We pulled up outside my place. It was in darkness, the windows showing only the distorted reflection of the houses opposite. Houses in which normal things were happening and people were going about their lives. How had I lost that?

Flood got out and, coming round, opened my door.

'Get out.'

'I'm not going in,' I said.

'It's your fucking house.'

'I'm not going in there. You need to tell me what's going to happen.'

He leaned into the car and grabbed me by the arm. 'I don't need to tell you anything. Get out of the car.'

He pulled me from my seat and closed the door behind me. I tried to stop, tried not to move towards my own doorway, looming in front of me, but he shoved me along.

'I'm not going in there,' I said.

'What the fuck are you so afraid of?' Flood sneered. 'It's your own house.'

I tried to pull the keys from my pocket, deciding that my chance might be to go in, quickly, and pull the door closed before Flood could follow me. But my hands shook so violently the keys spilled to the ground.

Flood bent and picked them up.

'She's shitting herself,' one of his mates said, still standing at the car, watching.

Flood took the keys and, trying each in the lock, eventually found the one he needed and turned it, pushing the door. It yawned open, the hallway in darkness. I was sure there was someone in there. Someone waiting to take revenge for Mickey. Or to punish me for Black-Hair and English. I cursed trusting Kenneth, cursed agreeing to Black-Hair's demands, cursed the day I set foot in O'Reilly's bar.

Flood stepped away from the open door, handed me my keys and pushed me inside.

'Your time's coming,' he said, closing the door behind me. I stood there, in the dark, petrified, waiting for the shot to come.

I heard Flood walking back to the car, the roar of the engine. Then I heard footsteps inside the house, coming from the kitchen. The door creaked open and Mark appeared in the doorway.

'Katie,' he hissed. 'Get in here.'

He wore a blue T-shirt, the front of which was covered in blood. As on the morning of Leon Burke's death, I looked at Mark and saw only a butcher.

# Chapter Forty-Six

'Get in here,' Mark said, wincing as he turned from me and retreated into the darkness.

Each step I took from the hallway to the kitchen seemed leaden. I could hear groaning in the kitchen and the scrape of a chair against the linoleum floor. Then long shadows jumped across the wall nearest as someone turned on a torch inside. I could make out a second figure. Mark was not alone.

'Hurry up,' he said, and, behind that, I could hear someone moan low.

I pushed open the doorway and saw the extent of the carnage.

Terry lay on my table. His shirt had been ripped open and his stomach bared. Blood pooled in the hollow of his guts, and I could see more pulsing from a wound in his stomach. A second wound, on his shoulder, trickled blood, but the skin beneath was already marbled purple.

'You need to help him,' Mark said. 'Get your mother up here. She was a nurse, wasn't she?'

Instinct took over and I rushed in, my concern at Terry's state significantly less than my relief that I was not the target of a bullet myself.

I grabbed tea towels from the drawer and pressed them to Terry's stomach, trying both to soak up the blood there so I could see the extent of his injuries and to stem the flow of blood from the wound.

'What happened?'

Mark winced and I saw that he had a wound to his arm, which hung by his side where he sat.

'We were pulled over by a cop.'

'They shot you?'

'Said he was a traffic cop,' he said, shaking his head. 'Bullshit. He was plain clothes. Looking for us to get out of the car.'

It must have been Black-Hair. I stopped myself asking what he looked like. 'Why?'

'He fucking knew,' Mark spat. 'He knew why we were there. We'd cash in a bag. Money to take to Spain. He knew why we were there.'

'How did this happen?' I asked, indicating Terry's stomach with my own bloodstained hands.

Terry groaned as I pressed on the wound, trying to clean it. His eyes fluttered open. His face was damp with sweat, his skin clammy and cool to the touch.

'Tel pulled on the guy and he started shooting back. I drove on and hit him. But he got shots off.'

'Terry needs a hospital, Mark.'

'No hospital. Get your mother up here.'

'I can't, Mark,' I said. 'I can't get her involved in this.'

'Then fucking help him. Stop the bleeding.'

'He's going to bleed out,' I said. 'I can't do anything about that.'

Mark winced and I could see by the light of his torch that he too was paling. 'Help him, Katie.'

I nodded and moved across to pull the blinds and put on the kitchen light. Any neighbours looking at the back of my house would find a torch light in the room more suspicious that a closed blind.

Mark shielded his eyes from the light with one arm, but the other hung useless by his side. I could see clearly now the poppy-shaped stain on his upper sleeve. I brought him over a cloth.

'Were you hit anywhere else?'

He shook his head. 'I think it's chipped a bone or something though. I can't lift my arm above this.' He tried raising his arm, not even managing horizontal before he winced with the pain and lowered it again.

I went over to the cabinet and pulled out packets of painkillers. I had a mix of paracetamol and ibuprofen, and gave Mark two of each. I remembered the doctor who had treated Hope's arm telling her it was okay to mix them so I figured Mark could handle them.

'Terry,' I said. 'Do you need a painkiller?'

His eyes fluttered again, and his lips moved dryly, but no sound came out.

I turned again to Mark. 'He's going to die,' I whispered. 'You need to take him to hospital.'

Mark shook his head. 'The cops will have him for good if they get hands on him now.'

'He's dying,' I snapped, not quite able to believe that he wasn't grasping what was happening to his brother.

'Just stop the bleeding,' he said. 'Your mum's a nurse.'

'That doesn't mean I am,' I said, but he had stopped listening and was looking at his brother.

Terry's stomach rose and fell more rapidly now, his breaths puffing on his lips. I wiped the wound and tried to work out how to seal it, but its shape seemed too irregular, and Terry too thin to pull together excess skin to try to sew it shut. Instead, and thinking of Leon Burke the whole time I did it, I got some superglue from the drawer and, pinching the edges of the wound together, tried to glue it closed.

I held it like that until I could feel my own fingers become tacky against Terry's skin. Then, as gently as I could, I unpicked myself from the wound, peeling back each finger one by one so as not to disturb the seal the glue had created.

There was no more I could do for him.

I came across to Mark and repeated the process on his arm, an easier task this time as the wound was already starting to dry a little. I dressed it, covering it with antiseptic cream.

As I was working, I heard movement outside. Perhaps Black-Hair had managed to follow Mark and Terry here and had gathered reinforcements. I moved across, then realised that the door lock had been broken, which at least explained how Mark and Terry had got into my kitchen. And just as I reached the door, it was pushed open and Ann came in.

'My boys,' she yelped when she saw them and rushed over to Mark first and then to Terry. 'What did they do to you, Tel?'

'Fucker came out of nowhere,' Mark said. 'He didn't even have his blues on. Just pulled in in front of us, pushing us off the road.'

'Someone talked,' Ann said. 'If he knew to pull you over, someone talked.'

'Would there not have been a whole squad of them?' I said. 'If they knew anything, surely it would have been a whole big operation. Not one man just turning up.'

'Was there only one?' Ann asked, turning to Mark who nodded. She considered this a moment, then shook her head. 'Naw. Someone definitely talked.'

Mark tried to stand to come across to Terry, but he staggered when he did so, and could not raise his arm enough to steady himself against the kitchen chairs next to him.

'Come on, Tel,' he said. 'Fight it, big man.'

'You need your arm in a sling,' I said. 'I'll make one up.'

I took Mark across and helped him sit, then under Ann's watchful gaze, I tended to his arm, showed him affection and all the time tried to work out how I was going to escape from the hell of my own house.

## Chapter Forty-Seven

The first light of morning bled into the sky just after 6 a.m. Terry had survived the night. Ann, Mark and I had sat vigil beside him while he puffed and panted next to us, his wound holding even as his skin paled and marbled.

I made us tea and we waited. During the night, Flood had arrived to discuss things with Mark. I'd used the chance to go to the toilet, checking my phone as I did so in the hope that Black-Hair might have made contact, but there was nothing.

Mark said he had hit him with the car. That Black-Hair hadn't gone after them suggested he was either too badly injured to do so or that Mark had killed him. Either way, he would not be coming to help me. And I knew English certainly wouldn't. I had made my choice, as he had put it, the moment I set Black-Hair after Mark and Terry. What happened now would be all my own fault.

Despite being in my own house, I felt exposed. I also was aware that my old handset was still sitting in the drawer next to my bed. I crept into my room, and pulling open the drawer, lifted out some of my underwear and stuffed the phone right to the back, covering it as best I could. My dad's penknife lay there, and I lifted it. It might be useful to have, albeit how blunt I knew it to be, if things went badly downstairs.

I was just coming out of my room when the phone Black-Hair had given me rang. It was my mum.

'Did you not get home last night?' she asked, jokingly.

'I did, Mum,' I said. 'I had a few unexpected guests though.'

'Are they still there?'

'Uh-huh.'

'Will I take Hope on to school, or what do you want me to do?'

'No, take her to school. I can collect her later. I'm sorry I didn't call last night. I got tied up and . . . but I really wanted to see you before I leave.'

I turned the corner on the stairs to find Ann, waiting.

'Yeah, back on Monday,' I added. 'But I don't know if we'll be able to go now.'

Ann covered the stairs between us in surprising time and grabbed the phone from me. I tried to pull it from her, but she was stronger than she looked, and she tore it from my grasp.

'Who are you phoning?'

'My mum called to see what I wanted her to do with Hope,' I said.

But Ann was not convinced. She stomped back down the stairs and into the kitchen where Mark was still sitting, watching his brother, Terry's hand in his own.

'She had a phone,' she snapped. 'She was talking to someone.'

Mark looked to me for explanation.

'Mum called me,' I said.

'She told her about being away this weekend.'

Mark straightened up in his seat. 'Did you?'

'She'd think it was bloody odd if I took Hope away for a few days and didn't tell her. I thought the whole point was to make it look like a family holiday.'

'Give me the phone,' Mark said.

Ann handed it to him. I was going to protest, aware that if he checked my call history closely, if he paid attention, he'd notice that there were times he had called me that would not be in this handset's history.

He looked to me once more. 'Am I going to find anything on this?'

'Like what?' I said, swallowing dryly. I tried to remember if I had deleted all the voice messages I'd left for Black-Hair and English but could not be sure that I had.

'Old boyfriends looking to catch up?' Mark said.

'No,' I said. 'Of course not. I only ever ring Mum or work.'

He handed me the phone and I thought for a moment that he trusted me. Instead, he shook it once in my direction. 'Unlock it,' he said.

I did so and handed the phone back to him, like a scolded child. He spent some time going through it, reading messages, checking calls. All the time, Ann stood between us, hands on hips, watching from one to the other, as if waiting to have her suspicions confirmed.

Finally, Mark turned off the handset altogether and tossed it on the seat next to him. Then he leaned over and took his brother's hand again.

'What are you going to do now?' I asked. We had avoided the question all through the night and I had been afraid to ask. But now, the dawn brought with it a sense of reality.

They could not remain sitting in my kitchen indefinitely. Terry, groaning and moaning on the table, would die soon without help. In fact, even then, I knew he would die anyway. It had been left too long, the blood loss too great. His death, like Leon Burke's, would be slow and painful. And though I was horrified by being close to it, I could not but think that on some level it was wholly fitting that this is how it should come for Terry O'Reilly.

'Floody is taking too long,' Ann said. 'He should have been back by now. It's getting too bright. People will see.'

'Where is he?' I asked.

'Trying to get clean transport,' Mark said. 'And collecting our things. We'll need to clear out. Where's Hope?'

'Going to school,' I said. 'We're not travelling till later.'

'We're not going to Marbella,' Mark said, as if I could not have guessed as much myself. 'We're going to clear out altogether.'

'What about Ross?' Ann asked.

'Fuck Ross. I told Terry it was bad news, lifting our heads up over the trench. No one cares when you keep things small, local.'

He cupped his brother's limp hand in both of his and repeated, 'No one cares.'

I knew then I had to do something to get myself and Hope away from him. If we waited for Flood to arrive back, there would be no escape. And I was aware that I needed to be at the cemetery for 9 a.m. to meet Kenneth and get the passports from him.

Terry moaned almost constantly, punctuated by breaths that had regulated a little, though not in a good way. It had become increasingly mechanical and even, and I suspected he was already drifting into deeper and deeper unconsciousness. I remembered my father doing the same in his last days when his liver had given in after years of abuse. Abuse Terry and Mark had fed and which Mark had tried to justify to me on that day on Inch Island.

I moved over and stood with Mark, my hand on his uninjured shoulder, offering a show of support and solidarity. Then I looked at Terry's hands more closely. His fingernails were blue now, the skin cold to the touch.

'I can get him antibiotics,' I said, seeing a possible escape route. 'And stronger painkillers. From Mum's house. She had stuff from when Dad was sick.'

'It'll be out of date,' Ann said. 'That was years ago.'

'It never really goes out of date,' I said. 'Besides, anything would be better than this. At least it'll ease his pain, let him go to sleep without suffering.'

'You said you didn't want your mother involved,' Mark said.

'I don't,' I agreed. 'But she'll be taking Hope to school around nine. I could go over then and get the stuff. I'll be away before she comes back home.'

'I'll drive you,' Ann said.

It was the last thing I wanted. But a car would be handy, though it had been a few years since I'd last driven one.

'I can drive myself if I can use your car,' I said.

'You don't have a licence.'

'I do. I just can't afford a car myself, but I can drive.' The licence bit wasn't true either; I'd lost it and not reapplied for the test. But then, if the police pulled me over for driving without a licence, it would not be the worst thing to happen.

'I don't trust you,' Ann snapped.

'Fine,' I said. 'I'll stay here. We'll let Terry suffer.'

'Just give her your fucking car,' Mark said.

'I want to come with you.'

I nodded towards the hall, indicating that she should follow me. She did so, remaining a few feet back from me, as if worried that I was going to lurch for her.

'Ann, I don't know if Tel is even going to make it long enough for me to get back. He might and, if he does, at least we can ease things for him. But if he passes before I get back ... would you not rather be here? With Mark? Tel would want you with him.'

I could tell she was torn between her mistrust of me and the emotional pull of her brothers. Eventually, she took her keys from her pocket and threw them to me.

'Don't damage it,' she said, as if in all that was happening, a scratch on her car would make things so much worse.

'I need my phone,' I said.

'Why?'

I wanted to have it in the hope I could contact Black-Hair. Once I was clear from here, I'd get the passports, collect Hope and head straight to the airport to book the first flight to wherever was available. I hoped that if I could speak with Black-Hair and English to tell them where Mark was, English at least might realise that his surveillance in Spain was not going to work now, and might want the compensation of arresting Mark and Terry. By that stage, Hope and I would be long gone.

'In case you need to contact me, God forbid,' I said instead, glancing towards the scene in the kitchen.

She nodded and going in, lifted the handset. 'I'll check it when you come back,' she said.

'Of course,' I said. I just needed to get upstairs now to my case, for I'd hidden the money Mum gave me in it. I wouldn't be able to book flights if I had no money.

'Where are you going?' Ann asked, having followed me out to the hallway once more, keeping careful watch on all that I did.

'I need to get my bag.'

'Stop wasting time and go and get my brother what he needs,' she said.

'I need my bag.'

'Get the fuck out of here,' Ann said, shoving me towards the door. 'And hurry back with that medicine.'

I had no choice but to walk out into the morning air, leaving behind the cash with which I had hoped to buy our way out.

## Chapter Forty-Eight

It took several attempts for me to get the car into gear and, once done, another stuttering attempt at pulling away from the kerb. I could see Ann, standing at my living-room window, watching me.

Once moving, the rustiness soon passed, and I drove to the cemetery. I parked in the parking area at the entrance, nearest where I had met Kenneth two days earlier. Then I waited.

I began to worry that he might be delayed. Realistically, Mark and Ann might, at best, allow me forty minutes to get to Mum's, wait for her to leave, get the stuff Terry needed and get back. Perhaps an hour at a stretch. In that time, I needed to get passports, collect Hope and get on the road. I had hoped that, by the time they realised I wasn't coming back, I'd have had a decent head start on them.

I was acutely aware that I had no luggage and no money. I would have to deal with that once I made it out of town. I hoped Mum might be able to transfer some to my account and, if needs be, bring my luggage, or at least Hope's things, with her when she came out to join us.

If she joined us.

I saw a figure shuffling in through the front gates and was almost out of the car, assuming it to be Kenneth, when I realised it was an older man, a bunch of roses in clear cellophane in his hand. He struggled his way to the first step up the steep incline towards the first row of graves, lifting one foot and planting it firmly, then drawing up the other onto the same step.

I looked up, beyond him to the top of the incline. There must have been at least thirty steps to get to the top. Meanwhile, the man painfully lifted his foot and planted it on the second step.

I couldn't watch. Getting out of the car, I went across to him.

'Are you going up the whole way?'

He turned and smiled, gently. 'Aye. This row and the next.' He indicated up towards the steps with a curled finger, yellowed with tobacco. It would take him ages to climb and probably just as long coming back down. His chest was already heaving from the exertion of making it into the cemetery, a wheeze catching in his throat as he coughed.

'Do you want a lift up?'

He smiled. 'I would, love,' he said.

And so, keeping an eye out for Kenneth, I linked arms with him and tried my best to hurry him to the car. Then we set off, up the incline towards the higher row of graves.

'I know your face,' he said. 'You're the spit of your father.'

I looked at him, bemused: I was nothing like my father. 'Okay,' I said, assuming he was mistaking me for someone else.

'The footballer,' he insisted, aware that I didn't believe him.

'That's right.' I was surprised. I looked at myself in the mirror, searching for something of my father among my mother's features.

'He was a gentleman, too,' he concluded, nodding as if that was the final word on the matter.

And it was. All the pain and sickness, the drinking and the loss, abated in this stranger's memory of my father's goodness.

'He was,' I said.

The man smiled mildly once more. 'Sure, who else's daughter would you be? Apples don't fall far from trees.'

In spite of everything, in spite of the panic, I felt a moment of calm, as if the man had, in some way, absolved me of whatever faults had led me to this place.

'This is my Mary here,' he said, pointing towards a grave, tidier than those near it. A bunch of roses already lay on the marble plinth of the headstone, wrapped in cellophane.

'Is it her anniversary?' I asked, indicating the bunch he carried.

'I bring her a bunch every week,' he explained. 'To make up for the ones I didn't bring her when she was alive.'

'Do you want me to wait?' I asked, glancing down towards the cemetery gates far below. There was still no sign of Kenneth.

'No. I'll take my time going back down,' he said. 'The hard part is done. Thanks, love.' And he climbed out of the car, then pulled a single rose from the bunch he carried and handed it to me, his eyes twinkling. 'Mary wouldn't mind, I'm sure,' he smiled.

'Thank you,' I said, taking it. Things would be okay, I told myself. It was a sign, a moment when the universe had seen that I had done an act of kindness and would repay me in kind. Or at least that's what I tried to believe.

As I drove off, I saw a figure walk in through the bottom entrance. By the gait, even at this distance, I knew it to be Kenneth. I circled round and drove back down to find him sitting at the bottom of the set of steps, as if preparing himself for the climb.

He stared as I stopped the car and got out. 'I didn't know you drove,' he said.

'It's not mine,' I said.

He considered this and shrugged, then he pulled an envelope from his pocket and passed it to me.

'Two passports for you and the little one. And I managed to rush through your mother's.'

'That's amazing, Kenneth,' I said. 'Thank you. But I'm so sorry; I wanted to pay you. I had money in the house but . . . I can't get it.'

'In your own home?'

I nodded, hoping he understood the inference. He did.

'Why don't you phone the police?'

'I can't,' I said. 'It's . . . it's complicated.'

He did not speak for a moment. 'Have you bought your flight tickets yet?'

'No,' I said. 'It's okay. I'll sort something out.'

He took out his wallet and opening it, removed some notes. 'There's two hundred pounds there,' he said. 'It's not much, but it's all I have on me.'

'I can't take it,' I said.

'It's not for you,' Kenneth said, seemingly bemused by the suggestion. 'It's for the little one. Take it.'

'I'll send you money once I'm settled,' I said. 'I will repay you everything I owe you.'

335

Kenneth dismissed the offer. 'I owed your father a few pounds that I never got squared up before he died. That debt is repaid now.'

I didn't know whether that was true or simply something to make me feel better about taking his money. Either way, I didn't feel I could refuse it. So I accepted the notes and, as I did, I leaned in and kissed him on the cheek.

'Thank you, Kenneth.'

'It'll not get you far,' he said. 'But maybe far enough. You take care.'

And he turned and set off up the steps.

'Thank you,' I repeated to his retreating back.

I wanted to phone Mum but couldn't risk doing so on Black-Hair's handset. If I alerted the police to what I was doing, they might try to stop me.

Once in the car, I checked the three passports. They were remarkably real-looking. I would not know whether it was enough to fool the customs and computers until we reached the airport – if we reached the airport – but at least I was a step further on than I had been.

Perhaps the universe was rewarding me, I thought.

In that frame of mind, I drove up to Hope's school. The main road was blocked where a bus had pranged the back of a delivery van, so I was diverted along a warren of small streets, trailing at the back of a line of cars. Forty minutes had passed since I'd left my house and I suspected that Mark, or Ann, would soon be wondering where I had gone.

I parked up on the street outside the school and went to the main office. The receptionist, whom I had met several times before, smiled a little uncertainly when she saw me. I guessed she was wondering why I was collecting Hope so soon after her having been left in by my mum.

'Katie,' she said. 'Are you here to see someone?'

'I wanted to collect Hope,' I said. 'She has an appointment.'

She seemed relieved, smiling as she nodded. 'She's already been collected for it.'

'What?' I couldn't understand what she meant. Had Mum come back down for her?

'She was collected about ten minutes ago. She got signed out.'

I looked down at the logbook kept at the front desk, automatically going to the most recent name. Sure enough, Hope had been signed out at 9.30 a.m. By Ann O'Reilly.

'Why did you let her take Hope?' I asked. 'Why did you let her?'

The woman looked panicked again. She turned the logbook towards her to read the entry herself. 'Ann O'Reilly. You told the school she had permission to collect Hope if you or your mum couldn't.'

'Jesus,' I said, my own panic building now. 'You shouldn't—'

I turned and ran out, heading for the car. They had only left a few minutes earlier. But I hadn't seen them walking up the street from the school, which meant Ann hadn't been walking. Someone had driven her to get Hope.

Why?

I jumped when my phone started ringing. Surely it was Mark, calling to tell me Hope was with him. I lifted it as I drove and looked at the caller ID.

I almost lost control of the car when I saw who was calling.

Somehow, despite not being in my contacts, the name on the screen read *Maybe: Alex Duffy*.

# Chapter Forty-Nine

'Alex?' I asked, answering. 'They have Hope.'

There was a second's silence, then the accent. English.

'Katie.'

'They have Hope.'

'So you've said.'

'You need to help me. I need to get her back. Please.'

'Who's with you?'

'Just me. Mark is in my house. Terry's there, too. He's dying.'

'They're both dying,' English said.

'Not Mark,' I began, wondering at the comment. 'He has a broken arm, but . . .' The sentence died as I started to tease out what he could have meant.

'You sent Alex after them, didn't you?' he asked.

'Please. They have Hope. Will you help me?'

'You sent Alex after them, didn't you?'

'Mark was planning on staying out of the country,' I said, hoping the bluff might work twice.

'That's not true.'

'It is,' I said. 'Please help me get my daughter back.'

'It's not true, Katie. I *know* it's not true.'

'Okay. I sent him. Please, Hope—'

'I warned you what could happen.'

'I need your help,' I screamed. 'Help me.'

'No,' he said, simply.

I stared at the handset in disbelief. 'But ... you're the police.'

'And you're an informant. And I told you what happens when an informant's intel is of no value anymore.'

'Please,' I sobbed. 'She's only a child.'

'You thought you were clever,' English said. 'That was your mistake.'

'What?'

'Did you really think we didn't know you'd kept the other phone? Did you really think it wouldn't be found?'

The line went dead.

I was panicking by then, my breathing so fast and shallow, the cars in front of me twisted out of shape and seemed to lurch across the road towards me.

Hope was with Ann. She had help. It must be Flood. Flood who hated me. Flood who said he'd get revenge for Mickey. He'd take it out on Hope. My beautiful Hope. Ann who used women, sold women. What would she care for my girl? They'd killed Benny. Stripped him and shot him and left him hanging on a fence, like a scarecrow, to frighten off anyone else who would stand up to them. They'd stripped me. The cops had stripped me. Ann and Flood had Hope. Someone higher up the chain. Ann. Flood. The chain. They had Hope. Ann and Flood had Hope. What would they do? What would they do to her? They'd stripped me. Both had stripped me. Taken everything I thought made me *me*. Benny. Kissing, fucking, shooting, dying. Naked. Me stripped naked. The girl in the bar toilets, naked, watching me in the doorway. Ann and Flood. Someone higher up the chain. Ann or Flood. I was higher up the chain than Benny. Benny. Shot. Beautiful Benny. The bank card. The phone. My phone. Ann or Flood. The phone. Hope.

A thud and jolt.

I had driven into the rear of a car parked by the roadside.

The sudden stop paused my thoughts, stopped me spiralling ever further into my panic. I looked in the mirror but there was no one else about. I shifted into reverse, the gears screaming in protest.

Ann and Flood had Hope. They might not be back at my house yet if that was where they were going. If the roadway was still blocked, they too might be creeping along the side streets, inch by inch, like the old man going step by step up the cemetery.

I had to draw them away, out into the open. If they brought Hope with them, I might have a chance to rescue her or get someone else to help me. If they didn't have Hope, if she was already with Mark, I would have a better chance convincing him I wasn't going to betray him without Ann and Flood there.

Someone higher up the chain, English had said. It could only be Ann or Flood. One of them. And if Mark was sure someone had talked, someone had informed on him and Terry going to Belfast, he would want someone to pay. Benny had paid the cost for my hiding Burke's phone; the cops had seen to that with the bank card. Had they told someone to look for my phone? Hidden in the most obvious place in the house: my bedroom drawer.

As if to confirm my panicked thoughts, the phone buzzed to life. Mark.

'Where are you?' He was out of breath.

'I'm at Mum's,' I said. 'The roads were blocked. I'm trying to find something strong for Tel.'

Mark snorted, a long low sound which became a sob. 'Don't. He's already gone.'

'Mark, I'm so sorry.'

'You need to come back here now,' he said, ignoring my comment.

'I'm on my way,' I said, choosing my words carefully. 'The school phoned me. There—'

'Get back here now, Katie,' he said. 'Hope will be here.'

Hope *will* be here. They weren't back yet. I had time. I pulled away from the car I had hit, dragging a small part of the bumper onto the ground as I did so. Then I sped along the roadway into town. I knew what I had to do.

## Chapter Fifty

I drove up Carlisle Road and parked opposite the turn in at the cul-de-sac of terraced houses on the left. I recognised the one the taxi man had stopped outside, on the night of Flood's party, when he'd collected the two women. Now I watched as a man walked up the pavement towards it, rang the bell and, after speaking into an intercom on the doorframe, was allowed in. I couldn't see who had opened the door, so did not know whether there might be security men there, or perhaps one of Flood's people.

The one thing I did know was that, based on what Mark had said to his sister that night, this was Ann's business. And if there was a problem, I suspected it would be Ann the people inside would call. I had her car, which meant that if she needed to come down to deal with an issue, Flood would have to drive her. I hoped that if I was quick enough and caused enough of a problem, they might still be on route to my house and would have to turn and come back with Hope in the car.

I got out and ran across the road, dodging a car which shrilled its horn at me as I did so. I went straight up to the door and began knocking. I could see there was a camera on the intercom, so I covered it with my hand and pressed the button repeatedly. Eventually, with a buzz of static, I heard someone speak.

'You've the wrong house.'

'My husband is in there with your whores,' I shouted, wincing at the word even as I said it. 'Let me in.'

'Go away, please.' The voice was accented, though I couldn't tell the origin.

'Whores,' I screamed. 'Whores.'

Glancing across, I could see people on Carlisle Road looking over at me.

'Go away,' the voice snapped, and the intercom went dead.

'Whore,' I shouted, banging on the door.

Nothing.

I didn't know what to expect. How would I know if they had called Ann? And what if she arrived to find me standing here? What good could I do Hope? I needed to do something they could not ignore and then wait, away from the house, in the hope Ann and Flood came.

Looking around, I could see nothing useful to hand. Across the roadway, a few onlookers had stopped to watch the performance. Behind them, I could see a vape store. It gave me a thought.

I ran back across the roadway and into the store.

'Do you sell lighter fluid?' I asked from the doorway.

The young lad behind the counter stared at me as if I was stupid. 'You don't need a lighter for vapes,' he said.

'Do you sell fucking lighter fluid? It's an emergency.'

'Sorry,' he said. 'The shop up the street does though,' he added, coming round the counter to indicate the direction in case I was so stupid I couldn't tell which was up and which was down.

'What kind of emergency?' he shouted after me.

I went to the shop he had mentioned and asked for a bottle of fluid for a Zippo lighter and a box of matches.

'Why do you need both?' the woman behind the counter asked.

'In case my lighter is properly broke and not just empty,' I said, and that seemed to satisfy her.

I jogged back down the street and up the terrace to the left, back to the brothel. I buzzed the intercom once more. 'Whoever is in the front room better get out,' I said.

Then I moved round to the main window, the occupants inside obscured from view by a thick lace blind. I hoped it wasn't one of the rooms the girls used, guessed it would not be, so close to the pavement. Perhaps it was a waiting room, if brothels used such things.

I banged on the windowpane several times as a warning. Pain stabbed through my bandaged hand. A face briefly appeared from a gap pulled in the blind. She was not one of the two girls I'd seen at Flood's party.

'Go away,' she shouted.

I pulled off my coat, wrapping it round my uninjured hand and thumped on the window, hoping to break it. But it was my weak hand, and the impact did nothing. The glass held firm. I tried again, but with no luck. Even had my other hand not been injured already, I doubted I could break it with my fist alone.

I considered squirting the lighter fluid in through the letterbox, but to do so would trap the girls inside and I did not want to hurt them. I just needed to create a distraction big enough that it would draw Ann and Flood to me.

I tried hitting the window with the can of fluid, hoping its hard metal edge would crack the glass. But still, I had no luck. Finally, in a panic, I looked around the street, hoping there might be a rock or lump of stone I could use.

There was nothing. The gutters were free from debris. In desperation, I reached down and tugged at the metal grill of the drain at the kerb. I felt it give, felt the tug of the mud encasing it as, slowly, I pulled it up from its place. Hefting it up, I angled it so the hard edge of one of the crossbars was pointing at the glass and I thumped it against the window. Once, twice.

The glass spiderwebbed under the impact.

Again.

The lines widened and spread with a sharp crack.

A final heft and the grill went straight through into the room as the shards of glass shattered to the ground.

Wasting no time, I lifted the lighter fluid and sprayed it onto the lace blind. Then, striking a match, I held it to the dampened material.

It took with a whoosh.

I could smell the singeing of my own hair as I made my way back to Ann's car. Someone across the street from the brothel had come out now and was on his phone, presumably calling the fire service or the police. I could only hope that someone inside the brothel had phoned Ann already.

All I could do now was wait.

The next minutes were the worst of my life. Every doubt about my plan strengthened and multiplied to the point where, several times, I started the car's ignition to leave, sure that I had made a mistake and was wasting time. Time Hope might not have.

Then I would convince myself that this was my only option, and I would wait until the doubts built once more.

I'd waited eight minutes by the clock in the car when I decided I had made a massive mistake. Hope would be with Mark, Ann and Flood. She would be standing in her own kitchen, staring at Terry O'Reilly's dead body. How would I bring her back from this? How could I wipe all of this from her memory?

Across the way, two men had hurried out of the brothel, scurrying up Carlisle Road. The women were gathered out on the street by now, some of them wrapped in housecoats, one in Uggs and heavy pyjamas. They were being spoken to by an older woman, who I assumed was running the place for Ann. It was obvious they were waiting for someone. It could be Ann, or it could be the fire service.

I couldn't take the risk, waiting any longer. I wiped the tears from my face and started the engine once more. I was just pulling out onto the roadway when a car sped past and pulled into the side street.

Ann was straight out of the vehicle, ushering the women back inside the house, which, I presumed, meant the fire had gone out. Flood followed a moment later, taking a second to scan the street first. Perhaps they'd been told it was me who'd started the fire by whoever had seen me at the window or in the camera. The two from Flood's party might have recognised me as the barmaid in O'Reilly's.

Taking a risk, I got out of the car the moment Flood stepped inside the house. I ran across the road, heading straight for his car, hoping, praying that Hope would be sitting inside. I had my penknife in my hand, blunt as it was, to defend myself against Flood or to cut his tyres and prevent him following Hope and me.

I was nearly there. Wisps of white smoke drifted from the house out onto the street, obscuring my view of the car enough that I couldn't tell if Hope was sitting in it. I thought I saw movement and felt my pulse quicken at the thought that she was so close.

Another few steps.

I reached the car and wrenched open the rear door.

It was empty inside.

She was not there.

## Chapter Fifty-One

I banged on the rear seats in panic, hissing Hope's name, worried that they had put her into the boot of the car, but there was no sound. Where was she?

Nearby, I could hear the growing wail of sirens and realised that either the police or the fire brigade were close.

I opened the knife and, crouching down, stabbed it at the rear tyre closest to me with the knife in my bandaged hand. The first thrust bounced off, causing me to thump my wrist off the open door. Wincing, I shifted my balance and tried using my other hand. This time, the tip of the knife wedged in the rubber, but not deeply enough to pierce right through. I had to stand up and kick it with the heel of my foot until eventually it sank in as far as the hilt of the blade. Crouching again, I wiggled it until it pulled free of the tyre with a sucking sound, followed by the loud hissing of the air escaping.

The sirens were louder now, and I knew Ann and Flood must surely hear them too. While I'd wanted to slash the second tyre, I did not have time. I gave up and scurried back over towards Ann's car as, at the top of Carlisle Road, the first fire engine appeared, its lights flashing. It roared down the street, and I just had time to pull out and get past it when it swerved across the roadway, effectively blocking the terrace and, thankfully, trapping Flood's car in the cul-de-sac.

Coming behind the fire engine, a police car, blue lights flashing, sped down and also pulled in sharply. With any luck, they would deal with Ann and Flood.

Mark must have Hope. I knew that now. I'd been too slow in drawing Ann away from him.

He had Hope. He had reason to hurt her.

No one was going to help me. I knew that now, too.

But if Mark did hurt her, if he so much as laid a hand on her, I knew one final thing: I would kill him for it.

Everything looked normal from outside as I pulled up opposite my house in Ann's car. I'd considered phoning my mother but couldn't be sure English wouldn't eavesdrop on our conversation. I knew too much about him allowing Shaw and Benny to die for no reason. I'd thought of calling the police but couldn't be sure that English wouldn't have already instructed them not to get involved. Besides, if Mark saw the police outside, he would have nothing to lose. He would kill Hope just to hurt me before they could do anything to stop him.

He didn't want Hope. He wanted me. I was the one who had let him down, just as he had believed Leah Duffy had let him down.

I got out. My instinct was to go in the front door, but I couldn't be sure what would be waiting for me. I knew the back door was unlocked, the bolt broken by Mark the previous evening. I crossed the road and went down the side of my neighbour's pathway and stepped over the low fence, which had marked the boundary between her garden and mine.

Cautiously, knife in hand, I edged towards the door which still remained a little ajar. Dipping down, I tried to catch a glimpse into the kitchen. All I could see was Terry's lifeless form on the table and the floor marked with bloody rags.

I leaned a little closer, dreading what I might find, but the corner chair, where Mark had been sitting when I left, was empty now. Next to it, the bag I had seen the previous evening remained.

I pushed the door open, slowly, gently, hoping that the hinges might not cry out my arrival as I did. The kitchen was empty. From the living room beyond, I could hear the television. Hope must be there. And, if cartoons were playing, there was reason to believe she was okay.

I stepped into the kitchen now, trying not to focus on the dead man. Moving across, I opened the bag lying on the floor, hoping that, perhaps, there might be something more useful than a blunt penknife in it. A gun maybe. I'd not know how to use it, could not trust that I wouldn't panic if I found one, but it might convince Mark that I was serious. But the bag contained only money, rolls of twenty-pound notes, their scent earthy and damp.

Ross's money, intended for Marbella. I was underwhelmed by the size, even though I suspected each roll contained a thousand pounds and there were at least a dozen of them lying in the bag. All of this for something so insignificant-looking? Terry, Benny, Burke, Shaw, Millar, all had paid with their lives for *this*?

I moved over to the cutlery drawer and, after pocketing my dad's penknife, took out a more useful blade: one which I used for cutting chicken. The rattle of the drawer must have been audible in the living room though, for Mark suddenly called, 'In here, Katie.'

Holding the kitchen knife on my bandaged hand, I moved out into the hallway and, again, leaned in at the doorframe of the living room to see what lay inside.

Hope was sitting on the floor, in her usual position, in front of the TV, but she had her head turned towards the doorway in expectation that I was coming. Mark sat on the seat closest to her, his thick hand resting on her shoulder, seemingly to stop her running to greet me. In his other hand, he held a gun, pointed lazily towards the door.

I lowered the kitchen knife as I came in. I didn't want to scare Hope any more than she already was and, if Mark's gun was loaded, there was no chance for me to reach him before he shot me.

He saw me doing so. 'Smart girl,' he said. 'Toss the knife and sit down.'

I dropped the knife, went to the seat he had indicated and sat. 'Hey, Hope,' I said. 'Everything's okay, love.'

'I want to go to Nana's, Mummy,' she said, and a fat tear dropped onto her cheek. She sniffled as she wiped it away.

'I know, love,' I said. 'We will.'

'The fire at Ann's place. That was you?' Mark said.

I nodded.

'Give me your phone,' he said. 'Toss it over here.'

I pulled it from my pocket and tossed it to him, though the dressing on my hand made it awkward to do and it clattered to the floor between us.

'Pick that up for Uncle Mark, Hope,' Mark said, always watching me.

Hope looked to me for approval and I nodded. She lifted the phone and handed it to him.

'Good girl,' he said. 'What's the code?'

I told him and heard the click as he unlocked it. He looked through the calls, then turned the phone off.

'Alex Duffy,' he said. 'Who's he?'

'Leah Duffy's brother,' I said. I didn't mention he was a cop, hoping that Leah herself would not have told Mark.

'I thought he vanished,' Mark said. 'How did he find you?'

'I found him,' I lied.

'I should have known,' he said. 'There were calls missing from your phone when I looked at it earlier.' He reached down the side of the chair and, feeling the weight of his hand off her, Hope motioned to come to me.

'Sit,' Mark cautioned. 'Hope!'

'She's not a dog,' I snapped. 'Don't talk to her like that!'

Mark laughed hollowly. 'You always have fight about you, Katie, eh? I should have just fucked you the first night.'

'It would have been your last,' I said.

He laughed again, reaching once more and tossing something at me. Again, it fell short, landing at my feet.

My own phone. Someone had found it in my drawer.

'Why do you have two phones?'

'I fixed this one,' I lied.

He saw through it. 'You've been swapping calls between them. Are you working with the cops?'

My thoughts were racing. I looked again at the gun and realised it had not moved. He was holding it in his injured arm, his broken arm. It did not mean he would not be able to pull the trigger if needs be, but it did mean his mobility was reduced. It explained why he was using one hand for everything.

'Who found the phone?'

'Floody,' he said. 'Are you with the cops? Are they listening now?'

'Why did he go looking?' I asked.

'What the fuck does that matter?'

It was Flood; the person higher up the chain. English told me they knew about the second phone and at the same time Flood suddenly found it. There was no coincidence there.

'You can't trust Flood, you know,' I said. 'He's working with them too.'

He swallowed, licked his lips. 'I don't believe you.'

'I've no reason to lie. Not now.'

He said nothing and I could tell he was thinking.

'The cop who stopped you last night. What happened to him?'

'He's dead,' Mark laughed. 'I went over him like a speed bump.'

'I didn't tell anyone you were in Belfast,' I said. 'That didn't come from me. Who else knew you were going up?'

Again, he said nothing. He laid his hand on Hope's shoulder though and I knew I had to be careful. The gun twitched in his other hand, and I saw him try to hide a wince. The worst thing would be if it fired accidentally, if whatever pain he felt caused his fingers to clamp together and pull the trigger. Hope sat between me and it, in the line of the muzzle. I needed him to let her move.

'Ross wanted to see the organ grinders, not the monkey. Who told you that? Flood? He convinced the pair of you to go up to Belfast.' I allowed the thought to settle. 'Then when you do, the cop pulls you over. So, who was dancing to whose tune?'

'Don't try to be smart with me,' Mark said. 'You're not.'

Both English and Mark had reminded me that morning that I was not smart enough for them. Yet the situation I was in was one they had created.

'So, what now?'

'Floody is coming back to get me.'

'And take you where? A safe house? You'll not be going to Spain now.'

'Where *I'm* going isn't the issue.'

'It should be. Do you think he'll let you live? He's in charge now. He has the cops behind him, and Terry is gone. You're all that stands between him and running this whole place. He's the obvious one to take over.'

He stared at me, his gaze level and unmoving.

We both started when there was a sudden knocking at the front door.

## Chapter Fifty-Two

'Don't answer it,' Mark said. Then to Hope, 'Turn that off.'

I wanted to shout out, call for help, run. I hoped it might be Black-Hair, even though I suspected he was already dead. English? He'd be no help. I began then to panic that it was my mother, though she had her own key and wouldn't need to knock.

Another knock, hard, businesslike. I itched to answer it.

'Don't,' Mark said.

I heard the letterbox rattle. 'Ms Hamill?'

I recognised the voice but could not place it.

'Ms Hamill? It's Marie Doherty.'

'It's Hope's school principal,' I said. 'She's probably wondering why someone took her out of school. If I don't answer, she'll report it to social services and the police. Especially after everything that happened with Mum.'

'Wait,' Mark said.

Another series of short raps. 'Ms Hamill? I could hear the TV when I got here. Can you answer the door, please?'

I looked to Mark, who gripped Hope's shoulder, tightly.

'You only. Everything is fine. Tell her to go. Any shit, Katie, and . . .'

He nodded towards Hope who stared between us.

'I won't do anything stupid,' I said. And I meant it. I

didn't want Marie getting caught up in this. Even in the thing with my mum, she'd only ever been concerned for Hope.

I went out to the hallway, using the chance to take out Dad's penknife and open the blade, slipping it back into my pocket carefully. If I needed to act quickly, I wouldn't have time to waste.

I opened the door.

Marie seemed surprised by the motion, and I could see she had been on her phone. 'Oh, Katie,' she said. 'I was worried about Hope.'

'She's fine,' I said. 'Thanks.'

'Are you sure? Eleanor said you called looking for her after Ann O'Reilly had already signed her out.'

I guessed that Marie knew who Ann was, knew the family connection.

'That's right,' I said. 'Crossed wires.'

'Is Hope okay? I was worried that maybe we had done something wrong in allowing her to leave, but you did say that Ms O'Reilly was—'

'She's fine,' I said. 'Look, she's been sick, and I'm elbow deep in vomit so, you know . . . But thanks.'

'Is Hope there?' Marie asked, glancing past me towards the open door of the living room. 'Just so I can content myself that she's okay.'

'Trust me,' I snapped. 'She's okay.'

I went to close the door, but Marie had placed her foot between it and the frame, and she pushed it open against me.

'I'd like to see Hope myself, Ms Hamill,' she said.

What could I do?

'Hope?' I called. 'Mrs Doherty is here to say hello.'

I waited and, after a moment, heard the creak of the chair. Hope appeared in the doorway, Mark standing awkwardly behind her, his hand on her shoulder.

When Marie saw him, noticed his clothes stained with blood, she glanced to me once more, realising something was not right.

'Hello, Hope,' she said, keeping her voice neutral and lowering herself to Hope's height. 'Are you okay?'

Hope nodded from the doorway.

'Are you sick?'

Hope shook her head, then looked to me to see if she had done right.

'Can you come to me a wee second, pet?' Marie asked.

Hope started to move, but I saw Mark's hand tighten.

This was a way out for Hope, I realised. If I could get her to hug Marie, I could close the door on them, keep her outside, safe from whatever Mark would do to me inside the house. Marie might even run with her and call the police. It would make no difference at that stage.

'Isn't Mrs Doherty very good, calling to see how you're feeling, Hope? Give her a hug to say thank you,' I said.

Hope began to move once more and, reluctantly, Mark allowed her to, stepping behind her, his hand on her shoulder. His broken arm hung limp by his side, and I realised that he was holding the gun, quite uselessly, in that arm, hidden behind Hope's back.

As he neared me, I put my own hand reassuringly on

Hope's shoulder, then pushed her towards Marie, who leaned a little off her balance to accept Hope's hug. I knew what she was doing, getting close to her to see if she was hurt.

Hope stretched out to her as Marie leaned closer. I could see the gun in Mark's left hand, pointed at the floor.

I shoved Hope forward, knocking her and Marie out onto the step. I laid my weight against the door, closing it on them, even as I turned and pulled the penknife from my pocket with my uninjured hand.

Mark was, in that second, reaching to take the gun from his weak hand.

I had to act.

A blunt knife.

Soft skin.

With my left hand, I wedged the penknife hilt-deep into the space just under Mark's chin, pushing it up, into his mouth and through his tongue.

He squealed with the pain, the gun clattering onto the ground.

'Ms Hamill!'

I heard the rattle of the door handle, felt the weight of the door shift behind me. I slammed against it, closing it, while Mark flailed, his good hand reaching up and drawing the knife from beneath his chin. Blood burst from his mouth, his jaw slack, his tongue lolling.

He lunged for me, swinging the knife wildly, while I dipped to avoid his blow. I squeezed past him, kicking the gun further towards the kitchen, then rushing to grab it before he could catch up with me.

I got it and turned as he loomed above me. I couldn't risk shooting in case I missed him, and the bullet hit Hope or Marie, standing outside.

The front door opened, and I yelled, just as Mark dropped to his knees and, discarding the bloodied knife, reached to take the gun from me.

I pulled the trigger, but nothing happened. It didn't even shift.

He wrenched it from me.

'You bitch,' he said.

My fingers scrabbled along the floor, searching for the knife as Mark looked down to take the safety catch off the gun.

I felt the stickiness of the blade, the hilt.

I gripped.

Mark turned the gun towards me.

I struck him on the neck.

I must have hit the artery for the spurt of blood was instantaneous. I could feel its heat, the stickiness of it. It hit the kitchen cabinets, even as Mark's hand slapped against the wound, trying to stop the bleeding.

He looked at me, his eyes rolling.

Then he fell onto the floor.

## Chapter Fifty-Three

In the shock of what had happened, I looked up and saw Marie appear in the doorway.

'Jesus Christ,' she said.

'Keep Hope out,' I shouted.

'She's in my car. Are you okay?'

I hadn't thought to check. I wasn't injured, I knew that. But adrenaline coursed through me, my nerves buzzing, my movements jittery as I stood up and moved away from Mark.

'I have to get away,' I said.

'I'll call the police,' Marie said.

'Please, don't' I said.

'What? Why not?' Marie said.

'You see who I've killed.'

Marie glanced at Mark. I knew she would recognise him.

'I was an informant,' I said. 'I tried to tell you, that day you got the complaint about my mum and Hope. That was them: the police. They did that to force me to spy on the O'Reillys.'

I could see Marie remembered our conversation from that day. She stared at me, as if wondering what path had led her from her normal workday into this hell.

'I'm not lying. I tried to get out so many times, but they wouldn't let me. Now, someone else will take over from the

O'Reillys. How safe do you think I'll be? Or Hope? Please, I need to get away from here. Get *her* away.'

'I can't.'

I lifted the gun. Marie took a step away from me, thinking perhaps that I intended to hurt her.

I walked across and left it on the countertop. 'That has my fingerprints on it now. You can tell them I threatened you. You had no choice but to let me go.'

'What about Hope?'

'Hope is more at risk here than she is anywhere. I know information about the person who will take over from the O'Reillys. He won't let me live.'

'But the police—' she said, once more.

'The police helped put him in place,' I said. 'They're controlling him.'

'Where are you going to go?'

I could see she was wavering. Perhaps she thought I wouldn't get far anyway. Or perhaps, having lived in this place her whole life, my story sounded more depressingly plausible than it might seem.

'Away,' I said. I looked at the mess of my kitchen and felt outside of myself, as if all of this was happening to someone else. 'Far away from this,' I said.

'I can give you a few minutes before I phone,' she said. 'Your neighbours will have seen me come in.'

I nodded and fought my instinct to hug her, covered in blood as I was. I sprinted up the stairs and grabbed Hope's small case, emptying the contents into my own half-filled one. I stripped off and washed Mark's blood from my face and hair as best I could, pulling on the nearest clothes to hand.

When I went back downstairs, Marie was standing in the hallway with her phone. She held Mark's bag, the one that had been in the kitchen.

'Is this yours?' she asked.

Tempted as I was to take it and put it to use, I did not, in all conscience, feel that I could, filled with blood money as it was.

'No,' I said.

'I think it *is*,' she said, clearly having seen the bag's contents. 'For a fresh start.'

'People died for that money,' I said.

'Then it needs to be used to help people instead,' she said. 'How else are you going to survive?'

I hugged her then, tightly, and felt her arms slip round me.

'Thank you,' I wept against her cheek.

Then I took the bag and went out the back door.

Hope sat in Marie's car, her face pale and frightened at the window. When she saw me, she climbed out and came running across to me.

She hugged my legs while I threw our bags into Ann's car and then hefted Hope in, buckling her seat belt. I had no child seat, but what could I do?

Then we set off while Marie, inside the house, finally called the police to the scene of devastation which lay there.

## Chapter Fifty-Four

I drove up the motorway, towards the airport. It was my instinct, the obvious escape route. But as I drove, I realised that it was *too* obvious. If English wanted to stop me, and I imagined that he might, once news of the deaths of Mark and Terry became common knowledge, all he had to do was have someone watch the airport and sea ports until I appeared.

I needed to get across the border. If I flew out from the south, I'd have a greater chance of escaping. But I needed English to think I'd done the obvious. He believed me to be stupid; let him keep believing that.

I drove to Belfast airport and parked in the long stay car park. Then, Hope and I walked across to the bus stops and waited for the bus back into Belfast city. Once there, I took us straight from the airport bus to the Dublin express. This bus was quieter, and, after a while, Hope drifted to sleep.

I could not, though. Not until I saw the speed signs change from miles per hour to kilometres and, for the first time, I allowed myself to relax even a little.

We reached Dublin airport about two hours later. As Hope and I headed to Departures, I looked around, watching every face, wondering if any were working with English. He and Black-Hair had picked me up, that first time, in

Donegal after all; there was nothing stopping them coming to Dublin, even if it was in a different jurisdiction.

But no one approached us, no one held my stare too long. I realised that I needed euros if I was to pay for flights. I couldn't risk unrolling Mark's money so hunted through my suitcase and took out the stash which Mum had given to me. I took one thousand and walked with Hope across to the Bureau de Change.

'Can I change this to euro, please?' I said.

The man looked at the notes I'd laid on the Perspex drawer.

'The rate here is shite,' he said. 'You'd be better holding on to it until you get to town.'

'I missed my flight,' I lied. 'I need to rebook. The rest of our family is already on their way to Paris.'

He accepted the excuse with a nod. 'I'll need ID for a transaction of that size,' he said. 'Money laundering, you know?'

I swallowed as I handed him the passport which Kenneth had made for me. This would be the test, I thought. If anyone would spot a fake ID, surely this man would.

He took it and looked at it, then at me. Then he jotted down some details from it before handing it back to me. He pulled in the drawer, taking my sterling and checking it, then counted out the euros, placed them in the drawer and pushed it across to me.

'Enjoy Paris, Mrs Porter.'

I went to the sales desk of one of the budget airlines and booked two flights for Hope and myself and one for Mum under the name on her new passport, Rosie Coyle: her late sister. I used the same excuse of having missed an earlier flight and needing to get across quickly to Pisa, it being the closest airport to Florence that had direct flights.

'It'll not be cheap,' the stewardess said.

It wasn't. But she sold us the tickets for the first flight the following morning.

'Is there nothing earlier?' I asked, but already knew the answer.

'The airport hotel's not bad,' she said. 'Your wee lady looks dead on her feet.'

I considered the choice. Sitting in the airport would leave us exposed, visible. Booking into a hotel would cost money for sure, but at least we'd be out of sight. It would allow Hope to sleep and eat something, and would give me a chance to call my mum and wait for her to arrive.

I went back to the Bureau de Change and explained I needed more money to stay the night. The man did not require my passport this time, but simply copied out the details from the previous transaction.

At the hotel desk, I explained that I had lost my wallet with all my cards but could pay in advance with cash. We left our bags in the room and then I needed to call Mum.

Although we had a phone in our room, I went back across to the airport and called her from a payphone there.

'Yes?'

I didn't dare speak, assuming that someone would be with her, quizzing her about where we had gone. What could I say?

'Maggie Hamill?' I asked, using the pet name my dad used for her.

'Oh,' I heard her sob lightly, but she didn't say anything further. Perhaps she too was afraid to speak, not knowing who might be listening.

I thought back on the code we agreed that she should post on Facebook that she had work the next day whenever she was planning on coming to Italy.

'I need you to come in to work tomorrow morning. Early.'

'How early?' she asked, and I knew she understood.

'Ten past nine. It'll take you a while to get here, though, so be early.'

'I see that,' she said. I guessed the caller ID on her phone must have shown I was calling from a southern number. She'd know it was Dublin from the prefix, would guess we were leaving from the airport here rather than Belfast.

'I'll see you then,' I said, then hung up.

Once we went back to the hotel, we ordered room service, and Hope and I stayed in our room for the rest of the night. After she'd eaten, I got Hope snuggled into her own bed, I turned on the TV in our room and changed the channel to BBC One Northern Ireland.

At 10.30 p.m., the news began. The first story caught my attention.

> *'Police are investigating the circumstances surrounding the deaths of two men whose bodies were discovered in a house in the Blackthorn Terrace area of the city. It is believed that both men died from gunshot injuries. Police say that inquiries are ongoing.'*

At least they hadn't mentioned me or Hope. I'd worried that they might release pictures of us to the press. They still might, I realised.

I left the news playing and was glad I had done so, for towards the end of the programme, another story caught my interest. Police responding to reports of a fire on Carlisle Road earlier had been shocked to discover a brothel operating in the burning house. Several women, suspected of being victims of human trafficking, had been rescued and two people had been arrested. I assumed it to be Ann and Flood until the newscaster continued. 'The two women, both in their thirties, are to appear at court in the morning. One is believed to be a local woman, the other a foreign national.'

Ann had been arrested then and the clear-out of the whole family was complete. And, more interestingly, Flood had not. He was free to take his place at the head of the O'Reillys' gang and provide English with whatever intel he needed on Ross and whoever lay further up the chain. And so it would go on.

With that, I knew I had made the right choice in leaving. To have stayed in the city would have risked both my and Hope's lives.

And so I sat awake all night, watching the door in case someone should come looking for us. And the following morning, we left early and went to the bus stop at which travellers from Derry would be dropped.

Just after 6 a.m., Mum stepped off the bus and ran to hug the pair of us.

'Don't,' I said, as she approached. 'Not yet.'

She nodded and walked a few paces in front of us towards Departures.

'I need you to take Hope through Security,' I said. 'They will be looking for me and her.'

I handed Hope the envelope with passports for her and Mum and their two tickets, as well as a letter of authorisation which I'd written giving her granny permission to travel with her. I'd also divided the cash between Mum's bag and mine, in case either of us got searched; at least the other would get away with something to live on. They walked ahead, hand in hand, while I followed, not far behind. Hope stayed with Mum while we waited for our gate to open and I went through a separate security gate from them too, just in case someone was looking for a woman of my age with a child.

I'd checked in online, with hand luggage, so it was only when we reached the gate and were being called for boarding that I had to show my passport for the first time. I thought I would be sick as we queued. I felt certain that English would be watching, that the fake passports would be recognised. I decided it best to go ahead of Mum and Hope. At least if my passport did not work, they would see and might, perhaps, have time to quietly leave the queue, even if I was arrested.

I reached the desk. The attendant held out his hand and took my passport. He opened it and stared at me, then placed it face down on the scanner. He stared at the screen in front of him, then back at me.

I could feel my legs go weak and had to lay my bandaged hand on the counter.

'What happened?' he said, and it took me a moment to realise he was nodding at my injured hand.

'I closed the car door on it,' I said.

He nodded as if this might be a normal thing to do, then lifted my passport and looked at it. 'Enjoy your flight, Hannah,' he said. 'Safe travels.'

I could barely believe it had worked. I walked on through the gate and joined the queue to board, all the time looking back, fearful that Mum and Hope had not made it. Then I saw them pass through the boarding gate. Mum gave me a thumbs up and Hope smiled and waved.

We did not sit together until we got onto the plane. Even then, I worried that English might halt it at the last moment. Hope though was buzzing with excitement while Mum was doing her best not to show her own anxiety.

Then we were taxiing onto the runway, and with a surge the land tilted, and the sunlight slanted across our seats as we took off.

I looked out the window, down at the only home I'd ever known. The land that held my father, that held Benny and Shaw and the Millars, Mark and Terry. Alex Duffy. And though it was my home, I felt little but relief to be leaving it behind. I had my mother and Hope with me and that was enough.

The future stretched ahead, rich with promise, even as I hoped that the past fell away from us with the earth below.

# Epilogue

The last of the Christmas season tourists had dried up now but the early January sun offered some relief from the rain which had fallen all week. We sat in the café on the Piazza Santa Croce just opposite the Basilica; Mum had wanted to do all the touristy things with us that she and Dad had done on their honeymoon, but I'd convinced her to leave it a few weeks until the chances of bumping into someone from home over here on holidays had lessened. Now, on a Thursday morning in January, the three of us had risked coming into the centre of town to let Mum take us on a tour.

Once we'd rented an apartment, after we first arrived, both Mum and I had managed to find cash-in-hand jobs: one of the post-Brexit benefits of having an Irish passport. We were able to open bank accounts and, bit by bit, exchange and lodge Mark's money which Marie had given me the morning we left, more than enough to ensure we had the six thousand euro needed in each account in order to apply for permanent residency in the municipality in Borgo San Lorenzo where we'd settled, thinking a smaller town might be safer. Hope hadn't started school yet, but if we got our residency permits and *codice fiscale*, I'd be able to get her registered for the following academic year.

In the days after we left, news began to emerge, piecemeal, about the death of Alex Duffy on the M2 and how it connected to the discovery of the O'Reillys. About a week after we arrived, I read a report online from a Northern Irish newspaper which concluded:

> Police have now accepted that Alex Duffy had been running illegal surveillance on the O'Reillys over the past number of months, which resulted in both his death and the deaths of Terry and Mark O'Reilly. Details had been passed to the Police Ombudsman but at this time, police were keen to stress that Duffy had been working alone and that they are not looking for anyone in connection with the investigation into the three deaths.

Duffy had been working alone? So English had managed to scrub both his involvement and mine, presumably because I could connect him to the whole thing. The question was whether he would be content to let me live my life or whether he would come looking for me, knowing what I knew.

I could see no reason why. Flood was in place, where English wanted him. I'd disappeared and, I figured, so long as I kept my head down and stayed away, neither of them would have cause to come looking for me. What was I to them? What possible value could I have?

'Shall we go?' Mum asked, placing Hope's baseball cap on her head and earning the reward of her smile in so doing, her nose covered with cream from the chocolate she'd been drinking, her eyes squeezed almost shut behind the pink sunglasses she wore.

We stepped out onto the square and made our way across towards the ticket office along the side of the Basilica. One of the guides let us join a tour along with a group of English sightseers, all past retirement age.

We stopped in front of the church as the guide pointed out some of the architectural features, but Hope's attention had already wandered. She'd moved across to where, towering over us near the steps, was a statue of a man clasping his cloak while an eagle looked up at him.

'Who's he?' Hope asked.

'That is Italy's supreme poet, Dante Alighieri,' the tour guide said. 'He is one of Florence's most beloved sons, though he was exiled from the city for much of his life. He wrote *The Divine Comedy*, in which he travels through Hell and Purgatory to reach Heaven.'

'Sound familiar?' Mum whispered, standing next to me.

The tour guide continued, heading up the steps. 'We'll see his tomb inside the Basilica, though his remains are not actually there. His burial spot is in Ravenna.'

She had moved on now, the English tourists following and, behind them, Mum, taking Hope's hand as she climbed the steps. I watched them, for a moment feeling as if I had been pulled out of myself. I knew what Mum had meant, about travelling through hell. But it was the other part of the tour guide's story which had stuck with me.

How had I ended up here, an exile from my own city? I'd said that so long as I had my mum and Hope I was home, and that was true. But at times I missed the familiarity of my old life, the ease with which each day had hung like well-worn clothes. My history was there, in Derry, just as

Kenneth had said to Hope that day in the cemetery. Black-Hair and English and the O'Reillys had robbed me of my past and, in doing so, had stolen a part of my identity from me.

But then, I also knew that so long as Flood and Ross and English played out their games, I could not go back. The O'Reillys might be dead, but there would always be more like them. More Andy Floods. More like English and Black-Hair fighting their dirty war to try to stop them. Most would meet their end on the street, or a bar, or a kitchen floor, in a pool of blood. Such men did not die in their beds, forgiven.

Their greatest sin was that they dragged so many others to death with them: Benny; Leon Burke; Shaw; the Millars. How many before? How many to come?

And so, as I stepped in through the wooden doors of the Basilica and dipped my fingers in the holy water font at the entrance, I said a quiet prayer for all those lost souls, and then a second for Mum, Hope and me, in thanks for the new start, and in anticipation for what lay ahead, filled as it was with possibilities. Prayers of grief and hope, for past and future.

Now, in this moment, we'd been given a chance to start over, to build a new life on the foundations of our family of three. I had to make the most of it, for my mother, for my daughter, for myself. As I watched Mum and Hope stand, hand in hand, staring in wonder at the beauty of the building, I promised that I would.

The air around me was cool and heavy with the smell of incense. Above us, the late winter sun shone through the stained glass, bathing us all equally in scarlets and blue.

# Acknowledgements

My thanks to everyone in Constable who helped bring this book to life, particularly Krystyna Green, Beth Wright, Amanda Keats and Tara Loder. I'm especially indebted to Hannah Wann, without whose editorial expertise and insight this book would be so much the poorer and to whom I'm very grateful.

Thanks to David Headley and Emily Glenister of DHH Literary Agency and to Emily Hickman of The Agency for all their continued support and tireless efforts on my behalf. Thanks, too, to Dave Torrans, to whom this book is dedicated, for his continued support and friendship.

Thanks to my mum and to Carmel, Joe, Dermot and families.

Finally, my love and thanks to Tanya, Ben, Tom, David and Lucy. I'm a lucky man.

# CRIME AND THRILLER FAN?

## CHECK OUT THECRIMEVAULT.COM

The online home of exceptional crime fiction

# KEEP YOURSELF IN SUSPENSE

Sign up to our newsletter for regular recommendations, competitions and exclusives at www.thecrimevault.com/connect

Follow us
@TheCrimeVault
/TheCrimeVault
for all the latest news